The Time Thief

&

A Change of Face

Jacqueline R. Richardson

Book 1

The Time Thief

Chapter 1

The first time I met him, there weren't any butterflies. Angels didn't sing. Sparks didn't fly. My heart didn't beat from my chest, and my breath didn't catch in my throat. No, time did not stand still, not even for a moment. He seemed positively ordinary at first glance, but it wouldn't take me long to discover that he wasn't at all, not even remotely, ordinary.

I had just been through a nasty divorce, and I was getting settled into my new house. Admittedly, I was having a hard time settling. The house was out in the middle of nowhere in Michigan's Upper Peninsula, and I was already feeling isolated. I had intended for it to be a fresh start, but I hadn't anticipated how lonely I would be in a new town by myself. I did enjoy the peacefulness of the woods, and the quiet of a home free of arguments and name-calling, but there were times that the silence seemed overwhelming.

Perhaps it was my loneliness that prompted me to open the door when the stranger came knocking. Or perhaps it was his suit – throughout the divorce I met with several men in suits, and thus it became almost normal to expect to see a man in a suit from time to time. Whatever it was, I opened the door when ordinarily I would have ignored it. That was how I met Trent Morgan.

He was around 5'11" and a little on the lanky side. He looked to be in his early 30's. His dark brown hair was shorter on the sides and longer on the top – long enough on the top for his bangs to dangle in his hazel-green eyes when he moved his head about. But he had it well styled with the lengthy top combed sideways from the part on the left side of his head. His face was clean-shaven and his dapper brown tweed suit was impeccable. Upon first impression, though, I thought perhaps he was a bit…plain.

I opened the door partially, peeking only my head out. "Can I help you, sir?" I asked, brushing my long blond hair from my face.

He smiled at me, revealing straight white teeth. It was as though his whole face lit up with that smile, and I couldn't help but smile in return. He had kind eyes that gazed at me as though we were old friends.

"Yes, hello! I'm Trent. Trent Morgan. We haven't met, have we?" He offered his hand to greet me, and I paused, surprised by his English-like accent.

"No, I don't believe so. I'm Roselyn," I responded, shaking his hand. I suddenly felt a little wary of this man who seemed quite out of place in the U.P. "Where are you from? You don't hear a lot of English accents in the U.P."

"Oh, it isn't English, per se. It's Nohkean. You've probably not heard of it. No matter! Now, I hate to bother you, but I was hoping you could help me."

"With what?" I was starting to wonder if I had made a mistake in opening the door. "If you are going to grill me about religion, I'm not interested."

Trent chuckled. "No worries. I'm not here to talk religion. I do fear it may seem a bit stranger, though. Have you noticed anything odd going on around here?"

"Odd like what?"

"Like strange time discrepancies, namely."

Was he nuts? "No, I don't think so. I've only been here a couple of weeks." I tried to shift my body as much behind the partially opened door as I could without being obvious. I wondered if I was going to have to shut the door in his face.

"Ah. All right. Say, did you ever meet the previous occupants of this house?"

"No, I didn't."

"Do you by chance know their names?"

"I don't recall off-hand," I replied, feeling uneasy. "Is this conversation going somewhere, or are we done here?"

"My apologies. I know this all seems a bit bizarre. I'll be off then." He held out a business card to me. "If you notice anything out of the ordinary, please give me a ring. I have a sneaking suspicion that something is afoot, and I'm rarely wrong about these things."

I hesitantly took the card from him. I knew I must've been giving him the most obvious look of disbelief, but he just smiled again at me and bowed his head slightly before turning on his heel and walking down the driveway. I shut and locked my door and watched him from the window, peeking from behind the curtain. He had a confident gait, but it was almost amusing how disproportionately large his feet were and the way his legs bowed slightly when he walked. He walked a short distance down the driveway and then stopped. He turned and looked back at the house, a look of puzzlement contorting his face. His brows drew together and he looked down at his watch. He glanced back at the house one more time before he walked to the end of the drive and headed up the road to the north. The trees around my house and along the road quickly obscured my view of him and I lost him. He had appeared to be on foot, but who walked around on foot in a tweed suit down an old dirt road out in the middle of nowhere? My closest neighbor was three miles to the south of me, and there was nothing but state forest in the direction he was headed. Where was he going? Where had he come from?

I looked at the card he had given me, which I was still clutching in my now clammy hands. It was only a phone number – or at least

I assumed it was supposed to be, but it had too many digits. No name, no explanation. I ran around the house locking all the windows and the basement and back door. I took my handgun from my purse and holstered it at my hip. I was a strong, athletic woman with some martial arts training, and I could hold my own if I had to – but no one was a match for a gun. I looked out the window again, where my fluffy white cat, Cattiel, was now sitting on the sill. He looked up at me with palpable contempt for invading his space, and it was then that I realized just how much I wished I had a big, intimidating dog.

I was on high alert all afternoon and evening. I checked my windows every few minutes. Had that man been sent by my ex-husband? It was possible. He had always been a bit off mentally, but the divorce had really brought out the worst in him. Psychological warfare was his specialty, and after being married to him and enduring his abuse for over two years, I had come to expect that everything out of the ordinary was either a trick or a test. I may have had a restraining order against him, but he was maliciously inventive and I couldn't rule anything out at this point. I was prepared for the worst.

That night, everything was quiet. I had turned on every outside light I had, including the light on the detached garage, but nothing crossed a single beam. By 2AM, I was barely able to keep my eyes open, and I grabbed Cattiel and crawled into bed. All the lights in the house were on save for my bedroom and hallway light, and I had my door closed, my .45 near my bedside, and my phone under my pillow. I wished I had a burglar alarm, but the tripwire I rigged up in the hallway outside my door would have to do for tonight.

Some time later, I awoke with a start. I lay frozen in my bed, listening, trying to gain my senses and figure out what had awakened me. I turned my eyes toward the clock, trying not to move, and saw that it was a little after 3AM. Then I heard it. It sounded like voices talking, but it was faint and muffled. I sat up in bed and looked around, reaching for my .45. I racked a bullet into the chamber and slipped carefully out of bed, keeping the gun pointed at the ground, safety on. The sound of Cattiel growling caught my attention. In the darkness, I could make out only the outline of his body, but it appeared that his ears were back and he was flattening himself against the bed. It was clear something was upsetting him. I tip-toed closer to the door, hoping to be able to hear what the voices were saying. As I listened, however, it became apparent that the voices weren't coming from a particular place. They were all around. They were muffled, like listening to a dinner party from under a pool. It was like a hundred conversations going on all at once all throughout the house, inside and out.

I didn't know what to do. I stood in the darkness with my sidearm, feeling fairly certain that it would do me no good in this situation. The voices didn't seem to grow or wane in volume, but they did seem to move and change, like people mingling about. I heard laughter. I heard excitement. I heard arguing. But none of it was quite loud enough to make out what was being said. I only got tones and pitches and syllables, and I stood and listened for what felt like an eternity.

Finally, I gathered up enough courage to open my bedroom door. I peeked out into the hallway, and it was empty. I stepped out of my room and sneaked down the hallway, being careful to avoid the tripwire. I investigated the living room. Nothing. The kitchen was clear, too. Everywhere in the house was empty, but the voices emanated throughout the entire place.

"I bought a goddamned haunted house," I whispered shakily under my breath.

Everything went instantly and eerily silent. It felt like a thousand eyes had just turned their attention to me.

"Oh, hell no," I declared, suddenly panicked. I ran to my room to get Cattiel and my car keys, and in my haste, I forgot about the tripwire. It sent me sprawling over the floor in what I can only imagine was the most graceful tumble nobody ever saw. I felt a sharp jolt in my wrist when I landed on it, but the adrenaline coursing through my veins helped to dull the pain. I scrambled to my feet, forgetting about the gun I'd left laying on the floor, and ran into my room. I clumsily fumbled with my keys and snatched my phone from under my pillow. As I reached for Cattiel, he bolted.

"Dammit, cat! I will leave you! I'll do it!" I dropped down and looked under the bed, but it was too dark to see the cat. "Fine, fend for yourself, butthole," I said in exasperation as I stood up. I took the keys and my phone and hurried out of my room – and hit the tripwire one more time. With a slurry of swear words and self-deprecation, I finally made it down the hallway, through the living room, and out the front door. I rushed down the front porch and ran to my car, diving in and locking the doors behind me. I jammed the key into the ignition and started it up.

Just then, my phone started ringing. Surprised, I looked at the screen. It was a jumble of numbers and symbols on the caller ID.

The ghosts are calling! I thought to myself in horror.

I juggled with what to do briefly, but ultimately my curiosity won out. I answered the phone.

"Hello?" My voice sounded higher pitched than usual.

"Has something odd happened?" an English (or Nohkean?) accent asked from the other line. "I feel like something odd has happened."

"Who is this? What kind of sick joke is this?!" I demanded.

"Oh, where are my manners? This is Trent Morgan. I take it something did happen, then? What happened?"

"How did you get my number?" I asked in disbelief.

"Roselyn, we can ask each other silly questions all night or you can just get to the point and tell me what has happened. I can't help you if I don't know what I'm dealing with."

I was taken aback. I stammered, "Voices…voices everywhere. I…I think it's haunted." I noticed that my fear had somewhat dissipated with this distraction, and I realized how crazy what I just said sounded.

"Voices? Oh! Well that's interesting. I wasn't expecting that. Give me a moment. I need to check this out."

"…What?" The call ended before I could give any more of a response. I looked down at my phone, perplexed, and then set it aside.

While the car idled and I sat with my hand on the shifter, I contemplated where exactly I was going to go. I didn't really know anyone around here yet, and my family members were all hours away from me. What on Earth had made me decide moving out to the middle of nowhere would be a smart life choice?

I jumped out of my skin and shrieked when I heard a tapping on the car window next to my head. I continued to shriek until my widened eyes registered what they were seeing outside the car. It was Trent.

...Wait, Trent?!

"Where the hell did you come from?!" I shouted through the closed window.

"I was out and about," he shouted to be heard over the car engine and the closed window. "I told you I was coming to check things out."

"You didn't say you were coming! How did you get here so fast? It's three o'clock in the morning! Who the hell are you?!"

"Can we maybe do this with the window down? Or the car off? I'm afraid I'm not terribly fond of shouting my conversations if it isn't absolutely necessary."

"Go away!" I commanded. I threw the shifter into reverse and hit the accelerator. The car rocketed backward down the driveway, and I saw Trent Morgan throw his hands into the air in exasperation. I slammed on the brakes at the end of the drive and watched him in my headlights. He put his hands on his hips and hung his head slightly, like a parent who has just about had it with his kid's nonsense. He looked at his watch and then looked up at the car. He raised his hands to me as if to say fine, you win, and then started walking toward the house.

What was he doing?

I drove the car back up the drive and jammed it in park, rolling down the window to yell, "Hey! I'm calling the cops!"

His pace didn't falter as he replied, "I wouldn't bother. They really won't be of much assistance to us. Now, quit messing around and come on."

I was beyond frustrated. I wasn't even scared anymore. I turned off the car and jumped out. "Trent! You stop right there!"

"Are you coming?" he asked as he stopped in front of the basement door.

"You can't go in there!" I said defiantly.

He started walking toward me again, and I retreated back to the car.

"For the love of..." he said as he stopped and rubbed his forehead in annoyance. "Roselyn. I'm not here to hurt you. There is something infinitely interesting going on in that house, and I'm dying to figure out what it is. It's kind of my thing. Now, you can come with me and help me to help you, or you can get in the way and be a big old annoying nag. I'll let you in on a little secret: the first option is way more fun." Despite his obvious irritation with me, he smiled and held his hand out to me invitingly.

"What do you even want?" I asked contemptuously.

"I'm sorry, I thought I had made that fairly clear. I want to know what is going on in that house," he said, pointing behind him. He stood and looked at me with a pleasant smile on his face.

"Who are you?" I asked in wonderment. He was unlike anyone I had ever met.

"I feel like we are going in circles again. I am Trent, you are Roselyn, and together we are going to figure out the mystery of this house!" he declared, jutting a finger into the air excitedly.

"No," I said, approaching him finally. "Who are you, really? I know your name, but where did you come from? How did you get here so fast? Have you been watching me? How did you get my phone number?"

Trent gave me a tight smile and looked away. "These are all things that will be answered in due time, but there are more pressing matters at hand. Please just trust me. I'm here to help."

"Tell me now," I demanded.

"You wouldn't believe me if I did."

"Try me."

Trent sighed. He walked away from me toward the basement door.

"Hey, where are you going? Answer me!" I shouted.

He stood in front of the basement door and turned to look back at me. He then pressed a button on his watch and disappeared in an instant.

Chapter 2

I blinked several times, expecting him to still be there, but he wasn't. He was gone. I looked around me, thinking he had performed some kind of illusion and was going to pop out from behind a tree. That was when I heard a rapping coming from one of my living room windows. I looked up and saw Trent standing in the window, waving to me.

...How?

I ran up my front porch steps, knowing that I had failed to lock my front door in my haste to escape the house earlier, and burst through the door. There was Trent, standing in my living room.

"How did you do that?"

"I have a thing that does a thing. You said there were voices. I don't hear voices."

"You didn't—"

Trent shushed me mid-sentence. He tilted his head and moved around the living room. "No, I definitely don't hear voices. Are you sure you aren't going mad?" he asked me as he climbed onto the couch and stuck his ear to the wall.

"Me?! You're asking me that?! You're the one listening to walls right now!"

"Because you told me they were talking."

"I never said the walls were talking!"

He stopped and turned to me, still standing with his shoes on my couch. "Well, when you said 'voices everywhere,' I assumed that walls were part of 'everywhere.' Where exactly were the voices coming from, then?" He hopped down with the energy of a five-year old.

"Just...I don't know...everywhere. The air, I suppose. Inside and outside the house it seemed."

"But they aren't talking now. What were they saying?"

"I couldn't make out the words. As soon as I spoke out loud, though, it all stopped."

Trent furrowed his brow. "No, that's wrong. That's not supposed to happen."

"Don't tell me I'm wrong. You weren't even there," I said defensively.

He stepped uncomfortably close to me and looked me in the eye. "Are you sure it wasn't in your head?"

"I'm not crazy!"

"No, that's not what I mean. I'm wondering if the voices you were hearing were coming through telepathically."

"You're nuts, aren't you? This is one hell of an elaborate joke."

"You know this isn't a joke, and I wish you would find a better coping mechanism because this is getting tiresome." Trent looked over toward the hallway and his face lit up with a smile. "Oh, who's this?"

I followed his gaze and saw Cattiel sauntering out of the bedroom.

"There you are, you jerk," I said to the cat. "That's Cattiel. He ran off on me when I tried to rescue him from the voices."

"So he heard them too?"

"He must have. He was growling and seemed scared."

"Hm." Trent rested his chin in his hand, covering his mouth with his fingers. He crossed the other arm over his chest and rested his elbow on it, standing in contemplation.

"Hm? That's all you have is 'hm'?"

"At the moment, yes."

"Should I be worried?"

"Not unless you hear me say something colorful." He looked at me and pointed. "Did something hurt you? I notice you seem to be favoring your wrist."

I looked down and realized I was holding my wrist in my other hand. I must've sprained it when I fell, but I had been mentally blocking the pain. Now that someone had brought attention to it, I felt the ache of it.

"Oh, this. This was just me being clumsy," I said as I inspected my hand and arm for further damage.

I suddenly heard a loud crash and felt the floor shake. My head snapped up and I saw that Trent was no longer in the room. I whipped around just in time to see him scrambling to his feet in the hallway, his hair going every which way and a look of surprise on his face.

"It was that, wasn't it," he stated rather than questioned as he pointed down to the tripwire at his feet. "That's what happened to your wrist." He smoothed his hair and straightened his tie, trying not to look embarrassed.

"It's rather effective, though, isn't it? Got me twice."

Trent bent down to pick something up. It was my gun. As soon as I saw he had possession of it, my heart jumped into my throat and I became conscious of the fact that I was in a situation that didn't warrant the level of comfort I had allowed myself to fall into. I took an instinctive step away from Trent.

He wasn't looking at me, though. He was giving the gun a distasteful look as he held it away from him like it was a dirty diaper. He brought it to me and held it out for me to take it.

"You shouldn't leave these things lying around loaded like that. That was incredibly irresponsible."

I took the gun and stared at him as he turned away from me and started pressing buttons on his watch. Was he for real?

Trent pulled a pair of thick-framed glasses from his jacket pocket and slid them onto his face. I watched as a holographic interface appeared, projected above the watch. Trent was using his other hand to manipulate the images and quickly sort through what looked like a whole lot of nonsense to me.

"What is that?" I asked, dumbfounded.

"Data," he replied without looking at me.

"What does it mean?"

"I don't know yet. It doesn't become information until it is interpreted, and that could take me a bit." He pressed a button and the holographic display disappeared back into his watch.

I couldn't help myself. I had to ask one more time. "Who are you?!"

Trent gave me a smile that seemed to be hiding a thousand secrets and the kind of wisdom only time can bequeath. "I'll see you again, Roselyn." He pressed another button on his watch and was gone.

It was like he'd never even been there. I looked at the clock on the wall. It was 4AM. Was I dreaming? Was this some kind of convoluted sleep walking hallucination? I looked out at the driveway and saw the tire tracks and agitated dirt and gravel from when I was in the car earlier. The couch was still in a state of minor disarray after having giant feet walking all over it. Cattiel was rubbing against my legs, assuming that it must be time for breakfast. This didn't feel like a dream. But then again, when did dreams ever feel like dreams while you were in them? I went back to the bedroom to try to sleep away whatever this was, but not before catching the tripwire just one more time.

I didn't wake up until noon. Thank god for Sundays. Cattiel and I investigated the house, and it was obvious to me that whatever it was that had happened last night had really happened. I started a pot of coffee and took down the tripwire before I could trip over it again and break my face. It wasn't going to do any good against disembodied voices anyway.

I sat down on the couch with a hot cup of black coffee and a warm, fuzzy, grumpy cat and turned on the television. As I flipped through the channels, however, I began to notice that the television was playing shows for 3PM. That couldn't be right. I looked over at the ticking clock on the wall. It said 12:24. I pulled out my phone and checked the time. I frowned when I saw it showed 3:06PM. I jumped up and checked all the clocks in the house, and every other clock showed 12:24 – even the atomic clock at my bedside.

Were these the "time discrepancies" Trent had mentioned upon our first encounter? What did it mean? Had I really slept until 3PM in the afternoon? I went outside and looked up at the sky. The warm summer sun was hanging high in the western sky. It wasn't noon. I had lost a big chunk of my day somehow…or had I lost a chunk of my night? Or morning? When did this happen?

I went back inside and looked at my phone again. I should call Trent…shouldn't I? He was weird and mysterious and I had no idea what his story was, but he seemed to want to help. This whole situation was absurd, and he seemed to be ok with absurd. Besides, I had to work tomorrow and I wanted to make sure I had my time correct. I had just started on as a trainer at the fitness center in town, and I didn't want to show up three hours late and lose clients or my job. I was going to call him.

No. No I wasn't. He was basically a stranger! A strange stranger, at that! This house had been completely normal until he showed up on my doorstep – maybe he was the one causing this! Maybe it was some kind of elaborate trick orchestrated by the psychopath I was trying so hard to leave in my past. Trent could have switched my clocks when he was in the house last night. The voices could have been some kind of sound system he rigged up before he knocked on my door. That would explain why he was at my house so quickly, and how he knew that something had happened last night. I glanced up at my ceiling and light fixtures suspiciously. He could be watching me right now.

But what about the teleporting? How did he get from outside my locked basement door to inside my living room? Where did he go when he disappeared from my living room? There was still something about the whole situation that didn't add up. Perhaps I did need to call him. Keep your friends close and your enemies closer, right? I would pretend I believed this was all real until I could figure out how he was doing it.

I looked at my call log. The number Trent called from last night appeared to have been scrambled. I tried to call it anyway, and I wasn't surprised when it wouldn't go through. I found his card sitting on the table where I had left it when I'd gone around barricading the house, and I entered the oddly long series of numbers into my phone. When I put the phone to my ear while it was dialing, I heard strange sounds on the line. It wasn't the typical "ringing" you hear on the other end, but rather a crackling and beeping.

"Yes! Hello! Who's there?" I heard an out-of-breath English voice answer the other line impatiently.

"Trent? Is this Trent Morgan?"

"Last I checked, but I've been wrong before. Who might this be?"

"It's Roselyn."

"Roselyn? I don't know a Roselyn. Are you from housekeeping?"

"Seriously?"

"No, I'm just having you on," Trent said with a chuckle. "It's Roselyn with the voices in her head. But, for future reference, if you ever do run into me and I don't seem to know who you are, don't be cross with me. It happens occasionally."

"…What? That doesn't make any sense."

"It makes perfect sense, you just aren't quite there yet. What can I do for you, Roselyn?"

I had to take a second to remember why I called. He kept my brain moving in all different directions when he spoke and it was hard to maintain my train of thought.

"Are you there? Did I lose you?" he asked.

"I'm here. The time. Something is weird about the time," I said vaguely. I didn't mean to be vague, but those were the words that came out of my mouth.

"Time's gone wonky, has it? That was what I was waiting for. Tell me about it."

"Well, I noticed this afternoon that my phone and my TV were about three hours ahead of the rest of the clocks in my house."

"That makes sense. Your telly and smart phone get time updates from a source outside the bubble. The clocks in the house are inside of it and therefore only advance according to the passage of time experienced in the bubble."

"Excuse me? Bubble? What do you mean bubble?"

"I'm not sure yet. But after looking at the data I gathered last night, it appears there is some kind of weird gravitational force in the vicinity of your house. The gravity is affecting time, but only time inside a certain space. Namely, your house."

My disbelief took a brief hiatus as I was drawn into his explanation. "Why only my house? What kind of gravitational force?"

"I don't know. Isn't that exciting? I love it when I have to figure it out."

"Does that mean I weigh more when I'm in my house?"

"Strangely, no. The gravity doesn't seem to be affecting objects in our three dimensions. It's coming from somewhere else."

"Where?"

I heard a knock on my front door. My brows snapped together and I walked to the door, parting the blinds over the window on the door to see who was out there.

Trent smiled at me through the window. "I don't know where!" he exclaimed excitedly. He wasn't holding a phone to his ear, but I could still hear him on the other line as though he was talking to me through the phone as well. I quickly hit the button to end the call on my phone. I inspected him through the window. No Bluetooth device in his ear, no visible microphone on his suit. It could be under his tie, I supposed. He was wearing another tweed suit today, and there were a lot of places one could hide a microphone or Bluetooth device on a suit.

"Why are you here?" I demanded.

"You rang me. I thought you wanted me here," he said loudly through the window. "Are you going to let me in?"

I paused. "I don't know yet."

"Well that's rude," he said.

"How did you get here so fast?"

"You've seen it. I have a thing that does a thing, remember?"

"Not good enough."

"You wouldn't understand. It's…classified."

"Are you just making that up?"

"Nnnoooo," he said unconvincingly.

"You're a terrible liar," I said.

He smiled with amusement. "Yeah, well, it isn't my favorite thing to do."

"Ok, enough is enough, Trent," I said, fed up. "I know you must be working with Barry. The jig is up. You can go home now." I had intended to play along until I figured out what he was up to, but this was just getting too weird.

Trent looked at me through the window with genuine bewilderment. "Who?"

"It's obvious he set this all up to mess with me and try to scare me. I'm not going to lie, it worked for a minute. But I'm over it. You can tell him to screw off."

"I'd rather not tell anyone to screw off. Who is Barry? Is he a friend of yours?"

"My ex-husband. Barry Schmidt. I know you're working for or with him. You can quit with the act now."

Trent stared at me. After a long pause, he said, "I'm sorry, what? I'm not sure what you're talking about. I don't know Barry Smith."

"Schmidt."

"I don't know Schmidt either."

Despite my current mood, I still had to suppress the snicker that threatened to bubble up my throat. It seemed that he might have been being truthful, but what was he up to? "You obviously don't know Schmidt," I said, unable to resist the joke.

Trent raised an eyebrow at me, my pun apparently going right over his head. "Are you having a laugh?" he asked in confusion, an expression of mild irritation on his face.

"A small one, yes."

"Well, are you done now? Can I come in yet?"

"No."

"What do you mean no?"

"No."

"Why not?"

"Because you're weird and I barely know you and this could all be a trick."

"Not with the trick thing again," Trent said, running his hands through his hair in exasperation. "It's not a trick! What reason would I have to trick you?"

"I don't know! That's what people do! They play games and trick each other and hurt each other. I don't know what you're playing at, but you can count me out."

Trent's face became somber. He gave me a sad, empathic look. "I'm sorry." He shoved his hands in his trouser pockets and leaned his shoulder against the door.

I took a step back from the door. "'I'm sorry'?" I questioned.

"I know this level of mistrust doesn't just happen overnight. Someone made you this way. Jerry, was it?"

"Barry. And I'm behaving perfectly rationally. Why won't you just go away? Your persistence is raising all kinds of red flags."

"Why did you ring me if you don't want my help?"

"I called you. I didn't ask you to show up at my door."

"You know what? Fine. Fine! Have fun dealing with this yourself. I'm not going to beg."

I watched him straighten his tie and walk away from the door. He looked down at his watch and stopped as he was on his way down the porch steps. He turned around and came back to the door.

"Ok, I might beg a little," he amended, looking at me through the window with pleading eyes.

"No."

"Ugh. Fine." He threw his hands into the air and walked away.

I went to the window and watched him walk down the driveway. I threw open the window as a thought occurred to me.

"Hey!" I yelled to him.

He stopped and turned toward the house. "Change your mind?" he asked, a hopeful smile spreading across his face.

I ignored his question. "If you have a 'thing that does a thing,' then why didn't you use it to get in the house again?"

"You told me no."

"It didn't seem to matter to you last time."

"You weren't inside the house last time. It wasn't the same."

"What, are you like a vampire or something? You can only enter when invited?" I challenged.

He looked up at me like I had said the most ridiculous thing. "No. I just have manners."

"Why aren't you using it to disappear out of here? Why are you walking to the road?" I asked, thinking I had caught an inconsistency in his game.

He shook his head. "I was hoping to give you time to change your mind, but it appears you have no intention of doing so. I'm sorry you have chosen to be a big annoying nag. I'll be off now," he said curtly. Before I could scold him for calling me an annoying nag, he touched his watch and disappeared, much to my surprise.

And there I was, alone again. I thought about what Trent had told me about the gravitational field and how it affected time, and I wondered if it were possible that this wasn't all a hoax. Had there been weird things going on before now, and that's why the house was for sale? I picked up the phone and called my realtor. I hoped she accepted calls on Sundays.

When she picked up, I introduced myself. "Hi, it's Roselyn Schmidt...excuse me, I mean Wolff. Roselyn Wolff. I bought a house through you a few weeks ago—"

"Oh yes! How are you Roselyn? Are you enjoying your new home?"

"Yes, thank you. I was just wondering if you had any information about the previous owners, or if you had heard anything…strange…about the house."

"Oh dear, is something wrong?"

"No, no. Some things have just come to my attention and I was hoping I could find out more about the house."

"With foreclosures I have very little information about the previous owners or the house itself, really. I can probably find you a name, but that's about all I can do."

"That's all right," I said. "I recall seeing the name on some of the forms. I was just wondering if you'd heard anything, being a small community and all."

"No, nothing of the sort, I assure you. It's a perfectly lovely home."

I thanked the realtor for her time and hung up the phone. It seemed that if there was something wrong with this house, and people had been living here before me, surely someone would know something.

I went rummaging through my papers from when I closed on the house, and eventually I found a name. The home had been foreclosed on a woman named Tilda Titus. I got online and did a search on her. It didn't take me long to find her. My address was listed as her previous address, and her current address was at some retirement home about forty-five minutes away.

What was I doing? I wasn't actually going to go bother some old woman about a house she lost to the bank, was I? And spouting nonsense about voices and lost time and a strange man at my doorstep, no less! No, I couldn't do that. I wouldn't do that. Everything was fine. I'd sent Trent away, this was all a hoax, and it was over. This will be the end of it, I convinced myself.

For the next week, everything was quiet. Trent Morgan had disappeared, I heard no voices, and my clocks all stayed perfectly in sync…sort of. The house clocks did seem to run a little slow for some reason, but they were only off by a minute or two each day by the time I got home from work. Admittedly, it was odd, but nothing I couldn't deal with. I adjusted them and went on with my day.

I should've been perfectly happy, but I wasn't. I found myself thinking about Trent on a daily basis, and I wished I hadn't run him off. It was probably just my loneliness affecting my logic, but I kind of missed the excitement of having him show up. He was weird and he never said what you thought he should say, but…I realized I kind of liked that about him. If I hadn't been so suspicious of him, I might've become friends with him, even if he was a complete mystery. But now, the more I thought about him, the more I wanted to know who he was. I worried that I might never find out, and I knew it would always bother me if I never saw him again.

Suddenly, as I sat absent-mindedly petting Cattiel on the couch next to me while I day-dreamed with the television on in the background, the house was filled with the low murmur of voices. As I froze and listened, I caught movement out of the corner of my eye. My head swiveled around just in time to see a shadowy figure glide across the kitchen and disappear into a wall, and the voices were silenced in an instant.

Chapter 3

I sprang from the couch almost as quickly as my heart had leapt into my throat.

"Hey!" I yelled at the vanished entity, because…well, that's just what you do when something like that happens.

I watched the kitchen and hallway for several minutes, expecting something more to happen. But that was it. There wasn't anything else. I glanced over at Cattiel, and he seemed perfectly unperturbed. I looked over at the front door, wondering if Trent was going to magically show up. I wouldn't have minded if he did.

I sat back down and took a few deep breaths, trying to calm my nerves. In an attempt to distract myself from my racing heart, I returned my attention to the television show I had been half-watching earlier, but it was over already. I checked the channel guide, but it was on the five o'clock block of shows. That wasn't right. It was only supposed to be 2:30PM.

"No, no, no! Not again!" I cried. I looked at my phone and felt an overwhelming uneasiness when I saw it said it was 5:26PM. It hit me right in the gut to finally accept that this time it absolutely wasn't a trick. This was real.

I quickly scrolled through my phone log and called the ridiculous number that I knew would connect me to Trent. The line crackled and beeped for a while, and just as I was beginning to think maybe he wasn't going to answer, I was greeted by his jovial voice.

"It happened again, didn't it?"

"Yes. Well, kind of. Did you know I was going to call? I feel like you were expecting this."

"I knew you'd need my help eventually. What happened this time?"

"There were voices and an apparition in my kitchen, just for a moment, and then the time changed by almost three hours. Are ghosts causing the time changes?"

"Time 'change' isn't really what's going on. The rate at which time passes in relation to the rest of the world is what is changing. It isn't that the time on the clock just suddenly 'changed.' You do understand that, right?"

"I don't care about the semantics. All I know is that I've lost three hours of my life in an instant and I want this to stop!"

"Oh, no, you haven't lost those hours. Well, you did lose them from today, I suppose. But you aren't 'out' that time in the biological sense. Actually, you're three hours younger than you should be now."

"I'm sorry, what?"

"Do try to keep up, will you? You only age as quickly as the time you experience. If you experience a twenty-one-hour day, then you have only aged twenty-one hours rather than twenty-four. In other words, you've discovered the fountain of youth."

"Why, though? Why is this happening?" I asked.

"Gravity."

"Yes, but gravity from what?"

"I don't know," he said simply.

"I thought you were going to figure it out!"

"You told me to go away!"

"I thought you were the one responsible for the things happening!"

"Obviously I'm not!"

"I know that now!"

"Then why are you yelling at me?!"

"I don't know! You're yelling at me!"

"You started yelling first!"

I stopped and took a deep breath. "Ok. Ok. I'm sorry," I said calmly.

"You should be. You've been quite cross with me, and I've done very little to deserve it."

"You're right."

"I beg your pardon?"

"I said you were right."

Trent chuckled from the other end of the line. "I know. I just wanted to hear you say it again. I do enjoy being right. I mean, I am most of the time, but it's still nice to hear it once in a while."

"So are you coming or not?" I asked impatiently.

I heard him gasp. "Are you actually inviting me to come help? But you usually get angry with me when I do that."

I sighed. "You've made your point. Just come help me."

"Be there in a jiff."

I ended the call and turned around – and Trent was standing in my living room.

I gave a quick gasp of surprise and threw my hand over my startled heart. "Good lord, I cannot get used to that."

"The fact that you aren't shouting at me right now indicates that perhaps you are starting to get used to it." Trent smiled slyly.

"How do you do that? How?"

"Let's wait until we know each other a little better before we start divulging our secrets, eh?" he suggested as he looked at his watch and walked to the kitchen. He walked through the path the apparition had taken through the kitchen and stopped, backing up again until he was right in the middle of it. "It was here, wasn't it?"

"The ghost? Yes. It floated through the wall over there and disappeared," I said, pointing.

"Disappeared? Or did it pass through the wall and go into…" Trent glanced around, then walked down the hall and looked into the door to his right. "…The loo? And then right through the loo to the next room, and so on? I don't think these walls exist to whatever came through here. Or perhaps it just doesn't have enough solid form to be affected by the walls." Trent pulled his glasses from his pocket and put them on. "Is this a dimensional overlap or a parallel problem?" he muttered to himself as he activated the holographic display on his watch. The fingers of his right hand flitted through images and numbers and symbols as he looked at the display pensively. He stopped for a moment to turn and look at the clock on the wall, then the clocks on the appliances in the kitchen. "Parallel. Definitely parallel," he said as he returned his attention to the watch.

"Do you know what it is?" I asked. "Is there anything I can do?" I felt completely useless standing in the living room just watching him. I wasn't accustomed to feeling useless.

He held his finger up in the air to quiet me. "I'm thinking."

I frowned at him but kept my mouth shut.

He stared at the display before him and scowled. "I know I fix this eventually, but I can't seem to crack it!" he complained.

I gave him a puzzled look. "How do you know you fix this eventually?"

He looked at me with raised eyebrows, like he had just remembered I was still in the room. "Oh! Well…I fix everything eventually. Usually. Most of the time. I've had a lot of time to ponder this query, so I should have figured it out by now!"

"It doesn't seem like that long to me. You've had, what, a week?"

He smirked mysteriously. "Something like that."

"Is there something you aren't telling me?"

He glanced over at me, still smirking, and winked at me through his glasses without saying a word. In that moment, I realized he no longer seemed "plain" to me. I felt the corners of my mouth lifting slightly, wanting to smile back at him.

Stop it. He's weird, remember?

"Shall we go see what Tilda Titus has to tell us?" Trent said cheerily as he deactivated the holographic display on his watch. He tilted his head to the side and raised his eyebrows. "That was oddly satisfying to say. 'What Tilda Titus has to tell us.' Tilda Titus. That's quite a name," he mused.

"How did you know about Tilda Titus?"

"I'm very clever," he said simply. He took off his glasses and slid them back into the inside breast pocket of his jacket. "Come along now. Grab on," Trent instructed, gesturing for me to come to him.

"What? No. Why?"

"If you want to take the long way 'round, be my guest. Last chance." He tinkered with his watch briefly, then looked at me expectantly. "You can't tell me you don't want to give it a go."

"Are you serious? You're going to zap us there, just like that?"

He cringed at my terminology. "Zap, no. No zapping. We're going to teleport."

"Using the thing that does a thing."

"Yes! Now you're getting it," he exclaimed, pointing at me approvingly. "Let's go!"

I approached him somewhat timidly and stood next to him. I was afraid of what this was going to feel like. Did it hurt to teleport? Was there a flying sensation?

"Do you have an aversion to physical contact with strange men?" Trent asked, looking down at me.

"I think I can give a universal yes to that statement on behalf of all women everywhere."

"Well, time to get over it," he said as he put his arm around me and pulled me to him. He was stronger than I had expected. "Hold on tight! Here we go!"

I squeezed my eyes shut and shamelessly threw my arms around Trent's torso, hanging on for dear life. Adrenaline shot through my veins and my heart raced and…nothing happened.

"You can let go now," I heard Trent whisper with amusement.

I opened my eyes. We were outside. I quickly released Trent and took three steps back, looking around. We were around the side of a large building.

"Was that it?" I asked, confused.

"That was it," he replied with a big smile.

"But…it didn't feel like anything. I thought it would be…exciting," I said with disappointment.

"That weirdly hurts my feelings," Trent said, looking a little surprised.

"Why?" I asked with a short laugh.

"You think my thing that does a thing is inadequate. I thought you'd be impressed." He looked down at his watch and frowned. He gave me a disgruntled look and waved for me to follow him. "Come on, let's meet Tilda," he said flatly as he started to walk away.

I laughed unapologetically for a moment and then followed him around to the front of the building.

We went inside and approached the receptionist.

"Hello," Trent said. "We were hoping to visit with Tilda Titus today. Would that be possible?"

The man behind the counter looked at us sympathetically. "I'm sorry to be the one to tell you this, but Tilda is no longer with us. She passed a few days ago. Are you family? You were here just last week, weren't you?"

"Oh, dear!" Trent said in surprise. "Oh, I'm sorry to hear that. We were acquaintances. When is the funeral?"

The receptionist gave us details on the wake and funeral, and we left quickly after that. Trent headed around to the side of the building where we had arrived.

"Why did you ask about the funeral? Are we going?" I asked.

"No, of course not. But it would've seemed callous to not ask about it, now wouldn't it?"

I scrunched my face. "Really? Well, I suppose, maybe."

"Do you have feelings?" Trent asked me sardonically.

"Of course I do. I'm not a sociopath."

"I do wonder," Trent muttered.

I ignored him and asked, "Were you there the other day, like the receptionist said? Is that how you knew about Tilda?" I asked Trent.

"Apparently I was, but I figured out who she was before that."

"What did she say to you?"

"I don't know yet."

I stopped and crossed my arms. "Excuse me? How do you not know yet?"

"I haven't done it yet."

"But you did it just the other day."

"Correct." He looked at me blankly. "…Is there a problem?"

I waved my arms dramatically. "Yes! How does any of this make sense to you?! If you did it the other day, how can you not have done it yet?!"

"Oh," Trent said, realization washing over his face. "I forgot that you don't know yet. All right, off we pop to the past. Grab on."

Before I could protest, Trent pulled me to him and pressed a button on his watch. It was almost like watching a single frame change of a time lapse video. We were in the same spot, and things looked mostly the same, but minor things like cars parked in the street and the wind speed had changed in an instant.

"Did we just time travel?" I asked in awe.

Trent ruffled my hair as though I was a child. "Sure did!" He started to walk away.

I scowled and quickly combed my fingers through my long, straight hair to fix whatever mess he had made of it. I hurried after him.

We followed the same procedure as last time, only now we were able to visit with Tilda. As we were being led by a nurse through the corridors to the sitting room where we were told Tilda was drawing, I felt strangely. I knew she would be dead soon. Trent knew she would be dead soon. But no one else knew. This felt wrong.

"Aren't you bothered by this?" I whispered to Trent. "We know when she's going to die."

"But she doesn't, and it needs to stay that way," he warned.

"You and I have a lot to talk about when we are done here."

"I suspect we do."

The nurse led us into a large room with a television, comfortable chairs, a bookshelf, and tables. There were only about five people in the room at the time.

"Where is everyone?" I asked the nurse.

"You came at a relatively quiet hour. Many of our residents like to rest in their rooms around this time," he said.

He took us over to a woman who looked entirely too young to be in a retirement home. She had very little gray mixed in her saffron hair, and her skin was fairly smooth still. She only looked to be in her early sixties, but she was supposed to be close to eighty. She was sitting at a table with paper and pencils scattered about her, her attention completely focused on the artwork she was creating.

"Tilly," the nurse said in a soft voice as he rested his hand gently on her shoulder. Her head shot up and she looked around wildly, eyes wide with fright. "Tilly, these nice people are here to visit with you. Are you all right with that? Is it ok if they sit and visit with you?"

Tilda looked at Trent and squinted her eyes. "Are you one of...them?" she asked in a hushed whisper.

Trent pulled out the chair next to Tilda and sat down. "No. But I'm here to figure out who they are," he replied calmly. "I just need your help in understanding when they first showed up."

I was already lost. Who were "they"?

The nurse came to me and said quietly, "I'll be around the corner if you need me. Tilly is prone to delusions, but she's harmless. I'll come check on you in a little while." He turned and walked away.

I pulled out a chair next to Trent and sat down, feeling uneasy. What did he mean she was "prone to delusions"? Did she have dementia? Alzheimer's? I looked down at the pictures she was drawing, and I immediately recognized what she was depicting – shadow figures, like the one I'd seen earlier today. Or, not today, but whatever day I had come from. One of them, however, was more frightening than the others. The one that particularly drew my attention was the drawing of a tall, broad-bodied shadow figure with long arms and long, gnarly fingers, red eyes, and a wide, gaping mouth. Was this something she had seen in that house? In my house?

"When did you start seeing them, Tilly?" Trent asked, indicating the figures in the pictures she had drawn.

"Oh, right from the get go," she said. "I bought that house back in 1971 after my husband died in an accident. He had been the love of my life. I never did remarry. The house he had built for us just held too many memories for me, and I thought a change would help me move on. At first, I thought the Time Thieves were the ghost of my late husband. I would talk to them when I saw them, and it made me feel like he wasn't really gone. They never spoke back, of course. Never paid any attention to me. None of them but the one," she said ominously. She looked over at the picture she had drawn of the tall, frightening shadow figure. "That one...I still have nightmares about him. The Big Bad, I called him. He wanted something, but I never could figure out what it was. Whatever it is, it ain't good." She was thoughtful for a moment. "No one ever believed me. Truth be told, sometimes I miss the Time Thieves. They kept me young. But I will never miss the Big Bad." Tilda looked over at Trent with a slightly confused, almost suspicious expression. "You know, I spent a long time around them. As I got older, I found I could sense them coming. When you came today, I felt that same feeling."

"Maybe you were just sensing that we have seen them too, Tilly. I assure you, I am not one of them. This young lady here," Trent gestured toward me, "is Roselyn Wolff. She bought your house, and she saw her first Time Thief recently. I'm trying to help her make the Time Thieves go away. I was wondering if you had any suggestions for us?"

It surprised me when Trent used my last name. I was unaware that he knew it.

"They won't go away," Tilda asserted. "They live there. Why would you want them to go away? If I had the choice, I would still be living there too. I probably would've lived forever if the bank hadn't taken the house from me."

I felt a lump in my throat. She was going to die soon, and she had no idea. Not a clue. She looked perfectly healthy, but she was going to die. In fact, in my time, she is dead. I'm sitting here talking to a dead woman. It made my skin crawl.

Tilly continued, "Just watch out for the Big Bad. Whenever he shows up, you'll be sick for days. He's going to really hurt someone someday, I just know it."

"Sick? What do you mean sick? What kind of symptoms?" Trent asked.

"Weird symptoms. Throwing up, bloody nose, and just feeling completely wiped out for days. One time he showed up and hung around for longer than usual, and after that I noticed a lot of hair loss when I was in the shower. It all grew back eventually, but that one had me worried."

"That is odd. Very odd. Say, Tilly, can you tell me about the time loss at the house? Did it only happen when the Time Thieves showed up?"

"It was sporadic. All of it was, really. I would have weeks, sometimes months of relative calm, and then the whole house would go haywire for days on end. The most time they ever took from my day in one go was a 16-hour block. I had no night that day. It went from evening to the next morning just like that," Tilda said with a snap of her fingers. "That was the time the Big Bad showed up and made my hair fall out."

"Wow, that's incredible," Trent said. "Now, you said the Time Thieves never paid you any attention or responded to you when you talked to them. Have you ever heard them make any noise, or ever heard any unexplained voices in the house?"

"No, nothing like that. They were always silent."

I heard voices, though. What does that mean? I wondered to myself.

"Tilly, thank you so much for taking time out of your day to share your wisdom with us. You have been such a tremendous help. It was so wonderful to meet you. I'll let you get back to your day and your drawings. Thank you," Trent said as he stood and gently shook Tilda's hand.

I thanked her and shook her hand as well, trying to keep my emotions in check. I didn't want to stay at my house. Tilda's story had terrified me. I could handle Time Thieves if I had to, but the Big Bad scared the hell out of me. I wanted to run home immediately and get Cattiel out of the house. Poor Cattiel was there all by himself in that creepy house!

…But wait, he wasn't, was he? If I was in the past, then I was also at home with Cattiel right at that very moment. I was in two places at one time.

I walked with Trent down the corridor back to the lobby. How could he seem so calm and collected right now? He had a pleasant smile on his face as though he had just visited his grandma and was headed out for a nice walk in the park – when in reality he had just visited with a dead woman in the past and was returning to a house in the present that was full of potential horrors. Who was this guy?!

Chapter 4

We walked out the front doors and headed around the side of the building. As soon as we were out of earshot of anyone else, I started in on him.

"How did you know my last name? I never told you that."

"I found Tilda Titus, but you didn't expect me to find out your last name?"

"Most things still have Schmidt as my last name. I just recently changed it back to Wolff. Even I sometimes forget it isn't Schmidt anymore."

"This is what you're hung up on? After all that has happened today, you are upset because I know your last name?" He stood in front of me with his arms hanging at his sides and his head tilted slightly to the side in exasperated disbelief.

"No. I'm not upset. I just don't understand how you just know things."

"Get used to it. It's my job to know things."

"What is your job, exactly? Where did you come from? And what's with the tweed suits?" I said, pointing at his outfit.

"Oi!" Trent objected with a look of injury. He looked down at his suit. "What's wrong with my suit? This suit is cool." He tugged at his lapels to help emphasize his point.

"Are you ever going to tell me anything about yourself?"

"I suspect so, but not right now. You've gone and insulted me."

"I didn't say there was anything wrong with your suits. I just asked about them," I countered.

"It was the way you asked about them. 'What's with the tweed suits?'" he said, mimicking me in an exaggerated high-pitched voice. "There's nothing 'with' them. They're fantastic."

"Ok, ok! They're lovely."

He gave me a disgusted face. "They aren't lovely! A woman's blouse is lovely. A floral summer dress is lovely. My manly, cool, stylish suits are not lovely."

"You're right. They're horrid."

Trent opened his mouth in brief outrage. "Sociopath," he mumbled as he turned his attention to his watch.

I chuckled to myself, and I saw the corner of his mouth curve upward slightly in the beginnings of a smile. I think he enjoyed the banter almost as much as I did. I really needed to stop finding new ways to like this madman.

"Let's get you home," he said as he held his arm out to me, "…before I decide to leave you here."

I walked up to him and he wrapped his arm around my waist, nestling me next to him snugly. I noticed he smelled pleasant. He had a clean and faintly woodsy scent.

"You'd come back for me," I said.

"I'd have to. Two of you in the same timeline would be a bloody nightmare."

In an instant, I was in my own living room again. I thought I would feel more apprehensive about being home after hearing Tilda's story, but I wasn't. With Trent there, things didn't seem quite as scary. His perpetual ridiculousness kept my mind distracted from the possible dangers we could face.

I slid out from under Trent's arm and walked over to the couch, plopping down next to a slumbering Cattiel. Cattiel opened his eyes and looked at me contemptuously.

"I love you, too," I said to the cat sarcastically.

Out of the corner of my eye I saw Trent – who is normally gesticulating about and fidgeting with his watch and just generally a wiry ball of energy – freeze in his tracks. He glanced over at me with a strangely startled expression, and quickly looked away again.

"What is it?" I asked, concerned.

"Nothing. It's nothing. How has Cattiel fared in our absence?"

"He hasn't budged since we left."

"I wouldn't imagine so. We've been gone less than a minute."

I raised my eyebrows at him. "Really?! But it seemed like half an hour!"

"Well, it has been half an hour for us. You remember when I said that you only age as much as the time you experience? Well, it applies in this case too. In your present time, only a minute has passed, but you have aged half an hour."

I ran my hand through my hair and thought about what that meant. "So, does that mean you're the real Time Thief? Time travelling with you takes time away from me biologically? If I were to go to the past with you repeatedly and be gone for hours at a time, and you always brought me back to the moment after we left, I would age faster than other people, wouldn't I?"

"Yes." He was avoiding my gaze.

"How old are you?" I asked him.

"Don't you know it's rude to ask someone their age?"

"How old are you, Trent?" I repeated firmly.

He gave me a tight smile. I didn't know how he could manage to look so sad with a smile on his face. "Older than I look."

"…how?" I asked.

Trent's demeanor suddenly became more playful. He clapped his hands together. "Here I am, spending all this time talking about myself. What about you? What's your story? You and your," he pointed awkwardly, "cat…Cattiel. How did you end up here?"

He started to wander about the kitchen before I even opened my mouth. "You're trying to avoid my questions," I said.

"Who's doing what?" he asked as he began rummaging through my cupboards.

"You heard me," I said.

"Blimey! What's with all this health food? Where are all your fabulously fatty American essentials? Your snack cakes and cereals and biscuits and crisps?"

"I'm a fitness trainer. I don't buy a lot of that stuff."

He turned to me with his face contorted in disgust. "You only eat kale, don't you?"

I laughed. "No. I don't like kale."

"Oh good. I thought for a moment I was going to have to end our friendship."

"We're friends?"

"As long as you don't try to make me eat kale. Kale is rubbish. Oh! Look! You do have treats!" I heard plastic wrappers crinkling and knew immediately he had found my secret stash of chocolate toaster pastries.

Trent came out to the living room and flopped down on the other couch across from me. My living room seemed so much smaller with two people in it. He happily and noisily unwrapped a packet of pastries and took a ridiculously huge bite out of one. He sat there staring at me while he chewed.

"You didn't bring me one?" I asked jokingly.

"Oh." He pulled the second pastry from the crinkly wrapper and tossed it at me. "How convenient. It comes with two so if you're with someone, you can share. And if you're not, you can eat two because you're sad and lonely."

I laughed as I took a bite, and we sat without speaking for several minutes. Usually, when you're first getting to know someone, sitting in silence for any amount of time is uncomfortable. That was oddly not the case with Trent. He was usually talking or ranting or arguing, and I would have thought a moment of silence with him would be awkward, if not insufferable. But it wasn't. It seemed so perfectly, completely bearable.

"Ok, here's the thing, and you aren't going to like it," Trent broke the silence.

"Oh goody."

"I need to stay here."

I furrowed my brow. "What? Why?"

"I need to get measurements from the actual Time Thief events. Since we can't predict when they're going to happen, I need to wait it out. Think of me as a temporary roommate. I'll compensate you."

"Why don't I just call you when it happens, and you can go back in time and show up right before it happens to collect your measurements?" I suggested.

Trent grimaced. "Eh, that's probably not the best idea. The energy used to make the trip may end up affecting my measurements. It might also create a minor paradox and I really hate creating paradoxes."

"I thought a paradox indicated something was impossible."

Trent see-sawed his hand and said, "Well, not quite." He failed to elaborate.

"So you're going to be sleeping on my couch until something happens?"

Trent looked disappointed. "Really? You don't have a guestroom?"

"I have two spare rooms, but there aren't any beds in them."

"That's all right, I don't need a bed. I don't sleep much anyway."

"Can I ask you something?"

"If I say no are you going to ask me anyway?"

"Do you have a home?"

"Yes."

"Oh."

"You sound surprised. You thought I was homeless?!" he said with indignation.

"I don't know!"

"Well, for your information, I have several homes."

"Where do you live?"

"Wherever I want."

"What do you do for money?"

"It depends. How much do you have?" Trent asked with a raised eyebrow.

"You know what I mean," I smirked. "How can you afford several houses? Where do you get your money?"

"I have my ways."

I inhaled sharply. "Are you a criminal?"

"No, I'm not a criminal. But I'm not going to say I've never broken any laws. Say, how is it we always end up talking about me?" Trent wanted to know.

"You are a walking impossibility. Of course I want to talk about you," I replied.

"You have a house enshrouded in an inexplicable mystery. Let's talk about you and this house." Trent held up his index finger. "First thing I need to know, though, is whether I am going to have to be wary of tripwires throughout the house at any point during my stay."

I laughed. "No, I took that down."

"You know what I wonder, now that I'm thinking about it? Why, if you were so suspicious of me at first, you never once threatened me? You have a gun."

"I didn't find you threatening. Not physically, anyway. Plus, you have a way of disarming someone with your delightful weirdness."

"I'm not sure whether you just complimented me or insulted me."

I stood up and went to the fridge. "Do you drink?" I asked.

"Not usually."

"Well, I'm having a glass of wine. You're welcome to a glass if you're interested."

"Thanks, but I'm all right."

"You aren't sitting out there judging me, are you?" I asked as I poured myself a fairly full goblet of Sangria.

"I wouldn't dream of it."

I returned to the couch and sat down, careful not to spill my drink.

Trent leaned forward and rested his elbows on his knees. "I have to ask: why did you think I was working with someone to trick you? What was that all about?"

I took a long drink of my wine. "Have you ever been in a relationship with a toxic person, Trent?" I asked.

"Relationships aren't really my forte."

"Let me paint you a picture, then. I married a man because he made me feel so badly about myself that I thought no one else would ever want me, and after I realized how unhappy I was, I was afraid to leave because I didn't know what he would do. He couldn't hold a job for more than a few months before either causing a scene and walking out or getting fired for being confrontational. When I was sleeping between working or college classes, he would go online and chat with other women. I wasn't allowed to mention the name of any other man, even classmates or coworkers. If I did, suddenly he thought I was having an affair with them. If I was two minutes later than usual getting home from work, he thought I was having an affair. I became obsessive about how I managed my time just to prove to him I wasn't cheating and I wasn't a bad person – trying to prove him wrong. If a man tried to talk to me, regardless of how innocent the exchange was, it made me nervous because then I had to decide whether to tell him about it or not. If I told him, eventually it would turn into 'you're having an affair with him!' If I didn't tell him, I would constantly worry that he was going to find out about it and then accuse me of trying to hide it – because 'you're having an affair with him!'

"I remember one year we had a neighbor living in our apartment complex who went to school with me and was even in the same degree program. He was a nice guy, and I liked him quite well. One day, Barry had taken my car and left me with his crappy one, and of course when I went to start it, the battery was dead. I had class that day, and no way to get there. Luckily for me, though, my neighbor happened to be heading to the same class, and he saw me with the hood up. He asked if I wanted a ride, but heavens no, I knew I couldn't do that. Barry would bring down the whole complex if I accepted a ride from another man. So instead, he jump-started the battery, and I thanked him and was on my way. Well, later that evening, as I waited for Barry to get home from whatever random job he had at the time, I wrung my hands in anticipation of having to tell him about our neighbor helping me. He came home, and I gave him a detailed account of what had transpired earlier that day. It was all completely innocent. You know what he did? He stormed out the door and stomped halfway to our neighbor's building, screaming and shouting about how he was going to kick his ass! I was so embarrassed, and I fought to keep him from ruining anyone else's day aside from my own. I finally managed to get him back to our apartment, but not without a lot of yelling in the parking lot and storming back and forth. I think I got accused of having an affair with that neighbor fairly regularly because of that one incident.

"He didn't just scare me away from other men, though. He cut me off from all of my friends, too, and now no one wants anything to do with me," I continued. "He wanted all of my passwords as proof that I had nothing to hide from him, and he then used them to go online under my social media accounts and pretend he was me, sending hateful or strange messages to people. Most of them didn't realize it wasn't me. They all just thought I'd lost my mind and they stopped interacting with me.

"He was so incredibly manipulative. I have no idea how he did it, but he always made me feel like I needed to prove myself to him. Instead of feeling like I needed to get the hell out of there, I just kept trying harder. I cried a lot, yelled and got yelled at a lot, and spent a large portion of every day with a huge knot of anxiety in my chest." I stopped to wipe the tears that were suddenly streaming down my face.

"I'm sorry, I didn't mean to bring up something so obviously painful," Trent said apologetically. "You don't have to talk about it. I understand now why you were so suspicious of me showing up at your doorstep."

"No, I think I need to get it out. I've never told anyone all of this. Everybody knew he was awful, but nobody ever got the full story. I think it's time to get it off my chest."

"Then by all means, please continue," Trent said soberly.

"I think the worst part was wondering what he was going to do next – what trick he was going to pull, or what outlandish story he was going to concoct about me that I was supposed to prove wasn't true in order to clear my name. He called me horrible names and accused me of horrible things. He would turn my words around and then repeat them to me, declaring that that was what I had said, even though I knew it wasn't true. He made me question what was real. I remember him calling me 'a pile of dog shit' one Christmas because I had bought him a $20 bag of tobacco. We were dirt poor at the time, and that was all I could afford. He had bought me an $11 necklace from Walmart that I apparently didn't deserve. As I recall, he threw it out the window of the car as we drove down the highway. Another Christmas, we had used money I had earned as a waitress to buy a digital camera as my gift. He threw it at me and broke it on Christmas day shortly after I opened it.

"He made me crazy. He changed who I was. I wasn't me anymore, and the longer I was with him, the more I lost myself to his insanity. It started to leach into my brain, and I started thinking like him – not because I wanted to, but as a survival mechanism. I needed to know what he was going to do. I needed to be able to predict the unpredictable, and it drove me to the brink of madness. Sometimes I worry that I've been completely broken and I won't ever be able to have a normal relationship again. I feel like I'll always be in a state of recovery – never completely healed from this," I choked out the words.

Trent came and sat near me on my couch. He leaned over and put his hand on my back and rubbed it gently in a comforting gesture. "I am so sorry you were ever treated that way. But can I tell you something? You aren't broken. From what I have observed, you are strong and independent and absolutely wonderful. If you ask me, I think you are strong as steel."

"That's the thing, though. I don't feel strong. I can't believe how incredibly weak I was for allowing him to keep me under his thumb for so long. Why didn't I just walk away at the first sign that something was off? Why didn't I? Why the hell did I stay so damn long?!" I couldn't stop the full-on snot-spewing sobbing that ensued.

Trent got up and took my wine glass from me, setting it down on the end table near the couch. He stepped in front of me, grabbed my hands, and pulled me to my feet. The next thing I knew, my face was buried in his shoulder and his arms were wrapped tightly around me.

"I'm going to get snot on your tweed suit," I blubbered.

"It's all right. I have other suits. Snot away."

I knew I should restrain myself and find my composure. I knew I had no reason to feel this comfortable with someone I had only just met recently. But, by god, it felt so good to be held and let it all out. I didn't feel judged or looked down upon. He held me close and embraced me without reservation. I cried until I felt like I had run out of tears. And snot.

When Trent finally released me from his arms, I immediately checked his jacket.

"Oh, gross, I'm so sorry," I apologized profusely as I looked at the big wet mark my face had left.

"Trust me, I've had worse," he said.

As I settled down, I felt it was important to finish my story. "After all this and I haven't even recounted the horrible things he did when I did finally leave him," I said. "This is the part where my mistrust of you begins to make sense.

"After I found out he had been physically unfaithful, I finally found the courage to leave. It wasn't easy though. He made sure of that. He threw a fit, of course, breaking things and yelling in my face the entire time I was packing things in boxes. He'd stop and cry, trying to make me feel bad, and then he'd turn around and threaten me when that didn't work. He made promises to change, then made promises of revenge against me. He tried to force himself on me, then called me names when I fought him off. It was a nightmare.

"When I finally did get out with whatever belongings I had that he hadn't broken yet, I still wasn't out of the nightmare yet. I moved in with my parents briefly, and at night he'd drive up their driveway just far enough for his headlights to fall on my car so he could see I was there. He'd then back out of the driveway and drive off. He'd call from payphones so the caller ID wouldn't register that it was him. He'd call and leave long, creepy messages on my parents' answering machine. If by chance you did answer the phone to try to tell him to stop calling, he'd just hang on the line so you couldn't hang up or make any other calls because my parents have a landline. He was relentless.

"Then came the games. He'd show up at my work and put things under or in my car. He posted an ad on the internet that gave out my name and phone number and wrote that I hated certain religious groups. Calls poured in with death threats against me, and of course I had no idea what the hell was going on. Then he went online and signed up everyone I knew for dirty magazine subscriptions. Some of them he even had sent to their places of employment. They were then sent bills for the subscriptions and had to deal with trying to get those cancelled. He just wouldn't let things go. I've spent every moment since I moved out wondering what new hell was coming next.

"So now you know the whole story. Now you can fully understand why I would be so wary of you and why I would believe so whole-heartedly that this was all some kind of trick or game," I said.

"I have no words," Trent said. "I'm sorry I pushed you so hard at first. I had no idea what kind of psychological and emotional torment you had just been through. I didn't fully understand. Now I do. Thank you for sharing with me. I know that couldn't have been easy."

"I feel a lot better right now than I have in a long time. I needed to do that. I needed to talk about it. I'm sorry your jacket had to suffer for it," I said, trying to lighten the mood.

Trent looked down at his jacket. "Yeah…but it was worth it."

"I probably look like a damn train wreck now, though, don't I?"

"Eh, a bit blotchy and puffy, but that's to be expected, isn't it? I don't mind if you don't."

"Honestly, I really don't." I looked over at the clock on the wall and realized I still needed to change all of the clocks ahead almost three hours. Then I mentally calculated the actual time. "Oh shoot, I need to eat," I said as I leapt up from the couch, wiping away the last of the tears from my eyes. "Are you hungry?"

"I could eat. Should I pop out for some takeaway?" he asked as he stood up and jutted his thumb toward the door.

"No, no. I prefer to eat at home."

"Well that's a bit boring, isn't it?"

"Hey, at least I know what goes into my food if I'm the one preparing it. I have a hard time trusting other people with my food. People are disgusting and food poisoning is no joke."

"I suppose you're not wrong," Trent said as he followed me into the kitchen. "What are you making? It isn't kale, is it?" he asked, wrinkling his nose.

"What do you like? It's your first night as my temporary roommate, so I suppose I should try to make you feel at home."

"I like takeaway. Pizza or Chinese, ideally."

I put my hand on my hip and turned to him. "What do you like that isn't takeout?"

He pressed his lips together and his brows knitted thoughtfully. "Um…eggs? I like eggs."

"That's not a meal. You said you like Chinese, so what if I made some fried rice and stir fry? Would that be acceptable?"

"You aren't going to put k—"

"No kale!" I shouted.

Trent leaned away from me in mock surprise. "Good grief, what did kale ever do to you?"

I closed my eyes and took a deep breath. "Go sit down. I'll let you know when the food is ready."

"I can help! Probably. Maybe. Well, I don't really cook, but I can hand you things," Trent offered, hovering over my shoulder as I started rummaging through the fridge.

"I can do it by myself, thank you. You'll just be underfoot."

Trent folded his arms and leaned against the wall near the kitchen table where he was out of the way. As I started getting my pans ready and chopping up vegetables, however, he wandered his way back into the main part of the kitchen again.

"So the conversation with Tilda today - we never discussed it. Aren't you curious what I've deduced?" he said, looking over my shoulder.

"What have you deduced?" I asked.

"When Tilda was talking about the Big Bad making her sick, it sounded an awful lot like radiation sickness. I'm guessing that much exposure to radiation is what ended up killing her."

"She was almost eighty. It could've been anything age-related."

"But she wasn't really eighty, though, was she? She was much younger than that in actuality."

"I suppose so. But what is the Big Bad, then? Why is it giving off radiation?"

"I haven't the foggiest," Trent confessed.

"What about the Time Thieves?"

"I'll know more after we have another 'event.' Whatever is going on seems to be either getting closer or growing in strength. The fact that you heard voices, but Tilda never did, makes me suspect this isn't just a constant, repetitive occurrence. This is something that's changing. But what is the endgame? Where is it headed? What's the next phase? How dangerous is this going to get?"

That last line made me pause. "Should I even be staying here? Am I in danger by being here?" I asked with concern.

"I won't let anything happen to you," Trent promised. "If the Big Bad is emitting radiation, my gadget will detect it," he said, pointing to his watch, "and I'll protect you from it."

"How are you going to protect me from radiation?"

"I can move us through time and space in an instant, but you doubt my technology can protect you from radiation?"

I put my hands up in submission. "Fair point."

As I stir-fried vegetables in the wok, I realized Trent had been awfully quiet for an abnormally long time. I turned around to see what he was up to just in time to see him walking into the kitchen with Cattiel curled up in his arms.

"How did you do that? He hates strangers," I said.

"I'm not a stranger. I'm your roomie." Trent stood next to me with the cat.

I held my arm up to barricade him from the stove. "You need to get the cat out of here. He's going to get hair in the food!"

"Aw, he just wants to see what you're doing," Trent protested. "Fine. Come on, Cattiel," he whispered to the cat. "She's being cross with us."

Trent managed to stay entertained by the cat while I finished dinner. I called him into the kitchen to set the table while I put the food on.

"This is so domestic," Trent commented as he laid out the utensils. "I thought it would be boring, but I'm rather enjoying it!"

We sat down to eat and I began to serve up my plate. "You act like a night at home is an all new experience. What is normal for you? Don't you ever just chill?"

"There are far too many adventures and excitement out there to waste my time 'chilling.'" Trent took a bite of his rice and stir-fry. "Hey, this is actually good! Well done!"

"I feel strangely insulted by the way you said that, but thank you, I guess?"

"I see you didn't put kale in it," Trent said. When I glowered at him, he flashed a playful smile.

I noticed he was trying to redirect the conversation yet again, like he always did when I tried to talk about him. It wasn't going to work this time. "So what do you do with your time, Trent? You just time travel and be weird?"

"And know things. Remember, it's my job to know things."

"Why? What do you do? You never really got around to explaining that."

Trent hesitated briefly before responding. "This, Roselyn," he said with a sigh as he gestured his arms widely to indicate the house in general. "This is what I do. I fix things and protect people from things they don't even know they need protection from. This is my life." He looked down at his plate as he took his next bite, avoiding my gaze.

"So…you're some kind of hero?"

"No. I'm not a hero," Trent said with a disdainful face and a dismissive wave of his hand.

"Where did you get that watch? Is that where all of your superpowers come from?"

Trent almost spit out his food. "Superpowers? Good grief, you've been reading too many comic books. My watch is a piece of technology, not a superpower."

"Where did it come from, though? That's way more advanced than anything we're capable of developing right now."

"I'm a time traveler, remember? That includes both backward and forward."

"But you had to acquire it before you could travel, so you couldn't go to the future to get a watch if you didn't have the wa—" I stopped midsentence as I finally understood.

Chapter 5

"You didn't start out here, did you?" I inquired.

Trent raised an eyebrow at me. "What do you mean by 'here'?"

"Either you aren't from this time, or you aren't from this planet. Or is it both?" I asked as I set my fork down. I couldn't focus on eating and the conversation at the same time. "Are Nohkeans an alien race?!"

"Relax, I'm not an alien," Trent assured me. "But no, I'm not from this time. Nohkea is a country that hasn't been established yet. It includes what you currently call the U.K."

"What time are you from?"

"A long time in the future."

"So why are you here? And why aren't there more of you? If we have time-traveling watches in the future, shouldn't our entire history be riddled with time-traveling tourists?"

"If that technology were made available to the public, then yes, it would be."

"But it isn't. Why?"

"There are several reasons why, but mostly it's because I exist. Oddly enough, that's the same reason the technology exists as well."

"I don't understand."

"I made the watch, Roselyn. They made me, and I made the watch. They wanted it to 'fix' history. To kill Hitler, stop the plagues, take away the nuclear bombs, stop the climate crisis, et cetera. But they didn't understand the implications. They didn't understand that, without the past, the present would change, and they wouldn't even know it because their memories would change to reflect their experiences. The only reason I would know the difference is because traveling through time changes your perception of events. History in my brain is established because I've stepped out of the timeline. I've removed myself from play. Think of it as a simulation. If you change things in it, no one inside the simulation would realize it was different. They'd think it'd always been that way. But if you are on the outside, jumping from simulation to simulation, you'd notice that things had changed. If they changed history, some people would suddenly cease to exist, forever erased. Others would pop into existence, full of memories of a childhood that hadn't happened in the original timeline. It would be utter chaos on Earth, and no one would be any the wiser – but me."

Trent got up from the table and took his plate to the sink. He rinsed it and opened the dishwasher. "What? No, you've packed your dishwasher all wrong!" he complained as he started rearranging my dirty dishes. "They don't get as clean when they are facing that way."

I stared at him in disbelief. "Forget the dishes! Who are 'they'? Who are you?!"

He stopped what he was doing and paused briefly. Then he stood up and faced me, standing rigidly with his heels together. He crossed one arm in front of his stomach and one behind his back and bowed deeply toward me. As he rose, he said, "Trent Morgan: the original Time Thief, at your service."

I stood up quickly, knocking my chair over. "You're one of those shadow things?!"

"No, not like that. I just like the name Tilda gave them and realized when you called me a Time Thief that the name really does apply," he said with a grin. He continued his story, "You see, it wasn't until after I had created the watch for them that I learned what I was and what they were planning to do with the technology. I knew they needed to be stopped, so I nicked the time-warping watch and ran. Do you get it now? Time Thief? It's quite perfect, really," Trent said with a pleased smile.

I wasn't smiling. Every time I felt like I was starting to get to know him, he threw me a curve ball and I was lost again.

Trent continued, "I've been using the watch ever since then to keep them from ever acquiring this technology. Whenever the watch detects a disturbance in the continuum, I investigate. If it's them, I take whatever measures I need to in order to stop them."

I needed to know more. "What do you mean by 'them,' and what do you mean they created you? Are you human, or aren't you?"

"It's not that simple," he said.

"Yes, it is. You either are, or you aren't."

"I am human…but tweaked," he said, demonstrating "tweaked" by twisting his hand with his fingers pressed together like he was turning a screw into the air.

"Explain. Explain all of it," I demanded as I righted my chair and sat back down.

"Can I finish arranging these dishes while I talk? They are truly bothering me," Trent said, pointing to the mess in the dishwasher.

"I don't care! As long as you talk!"

Trent gave me a thumbs-up and bent down to work on the dishes. "'They' are a united force of the global elite - the supremely wealthy and top politicians from the most powerful nations around the world. They call themselves SABER – Sovereign Alliance for the Betterment of Earth's Republic.

"Now, in the time that I come from, genetic engineering is lightyears beyond what is possible in this time period. They use gene therapy to treat disease, and they can grow tissue specifically for an individual to replace parts of the body that have been damaged by age or trauma. People can live longer, but they still hadn't found that fountain of youth. The technology was available to alter human embryos in the same way they altered animals and plants, but ethics had always stood in the way of designing human embryos – until SABER. SABER ran an elaborate, secret experiment on thousands of human zygotes. They used human DNA to create me, but they manipulated it in order to expand my cognitive capabilities and to lengthen and strengthen the telomeres that protect my DNA. In other words, I would be smarter and age more slowly than other humans. But that wasn't all. They also injected an experimental technology into the zygote that would grow into me – self-replicating nanobots that repair damage to my cells and restore my DNA as my telomeres shorten, like telomerase without the associated cancer risks. Of all of those trials, out of thousands of zygotes, I was the only success. So, I suppose you could say I am human, but not exactly a 'normal' one."

"How old are you, Trent?" I asked quietly.

He closed the dishwasher. "Oh, I don't know. I lost track a long time ago," he said as he turned to wash his hands in the sink. I had the feeling he wasn't being entirely truthful.

When he shut off the water, I asked, "Are you going to just keep living forever?"

He turned to me while he dried his hands on the towel hanging from the stove handle and shrugged. "I don't know. I'm sure something will kill me eventually. We all have a weakness, right? Maybe a wooden stake through the heart," he said jokingly.

"That isn't funny."

"But you had compared me to a vampire once, remember? It's a little funny."

"I don't know how to feel about all this," I said.

"You don't have to feel anything about it. It isn't your problem. Feeling sad or angry or glad or worried isn't going to make my situation any different. Trust me – I learned that a long, long time ago," he said cynically.

The air felt heavy as Trent walked out of the kitchen. I was at a loss for words. I had gotten what I wanted, hadn't I? I wanted to know who he was, and now I knew. So why did I feel so much further from him now than I did only moments ago when we were sitting down to our first meal together? It felt like he'd become a complete stranger yet again, and it bothered me.

As I walked into the living room, trying to think of something to say to Trent, he suddenly jumped up from the chair he had just sat in, his eyes fixed on his watch.

"It's still slower," he said. "Not as noticeable as a big event, but it's definitely slower." He walked around the chair and headed to the front door. He was still looking at his watch as he stepped outside to the front porch without explanation.

I started to follow him, but he came right back in and we almost collided in the doorway. I quickly stepped out of his way as he came through, clearly on a mission.

"What are you doing?" I asked, following him into the hallway.

"The time doesn't just move slower here during singular events – it moves slightly slower all the time. You know what that means?" he asked as he turned to me excitedly, looking away from his watch for the first time since he left his chair.

"What does that mean?"

"It means I can use that difference in the rate of time passing in order to roughly map out the borders of the bubble!" Trent looked at me expectantly. When I looked back at him blankly, his face fell. "You don't look impressed. I thought you'd be impressed."

"Oh, sorry. Um, yay!" I said with unconvincing cheer.

"You have zero appreciation for how clever that was," Trent said accusingly.

"I'm sorry, I'm afraid I'm still trying to catch up. Borders of the bubble? Like, physical lines drawn out where we can stand on one side or the other?"

"Yes! See, you were all caught up! Now you can look impressed."

"How are you going to mark the lines?" I asked. "I'm not going to let you draw all over my house."

"Do you want to figure this out or not?"

"Of course I do!"

"Then you're going to have to let me make a bit of a mess."

I looked at him reluctantly. "I don't like a mess," I confessed.

Trent stepped close to me and took my face between his hands suddenly. He touched his forehead to mine. "I'm afraid life is messy, my dear. You're just going to have to trust me that it'll all be worth it." He released me and dashed to the kitchen. I heard him rummaging through the drawers hastily as I tried to ignore the lingering flutter in my chest.

"Chalk!" he shouted to me. "Don't you have chalk?"

"I have no use for chalk," I replied as I followed him to the kitchen.

"You most certainly do! What about a marker? Preferably washable?"

I cringed. "I can get chalk tomorrow, so let's forget the markers, ok?"

Trent turned to me and crossed his arms. "You know, I'm beginning to question your commitment to finding a solution."

"Tomorrow is another day. It's getting late, and I have to work in the morning. I can pick up some chalk on my way home in the afternoon," I reasoned.

Trent sighed and pressed a button on his watch, disappearing instantly. He reappeared only seconds later, holding a stick of chalk.

"Did you just time-travel for chalk?"

"No, I just popped over to my chalkboard and came back."

"Your chalkboard? Where?"

"In one of my houses."

"Why didn't you just do that from the start?" I asked.

"I don't want to be teleporting in and out of here if I can help it. I don't want to be out when something happens."

I cleaned up the table and put the leftover food in the fridge while Trent ran about the house like an over-caffeinated child, marking lines and X's on walls and floors. I brushed my teeth and got ready for bed, hoping he would be done soon so he could retire to his room before I went to bed. He was not.

"Trent, I'm going to put a sleeping bag and a pillow up in your room," I yelled down to him in the basement. "I set out an unopened toothbrush for you in the bathroom and hung a fresh towel for you on the rack."

"Thank you!" he shouted up to me, but I didn't see him.

"What are you going to do for clothes? I don't have any men's clothing other than a pair of athletic pants and a couple of t-shirts. You're welcome to them if you want, but—"

Trent stuck his head around the corner and looked up the stairs at me. "I have clothes, but thank you." He ran off again.

"Where did you get clothes?"

"Same place I got the chalk," he yelled to me.

"But…ugh, I don't even care," I mumbled to myself. I grabbed a sleeping bag and a pillow from the closet and trudged up the stairs to the bedrooms tucked away at the top of the house. There were two of them and they were both identical, so I just picked the room on the left. As I laid out his sleeping bag and pillow on the floor, I heard him galloping up the stairs.

He burst into the room with a smile on his face. "This is most interesting! It appears that there is a small patch of the bubble that extends beyond the walls of the north side of the house! Also, do you have a torch?"

"What? Why would I have a torch?"

Trent looked at me strangely. "It's not that uncommon to have a torch. Most people do."

We stared at each other in confusion for a few moments before realization hit me. "Oh! You mean a flashlight!"

"Flashlight. Torch. Same thing."

"Why do you need a flashlight?"

"It's dark outside."

"You need to go outside?"

"Obviously."

I sighed. "Are you going to be at this much longer?"

"Not terribly."

"Is this spot ok for your sleeping bag?" I asked him.

"Oh! Lovely! Yes, that will do just fine."

I stood up and walked past him, heading out of the room. "The flashlight is in the kitchen drawer nearest the back door. Please shut off the lights when you go to bed."

"Roselyn," Trent said. I stopped halfway down the stairs and turned to look up. He was standing in the doorway of his room, looking down at me with a pleasant smile on his face. "Thank you for trusting me. I know this hasn't been easy for you. I promise I will figure this out as quickly as I can and then I'll get out of your hair."

"That would be great," I lied.

I lay in bed with Cattiel slumbering quietly at the foot of the bed and listened to Trent tromping around the house. Yes, the man did have enormous, clumsy feet, but I think even an elephant could have been quieter. He had a habit of occasionally talking to himself, as well. I couldn't fault him for that, though, because I was notorious for it. I just never realized how oddly it sounded hearing someone else doing it.

I thought about what he had said about figuring things out quickly and leaving. It should've given me some comfort to be reminded that this was just a temporary arrangement, but it did just the opposite. It reminded me of how lonely it was here before he'd shown up. It seemed weird that I would want him to stay for any length of time, didn't it? He was a genetically engineered time-traveler from the future. Why didn't that knowledge scare me? I was living in a house that had the potential to unleash a radioactive monster from thin air at any moment, yet I fully trusted that Trent would keep me safe. Why? What reason did I have to trust him so fully and completely after only knowing him for such a short amount of time?

And why did my foolish heart start racing every time he touched me?

I was lonely, that's why. It had been a while since I'd allowed a man to come that physically close to me.

But…there was something about him. I hadn't seen it at first, but it was there. It was there in the way he smiled at me. It was there in the way his eyes lit up when something struck him. It was there in his childish and seemingly endless energy. It was there in the way he put to ease my misgivings with a wave of his hand and a silly grin. He wasn't a particularly tall or masculine man, but he seemed to fill a room with his presence. There was an indescribable appeal to him that I just wished I could ignore.

But I would ignore it. I would ignore the hell out of it. He was going to leave as soon as this was over anyway and move on to another wild adventure and forget all about me, and that was the way it should be.

I woke up in the middle of the night to the sound of a voice whispering my name. I reflexively reached for the gun at my bedside.

"No, don't shoot me! It's me!" Trent cried, throwing his hands into the air and dropping the flashlight.

I exhaled loudly. "Why are you in my room?!"

Trent bent down and picked up the flashlight. He bumped it against the heel of his hand and the light came back on. "You didn't wake up when I knocked. I wasn't up to anything nefarious, if that's what you're thinking. I want to show you something."

Trent walked over to my closet and opened the doors, shining his flashlight in. I climbed out of bed and went to his side. I looked in the closet. "Yeah, it's my closet. Woo. Go to bed." I turned to walk back to my bed.

"No, wait!" he said, and I stopped and turned back around. "Look closer. Look at the paint on the wall in there."

I rubbed my eyes and bent down to get a better look. "It's old paint. Is that a problem?"

"Look at the color, though. It's the same paint that's on these walls, but it looks so much older. Care to venture as to why that is?" Trent was giving me a giddy grin.

"The closet is outside the bubble?" I asked.

"Yes! How brilliant is that?"

I didn't share his same enthusiasm. "That's great. Can we talk about this tomorrow? I don't think you understand the concept of having to work in the morning." I closed the closet door and plodded back to my bed. I slid under the covers and pulled them up to my ear.

"You should get some sleep, too." My voice was muffled from under my comforter.

Trent walked to the door. "Sorry. I was just excited to share my discovery with someone. I thought you'd be excited, too. Goodnight, Roselyn."

"Goodnight, Trent."

Over the next few days, I had a hard time walking through my house without feeling overwhelmed. Everywhere I looked there were chalk marks. When I got home from work, they greeted my eyes as soon as I walked in the door. Trent had informed me that there was a small corner in the basement that was outside the bubble, in addition to my closet. Since there were only two small exclusion zones, I was at a loss for why he needed to mark up my entire house. However, he insisted it was necessary.

Aside from Trent being in the house, things were relatively quiet. He and I were beginning to figure out our roles in this new dynamic. He gave me money for food and utilities and I cooked dinner and didn't ask where the money had come from. We got along well enough, except for the times when I came home from work to find Trent had forgotten that he was perfectly capable of picking up after himself. We were fairly comfortable, but it was apparent that Trent was growing restless waiting for a time event.

Then, one night as I was settling down to go to sleep, something happened. Shortly after I closed my eyes and snuggled into my pillow, I noticed some kind bright flash in the room – bright enough to be detectable through closed eyelids – and I heard Cattiel jump down from the bed as though he'd suddenly been disturbed. My initial thought was that Trent had come wandering in with the flashlight to inspect my closet again. I opened my eyes and sat up in bed, ready to give him an earful.

There was a creature at the foot of my bed. I sat frozen in horror. The dark figure was almost as tall as the eight-foot ceiling, and it stared at me menacingly with glowing red eyes. It awkwardly raised its long spindly arms straight out to either side without bending where the elbows should be, splaying wide its seven elongated, gnarled fingers on each hand. The Big Bad had come for me.

Suddenly, Trent burst into the room and dived onto the bed, putting himself between the creature and me. Trent fidgeted furiously with his watch as I witnessed the creature beginning to open its mouth.

Terrified, I finally had the urge to flee. I started to scramble from the bed, but Trent grabbed my arm firmly enough to hurt. "Don't run," he commanded fiercely. It was the first time Trent had ever truly scared me. I sat there with his strong fingers digging uncomfortably into my arm while the creature's mouth gaped open impossibly wide.

"I'm going to let go of you, but you cannot run!" Trent instructed. He released me and returned his attention to his watch.

A shrieking sound accosted my ears suddenly from every direction, and I saw Trent flinch. It sounded like metal scraping violently against metal. I threw my hands over my ears, but as quickly as the sound had begun, it stopped. The creature disappeared along with it.

It was only then that I realized how badly I was trembling. Trent finished up whatever he was doing on his watch and turned to me.

"Are you all right?" he asked, putting his now-gentle hands on either side of my face and looking me over. Even in the dark, I could see his face was lined with worry.

"I...I think so..." I replied, but my voice was barely above a whisper.

"We got lucky that time," he said. "I was able to get here in time to block most of the radiation. I thought there would be more of a warning, but I only had a few seconds to get to you." Trent suddenly leaned over and looked under the bed at Cattiel. "There you are, you little scamp. You're lucky you didn't run." He sat back up and looked at his watch again.

"Five hours. That thing took five hours from tonight," Trent said in amazement.

I turned on him. "Why did you make me stay through that?!" I asked, my voice cracking. "You bruised my arm, and you wouldn't let me leave!" I was furious with him.

He looked at me with genuine bewilderment. "What? No, I was protecting you! I have a device that absorbs radiation, but you need to be close to me for it to work. If I'd let you run, you would've gotten the full dose of radiation from the Big Bad! Cattiel would've too, but he stayed right with us under the bed. I was trying to keep you safe, Roselyn. I wasn't trying to hurt you or traumatize you." He gazed at me with deep concern.

My anger quickly dissipated, but my fear remained. I was still shaken up by the whole incident. "I'm sorry. I…I didn't know," I apologized. "I had listened to Tilda's story about the Big Bad," I said shakily, "but I wasn't at all prepared for that." I felt tears welling up. I tried to fight it, but they cascaded down my cheeks anyway. "Great, now I'm crying," I said, embarrassed.

Trent scooted closer to me on the bed and pulled me to him. He leaned his back against the headboard and put his arm around me as I rested my head on his shoulder.

"If there were ever a good reason to cry, I would say that was right up there," Trent said.

I wiped my eyes and tried to gather my composure. "You weren't scared at all," I said. "How did that not terrify you?"

"I was scared. But you needed me, and that took precedence. It's easier to be brave when you have someone to be brave for."

I turned my head and looked up at Trent. I wanted to thank him for being there with me tonight. I wanted to thank him for keeping me safe. I wanted to thank him for helping me through this weird, impossible situation in which I found myself. I wanted to say all those things, but I couldn't, because Trent's lips suddenly pressed down against mine, stealing my words.

Chapter 6

It started out gentle and tentative, as though he were testing my willingness. When I didn't protest or pull away, his kiss became more urgent and needful. His fingers raked into my hair, holding me to him as his tongue found mine, and they engaged in a sensual dance.

As quickly as it had begun, Trent abruptly ended it, leaving me breathless. He leapt out of my bed and took a step away, toward the door.

"I'm sorry. I'm so sorry," he apologized profusely. "I just…forgive me. I shouldn't have done that." He hurried from the room before I could say a word, shutting the door behind him.

I had never been kissed quite like that before. I'd been kissed many times, of course, but this was different. It conveyed a desire and need of a magnitude to which I was unaccustomed. I had felt his longing, and it had lit a fire inside me. I sat and stared at the door, butterflies still fluttering in my abdomen, and wondered if I should go after him or if I should just lie down and pretend this never happened.

As much as I wanted to run down that hall and demand that he finish what he started, or at least make him explain why he ran off so suddenly, I knew I wouldn't. I would do what I always did – swallow these feelings and pretend nothing ever happened. My heart was safer that way. I straightened my bedding and lay down, my mind replaying everything that had happened tonight over and over in a loop.

It felt like I had finally just started to doze off when my phone alarm sounded. I had forgotten about the five-hour loss until I looked at my bedside clock and saw that it showed 2AM. It was a good thing I had decided to use my phone for my alarms or I would have slept in and been late for work. I dragged myself out of bed and trudged to the kitchen to make some coffee.

As I filled the pot with water, I noticed the chalk marks were gone from the walls. Had Trent spent the night cleaning? I looked over and noticed a note on the table and a simple gold-chain necklace with a small electronic device attached to it. I set the pot down in the sink and went over to investigate.

Dear Roselyn,

I have collected the data I need. I am working on finding a solution for your problem, and it should be resolved shortly. Thank you for your hospitality and for being a good friend. I'll be in touch. In the meantime, please keep this device on your person at all times while within the house. It will protect you from the Big Bad if he comes again, but I'm hoping I will have this taken care of before he has an opportunity.　　　*- TM*

My heart sank into my stomach. He'd left me? Just like that? No heartfelt goodbye, no hug, no explanation for last night – just a cold, initialed note? It was so unlike the Trent I'd come to know. How could he do that me?

I took the note and ripped it into tiny shreds. I picked up my phone and called him. He owed me a proper goodbye. The phone beeped and crackled for what seemed an eternity, but the cheery English-like voice I was waiting to hear never answered. He was ghosting me.

I bit back the tears, cleared my throat, and told myself that none of this mattered. This is what was always going to happen anyway, wasn't it? Right from the start, this was the endgame. He was always going to leave, and I shouldn't have been surprised. I tossed the shredded letter into the garbage can, picked up my coffee pot, and resumed my morning routine.

It wasn't until I was in the car heading to the fitness center that I lost the battle with my tears. All it took was a mediocre sappy song and the flood works began. I quickly changed the radio station and chastised myself for being so ridiculous. I wasn't in love. I didn't get dumped. There was no reason for me to cry! Regardless, my heart was of a different opinion and I showed up to work with puffy eyes and a blotchy face.

I got through the workday without incident. I was feeling much better after having interacted with other people all day, and I even sang along with the radio on my way home. When I walked through the door, however, it felt like walking into solitary confinement. Loneliness descended upon me, and I felt those blasted tears trying to make an encore appearance. I scooped up Cattiel and buried my face in his soft fur. He growled and tried to squirm away from me.

"Love me, dammit!"

Cattiel stopped fighting me and let me hug him for about ten seconds before resuming his tantrum. I released him, but not before warning him that I was going to start dog shopping.

That night, as I was getting dinner ready, I absent-mindedly set the table for two. I didn't even notice I had done it until I sat down and looked over at the empty seat across from me. I pulled out my phone and tried to dial him again. I just wanted to hear his voice, but I still didn't get an answer. I set my phone on the table and looked at the empty chair.

"Why am I so stuck on you?" I asked aloud to a man who wasn't there. "You weren't that great. You were weird as hell. And obnoxious. And annoying. And you had giant feet and bowed legs. And you moved your hands too much when you talked. And you made weird faces. And you had no concept of personal space. And your hair was always dangling just near the corner of your right eye and it bugged me. And you kept me up at night because you somehow never slept. And you kissed me and then apologized. And worst of all, you went and made me care about you and then you left. You just left. So screw you, Trent Morgan."

As I picked at my food, my eyes kept returning to the device he had left on the table. I hadn't touched it since this morning. It looked similar to an oval-shaped jump drive. It was metallic and ugly. And it reminded me of him, so I hated it. I grabbed it and stuck it in my pocket anyway, though. I might need it, and it made me hate it even more to know that because it was like still needing him.

The weeks passed, and life slowly went back to the way it was before Trent. I was still lonely, but I was used to being lonely now. The house had been quiet. There hadn't been any strange time events, and I had noticed recently that I no longer had to adjust my home clocks. But I always kept Trent's device on me, just in case. I had been wearing it around my neck as a daily accessory. Everything was...bearable.

Then, about a month after Trent left, the calm was broken. Autumn was beginning to tinge the leaves of the trees and the air had a chill to it. I came home from work on a blustery Wednesday afternoon and immediately made myself a pot of coffee. I went to my bedroom to change out of my fitness training clothes and into something warmer. When I came back out to the kitchen to pour a hot cup of coffee, I saw something in the kitchen that made me freeze in my tracks.

There was a Time Thief standing near my table. Just standing there. Even though it was only a faint, shadowy figure, I felt like there was something oddly familiar about this one. It appeared to be looking down and picking at something on its wrist.

No. No, it can't be…

"…Trent?"

The Time Thief moved its head. It looked like it was looking around.

"Trent, is that you?"

It looked back down at its wrist and started walking toward me. I stepped aside as it walked past me and disappeared into the hallway wall.

"Trent!" I ran to the office on the other side of that wall, but no one was in there. I ran around the house frantically seeking any sign of Trent, but I was alone.

It had been him. I knew those movements. It was Trent. But…how?! I grabbed my phone and dialed his number. I waited with bated breath as the line made its strange noises, but he didn't answer. I frowned. What was he up to? How had he ended up as a Time Thief?

I did a quick time check to find out how much of my day I had lost. I was perplexed when I realized my wall clocks still matched the phone. Same day, same time. Nothing had happened to the time. What the hell was going on?!

There was a knock at the front door. My heart leapt into my throat and I ran to answer it. I was certain it was Trent. I flung the door open without checking, and…it was a stranger. He wore a beige trench coat that looked like he had just quickly thrown it on and forgotten to button it, and beneath it he was dressed in a black suit with a blue tie. He was about 6ft tall and of average build. He had a somewhat round face and bright blue eyes that turned downward at the outside corners. It made him look mournful. His dark brown, almost black hair was cut short, and he wore it gelled in a spikey, bed-head style. He looked to be around thirty years old.

"Oh, hello!" he said with a big welcoming smile...and an English-like accent. "I'm Trent. Trent Morgan."

I panicked and slammed the door in his face. I didn't know what else to do. I stood there, staring through the door window at this man who couldn't possibly be Trent Morgan as a look of pure bafflement crossed his face. That was not Trent. This man was slightly taller and not as skinny and his eyes were the wrong color and his face was all wrong and...it wasn't him. Not even a well-executed disguise could change someone's appearance this much.

"I know Trent Morgan, and you, sir, are not him!" I yelled through the closed door.

The man on the porch furrowed his forehead and looked down at his watch. I pressed my face against the window to get a better look at that watch – and saw that it was Trent's watch.

"Where did you get that watch?! That isn't yours!" I shouted through the door.

"I'm sorry, who do you think I am?" he asked with his hands turned upward in a questioning manner.

"I don't know who you are, but you aren't Trent!"

"Listen, I just need to know something. Has there been anything strange going on around here? I received a distress signal from this area."

Why did he talk so much like Trent? "I didn't call you."

The man looked down at his watch again and started pressing buttons. As he turned away from the door, I saw him pull out a pair of glasses and slip them on before bringing up the watch's holographic display. It looked similar to the interface from Trent's watch, but there was something slightly different about it – but I couldn't quite put my finger on it. He flicked through the images just as quickly as Trent always did. Was it possible that this was Trent?

I opened the door a crack, and the potential imposter turned to me. "How old are you?" I asked.

"Don't you know it's rude to ask someone their age?"

"What is SABER?" I asked, watching for his reaction.

He gave me startled look. "How do you know about SABER?" he asked suspiciously.

"I told you. I know Trent Morgan. Why are you calling yourself Trent Morgan?"

"I've been Trent Morgan for as long as I can remember. It's the one thing I always remember."

I stepped outside onto the porch and walked around him, looking him up and down. "This is all wrong," I said.

"I feel strangely insulted. Is it the coat?" He looked down at it and swayed around in it. "It looks silly, doesn't it? I wanted to try something new, but it doesn't feel like me, you know?"

I gave him a deadpan expression. "Are you trying to be funny?"

"I wasn't. Am I?"

"Are you what?"

"Being funny."

I put my hand over my mouth. "Good lord, it is you, isn't it?"

"Well I certainly hope so. If not, I'm not sure who else to be."

"Why don't you look like you?" I asked, still suspicious. "And why don't you know me?"

He gave me a raised eyebrow. "You must not know your Trent Morgan all that well if you haven't figured that out by now."

I felt injured by that assessment. "What do you mean by that?"

"I swear I haven't met you before today. I don't know you. What does that tell you?"

I suddenly remembered an off-hand comment Trent made to me way back when I first called him. He'd said that if I ever ran into him and he didn't know me, not to be cross with him because it happens sometimes. Is this what he meant? Did that mean that this version of himself was from his past?

"You're his past," I guessed.

"The Ghost of Christmas Past!" he joked. Then he nodded. "Probably. Or I suppose I could be in his future. Memories get fuzzy when the change occurs."

I was still confused. "What 'change' are you talking about? Why are you different?"

"Didn't your Trent tell you how he came about?"

"Yes. He talked about SABER and genetic engineering and telomeres and robots—"

"Experimental nanobots."

"Yes, to keep him from aging."

"But he didn't tell you the side effects?"

"No."

"Well, let me enlighten you, then. See, there was a problem with the nanobots that didn't present itself until I was about 32 years old. I was working on the time-warping device, as that was my sole purpose at SABER, when I suddenly lost consciousness. When I awoke in the infirmary, I had changed. The nanobots had done their job, but not the way they were supposed to have done it. They weren't supposed to activate until my telomeres had shortened to a level when my aging would start causing damage to my system, but they activated much sooner. Instead of repairing the telomeres, they 'repaired' entire DNA strands in every cell. I was essentially a different person. It affected my brain – I retained some memories of my previous 32 years, but large chunks of information were missing. I knew what my purpose was, but I had 'forgotten' certain aspects of my research. These changes have continued to happen throughout my life at random intervals. I never know when it's coming. It just happens, and I wake up as someone else with only about half of my memories. That's why I say I could be from your Trent's future. It's possible I may have just forgotten you."

It broke my heart to hear those words.

It must've been written all over my face, because Trent looked at me with concern and asked, "Did I say something wrong?"

"No, it's nothing," I lied. I moved the conversation along with, "So how many times have you changed?"

"Eight times."

"Eight? In any of those phases were you ever a five-foot-eleven, skinny, bow-legged, swoopy-haired madman with an odd penchant for tweed suits?" I asked.

Trent crinkled his nose. "No." Then his face took on a look of utter displeasure. "Oh, you've got to be kidding me. Is that what I turn into?"

"So you haven't just forgotten me, then?" I said hopefully.

"Apparently not. Although I must say that I would find it rather difficult to forget a face like that. You're quite lovely," he said with a charming smile.

I gave him a half-smile, feeling flattered, but it quickly faded as a thought occurred to me.

"Wait. If you are Trent from the past, then why didn't he know me when he came knocking on my door? Shouldn't he have remembered something about me or something about this encounter?"

Trent grimaced. "…Yeah, I was hoping to distract you from that point since you seemed to be bothered that I would forget you."

"You did forget me! How could you forget me?!"

"Like I said, when I change, my memories don't always make it. It isn't as though I do it on purpose."

"It's still insulting," I pouted.

Trent sighed and looked around. "So why am I here? It can't just be to stand outside and listen to you yell at me."

I crossed my arms. "I don't know. You tell me. I didn't call you." I stopped and held my hand up. "Oh, wait! Maybe I did call you. I was trying to call Trent – my Trent – but he wasn't answering. I suppose if you're Trent, you must have the same number, right? Was I calling you?"

"No, it wasn't that. Even if it were, my calls get directed to me based on a chronological algorithm I programmed into my device. This was a distress signal that came from somewhere…else." Trent looked at his watch again. "Say, when was the last time you saw your Trent? Is he likely to pop back around anytime soon?"

"Why, is it a problem if he does?"

"Not for short periods of time, but it does add to my memory problem when I cross my own timeline. It does a funny thing to your brain when it tries to remember two different memories from the same place and point in time."

"So if you run into yourself, you don't remember it?"

"Not really, no."

We stood in uncomfortable silence for a moment as he stared at me.

"What?"

"You never answered my question."

"What question?"

"Has my future self been here recently? Am I coming back?"

"Oh. Um…I don't know how to answer that. You were here, yes. You came because—"

Trent quickly stuck his finger over my lips to shush me as he cried, "No no no! No! No spoilers! I don't want to know what happens or what I do in the future. I just want to know if I was here and if I am coming back."

"Wow, ok," I said, taking a step back from his reach. "Yes, you were here, but it's been a while. I thought I saw you in the kitchen a few minutes ago, but as a Time Thief."

"Time Thief? Wait, never mind. Don't explain that. I don't want to know. Actually, I really do. Time Thief?" He looked at me with heightened interest. When I started to open my mouth, however, he shouted, "No, no, don't tell me. It's better if I don't know."

"I was just going to suggest that maybe it was him that sent you the distress signal."

Trent raised his eyebrows. "Oh. Yes, it could be that. Can I come in and have a look in your kitchen?"

I nodded and led him inside. He walked through the kitchen looking at his watch. He suddenly stopped, as though he'd found something, and then started slowly following the same path I'd seen shadow Trent walk earlier that afternoon.

"I left a trail," he said as he stopped at the wall where shadow Trent disappeared, "but I'm not getting the entire message. I think I'm trapped somewhere."

I was instantly concerned. "What are we going to do?" I asked, wringing my hands worriedly.

Trent ignored me and walked around the house for a few more minutes before he gave up. "I don't know what to do yet. I need more information."

"What can I do to help? There has to be something we can do!"

"Relax," Trent said, holding his hands up. "If I know me, and I'm quite certain I do, I'll be just fine. I'll leave more clues and messages. We just have to wait for them." Trent pressed a few buttons on his watch. "When I get another distress signal, I'll teleport over here. If I don't show up, ring me. I've programmed this location in so your call will now be directed to me instead of him. I get the feeling he's probably not receiving calls wherever he is right now anyway." Trent held his watch up as though he was about to teleport out.

"Is that it?" I asked. "You're just going to leave?"

He turned to me with a puzzled look. "I told you, we'll have to wait. What more can I do?"

"You aren't going to stay and wait here?"

"It could be weeks before we get another message. What would I do here?"

"Wouldn't it be better if you were here when he showed up? You might be too late if you teleport. And wouldn't it screw up your data if you had to time travel to get here when the distress signal came?"

"I did have to time travel to get here today, and the message was still there. I'm very clever… – wait, what's your name again?"

"Roselyn. Roselyn Wolff."

"I'm very clever, Roselyn Wolff, so you can trust that future me is going to make sure that the message will get to me one way or another."

"Oh. Well, all right, then," I said, feeling a bit dejected. My Trent was a lot more fun than this one.

"Why are you doing that? Why are you making your face look so forlorn? What have I done now?" Trent asked, his brows drawn together in confusion.

"I was just hoping you might stay for a little while. It's been a while since I saw my Trent last and…well, truth be told, I kind of miss the weirdo. I thought maybe it would be nice to get to know the Trent before my Trent. I have coffee made if you wanted to stay and have a cup," I offered.

"I don't like coffee," Trent said.

"What are you talking about? Of course you do. You drank coffee every morning when you were here."

"The fact that I like coffee in the future doesn't hold any bearing on whether I like it right now." Trent must have seen the deflated look on my face, because he suddenly became more empathic. "I wouldn't mind a cup of tea, though, if you have it."

I looked in the cupboard as Trent removed his trench coat and sat down at the table. "Do you prefer an herbal tea or Earl Grey?"

"I love Earl Grey. That's great," he said amicably.

I put the kettle on to boil and then poured myself a cup of coffee. I stood near the stove, leaning against the sink, waiting for the kettle. I was holding my coffee cup, wondering if it would be rude of me to start drinking it before Trent had his tea. What an odd thing to worry about. I set the cup on the counter and folded my arms. I looked at my feet and tried to get my suddenly blank mind to think of something to say.

"So we just have to wait for Time Thief Trent to show up again, and then we can save him?" I asked.

Trent made an uncertain face. "Perhaps. Or it could take several appearances. Those messages might come through in fragments, like the one today, and I might have to piece them together over time. I just don't know at this point. Also, can we please stop calling my future self 'Time Thief Trent'? It sounds weird."

"What do you want me to call him?" I asked, annoyed.

"I don't care. Future Trent. Swoopy-Haired Trent. Literally anything else would be better."

"My Trent," I suggested.

Trent looked at me. "You seem to like the future me. Are you my companion?"

"What do you mean by companion? He's my friend, but that's it."

"Future me is lucky to have someone care so much about what happens to me. That doesn't happen very often. Ever, really. I'm a bit of a lone wolf."

The tea kettle started to whistle. "You must have someone," I said as I prepared his tea. I set the cup down in front of him, fetched my coffee from the counter by the sink, and sat down at the table across from him.

"Nope. There are only a handful of people who truly know what I am, and we don't keep in contact." Trent took a sip of his tea and leaned back in his chair. "No, the only people who give me more than just a passing thought are the members of SABER, and that's because they want to imprison me and steal my device."

"That's so sad. In all this time, hasn't there been anyone?"

"Eh, I try to keep to myself. It's just better that way."

"How is that better?"

Trent looked at me, and then looked around my house. "You look like you're keeping to yourself, too. That's not by choice?"

I frowned at him. "It's complicated."

"Isn't everything?"

He had me there. "Look, it isn't like I enjoy living by myself all the time. I would love to have someone around. It would just be nice if that 'someone' didn't up and disappear on me with nothing but a damn note on the table." I looked across the table at the other Trent, who was sitting in the same spot where my Trent used to sit, and he looked back at me blankly. He had no idea I was talking about his future self and that I was feeling angry with him for something he hadn't even done yet.

"That's unfortunate, but you should probably move on. If someone doesn't want to stay, you can't make them. And if you do, it isn't really fair to either of you, now is it?"

Trent was telling me to move on from my Trent without even knowing he was talking about his future self. It was an unusual conversation to be having. "I suppose you're right," I admitted.

"I usually am."

There was a lull in the conversation, so I blurted out the first thought that came into my head. "So what's it like to change?"

Trent's expression grew solemn. "A lot like dying, I suppose. I lose consciousness, and the person I was and many of the memories I made are lost."

"But you still have some memories. You continue on with your life when you wake up," I said.

"It's a lot more like starting over than it is like continuing. You might better understand it this way: imagine you spend your life building a house, a career, and start a family. Then, one day, your house burns down, your spouse leaves you and takes the children, and you get fired from your job. Yes, you continue on with your life, but you're basically starting over. It's a rough analogy, I know, but I want you to get the point that it isn't a wonderful, magical rejuvenation. It's hard, and scary, and no one else in the entire world can understand the way it feels but me."

"I'm sorry," I said. "I didn't know."

"Of course you didn't. How could you know? It's an unknowable thing for you." Trent sighed. "You know what the worst part of it is? It's in not knowing when it's going to happen. There is no warning. No time to say goodbye or to grieve what I am about to lose or accept that the change is coming. No time to warn those around you that they won't be seeing the 'you' they know anymore. It leaves you afraid to get close to people. It fills your life with a sense of uncertainty and impermanence, and it makes it damn near impossible to build an attachment to anyone or anything."

"How old are you, Trent?"

"It's hard to say. If I had to venture a guess, I'd say I'm probably somewhere in the ballpark of four hundred."

I couldn't imagine what it would be like to live for four hundred years. "Are you saying that in four hundred years, you've never fallen in love?"

"Who would put up with this?" he asked, raising his hands dramatically. "Who would be able to love a man who doesn't grow old with them? Who would be able to live twenty or thirty years with a man that never much ages, then be completely prepared and accepting when he becomes someone else?"

"It would be an unusual situation, I'll admit, but it isn't impossible."

"Isn't it? Look at you, for example. You care about Trent – quite a great deal, it would seem. You know that the man sitting before you is Trent. Yet you look at me as 'other.' I am not your Trent. I am just a Trent to you. Your brain and your heart aren't connecting us as one person. He is your friend and I am a stranger. I can tell by the look on your face that I'm right," Trent said as he looked away. "I usually am, aren't I?"

I was at a loss for words.

Trent stood up and hastily slipped on his coat. "Thank you for the cuppa," he said curtly. "I'll be seeing you." With that, he pressed a button on his watch and disappeared.

Chapter 7

I sat at the table and stared at the empty chair across from me. He had been right. He usually was, wasn't he? I did have a hard time seeing him as the same person as the Trent I knew. It bothered me to admit that to myself. But my Trent and this new Trent (or should I say old Trent?) seemed like two very different people. They were similar enough for me to truly believe that the Trent to whom I served tea today was indeed a past version of the Trent I knew. However, they had strikingly different personalities. The two seemed more like brothers – similar, but not the same.

I thought about how much a person must change in four hundred years just from life experiences. Hell, I am a drastically different person now than I was ten years ago. How old was the Trent I knew? Obviously older than four hundred, but how much older? How many changes did he go through to become who he was? Now that I knew more about him, I couldn't fault him for forgetting me – especially if he'd gone through several changes since first meeting me today. If he'd so easily forgotten me, was it possible that he had fallen in love before and has since forgotten? Is there a woman out there somewhere in time who had his heart?

I was surprised at the jealousy that quickened my heart with that thought. I had no right to be jealous. I didn't even know if a woman like that existed, but even if she did, what was it to me? Perhaps I was just one in a long line of ladies whose hearts had been stolen by the mysterious Trent Morgan.

And, just like that, I was angry with him all over again.

Three days passed with no sign from either Trent. I had spent most of that time worrying and wondering and over-thinking things. So, on this rainy Saturday, I decided to turn up the music on my phone and give the house a proper cleaning in order to get my mind off of Trent. Cattiel was of little help, as he hid under the bed in my room all day while I vacuumed and sang terribly at the top of my lungs. I couldn't really blame him. I mopped the kitchen, did the laundry, and even got dinner in the slow cooker right on schedule. I was on a roll.

As I stood at the sink, washing up the dishes that didn't fit into the dishwasher, I sang all the wrong words to the song on my phone and danced cheerfully. I hadn't felt this carefree in a long time, and I realized that living by myself definitely had its perks. I grabbed a large pan from the strainer and spun around, intending to do an electric slide across the kitchen floor to the towel drawer near the stove. Unfortunately, as I started the slide, my eyes suddenly locked with a very amused Trent, standing near the table with his hands in the pockets of his trench coat and a wide grin on his face. I dropped the pan with a resonating clang, and I came to a stumbling halt, cutting off the note I was so vociferously belting. I stood staring at him, mortified, while the dropped pan settled noisily to the floor. His face bore an expression of utter delight.

I quickly grabbed my phone and shut off the music. "How long have you been here?!" I demanded as I hurriedly fixed my ponytail and pulled my flannel shirt closed over the tank top I was wearing underneath.

Trent picked up the pan I had dropped and set it on the stovetop. "Long enough to hear you sing 'turtle on my knee' instead of 'dirt all on my name.' But don't worry, I won't tell anyone."

I could feel my cheeks burning in embarrassment, but Trent's smile just grew wider as I blushed.

"Why are you here?"

He held up his watch and pointed at it. "Distress signal. Did you see future me around anywhere?"

"Oh! No, I haven't seen anything today."

"That's all right. I'll find it," Trent said, looking down at his watch.

"I'm going to go change quickly while you look for the message," I said uncomfortably, my cheeks still burning. I wished I hadn't chosen to wear the "Bootylicious" sweatpants I'd had since college.

"Don't bother," Trent said as he started to walk away. "I've already seen the outfit. There's no point in trying to pretend I didn't." He headed toward the stairs to the second floor.

"Yeah, but I shouldn't subject you to that torture any longer than necessary."

Trent was halfway up the stairs, and he stopped and leaned over the railing to look at me. "Oh, I don't know," he grinned. "I kind of like it." He then continued up the stairs.

I desperately wished my cheeks would quit burning. I grabbed Cattiel, who had finally emerged from his hiding place in my room, and sat down on the couch, waiting for Trent to find the message from my Trent.

"I think I'm trying to send us coordinates," I heard him yell down to me. He dashed down the stairs and then hurtled the bottom rail athletically.

"You're way too springy for four hundred," I stated dryly.

"At least I'm not wearing trousers that say 'Bootylicious' across the rear." He stopped and put his hand to his chin thoughtfully. "Although, maybe I should be."

"What were you saying about coordinates?"

"Ah, yes! Look," he said as he brought up the holographic display on his watch. "Normal coordinates should look like this." He pointed at a set of numbers separated by commas. "But there are too many sets in the coordinates I sent."

"What does that mean?"

"I'm somewhere I definitely shouldn't be," Trent said ominously. "But I still have to wait. There's more to this message that I haven't received yet."

"Why is it coming through all broken up like this?" I asked. "Why wouldn't he just send it all at once?"

"Well, maybe I did send it all at once. There could be a delay due to traveling from wherever it is I sent it from. Or perhaps I only get fixed amounts of time to transmit information. Or perhaps I've sent the information multiple times, but only some of it makes it to us each time. It's hard to say. It could be any number of reasons."

"He hasn't indicated that he's in danger?"

"No, nothing of the sort. I'm trapped and obviously need help to get out, but there's been no indication of urgency or immediate danger."

"I wonder how he did it. He got the time changing to stop, but then he went and trapped himself. I just can't put together how he managed that."

"Time changing?"

I looked at him with a wry smile. "No spoilers, remember? Besides, you'll enjoy figuring it out…and I'll enjoy helping you figure it out."

I deposited Cattiel onto the couch next to me and stood up. "So, we're back to the waiting game, hey?"

"It appears so."

"The story of my life," I said. I went into the kitchen and started to fill the kettle with water.

"Are you making tea?" Trent asked.

"I am."

"Might I bother you for a cup?"

I turned to him with a grin. "Who did you think I was making it for? I'm having a glass of wine."

When the tea was ready, I poured Trent a cup and brought it to him. I grabbed my glass of wine and sat down at the table across from him.

"So here we are again," I said. "Last time I had to practically beg you to stay for a while."

"People don't usually want me to stay."

"I can't imagine why," I remarked sarcastically.

"Post hoc ergo propter hoc," Trent said and took a sip of his tea.

"Beg pardon?"

"It's Latin for 'after this, therefore because of this.' People assume that since I show up and weird things start happening that I'm to blame, when in reality I came because something weird was going to happen and I was only there to fix it. People don't want me to stick around because they're afraid I'll bring more mayhem down on their little world."

"Have you ever considered your personality might have something to do with it?" I smirked.

"Oi! I'm delightful, thank you very much!"

"Yeah, after someone gets to know you. But you are terrible at first impressions."

"I don't care what people think of me, especially if I'm not going to have to deal with them for long. I don't need people to like me."

"Then why did you stay for tea yesterday instead of just leaving?"

"You were making a sad face. I'm a sucker for a sad face."

"So you must care somewhat, then."

"I didn't mean I didn't care. I said I didn't care what people think of me. I still care about their well-being, though. I'm not a sociopath."

I smiled and couldn't help but mutter, "I do wonder." I knew he wouldn't get the call back to the conversation I'd had with my Trent outside the retirement home, but saying it brought a smile to my own face in remembering the exchange.

Then it struck me. From Trent's perspective, I was the first one to ever reply to "I'm not a sociopath" with "I do wonder." From my perspective, however, it was him. He was the one who said that to me, and that was why I was saying it now. But was it possible that the reason he had said it in the first place was because somewhere in his memory he remembered me saying it right now? Who said it first? Was "first" even an appropriate term for it, or was it just an impossible loop of cause and effect with no beginning and no end? More importantly, though, did it mean that my Trent actually had remembered me?

Trent's voice snapped me from my thoughts. "Are you literally wondering right now? Are you still with me?" He waved his hand in front of my face.

I blinked. "Yeah, sorry. I was just thinking about something."

"How dare you think of me that way while I'm sitting right here." Trent grinned at me playfully.

"You didn't smile much the first time you were here. I have to admit it's nice when you do."

"Dazzling, isn't it?"

I laughed. "You seem to be in a much better mood today than you were last time."

"Yeah, it turns out I'm rubbish at first impressions," Trent said.

"It's true. But you've redeemed yourself."

Trent and I sat and talked for almost an hour before he left. It was a lot more comfortable than it had been yesterday, but it still didn't feel like he and my Trent were truly the same person. I still couldn't see them as one and the same. I tried to avoid talking about it, though, because it seemed to bother Trent that I felt that way.

The next morning, I awoke to the sound of someone knocking on my front door. I looked over at the clock. Who was knocking on my door at 7:30AM on a Sunday morning? I rolled over and pulled my blankets up over my ear and ignored it, assuming it must be a solicitor.

"Roselyn?" Trent called. It sounded like he was in the living room.

I climbed out of bed and shuffled out into the living room, yawning. Trent was standing there in his trench coat and suit, holding a disposable cup of coffee or tea with foreign writing on it.

"Did you get another signal?" I asked, rubbing my eyes and likely flaking yesterday's mascara all over my face.

Trent was cringing at me. "Do you…need a moment?"

I frowned at him. "No. Why, is something wrong?"

"Did you just wake up?"

"What was your first clue, Sherlock?"

He pointed at my hair with a grimace, and then slowly ran his finger all the way down until he was pointing at my feet, indicating all of me.

"I know, I know. My hair is almost as perfectly chaotic as yours," I said, pointing to his spikey-styled hairdo, "but it doesn't look quite the same on me. Ugh, I'll at least go brush my teeth, ok? Thanks for the confidence booster, though."

Trent chortled. "You don't seem like the kind of person who needs confidence boosters."

"Everybody could use one now and again," I said as I went into the bathroom and grabbed my toothbrush. When I saw myself in the mirror, I was almost as mortified as I was yesterday. I quickly brushed my teeth and ran a brush through my hair. When I came out, Trent was still standing in the entryway of the living room, leaning against the couch.

"Trent, why are you here?"

He thrust the cup of coffee toward me. "I brought you coffee. It's from a shop in France that I remember I used to like in a previous life."

"My Trent forgets me, yet you remember a coffee shop from a previous phase?"

"I've told you, I don't get to choose what I remember and what I forget. Do you want the coffee or not?" Trent said, suddenly seeming agitated.

"Sorry. Yes, please." I took the cup from his hand. "Thank you. I can't say anyone has ever brought me hot coffee from France before."

"Not even your Trent?" he asked snidely.

"Wait, are we fighting? When did this happen? Did I nod off for a second? I blinked and you were mad," I sassed as I walked away from him to go look in the fridge.

"We're not having a row. It just frustrates me when you call my future self 'your' Trent."

I grabbed the carton of eggs out of the fridge and walked to the stove. "Why? Why on Earth would that bother you? You didn't want me to call him Time Thief Trent."

Trent was silent. I turned to see if he was still there. He was just standing in the living room with his hands in his coat pockets, his eyes distant.

"Cool. Great talk. Do you want some eggs?" I asked.

"Oh, uh, no thanks. I'm not hungry."

"Where's your drink?" I asked as I started cracking eggs into a bowl.

"What drink?"

"You brought me a coffee. Didn't you get a drink for yourself?"

"No. How is it, by the way? The coffee."

"It's actually quite amazing. Thank you. So why are you really here, Trent? It can't just be to bring me coffee."

"Why can't it just be that?"

I stopped whisking the eggs as the blood rushed to my cheeks. Cattiel took the ensuing silence as an opportunity to remind me with a noisy purrrrrt that he needed his food bowl filled.

"Oh, yes, Cattiel. You need breakfast too, don't you?" I said, avoiding Trent's question. I fed the cat and returned to my eggs.

I heard Trent walk into the kitchen behind me as I grabbed a pan and set it on the stove. "Are you sure you aren't hungry?" I asked, turning on the burner. "I can make some more—"

My words caught in my throat when I felt Trent's body come close to me and saw his hand reach across in front of me and turn the burner off. I looked up at him, and he was looking down at me with intense eyes that were as deep and blue as the Pacific itself. He cupped my face with his hands and brought his mouth to mine. It wasn't hesitant or inhibited. He kissed me with everything he had, holding nothing back. It made my head swim.

When our lips parted, he didn't let go of me or step back. He just looked into my eyes, searching for my reaction.

I wanted him to do it again. I wanted to taste his tongue and feel his lips crushing against mine again. But instead, I felt my lip tremble and I asked crossly, "Is this what you do with every woman you help out? Is this your go-to move?"

Trent furrowed his brow in confusion. "What are you talking about?"

I wrapped my hands around his wrists and pulled his hands away from my face. "I'm not going to lie – it's a great move. A really, really great move. But I've fallen for it before. I don't know what kind of game this is to you, but I don't want to play."

"Roselyn, what do you mean? I just…I like you!" he blurted as he took a step back. "Ok? I like you. Why is that a problem? Is it because of something I do in the future? Help me understand here, because I'm lost!" he demanded in frustration.

"How many women have fallen for it?" I asked as I turned the stovetop burner on again and slammed the pan onto it.

"What, you think I just run around snogging random women every chance I get?"

I dumped my eggs into the pan and started stirring them around with a spatula. "Yeah, I think maybe you do."

He brought his fingertips to his temples. "Why the bloody hell would you think that?!"

"Because my Trent did the same thing to me – exactly the same damn thing – and then he just ran off with nothing but a stupid note!"

Trent stood there, breathing heavily, nostrils flared, but I could see the irritation slowly dissipating from his features. His expression became disheartened. "It was me," he realized. "It was me you were talking about that first night." He gave a short, cynical laugh. "And

I told you to move on. I thought it was just some bloke." He sat down at the kitchen table and rested his chin in his hand. "If you are so obviously angry with me, then why do you care so much about rescuing me?"

"You can be mad at someone and still care what happens to them."

"Don't I know it."

I cooked my eggs while Trent sat quietly at the table. I tried to ignore the pleasant lingering taste of his mouth on my tongue and the tingle in my belly. Why did it matter so much to me if he had done this with other women? I was a divorced woman who hadn't been with a man in almost a year. My body was on fire for the man sitting only a few feet away from me – a man who obviously had carnal feelings for me – and I was standing here acting like I couldn't stand him.

It was because I cared about him. That was my hang up. I wanted to be more than just another woman to him. I wanted him to be more than just a warm body in my bed. It didn't help that I was still sorting through my feelings for my Trent. I still wanted my Trent to come back. Even though this Trent was right here laying his cards on the table, I still missed my Trent, and this Trent knew it. And I knew it bothered him. This was the strangest love triangle of which I'd ever been part.

I scooped the scrambled eggs onto a plate and stood at the counter to eat them.

Trent looked at me and sighed. "Are we going to talk about this or am I going to go?"

"I don't have anything to say."

"Yeah, you do."

"You should've had some eggs. They're good."

Trent's shoulders slumped in defeat. "Listen, I just want you to know that this is not something I ever do. All these 'other women' you speak of just don't exist. I don't have a 'go-to move.' I just like you. That's it. No secret motive or devious plot."

I stood there, trying to think of something to say. My feelings were all jumbled up, so what hope did I ever have of trying to articulate them to him?

All I could think to say was, "I don't know how I feel about any of this."

Trent gave me a tight smile. "I understand. Well, I suppose there's no point in me staying and making this any more uncomfortable than it already is. I'll be around."

And just like that, he stood up and teleported out of the house.

I couldn't eat all of the eggs I'd made, as my appetite had vanished just as quickly as Trent had. I sat down on the couch with the coffee he'd brought me and stared out the window. I shouldn't have pushed Trent away like that. I should've at least allowed myself to explore the possibility of him. And, good lord, why couldn't I have let him take it just a little bit further? My body was admonishing my heart for being such a sensitive fool.

I didn't see or hear from Trent for several days. I was grateful for the time to myself, however, because it gave me time to cool off and think with a level head. I thought about how everything that is happening between Past Trent and I right now has already happened from my Trent's perspective. If I was supposed to fall in love with Past Trent, wouldn't I have been an important enough part in his life for my future Trent to have remembered at least some of it? And if I was supposed to be with Past Trent, then my future Trent shouldn't have gotten so suddenly weird about kissing me, should he? None of what has already happened made sense unless I wasn't meant to be with Past Trent. As much as my body thought I had made the wrong decision, I knew in my head that no other choice was possible. This was always where I was going to end up because this has already happened before for Trent – and once an outcome is observed, it becomes reality, doesn't it?

As I dug through my closet, looking for a clean pair of athletic leggings to wear to the fitness center for work the next day, I pondered how much of my life for the next few weeks was already predetermined simply because someone else has lived it already and wondered if it applied to the rest of my life as well. The choices I made felt like free will, but were they? Were fate and destiny actually real things? Was it fate that had made me keep putting off laundry so I now had no leggings to wear for work tomorrow? Was it my destiny to find an old pair I had forgotten about buried beneath a pile of oversized t-shirts?

I turned around to toss what clothing I'd found onto the dresser, but as I did, the strangest thing happened. The clothes stopped and floated in midair, hanging as though frozen in time.

Chapter 8

I stared, dumbfounded, and it took my brain several seconds to piece together what was happening. Time was being altered again for the first time since my Trent left, but I was outside the bubble. Time was passing normally for me, but for my clothes, which were now in the bubble, time had slowed down relative to the rest of the world.

I stood in the closet, unsure of what to do. I thought of calling Trent, but I'd left my phone sitting on the nightstand. Would his watch pick up that something weird was going on here right now? Was my Trent any part of what was going on, and if so, was he sending a distress signal? Even if that was the case, Past Trent would probably teleport into the house and end up inside the bubble anyway, leaving me still trapped in the closet like R. Kelly to watch events unfold painfully slowly for the next three to five hours.

But what if I stepped into the bubble? Would it hurt me to make such a transition? It didn't seem to affect my clothes, but then again, they were just clothes – not living tissue. If I didn't make the transition all at once – if part of my body was on the inside, and part was on the outside – what would that do to me? It had the potential to be a biological disaster. I wished I had shown more interest in the closet when Trent had first shown it to me. Perhaps he would've had some insight into what one should do if they found themselves trapped in the closet during an event.

Suddenly, I saw a blinding flash of light, and from that flash, Time Thief Trent appeared. Even though everything else inside the bubble seemed to be moving at a snail's pace, that one particular incident seemed to be instantaneous. Once Trent had appeared and the flash was gone, however, his movements were almost too slow to be perceived. I sat in the closet and watched him, wondering what message Trent was going to leave this time and if it would be the final message needed to bring him back.

The longer I sat and waited, the more I speculated about why there was a time event around Trent's appearance this time when it hadn't happened the last couple of times. There was something odd about Trent's movements, too, aside from seeing them in slow motion. It looked like he was raising his arms, and the longer I watched, I saw it looked like he going to wave them as though he was attempting to get somebody's attention. Was he trying to tell me something? Was he trying to warn me? Was the Big Bad on its way?! What would happen if it showed up while I was outside of the bubble? I reached up and felt reassured when my fingers touched the small metal device on the chain around my neck that my Trent had left me what seemed like ages ago. Even if it did materialize, I was safe.

I tried to occupy myself by sorting through the clothes in my closet. I had several items that I never wore anymore, and I knew I never would even though I kept trying to tell myself that I might. I started making a stack of garments that I was going to donate to the local thrift store. When I got to the formal gowns, I found the beautiful dress I had worn to my senior homecoming event. I held it up and gazed at it, memories of a time full of possibilities and hopes for the future flooding my brain. I remembered how I'd felt when I wore that dress. I'd been overjoyed to be a part of something so important (as a high school senior), but I also remembered knowing that I wasn't quite special enough to actually win the vote for homecoming queen. I had been best at many things academically and athletically, but I was never best at being popular. As I stared at the dress I hadn't worn in almost twelve years, I wondered if my life would have turned out any differently if I had won the vote for homecoming queen.

I glanced over at the shadowy figure of Trent. If I had been homecoming queen twelve years ago, would I still have ended up here, in this house? Would I have ever met Trent? I tried to decide if it had been a good thing to meet him, or if I'd have been better off if I hadn't. He sure had made life a lot more interesting. He'd shown me things in the short time he was with me that had opened my eyes to a universe of incomprehensible complexity and a deeper perception of reality than I ever could have imagined before. And he'd made me believe that it isn't impossible for me to fall in love and trust a man again, even after what I had been through. He had hurt me, of course, but I was realizing that there was more to the story than I understood at first. So, I supposed I had been better off having met Trent. Perhaps it was a good thing I hadn't won homecoming queen after all.

Without warning, the trench-coat-clad Trent materialized in the bedroom near the doorway. He was just suddenly there. I waved my arms at him and yelled to him stupidly as if he were a plane flying over a deserted island I had been marooned on. He was inside the bubble, though, and he was stuck in the "time sap." He might be able to see me, especially if I stood in the same spot for a while, but there wasn't anything he could do to help me unless he teleported out of the bubble to the closet. By the time he figured it out, the time event would be over.

I threw my hands in the air in exasperation and started pacing. I had no idea what time it was getting to be, but I was getting a little stir-crazy just hanging out in my damn closet. I returned my attention to my formal gowns and proceeded to talk to myself to pass the time.

"Why do I even still have these?" I asked myself. "I'll never wear them again. I'm just clinging to a time that's long gone. Oh, but what a time it was, wasn't it? What I wouldn't give to feel the way I felt when I was wearing these dresses, just for a little while." I started to put the dresses onto the stack for donation, but I couldn't bring myself to go through with it. I hung them back on the rack. "I'm not ready to leave it behind. Not just yet."

I turned to the Trents moving slower than sloths in my bedroom. "Is that what you're going to end up being to me?" I asked them rhetorically, knowing that my voice would be talking so quickly to Trent from outside the bubble that he wouldn't be able to hear me at all. "Are you going to be like these gowns – a beautiful memory that I just can't seem to let go of even long after you've gone and left me behind? A feeling that I keep chasing even though I know nothing will ever quite replicate it?" I barely got the last words out before Time Thief Trent disappeared and trench coat Trent started moving at a normal pace. He looked down at his watch, his face bearing a look of bewilderment.

"What the hell just happened to time?!" he asked to no one in particular. He suddenly glanced over at me, looking surprised to see me there. "You weren't there a second ago," he said, baffled. "What just happened?"

"You'll find out some day," I said as I stepped out of the closet. Trent started to open his mouth to speak, but I interrupted him. "Hold that thought. I'll be right back." Not being able to leave the closet meant I also hadn't been able to use the bathroom that whole time.

When I returned to my room, Trent was peering through his glasses at the holographic interface on his watch. He turned to me, and he looked shaken. "Something's happened. My future self needs out. Now."

My heart was gripped by dread. "What do you mean? What's happened?!"

"I don't know exactly, but he's basically sent me an S.O.S. this time."

"Can we get him out?"

"I think so. It seems I have what I need now." After Trent looked through the information on his display for another minute or so, he turned to me. "I need to make sure to be right here in…" Trent glanced down at his watch again before continuing, "exactly 26 minutes, 32.46758 seconds – or thereabouts."

"Why?"

"Because that's when we'll be opening the wormhole."

I raised my eyebrows. "Excuse me?"

"Just a small one. He needs the energy from my watch to keep it open on our end, but it has to be at exactly the same time he opens it on his end or it won't work at all."

"Let me get this straight: you're going to open up a wormhole in my bedroom?!"

"Yes. Brilliant, isn't it?" Trent said with excited, sparkling eyes.

"Is it going to be dangerous?"

"Quite possibly. You might want to step out for a bit."

"Not a chance."

Trent smiled slightly. There was a hint of sadness in his expression, though. "That's awfully brave of you."

"It's easier to be brave when you have someone to be brave for," I said. When Trent looked at me like I was some kind of oddity, I asked, "What? What's wrong with that?"

"Forgive me. It's just that I'm not used to the idea of anyone being brave for me."

"Well, you don't exactly seem like the kind of guy who regularly needs people to be brave for you."

Trent's smile faded a little, but he didn't say anything.

"Do you want a cup of tea while we wait?" I offered.

Trent nodded. "That would be lovely."

I put the kettle on and sat at the table while I waited for it to boil. I perched my elbows on the table and rested my chin in my hands.

"Am I going to see you after this?" I asked.

Trent folded his hands and rested them on the table in front of him. He looked down at his hands instead of at me when he replied with, "Probably not."

"Why not?"

"I imagine your Trent will be planning to hang around, which leaves very little room for me. I can't spend much time around myself, remember?"

"What makes you think he's going to hang around?"

"Because I'm quite certain he has feelings for you."

I gave him a doubtful look. "You don't know that."

"I do, actually."

"How?" I challenged him.

"Because he fell for you when he was me." He looked at me with sorrowful blue eyes.

I felt my cheeks getting flushed. "But…he didn't even remember me."

"Are you quite sure of that?"

I hesitated. Was I? Now that I stopped to think about it, he had made some odd comments in that short while that he'd lived with me – comments that had indicated he knew more than he was letting on. But if he truly remembered me, there were so many things that didn't make sense about his behavior, too. Was it possible that he remembered just bits and pieces about me? Had he remembered this conversation Trent and I were having right now?

The kettle started to whistle, and I jumped up to get Trent his tea. I could feel his eyes following me as I poured the water over the teabag in his cup. When I brought him his tea, he looked at me regretfully.

"I'm sorry I upset you the other day. I knew this wasn't going to work. I knew I'd have to leave once I brought my future self back, but I just…I thought maybe you could feel the same way for me that you do for my future self. I thought maybe you could see us as the same person. I understand now that it was wrong of me to expect that of you."

I sat down across from him. "It's ok. I felt bad about snapping at you. It's not that I don't feel anything for you…it's just…complicated."

"To you, I'm not him. And I get it. In many ways, I'm not." He was trying to the hide the dejection in his voice, but he couldn't hide it on his face.

We sat quietly for a little while. It seemed that there should've been so much more to say, but when something is coming to an end, you can never think of what those things should be. It probably didn't help that I wasn't sad. Yes, I liked this Trent, and I probably would miss seeing him. But I was so looking forward to seeing my Trent again that it was hard to be properly upset about losing this one. I didn't want him to know I was feeling that way, but I was quite certain he did.

Trent stood up from the table, looking down at his watch. "It's time."

My heart leapt into my throat.

I followed Trent into the bedroom, my heart racing. Trent instructed me to stay back as he manipulated the display on his watch briefly. I stepped back to the doorway and observed as he stared at the watch in silence, his finger poised over a button on it. When the time came, I didn't even see Trent press the button because there was a sudden flash of light so bright that I had to close my eyes. When I opened them again, my Trent was standing in the room. Not a shadow of him – the real him.

When I saw his face, it was the strangest feeling. It was akin to the feeling you get when you walk into your home after being away for a while. There was a comforting familiarity and fondness. He may have looked a bit windswept and unkempt, but he still had that spark of mischief in his eyes and that smile that made his whole face light up.

His jovial laugh filled the room as he clapped his hands together once. "Ha! We did it! I'm back, baby!" He quickly patted himself down. "And I'm still in one piece! Brilliant!" He pointed to his past self enthusiastically. "Hey, I remember you! Or, I should say I remember when I was you! Things get a bit mixed up, don't they?"

"What was all of this? How did you end up in a parallel universe?" Past Trent asked.

My Trent winked at him. "You'll see. Besides, you know you wouldn't remember even if I told you." Trent's gaze moved beyond his past self and his eyes finally met mine. He grinned so widely it made my heart soar. "Roselyn!" He held his arms wide and started toward me.

I met him halfway and did my best to fight the urge to leap into his arms. He squeezed me tightly, lifting me off the floor slightly. I didn't want him to let me go.

"I have so much to tell you!" he exclaimed as he released me. "But first, I need a snack." He walked past me and left the room, heading toward the kitchen.

I looked over at the Trent from the past. He looked stunned. "That's who I become? I'm so…"

"Eccentric? Scattered? Ridiculous?" I filled in for him. "I know. Isn't it great?" I said with a grin. I turned and left the room, and Trent from the past followed me to the kitchen.

We found my Trent rummaging through the fridge, and it was almost like he'd never been gone.

"Roselyn, where's the kale? You seem to be out." My Trent stood up and looked at the other Trent and me. "I'm a bit shocked. She's obsessed with the stuff," he said to his past self as he quickly turned his attention to the cupboards.

I had almost forgotten how annoying he was.

"Listen," Trent from the past spoke up, "I should be going. Roselyn, I look forward to meeting you again." He held out his hand.

"A handshake?" My Trent commented around a mouthful of the toaster pastry he had just bitten into. "Ah, you forget how awkward your younger years were," he mused to himself.

I brushed past Trent's outstretched hand and hugged him. "Thank you," I said simply.

He hugged me back briefly, then stepped away. He smiled at me in a way that gave the impression he was holding back words that desperately wanted to escape his lips. Instead of speaking them, however, he gave a casual salute and pressed a button on his watch, disappearing in silence.

"You didn't show him very much gratitude," I said, turning to Trent. "He put a lot of time and effort into getting you home."

Trent laughed. "It was me. I don't think I'm obligated to thank myself for helping myself. I know I would've done the same for me," he jested.

I couldn't argue with that.

"So, how was it?" Trent asked me.

"How was what?"

"Everything. How was life while I was out? How was it getting to know my past self? Did anything exciting happen in my absence?"

"Everything was fine, but I suspect you already know that. Why didn't you tell me you'd met me in your past? Things could've gone a lot smoother if you'd warned me about what was going to happen."

"If I had, it would've changed the outcome. It would've changed my past and your future. It had to happen this way. Besides, I didn't really remember much of it anyway."

"But you knew your past self was going to show up, and you knew you were going to be trapped in another world."

"No, actually I didn't remember the part about me being trapped. I didn't know that was going to happen."

"Why did you act like you'd never met me before when you first showed up at my door?"

"You would've thought I was mad if I'd told you the truth."

"I still think you're mad, so your argument is invalid. Why didn't you at least tell me once I got to know you?"

"Like I said, it would've changed everything. It needed to happen this way."

"Why? What would've happened if it changed?"

"Any number of things. You never know the magnitude of damage that can be done when the past is changed, especially when you mess with your own past."

I thought about the conversations I had been having with Trent's past self – namely, the conversations regarding my feelings for him. I asked, "What do you remember about your past interactions with me?"

"Not much. I remember that I met you, and I had to help you with something. I remember that you had met a future version of me, but I didn't know the circumstances around that. That's about it."

I recalled something he had said to me back in the beginning. "When you were trying to understand the time events, you once said that you knew you figured this out eventually. Why did you really say that? I know it isn't because you figure everything out eventually."

"I thought I must have figured it out if my future self had been gone when my past self showed up here. I never leave anything unfinished."

"So, you don't remember anything I talked about with your past self?"

Trent gave me a sly smile. "Is there something interesting I should remember?"

"Ugh, never mind."

"How is it that you don't seem to be the least bit curious about where the hell I have been this whole time? All you want to talk about is my past. I'm more interested in talking about what's going on now. Trust me, it is far more interesting!"

"Ok, you have my attention."

"I was in a parallel universe!"

"Yes, I gathered that," I said dryly.

Trent looked insulted. "Time travel was a shocking novelty to you, but parallel universes are just humdrum?"

"What can I say, you've desensitized me to the outlandish."

Trent conceded. "I suppose that's reasonable."

"Well, what did you find? What was it like?"

"I found out who the Time Thieves are. They're just people. Scientists, working for SABER. They don't even know you can see or hear them from this side." Trent waited for my reaction.

This time I was surprised. "Really? Just people?! What about the Big Bad?"

"Now that – that was not a person. That's the probe they were trying to send through the wormhole to collect data on the other side.

It was incredibly radioactive from the continual attempts at trying to send it through the wormhole, and they had to keep it contained."

"I'm confused. Why is it only my house? How are they doing this? Why were they doing this?"

"Why does anyone do anything? Curiosity! Well, that's why the scientists were working on it. SABER's involvement, though, pointed at some underlying malicious intent. And the reason it was only in your house is because this is the corresponding location for the SABER compound in the parallel world – like two giant membranes coming together and touching at a single point," Trent explained as he held his hands out in front of him, drawing them closer together. "They are able to accomplish this because they have a particle accelerator that is capable of reaching the Planck energy, and when they focus that energy, they're able to create a wormhole. Oh, and guess who was leading the research and experimentation?" Trent smiled proudly.

"...You?"

"Yes! Not me me, of course. But a parallel version of me. Of course, I had to have a talk with myself and warn myself about SABER. It turns out that the parallel version of me wasn't working on time travel at all. Just travel between parallel universes."

"How do you remember any of that? I thought you couldn't remember it when you encountered yourself."

"It wasn't me. It was a parallel version of me. Not the same person. Different memories, different life – different being entirely. And oddly, he actually doesn't change. He still looks like me before my first change. I guess they got the nanobot technology right in his world. Oh, and he even picked a different name than I did. He goes by Jaeger Novak."

"Wait, you picked your name?"

"Of course. I couldn't go around as Number Thirty my whole life."

"Number Thirty?"

"That was my embryo number. Out of thousands of trials, only embryo number thirty grew successfully. And here I am."

"What made you choose Trent Morgan?" I asked.

"Well, Trent means 'thirty.' It's also been interpreted to mean 'traveler.' I think it's pretty self-explanatory why I chose that. I chose Morgan as my last name because it means 'sea circle.' The waters of the sea flow, as time does, and a circle is never ending, as I am."

"You should've called yourself Justin Tyme."

"Bit on the nose, don't you think?"

"Yeah, but it'd still be funny. What does Jaeger Novak mean, then?"

"Jaeger means 'hunter,' and Novak means 'new.' Get it? Because he hunts for new worlds. It's quite clever, really."

"Can I ask how the hell you ended up over there in the first place?" I inquired. "I mean, if it took this much of a team effort to get you back, how did you make it over there on your own?"

"When looking through all the data I had collected that night the Big Bad came, I realized that we were dealing with a parallel world and an artificially created wormhole. I was trying to send a communication through to them, sort of a 'cease and desist,' but I accidentally ended up sending…well…myself."

"How do you accidentally send yourself?!"

"Hey, it happens! Teleporting is a tricky science," Trent replied defensively.

"But how did you get through and couldn't get back?"

"The technology they were using to create the wormhole was keeping it partially open on their end at all times, but they didn't have enough of an energy source to make the wormhole complete. In other words, some things could get through, but they couldn't send full, solid objects. What happened is I accidentally opened the wormhole fully to our side – and sent myself through it. But then I was stuck there because I needed that extra boost from our world to get me back through. And the only boost that could do that was my watch. Therefore, I recruited the help of my parallel self to program my watch to send information to our world in order to contact my past self."

"So why didn't time slow down when you would show up as a Time Thief? Why did it only do it this last time, right before we rescued you?"

Trent gave me a surprised look. "You saw me more than once?"

"Yeah. You'd show up whenever you left a message."

"Oh. I didn't realize I was visible to your side. That's interesting!"

"Why didn't time slow down?"

"I wasn't trying to transmit anything but the information, therefore the gravity of the parallel world wasn't affecting the time in this world. The reason it did the last time was because I tried to use the artificially created wormhole in the lab to transmit the information because I thought you weren't getting my messages. And I needed to get out of there before SABER figured out what was going on. They were starting to catch on that something was off."

"How did you get them to stop trying to send things through to this world? The time events stopped as soon as you left."

"I explained to my parallel self what kind of damage was being done to this world, and how much more damage would be done if they were successful in the future. He adjusted his wormhole generator to try for another parallel universe, but he was quite interested in time travel after I told him about my watch. It's possible he's now going to end up going down the same path I did, but that's not my concern."

"He adjusted the wormhole generator just because you said so? Just like that?"

"Just like that."

"Why would he listen to you?"

"You'd listen to yourself, wouldn't you?"

I thought about how often I ignored my inner voice. "Not necessarily, no."

"Yeah, but you have trust issues. I guess I was asking the wrong person. My point is most people would listen to themselves."

"I don't have trust issues. I'm just cautious."

"Not the point right now, Roselyn. Pay attention, will you?"

I rolled my eyes. "So, is this all over then? Am I safe?"

Trent smiled. "Yes, I believe so. See? I fixed it. I knew I could fix it."

"What happens now?" I asked hesitantly.

"You should be all set to get on with your life. What happens now is up to you," Trent said.

"But…what about you?"

"What about me?"

"Are you going to, you know, still be around?"

"What are you asking, Roselyn?"

"Am I going to see you again?" I blurted.

"…Did you want to?" Trent asked, surprised.

"Maybe. I mean, what if the time events start happening again?"

"You have my number."

I sighed in frustration.

Trent smirked at me. "If you have something you want to say, maybe you should just say it outright."

"Just…never mind. Forget it," I said with a dismissive wave of my hand. "Thanks for all your help. I'm glad you came when you did." I started to turn away, intending to go busy myself with emptying the dishwasher. I didn't want Trent to see my face at the moment because I was afraid it would betray my feelings.

Trent caught my hand as I moved away from him, stopping me. "Is that it?" he asked.

I pulled my hand out of his grasp and looked up at him. "That's it."

"You weren't going to ask if I could take you away on a holiday?"

"No, I wasn't."

"I suppose I'll have to ask then. Roselyn, did you want to, oh, I don't know…go somewhere with me?" He smiled invitingly, and there was a twinkle of mischief in his eyes that made my heart skip.

I swallowed hard and turned away from him again. I tried to laugh off his offer as I began to unload the dishwasher. "Very funny."

"It isn't a joke."

"Take a holiday with you? Why would I do that? Where would we go?"

"I think the more appropriate question is when would we go."

I forced a laugh. "That's just crazy. I'm not going on holiday with you. I have a life here. A job. Cattiel. No, it's a terrible idea." I almost had myself convinced that I didn't want to do it.

"Just one adventure. I'll take you anywhere or anywhen you want to go."

"Anywhen isn't a real word."

"When you have a time-travel device, anywhen most certainly is a valid word. Come on," Trent pressed, "you name it, and I'll take you there."

"The only place I'd want to go is back to before I met my ex-husband so I could warn myself to avoid Barry Schmidt."

"You know you can't do that."

"I know. Paradox. So what's the point then?"

"Do you really lack such imagination? Forget about your life for a minute and think about all the amazing things in the world there are to see. Or all the things there were to see. You know what? I have just the place. Come on, I want to show you something."

I looked at him reluctantly. "Where?"

"When."

Chapter 9

I sighed and walked over to him, taking my place under his left arm. "Only for a minute, and then we come right back here," I stipulated.

"Only for a minute," he agreed.

He pressed a button on his watch and our surroundings changed in an instant. We were no longer in my living room, but rather in what looked like a savannah with a few tall, fern-like trees. The air was warm and dry. I heard an odd birdlike screech off in the distance, but it was an unfamiliar sound.

"What is this place?" I asked, stepping forward and looking around in awe.

"Somewhere in Utah."

"This is Utah?! How far back did you go?!"

Trent looked around. "Oh, about a hundred fifty million years."

My eyes widened. "Are you kidding me?! When you said anywhen, I was thinking, like, Greece. Rome. Ancient Egypt. I wasn't thinking dinosaurs!" I heard another strange animal call from somewhere around us, and I moved closer to Trent. "Are we safe? I feel like this isn't very safe."

"Well, I can teleport us out of here in a pinch, but strictly speaking, 'safe' isn't a great descriptor for our current situation. But stay close and we'll be all right," Trent said cheerfully.

"I want to go home now," I whined.

Trent scoffed at me. "Where's your sense of adventure? We are in the land of dinosaurs and you want to go home before you've even had a chance to see one?! Look," Trent said, pointing to my right.

I glanced over and saw a large lake. My mouth fell open when I saw a group of six stegosauri ambling down to the water's edge.

"That's...those...those are real dinosaurs..." I stammered, dumbfounded. They were some distance away, but the sight of them was mesmerizing.

Trent chuckled. "Brilliant, isn't it?"

"How did you know?" I asked as I continued to stare, mouth agape.

"How did I know what?"

"It was my favorite." I could see Trent looking at me from the corner of my eye. I glanced at him briefly and elaborated, "As a kid, the stegosaurus was my favorite."

Trent grinned as he looked over at the magnificent animals. "Of course it was. Isn't it every kid's favorite?"

"My brother always favored the velociraptors."

"He wouldn't if he ever met one."

I stopped staring at the stegosauri to take a quick look around. "We aren't going to see any of those here, are we?" I asked nervously.

"Oh, no. They won't be around for another sixty million years or so. And they wouldn't be in this region anyway," Trent assured me. Then he added, "But, I wouldn't be surprised to run into a Utahraptor here in this time period, and that would be even worse." He looked down at his watch. "We should probably be going now. Your minute is almost up."

"Just...just one more minute," I requested.

Trent looked pleased as he nodded in acquiescence.

As I watched the stegosauri drinking peacefully at the water's edge, I understood why Trent had chosen to take me to this particular time and place. He knew it would fascinate and intrigue me. He knew it would be just enough to make me want to go on one more little adventure with him. What he didn't know, though, was that he could've taken me just about anywhere and it would've had the same effect simply because I knew deep down inside that I wanted to run away with him.

As I turned back to him and let him put his arm around me, a sudden movement over his shoulder caught my eye. I glanced back and saw a man standing about fifty yards away from us. I gasped and opened my mouth to speak, but we were already back in my own kitchen before the words erupted from my mouth. "There's a man over there!"

Trent whirled around, looking around the kitchen. "What? Where?"

"No! Not here! There was a man back there in Utah!"

Trent became very serious, and it was instantly concerning. He put his hands on my shoulders and looked me in the eyes. "Tell me exactly what you saw."

"I don't know, it was a man! I saw him for just a second before we teleported!"

"What did he look like?" Trent's eyes were locked on mine intently.

"I didn't get a good look at him. He just looked like a man!"

"Clothes? Hair color? Skin? Weight? Come on, give me something!" he demanded roughly.

"Trent, you're scaring me."

"You should be scared!" He shouted. He fidgeted with his watch, scowling. He turned around and started pacing. "There shouldn't be a man in Utah a hundred fifty million years in the past. The fact that there was one means that something is very very wrong. And when something is very very wrong, you can bet SABER is behind it. Or I am."

"What do you mean by that? Why would you be behind that?"

Trent looked at me. "Who was behind the Time Thieves fiasco?" He held up his hand. "Me."

"Yeah, but not you you."

"But some version of me. Enough like me to be a possible threat. The last person on Earth I would ever want to contend with is me."

"But you're a reasonable person. You're a good person. Why would any version of you ever be a threat?"

Trent looked at me with pained eyes. "Oh, my dear, you have no idea. There's a reason I am constantly working to stop SABER – and that's not just to keep them from getting their hands on a time-travel device. That's important, of course, but there's a far more essential purpose for my vigilance. I can't allow them to create another one of me."

I furrowed my brow. "Because you could create a time-travel device?"

"No. It's because I could create any kind of device they asked me to make." He pointed at his head. "This approaches the limits of what human intelligence is capable. My brain. This mushy gray mass I carry around between my ridiculous ears holds keys to doors that should never be opened. We have some wildly clever artificial intelligence in the future, but nothing that's able to surpass the raw creativity and ingenuity of the human mind. And this one is undoubtedly the most imaginative – and most dangerous." Trent stopped his pacing and rested his hand against the wall, his other hand on his hip. He looked down at the floor instead of at me as he said, "Pack a bag and grab your cat. You aren't safe here. We need to go. Now."

"What? Why?"

Trent turned to me with a look of urgency. "For once can you just do what I ask?!"

"Ok!" I cried.

I ran to my room and started tossing clothes in a bag. I had never seen Trent look so rattled, and it scared the hell out of me. This was a man who faced off against the Big Bad and barely batted an eye, so I really didn't want to be around to meet whatever it was that did scare him. In my fear, I stuck my .45 in with the rest of my belongings. I threw my bag over my shoulder, rushed back out to the living room and scooped up Cattiel off the couch.

"I'm ready," I said as confidently as I could.

I barely got the words out of my mouth before Trent swept me up in his arms and teleported us out of the house. He released me and abruptly walked away as soon as the transfer was complete. I found myself in a small home library or office. There was a comfortable-looking beige chair sitting next to a window, and two large bookshelves full of novels and texts. The floors were hardwood, but they didn't appear to be well-maintained. There was a large desk near the wall with several half-burned candle sticks sitting upon it.

"When and where are we now?" I asked, following him over to the bookshelves as I tried to calm Cattiel.

"London, 1923. We are in my home." Trent replied distractedly. He began pulling unlabeled leather-bound journals from the shelves and stacking them in his arm.

"Is it ok for me to let Cattiel run around here?"

"Don't put him down yet. We aren't staying."

With that, Trent grabbed me and teleported us into yet a different location. This time, we were in what appeared to be a more modern apartment. We again were in some kind of library or office, as there were shelves of books along the wall and a desk nearby.

"More books? With all this running around, when do you ever have time to read?" I asked.

"There's always time to read," he replied. "You can let the cat down now. We'll be here a while."

Trent went over to the desk and plopped the journals down that he had taken from London.

"We aren't in 1923 anymore, are we?" I asked with a downward inflection as I set Cattiel on the floor.

Trent sat down at the desk and started thumbing through the journals. "No. This is 2361."

"I'm in the future?" I said, surprised.

"The future to you, yes."

"Where are we?"

"Vancouver."

"…Oh."

That got Trent's attention. He stopped looking through the journals and glanced up at me. "'Oh'? What, is there something wrong with Vancouver?"

"No, it's great."

"Then why did you say 'oh' like that?"

"Like what?"

"You had a tone."

"No, I didn't."

"You did. Is Vancouver not exotic enough for you?"

"I didn't say that! It's just that Vancouver is kind of…ordinary, you know? It caught me off-guard after all the excitement."

Trent gave me an irritated look. "You're 343 years into your future and you saw dinosaurs today, but hey, by all means, complain that I landed us in Vancouver."

"I wasn't complaining! You're the one making a big deal about it!"

"It bugs me! You expect me to give you over-the-top extraordinary all the time, but guess what? Sometimes ordinary is good too!"

"I don't expect anything!" I argued. "As I recall, I tried to turn down your offer of adventure, but you were the one who insisted! I didn't ask for dinosaurs! I didn't ask for the future! And I sure as hell didn't ask for you!"

I immediately regretted my words. I wished I could gather them all up and shove them back down my throat before they could reach his ears.

Trent gave me a tight, humorless smile. "I'm sorry I've caused such a disruption."

"I didn't mean that," I apologized.

"People say things they don't 'mean' all the time. The problem is that there is a part of them that does mean it…at least just a little.

Otherwise, the words never would've occurred to them. I think when people say 'I didn't mean that,' what they really mean is 'I didn't want you to know I felt that way.'"

"And sometimes," I countered, "people don't realize until after it's been said that they really, truly, don't feel the way they thought they did when they said it. You should know all about that, Trent. You know, like kissing someone because you think you like them, then realizing you don't and running off and leaving only a note. I think that's a pretty good example of what I'm getting at."

Guilt clouded Trent's face.

"What, nothing snarky to say now?" I prodded.

"It was a mistake. I told you I was sorry," Trent said quietly as he looked down at his journals. The word "mistake" shot through my heart like an arrow. I wondered if that was how he had felt when I had spit verbal venom at him only moments ago.

"Mistake or not, you owed me an explanation. A conversation. Not a note saying 'Hey, you're on your own now!'"

"What was I supposed to say? I was sorry. I said it. I meant it. I didn't want to cause any more complications."

"But then you come back and ask me to go on holiday with you? That's one hell of a complication if you ask me!"

"I know!"

I looked at him quizzically. "Then why did you ask?"

"I don't know! I thought maybe it would be fun!" He sighed. "You know, when I left you that note, I didn't know if I would be coming back, and I certainly didn't know you were going to help rescue me from a parallel world. None of those memories were retained from my past self. But I did remember one thing; and that one thing was that I kissed you back then and you did not like it. And I shouldn't have done it that night before I left, and I'm sorry I did. But, when I came back, and I saw you looking at me like...like you actually missed me, I thought maybe you had forgiven me. Maybe it would be ok if we were still friends. I thought perhaps you would like to accompany me on some of my journeys and see the things I see. I'm not expecting anything out of this, if that's what you're thinking. I just thought we could have some fun and kill some time – as friends." Trent looked at me earnestly.

"As friends," I repeated, trying the words out.

"That's all I'm asking."

"Trent, why did you kiss me?" I asked.

"Why does anyone do anything?"

"Curiosity?" I responded, puzzled.

Trent gave me a sly grin and tapped the side of his nose in reply.

I didn't understand the gesture, but before I could inquire, Trent's watch made a strange noise. He looked down at it and knitted his brows.

"What's wrong?" I asked.

"There's something going on at your house. Or rather, something is going to go on at your house."

"Wait, how does your watch know that?"

"I put up an alarm system when I was living there. I haven't deactivated it yet."

"So, what, you have cameras up around my house? Have you been watching me?"

"No, nothing like that. Just a couple of sensors to alert me if anything is amiss. I wasn't going to keep it up, I swear. I have alarm systems up at all of my houses in case anyone ever comes after me."

"Who would come after you?"

"SABER, of course."

"Is it someone from SABER at my house right now?"

Trent pulled his glasses from his breast pocket and slipped them on. He turned on the holographic display on his watch and examined the information. "No, it isn't anyone from SABER. The energy signal is all wrong. I think it's just your run of the mill intruder." He turned off the display and took off his glasses.

My heart thumped violently against my ribcage. He found me, was the only thought running through my head. The bastard found me.

"I should pop in and see if he's finding everything all right," Trent joked nonchalantly.

"No! He can't know about you!"

Trent looked at me with surprise. "Who can't what now?" he asked, confused.

"It's him. It's Barry. I know it is. If he sees a man in my house, he'll lose it." I was on the verge of a panic attack.

Trent stood up from his desk and walked over to me. "Say that last sentence again."

I gave him a puzzled look. "If he sees a man in my house—"

"Your house. Exactly," Trent said. "He doesn't have control over you anymore, Roselyn. Besides, we don't even know that it's him."

"It's him."

"All the more reason for me to go have a chat with him," Trent said with a defiant smirk.

"No, Trent. Please. Please just leave it alone."

"Will he stop if I leave it alone?"

"He won't stop if you don't."

"I can be very persuasive."

"Leave it, Trent. We need to focus on finding out who the man from the Jurassic was."

"We have time for a side quest. This is important."

"Important to me. Not to you."

"If it's important to you, it's important to me."

Those words made me pause. "…Even after I said those mean things to you?"

Trent grinned. "If you didn't say mean things to me, I'd think something was wrong."

"You don't know what you're getting into," I said. "You don't know how he is."

Trent gave me a confident look. "I've been around for over six hundred years. Trust me, I've dealt with plenty of people like Barry."

Six hundred years old?!

"You don't understand. If you go in and start something, it's just going to make an even bigger mess out of this situation and I'm going to have to continue dealing with it long after you've left."

"Who said I was going anywhere?"

"Well, eventually you will."

"Roselyn, even if I'm halfway around the globe and a hundred million years from you, I can still be by your side in an instant. I'm never really 'gone' if you don't want me to be."

"You were just in a parallel universe and unreachable for like two months," I pointed out.

Trent paused, tilting his head. "Ok, you got me there. But to be fair, that was a first, and hopefully a last. And hey! A past version of myself showed up to help and I did come back eventually!"

I looked at him skeptically.

"My point is," he said, "you're not alone in this. He's going to try to direct his wrath at you. That's what weak men do. Let me take it instead. Trust me, I've had worse."

I took a deep breath. "Fine. But I'm coming with you. Just give me a minute." I quickly dug through my bag and pulled out the .45 I had acquired in anticipation of a situation like this. I hooked the holster inside the back of my jeans and pulled my shirttail out over it to hide it.

"You won't need that," Trent said.

"Let's hope not."

I steeled myself and stepped up next to Trent. He put his arm around me and we were instantly in my kitchen, standing in the dark, facing the back door. The door handle was jiggling as an unseen hand from the other side was attempting to jimmy it.

Trent stepped forward and turned on the kitchen light next to the back door. He opened the door. "Can I help you?" he asked, sounding irritated. His body was blocking my view of whoever was on the back porch.

"Who the hell are you?" The sound of Barry's voice sent a shiver of dread down my spine. I hated that he could still fill me with such incapacitating anxiety.

"Trent. Trent Morgan. What are you doing to the door back here?" Trent demanded.

"Where's Roselyn? Why are you in her house?"

"Why are you trying to get in?"

"I need to talk to Roselyn. Where is she?" Barry asked impatiently.

"You can talk to me."

"I don't want to talk to you. Look, I know she's here. That's her car in the driveway."

"It's a very common model."

"It's her license plate, asshole. I'm not stupid."

"A bit obtuse, though, aren't you?"

"If you think you're going to talk down to me with your accent and your weird words, you've got another thing coming. Just let me talk to Roselyn and I won't have to hurt you."

Trent threw his head back and laughed mockingly. "Oh, dear. You are a bit of a shit, aren't you?"

"Oh, really?! I'm a shit? You know what else I am? I'm a black belt, fucker." That was a boldfaced lie.

"And I think you'll find I'm rather indestructible," Trent said calmly. That was probably true.

"Who the fuck are you?" Barry shouted angrily. "Are you her new boyfriend? You know what a whore she is, don't you?"

"I'm not her boyfriend, but I would consider myself a lucky man if I were. I suggest you watch what you say from this point going forward. Or perhaps you could just keep your rubbish to yourself, get back in your vehicle, and leave this place and never come back."

"I ain't going anywhere, you prissy asshole! Do you think I'm afraid of you?" Barry mocked. "I could break you like the little twig you are."

Trent crossed his arms and leaned against the door jamb. "That mouth just doesn't stop, does it? Wow, you do test one's patience!" he marveled.

When Trent shifted to lean against the door jamb, it had created a clear sightline between Barry and myself. I saw him standing there in the dark, and we locked eyes. My heart stopped and I froze like a deer in the headlights.

"You little bitch! Sending someone else to fight your battles for you? You're a spineless—"

Barry was cut off when Trent put his whole hand over Barry's face and pushed him backwards. Trent stepped outside with Barry and shut the door behind him. I could hear Barry yelling terrible things about me and making threats.

I heard Trent calmly say, "You need to leave, and there's no point in ever coming back because you're just going to be dealing with me if you do. And if I have to deal with you again, I'm going to have to relocate you."

"What the fuck does that even mean?" Barry shouted.

"It's what they do with problem animals. They relocate them to somewhere they can't hurt anyone."

"I'm not going anywhere! I'll come back every goddamn day! How the fuck do you think you're going to relocate me, bitch?"

"Like this."

The silence that followed concerned me. I ran to the door to see what had happened. The porch was empty.

"Oh, Trent, did you just do what I think you did?" I asked aloud to the air.

"If you think I relocated him, then yes," I heard Trent say behind me. I turned around to find him standing in the kitchen, straightening the cuffs of his suit jacket.

"Where did you put him?"

"When."

I put my hand over my mouth. "You didn't…"

"No, I didn't. It would've been funny though, wouldn't it? I put him in Wyoming. With a little effort, he'll find his way home. But I told him if he came here or bothered you or anyone you know again, then next time he'd end up in Russia." Trent smiled at me. "Also, I thought it might please you to know that he cried."

That did please me. "We have a small problem though, Trent. What are we going to do with his truck?"

"It's being towed, of course. Already taken care of." Trent swiped his hand through his hair and straightened his tie. "Well, that was fun, but shall we get back to boring old Vancouver now before we get company that isn't quite so easy to be rid of?"

I nodded as I felt tears welling up in my eyes. It was like someone had released a pressure valve in my brain, and twelve different emotions came bursting out all at once.

Trent scrutinized my face. "Are you unhappy?"

"No, I'm…I'm just a weird mix of emotions right now." I waved my hand dismissively. "It's fine, I'll be fine. Let's go."

As I went to Trent to be teleported back to Canada, I realized just how grateful I was to have him in my life. I wrapped my arms around his torso, resting my temple on his shoulder, and whispered, "I'm sorry I said I didn't ask for you. I'm glad to be able to call you my friend."

Trent put his arms around me and squeezed me. "Ditto." He pressed the button on his watch to send us back to Vancouver, but he didn't let go of me immediately after we arrived. I didn't complain, though, because I didn't let go right away either.

When I finally did release him, he went to his desk to pore over his journals. I wanted to know what it was he was looking for within their pages, but at the moment I needed to go sit quietly by myself and find my composure.

"Is there somewhere I can go lie down?" I asked.

"Oh, you're probably tired, aren't you? I forget how much you lot need to sleep."

"I'm too riled to be tired. I just need some time to myself for a bit."

"There's a very comfortable bed in my room that rarely gets used. I'll put some fresh sheets on it for you," he said as he started to stand. "It hasn't been touched in a while."

"No, don't worry about it. Like I said, I'm not going to sleep. I just need a minute."

"Oh. Well, all right. Do you want me to bring you anything? I probably have some crackers or something nonperishable in the cupboard."

"I'm fine, Trent. I'll be out in a little bit."

As I followed Trent's directions to his room, I almost tripped over Cattiel.

"Crap, you need your food, don't you?" I bent down to pet the fluffy feline. "And a litter box. Damn."

I yelled to Trent about Cattiel's supplies.

"On it," he replied. Within moments, he yelled, "There, he's all set. Come here, kitty kitty! Come get your dinner!"

I chuckled to myself as Cattiel's ears perked to attention and he trotted down the narrow hall toward Trent's voice. I went into Trent's room and turned on the light. I was surprised at how…clinical it looked. The walls were bare. The bedding was plain. It was less personal than a hotel room. It was…sad.

I sat down on the bed and took a deep breath. As I exhaled, I let out the feelings I had been holding in. A flood of tears streamed from my eyes. It had been painful and difficult to see Barry again. I had wondered how I would feel when it finally happened, and it had been as bad as I had imagined. That man had tortured me for so long that now all it took was the mere thought of him to send me into a fit of anxiety. Seeing him again just brought all of those vile memories and horrible feelings of dread and despair boiling back to the surface. I had hoped facing him again would help to ease some of the damage he had done – like ripping off a bandage – but it did nothing but reopen the wound.

But Trent – glorious, wonderful Trent – had stood up for me when I couldn't. He had taken on a burden that wasn't his to take for the sake of my sanity. I pulled the holster out of the back of my blue jeans and laid it on the bedside stand. Barry had been the reason I had bought that gun in the first place. He was the reason I had acquired a concealed weapons permit. It wasn't because I was vengeful or trigger happy. It was because I was terrified. But now that I had Trent around, I didn't have to be nearly so afraid. It wasn't because he was a man and I was a woman. It wasn't as simple or sexist as that. It was because I knew I could count on him when I needed him. I knew he would put himself in harm's way in order to keep me safe. He'd already done it on more than one occasion. In just a short period of time, Trent had become the best friend I was never allowed to have.

I awoke to the gentle caress of fingers brushing hair from my forehead. My eyes shot open. I hadn't realized I'd fallen asleep.

"Did you have a good rest, Wyatt Earp?" Trent asked with a grin. He was standing next to the bed, looking down at me. He nodded toward the .45 on the bedside stand.

"Oh, ha ha," I laughed humorlessly. "What time is it? How long was I asleep?"

"About two hours. I got carried away with my research for a while before I realized you still hadn't emerged from my room yet."

"I'm sorry. I didn't mean to take your bed from you."

"No, it's all right. I don't use it."

"Why not? How is it that you never sleep?"

"I do sleep. Just not nearly as much as everyone else. It's absurd to me to think of wasting six hours a day just lying around."

"I need eight."

"Good lord! How do you get anything done?"

"I know. It's pretty inconvenient," I agreed.

"I get a good hour or two of sleep every few days, and I'm good to go. It's amazing how much you can get done in one go when you don't have to go to bed at night."

"Don't you ever just lie down and relax? It seems like you're always running around or pacing or calculating or waving your arms about like a madman. I don't think I've ever seen you lie down just for the sake of relaxation or contemplation."

"I don't need to lie down to contemplate. And yes, I sit in a chair and read to relax. I'm not always running around."

I scooted over and patted the bed beside me. "Sit. You're making me nervous looming over me like that," I teased.

Trent looked mildly uncomfortable all of a sudden. He sat down and folded his hands in his lap awkwardly.

"Am I making you uncomfortable?" I asked.

"No. Well, yes. A little."

"Why?"

"Because I feel like you're putting me in a 'sit down, we need to talk' kind of situation. You aren't going to tell me I'm adopted, are you?"

I laughed. "Everything is fine. It's just exhausting watching you sometimes because you're always so annoyingly full of energy."

Trent kicked his giant shoes off and swung his legs up onto the bed, leaning back with his hands folded behind his head onto the pillow. "There, relaxed enough for you?" he asked as he turned and smiled at me.

My body suddenly became aware of his closeness to me. I rolled onto my back to look at the ceiling because I was afraid my cheeks were about to turn beet red.

"Is something the matter?" Trent asked.

"No. I just…I can't think of anything to say now. Isn't that funny how that happens?" I sounded like an idiot.

"Am I making you uncomfortable?" he asked.

"No, you're fine. It's just that I had things I wanted to say to you. Things to ask you. And suddenly it's all…poof…gone."

"It's probably more relaxing if you aren't talking the whole time anyway," Trent said.

"Damn, you always know the right thing to say," I commented sarcastically.

"I know. It's your favorite thing about me."

"It really isn't."

We sat in silence for a while, and finally, I felt comfortable enough to roll over and face Trent without worrying about blushing. When he turned his head to look at me, it struck me at just how much my eyes enjoyed gazing at that face of his. The longer I knew him, the more handsome he became to me. How could I have ever not noticed how handsome he was? All I saw now was the delightful way he swooped his hair; the dimpled smile that made you feel like he was smiling just for you; the twinkle of mischief in his eye whenever something clever occurred to him; and the strong, masculine squareness of his jawline. The features I used to view as faults, like his big feet, bowed legs, and rather big ears, were now endearing.

It was time to admit it to myself. I was absolutely, unquestionably in love with Trent Morgan.

Chapter 10

"You're looking at me funny," Trent said, ruining the moment per usual.

"No I'm not."

"Yes, you are. You look like you have something you want to say."

"I don't. Oh wait! Yes I do. Why don't you have any pictures on the walls?" I asked, finally remembering one of the things I had wanted to ask him.

He looked up at the ceiling. "I don't have any pictures to hang."

"Six hundred years and countless adventures, but no pictures?"

"Nope. I don't need pictures. If I want to see something, I go see it."

"What about people, though? You don't have any pictures of people you care about?"

"No."

"Why not?"

"I'm not exactly a popular fellow."

"There must be someone."

Trent looked over at me with a smile. "There is."

I tried to calm the flutter in my heart. "I mean someone else."

Trent looked back up at the ceiling again and sighed. "Yes, I have had some friends throughout the years. But I don't keep their pictures."

"Why not?"

"Guilt, mostly. I outlive everyone, Roselyn. They die, and I keep going, and then I forget. It's not because I want to forget – I've told you how it works. I used to keep pictures, back when I was younger. But the first time I saw a photo of someone hanging on my wall and I didn't know who it was, I got rid of all of them. It's painful to lose a friend, but it fills you with the worst guilt you can imagine when you see a picture of someone you're sure was a friend of yours, and you have no memories of the time you shared together. That's how the dead live on – in memories – and I can't even provide them that."

"Why don't you keep a journal to help you remember? You obviously already keep some journals."

"I do keep journals, but only for certain subjects – things that help me keep history straight. If I kept a journal for everything, could you imagine the sheer number of journals I would have? I'd never be able to keep up on them. Besides, it doesn't help me remember. Like I said, those memories are gone. It's really no better than keeping photos on the wall at that point. It just becomes another story."

"What's wrong with being a story?"

A saw a sad smile cross Trent's lips. "Because it's always a sad ending."

I reached over and slid my hand into his. I didn't know what else to do to comfort him.

He turned and looked at me. "There is one friend, though, that I just can't seem to forget. Even after two hundred years and four changes, she's still stuck in my head after first meeting her." I started to smile, but then he added, "I think it was the terrible singing. I just can't erase that terrible singing from my memory."

I gasped in feigned horror. "I can't believe you remember that! Why would you remember that, of all things?!"

He laughed. "Good lord, how could I forget? And those sweatpants! What did they say? 'Luscious'?"

I giggled. "Bootylicious."

"Yes! Bootylicious. I rather fancied those sweatpants."

"I bet you did," I teased.

"If only you hadn't been all doe-eyed for someone else..." he said, jokingly.

I hesitated. "Do you really not remember?" I asked.

"All I remember is that it wasn't me."

"It was, actually," I confessed quietly.

Trent furrowed his brow at me. "What do you mean?"

I could feel my cheeks reddening. "It was you...this you," I said, gesturing to him.

It was like Trent suddenly put up a wall between us and closed himself off. "Oh." He swung his legs over the side of the bed and sat up. "No, I don't remember that part."

I sat up. "Where are you going?"

"Those journals aren't going to go through themselves. Work to do!"

"Wait!" I grabbed his arm as he stood up, stopping him from walking away.

"Please let me go," he said sternly, avoiding eye contact with me.

I climbed off the bed and stood next to him, continuing to hold his arm defiantly. "Why? Why are you running off all of a sudden?"

Trent looked at the floor instead of at me. "I don't want to do something we'll both end up regretting." He was breathing heavily.

"Like what?" I demanded.

Trent sighed. A strange look washed over his face – a look of both defeat and relief. It was the look of someone who was finally giving in to something they'd been fighting for a long time.

"Like this." He turned to me and cupped my face with his hands. His mouth was on mine in an instant, his tongue searching out mine.

I felt a surge of lust rush through my body. His kiss was passionate and needful, and it was making my knees feel weak. There was a tingling sensation that started in my chest and shot all the way down to my pelvis. I cast aside my inhibitions and reached up and started unbuttoning his suit jacket, slipping it off over his shoulders. He leaned into me, and I could feel his rigidity pressing against me through his trousers, which sent another surge of desire through my veins. He leaned down and kissed the side of my neck as his hands slid down and around to my backside. He cupped my buttocks and squeezed before running one hand around to the front of my jeans. As I felt his fingertips pulling at the waistband, it finally struck me that this was actually happening. He intended to take it all the way.

I pulled away from him briefly to pull my shirt off over my head, and I climbed back onto the bed. I grabbed his tie and pulled him down to me, and he climbed onto the bed over top of me. His mouth found mine again as he pressed himself between my legs. His hand slid under my bra and explored the soft mounds beneath. Everywhere he touched he left a trail of fire that fueled the burning lust in my loins. His lips left mine and moved to my neck, caressing the tender skin sensually as they made their way to my bosom. He unhooked the clasp of my bra and cast it aside as his hot, wet tongue descended upon my breasts. I arched my back and tossed my head back, submitting to him fully.

He kissed my neck again briefly before sitting back and loosening his tie. As he undressed in front of me, I could see the wild desire burning in his eyes as he looked at me. I'd never felt so wanted in all of my life. After he kicked off his trousers, he tugged at mine. I assisted him as he slid my jeans down over my hips, my panties coming off with them. He tossed the clothes aside and finally lowered his boxers, releasing his manhood. His giant feet made a lot more sense to me now.

He mounted me, his long bangs dangling down against my forehead, and he looked into my eyes intensely. His waist was poised between my legs, but he hesitated.

"Are you ready for me?" he whispered.

I nodded in consent, my anticipation and excitement rising.

That was all he needed. I felt his manhood pressing against my opening, and slowly, little by little, he entered me. It had been so long since I'd been with a man that it took my body a while to accommodate him. But once he was completely sheathed within me, it wasn't long before I felt a pleasant ache in my abdomen. I could feel the sensation growing in intensity, and I urged Trent on. As he quickened his pace, I entwined my fingers in his hair and buried my face in his shoulder. I bucked my hips wildly against his as I felt an explosion of pleasure and a cry of ecstasy escaped my lips. My response to him was enough to put Trent over the tipping point, and a guttural moan emanated from his throat as he found his release.

We lay there for several minutes afterward, panting and shuddering from the pleasant aftershocks, before Trent rolled over onto his back next to me. I turned to look at him, a smile on my face. It quickly faded, though, when I saw him wipe his hand down his face in a gesture he only made when he was feeling stressed.

"I can't believe I did that to you. I shouldn't have done that."

My heart sank. I felt completely rejected. "That bad, hey?" I snapped.

He turned to me. "No! No, not that at all! That was…that was brilliant! Fantastic! Which is why I shouldn't have done that." He sat up and moved to the edge of the bed. He reached for his boxers and slid them on as he stood up. "We can't do this again," he added as he grabbed his pants off the floor.

"Why the hell not? What's wrong?" I demanded angrily.

He turned to me as he zipped up his pants. His face looked troubled. "I knew it back then, and I know it now: you and I won't work. For some reason, though, I just can't seem to let you be. We can't be more than friends. It has to be this way, Roselyn."

"But…what the hell was all of this, then?!" I said, gesturing to the bed in general.

"This was me losing control. This was me not keeping a handle on my feelings. This was me inadvertently hurting you. I didn't mean for this to happen."

"Are we going to need to revisit the discussion we had on what 'I didn't mean it' really means? Because you most certainly did mean for this to happen," I said as I started furiously grabbing my clothes off the floor and getting dressed.

"Wanting something to happen and meaning for it to happen aren't the same thing."

"Then help me understand, will you? You wanted to do this, but you didn't mean to do it? How does that make any sense?"

"I want you, Roselyn! I do! I always have! But this," he said as he pointed between himself and me repeatedly, "wouldn't be fair to either of us."

"Why not?"

"Think about it! What do you want? At the end of the day, who do you want to spend your life with? What does it involve? Kids? I can't have kids. I was specifically designed to be sterile. A husband who climbs into bed and sleeps next to you all night? I can't do that. Someone who grows old with you? I can't do that either. Hell, I might not always be me! I could change at any time – today, or thirty years from now – and neither of us will have any idea who I will be when I wake. Will I be someone you can love, or will I have changed so much that you can't love me anymore? Will you even see me as me anymore?

"You know what the worst part is, Roselyn?" he continued. "The worst part is that I will either have to watch you grow old and die while I live on, or I will have to watch you fall out of love with the person I become. Either way, it's a heartache that I don't think I can possibly endure. You and I are so wrong for each other that it's almost funny. So what on Earth makes you think that this would ever be a good idea for either of us? I make a great friend, but I would make a lousy partner. Domestic life suits me ill, and my life would be dangerous for you. It was selfish of me to give in to my desire for you, and for that I deeply apologize. I just…I just wish I could be man you need and deserve."

The heartbroken way he looked at me shattered me. He'd meant everything he said. I was angry and hurt and I wanted to fight with him and argue that he was wrong, but I just couldn't – because he was right. I hated that he was right, but he was. Damn, here come the tears again.

I quickly swiped away the tear that rolled down my cheek and hurried from the room without saying a word. I didn't know where everything was in his apartment, so I just went into the nearest nook I could find, which happened to be the kitchen. I saw a teapot sitting near the stove, so I started looking through his cupboards for tea. I needed a hot cup of comfort right about now.

"There isn't much to be found in there, I'm afraid," Trent said from the kitchen entry.

"I'm just looking for tea," I said flatly.

Trent walked into the kitchen and came up next to me. I instantly reacted by assuming he was going to hug me or touch me in some way, but he simply reached up into the cupboard over my head and pulled out a container of teabags. I immediately felt foolish and took a discreet step back.

I reached for the container, but he held it away from me. "Go have a seat in the library. I can make the tea," he said softly without looking at me.

I found my way back to the library through blurry tears and sat down in his chair at his desk. I didn't know how to feel. I had just made love with the man I have so utterly and completely fallen for, and who I'm certain has feelings for me, yet here I was in tears, knowing that I was never going to be able to hold on to him. I should have let him walk away when he had tried to leave the room. He was right that we shouldn't have done that, because now it was even more painful knowing I could never have him again. But he was wrong about one thing: I didn't truly regret it. Maybe I should, but if I was never going to have him again, I took solace in the fact that he and I had shared that experience – that bond – together. It wasn't going to make things any easier going forward, though.

I dabbed my eyes and looked down at the journals spread open on the desk. The text was hand-written, and the pages were yellowed with age. It was written in a language I didn't recognize. I opened another journal from the stack and found the same handwriting. What did he need these for? How was this going to help him figure out who was following us?

I heard Trent walking down the hall, so I closed the journal. I found my composure and put on a brave face. I didn't want him to see the damage he had done. He walked into the room with a cup of tea in one hand and Cattiel draped over the other arm.

"I bring you offerings," he said as he set the tea in front of me and handed me the ornery cat. He gave me a hesitant smile, as if he wasn't sure if it was ok to smile at me yet.

I squeezed Cattiel and rested my cheek on the top of his head while he growled at me. "Oh, I love you too," I said to the cat, but when I saw Trent visibly tense up, I made sure to add, "kitty."

Trent continued to stand near me, but he didn't speak. There was a tension in the air that neither of us knew how to clear. I decided to do what I always did – ignore the problem and hope it goes away.

"What are these journals for?" I asked, trying to keep my sniffling to a minimum.

"Oh! Those are my notes. I have to keep notes on all of my dealings with SABER so I don't lose any important information and details that might be of use later on. I was looking through them to see if I've ever had anything like this happen before."

"Find anything?"

"Not yet, but I still have the rest of that stack to go through."

"What language is this?" I asked. "I don't recognize it."

"You wouldn't. It's Unilang. It's like the metric system for language, but it doesn't exist in your time yet."

"I thought Latin was like the metric system for language."

"Eh, in a way, I guess. But how many people do you know that actually speak Latin? Everyone speaks Unilang in the time I come from."

"What time is that, exactly?"

"I was created in the year 2886."

"Wow. I never thought the human race would last that long, honestly."

"Things do get a bit dodgy here and there between your time and mine, but humans are a rather persistent lot."

"How far into the future have you gone? Have you seen if we ever do get wiped out?"

"I don't venture past my own time unless my device detects an anomaly that I have to investigate."

"How can it know that something is wrong in the future if you don't go there?"

"The funny thing about time is that cause and effect don't flow in just one direction. The future affects the past, too, so if something in the future is changed from what it is supposed to be, it can cause ripple effects backward through history."

"I still don't understand why you don't go to the future. Aren't you curious?"

"Of course. But that's unknown territory, and there's always a possibility I could end up throwing a monkey wrench into the natural progression of events if I insert myself into the future. You see, time and events aren't necessarily set in stone until they are experienced. It's kind of like Schrodinger's cat. You are both alive and dead until you open your own box. Whatever you see on the inside is what becomes reality for you. However, it's the events that lead up to you opening that box that determine the outcome, and if you open the box too early, out of sequence, well...you never know what outcome you're going to be stuck with, and how it's going to affect the past."

"You insert yourself into the past and change things. How is that any different?"

"I'm a pretty good judge of what kind of changes will be catastrophic and what kind won't be because I have knowledge of what events are supposed to occur. I lose that advantage if I visit the future."

"What about other planets? There must be other habitable planets like this one out there in the universe. Have you ever teleported off Earth?"

"No. I'm not saying I couldn't, but I'd need to know the exact location I was teleporting to, and, as of yet, I have no such information."

"Really? You're from almost nine hundred years in the future, and we still haven't colonized other planets? What about Mars?"

"You lot have a bad habit of getting distracted by war and politics, not to mention the whole global warming catastrophe. Suffice it to say things happened. Mars took a backburner for a while."

"We haven't even made it to Mars yet?"

"Oh, yeah, we did go to Mars. Didn't go well."

"So, we just gave up?"

"No, not exactly. We're just working on making it more…habitable."

"Terraforming?"

"Bingo."

"But doesn't that take, like, forever?"

"Aye. Now you know why we don't have a colony on Mars."

"Couldn't you steal a space suit and go check it out? Just for a little bit?"

"I might alter something that shouldn't be altered."

"You know, for someone who claims to live so dangerously, you sure do set some restrictive limits on yourself."

"I don't play fast and loose with the fate of humankind."

The cat in my lap started to fuss, so I set him on the floor and got up from Trent's chair. As I reached for my tea, intending to take it and move to the chair over by the bookshelves, I bumped the cup and accidentally sloshed some tea onto Trent's opened journal.

"Oh shit!" I exclaimed. I used my shirt sleeve to quickly dab up the tea on the page.

Trent objected to my method. "Not your shirt, Roselyn! It's fine, just leave it!"

"I'm so sorry," I apologized.

"It's fine. It's just a little tea. These journals have seen worse." Trent came over and pulled a handkerchief from his pocket. He stood next to me as he wiped up the mess I had made. His tendency to stand in close proximity to me, I noticed, was becoming a problem for me. I wanted to touch him, and I wanted him to touch me. Images of us together flooded my brain, and I couldn't stop them. I quickly stepped away from him.

He seemed to notice my abrupt retreat, but he didn't comment on it. Instead, he said, "I should probably get back to reading. Are you sure you aren't hungry or tired? You do realize it's the middle of the night, right?"

"I know. I'm fine. Do your reading so you can get this figured out...so I can go home."

"As you wish," he replied with a hint of dejection in his tone.

I browsed the books on his shelves, and found an odd array of titles. He had classics, like Wuthering Heights and Jane Eyre, but he also had books I'd never heard of and books in different languages. I finally chose Pride and Prejudice and settled into the only other chair in the room. It wasn't until I sat in it that I discovered it was a rocking chair. It made a slight creak when it rocked, but it wasn't terribly loud and didn't bother me. I curled one foot under my other leg and left one foot on the floor to rock the chair. It wasn't long before I heard Trent plop his journal onto his desk loudly. I glanced over at him, and found he was staring at me with aggravation.

"Must you?" he asked.

"What?"

"The chair. Don't you hear the creaking?"

"It's not that bad."

"It really is."

"It's not bothering me."

"It's bothering me."

"If it bothers you, then why do you have a chair that creaks?"

"It didn't creak last time I was here."

He and I stared at each other in silence. Finally, he broke eye contact and looked back down at his journal.

Creak.

I couldn't help myself.

Trent exhaled loudly and looked at me from under his eyebrows. "Oops."

I waited a little longer this time, until he was really starting to get focused.

Creak.

Trent stood up abruptly, startling me. "Ok, we're leaving. Grab the cat...and his box."

"Where are we going?"

"To a house that doesn't have a creaky rocking chair."

Chapter 11

When we arrived at the new place, we were in yet another small library. "How many places do you have?" I asked.

"Several."

"Do they all have a library?"

"Shouldn't every home?"

I put the cat down and stuck his box in the corner temporarily. "So, tell me about this place."

"Alaska – 2515. And this is an actual house, not a flat. You can pick a room," he said as he sat down at his new desk and laid out his stack of journals.

"Why Alaska?"

"It's still fairly remote. I don't like a lot of attention, so I either choose a location that's so busy that no one will notice me, or so remote that no one is around to notice me."

"How do you afford all of these places?" I said as I started browsing through the books on the bookshelves.

"I told you. I have my ways. I'm very clever."

"But how? Do you steal it?"

"Not technically, unless cheating counts. I take advantage of the stock market and I gamble."

"Like in a casino?"

"And the lottery. It's quite easy when you can get the winning numbers whenever you want."

"Oh. Well, that's not so bad. I thought you were hacking bank accounts or something."

Trent shrugged. "I'm not going to say it's never happened."

"So you are a criminal!" I said accusingly.

"Not necessarily. I just don't remember if I've done it or not…and it kind of sounds like something I would do."

As I looked through the books, I found The Time Machine by H.G. Wells. "Is this really why you're afraid to go to the future?" I asked, holding the book up to him.

"What, because I'm afraid I'll find a dystopia with underground savages? No, more like I'm afraid that I'll be the one who's set the events into motion that result in a dystopia with underground savages."

I put the book back on the shelf and grabbed Through the Looking-Glass. I took it and curled up in the oversized blue chair near Trent's desk.

"Aren't you going to go to bed?" he asked.

"I'm not tired," I lied.

In truth, I was exhausted, but I didn't want to be alone with my thoughts. I knew if I went to bed, I would just lie there feeling homesick and heartbroken. There was an ache in my chest that was being kept at bay as long as I was near Trent, and I was afraid of what it would feel like if I left his side. I knew I was going to have to face these feelings eventually, but not tonight.

I opened the book and started reading while Trent flipped through his journals. I had a hard time keeping my eyes open by the time I got to the second page, and I was out cold before I ever reached page three.

When I awoke, I noticed I was covered with a blanket that I hadn't had before. I looked over and saw Trent was still sitting at his desk, but the journals had been moved aside. He now had papers scattered over the desk in front of him and he was furiously writing and sketching on them.

"What are you doing?" I asked groggily.

"Good morning, 'I'm-Not-Tired,'" he teased. "I'm planning."

"You found something?"

"I did. Apparently, I have acquaintances in SABER who were secretly working with me to bring it all down – moles, if you will. I had forgotten about them. If I can get some materials from them, I can build a cloaking device to install in your house to keep it off of SABER's radar. You'll be safe at home again."

"Why weren't we safe there, but we're safe in all these other places you have?"

"When I time travel, it leaves a brief 'trail' that can be followed if you have the right technology. If SABER has a time-travel device, it's entirely possible that they had the technology to track me from the Jurassic to your house."

"But what about from my house to the other places we went?"

"The 'trail' disappears quite quickly, so I'm fairly certain that if they did follow us to your house, the trail we left when we teleported out of there would've disappeared before they could get there."

"If they were going to follow us, wouldn't they have shown up at my house already?"

"Not necessarily. That's the fun thing about time travel. But this cloaking device should essentially give them a dead-end or a redirection on their 'trail.' You'll be safe to go home."

"I wonder if I'll still have a job when I get back."

"Why wouldn't you?"

"How long have I been gone? I never called in. People get fired for that, Trent."

"You didn't miss anything. Time traveler, remember?" he said as he pointed to himself. "Now, I have to grab a quick shower and get ready for the day. I have places to go, people to see!"

"What about me?"

"You can shower after I do. The water heaters in 2515 are much better than the ones from your time."

"No, I mean what am I going to do? I'm coming with you, right?"

"I'm not taking you anywhere near a SABER compound."

"You're not leaving me behind."

"Yes, I am."

"Hey, you're the one who asked me to go somewhere with you. What fun is that if you leave me behind?"

"This isn't going to be fun. Besides, I'll be right back."

"I'm going."

Trent sighed and ran his hand through his hair. "Why would you want to?"

"Because I don't know if I'm going to see you again after this," I confessed.

"Why wouldn't you see me again?"

I gave him a knowing look. "I'm not stupid. When you get the 'let's just be friends' speech, it never ends in friendship. It just ends. You're going to drop me off and never come back."

"I wouldn't do that," he said defensively as his brows snapped together.

"You're taking me with you, and that's that." I said with finality.

"Fine! Fine. Whatever. I'm going to go shower," he said as he turned to leave the room.

"Leave the watch," I ordered.

"Damn it."

I held his watch hostage while I got ready for the day to ensure he didn't sneakily leave without me. When I had showered and dressed, I returned it to him. He seemed incredibly relieved when I handed it back to him.

"I've never gone this long without my device," he admitted. "I feel a bit helpless without it. You didn't go galivanting around in the future with it, did you?"

"If I knew how to use it, I might've."

"Good thing you don't know how, then," he said. He pulled a small device that resembled a tiny hearing aid out of his pocket and handed it to me. "You'll need this before we go. Put it in your ear."

I grabbed it and did what I was told. "What is it?'

"A translator. Can you understand me?"

"Yes, why wouldn't I?"

"I'm speaking Unilang. Good, you must have it in properly. Are you ready?" he asked, holding his arm out to me.

I hesitated. "Will the teleport still work the same if we just hold hands?"

Trent looked wounded. "Oh. Well, I suppose so, as long as we are making physical contact. You still have to stand near me, though. Is…is that going to be a problem?" he asked.

His expression hurt my heart, but so did being close to him. "I'm sure it'll be fine." I held my hand out to grasp his and stood next to him. Out of the corner of my eye, I saw him give me a questioning sideways glance, but I pretended I didn't see it. He held up the hand I was holding, as it was the one with the watch on it, and pressed the button to teleport us.

We arrived in a cold, dark room with what felt like a concrete floor. My eyes hadn't had time to adjust to the lack of light before Trent started moving. I clutched his hand and stumbled along behind him, unable to see where we were going. Finally, however, I noticed we were moving toward a small red light. I could make out what appeared to be a doorway next to it. By the time we approached the door, my eyes had become accustomed to the darkness, and I could see the light was some kind of indicator for an ID scanner. Trent held up his watch, pressed some buttons, and the light turned green. The door opened and revealed a brightly lit elevator with shiny white, metallic-looking walls.

"How did you do that?" I whispered.

"I have a thing that does a thing," he said, flashing a smile at me.

"Where are we headed?"

"Quit talking," he said with a finger over his lips.

He led me through the door into the elevator. He looked at his watch briefly, then entered a code into the digital display on the inside of the door. The elevator began its descent.

"Down? I thought we—"

The doors opened and Trent quickly cupped his hand over my mouth and backed himself against the wall to our right, pulling me backward against him firmly. He craned his neck and took a quick look out the door before releasing me. He looked at me with a stern expression and put his finger over his lips again. I raised my eyebrows and grimaced to as though to say "oops." Then I pointed to the watch and tried to use my hands ask why we weren't teleporting where we needed to be. Trent looked perplexed by my wild gesturing.

I sighed and looked around before whispering. "Teleport?"

He shook his head but offered no explanation. He grabbed my hand again and led me quickly down a hospital-like corridor, glancing down at his watch often. We zigged and zagged down one corridor to the next, looking through doors and trying to evade detection. It was hard to walk quietly on squeaky-clean floors, and I desperately wished I had worn different sneakers for this mission.

"Hey! Where's your synsuit?" I heard a man yell behind us. Adrenaline instantly shot through my veins.

Trent whirled around, eyes wide.

There was a man standing in the hallway behind us, wearing a weird gray unitard-like outfit. It was a glossy material, and it covered him from head to toe, except his face. He looked rather ridiculous – like a big, shiny Teletubby.

"Please tell me you're Rick Rodriguez," Trent said hopefully.

The man gave us a strange look. "Do I know you?"

"Perhaps. But you probably knew me when I had a different face."

"…Trent?"

"That depends. Are you Rick?"

"I am. Wow, you really changed this time, didn't you? You don't remember me?"

"Sorry, mate. It's nothing personal. Listen, I need your help."

Rick ushered us into the hidden door he had emerged from. It was camouflaged to blend in to the wall, and you couldn't see it at all until he waved his hand over a small, barely visible sensor on it. It looked like the wall just opened inward, and we walked into a bright, circular-shaped room.

"Shayla, you won't believe who just showed up," Rick said.

A woman stepped out of a doorway to our left. She was tall and thin, and she was wearing the same ridiculous "synsuit" that Rick was wearing.

"Who are these people? Why aren't they wearing synsuits?" She demanded huffily.

"Shayla, it's Trent! He changed again," Rick marveled.

The look of irritation on Shayla's face drained away. For a moment she looked pleased, but then it faded into a look of sadness. "Trent," she said softly. Then she looked at me. "Who's your friend?" she asked curtly, her face returning to an expression of irritation.

"This is Roselyn Wolff. You must be Shayla Benlock."

"You ask that like you don't already know it."

"I'm afraid I don't," he replied apologetically. He pointed to his head. "Memories don't have the same longevity as I do."

"It's only been three years since we saw you last," Shayla said, sounding offended.

"For you. It's been just a tad longer than that for me," he said, holding his thumb and forefinger close together.

Shayla shot daggers at me. "Why did you bring a guest?" she asked Trent tersely.

"She's under my protection. I seem to have gotten her into a bit of a pickle."

"You're good at that," Shayla said reproachfully. "You shouldn't have brought her here."

Rick turned to Trent and tried to alleviate the tension. "So, what brings you here anyway, Trent? What did you need? I can't imagine we have much time for catching up."

"Probably not. I used the watch to scramble the signals from the monitors in the halls so the men upstairs didn't see us, but I'm sure they'll soon figure out something unusual is going on. Listen, I need some supplies. I was wondering if you could help me out," Trent said, looking at Rick hopefully.

Rick, Shayla, and Trent discussed what he needed and how they were going to get it while I stood off to the side feeling useless. I didn't understand any of what they were talking about, and it made me feel dumb. It also reminded me just how out of my depth I was with Trent.

The plan was set, and Trent went in the other room to don a synsuit. I laughed when he walked out and did a little spin.

"How do I look?" he asked.

"Ridiculous," I said. Then I noticed the glare I was getting from Shayla. "Sorry, no offense," I apologized with an inward cringe. "You guys look great. It's just him," I backpedaled. It wasn't working, so I just stopped talking.

"Roselyn," Trent said to me, "I'm going to grab some supplies with Rick, and you're going to stay here and help Shayla. I'll be back in a jiff." He and Rick left the room.

I turned to Shayla and forced a smile. "What can I help you with?"

"Nothing. I'll do it myself," she snapped as she started to turn away. "Besides, your Old American English is annoying to try to understand."

"What is your problem with me?" I blurted. "You don't know anything about me."

"Yeah, I do. You're my replacement."

"Excuse me?"

"I see the way you look at him. You like him, and you think he likes you. Well, I've got news for you, honey. You're dust in the wind to him. A flash in the pan. Temporary. He doesn't love you, and he never will. And apparently, he'll forget you just like that," she said with an angry snap of her fingers.

I felt the sting of jealousy. "You and Trent...?"

"Yeah. And I've put my reputation on the line for him time and time again to help him. And he doesn't even remember me now," Shayla said bitterly. "Do yourself a favor and don't fall in love with that one. He's a waste of your time, and you're a waste of his. He'll only hurt you in the end. He's incapable of anything else."

Shayla walked into the other room and started sorting through drawers. I stood there, feeling like a fool. Jealousy filled my heart, and Shayla's warnings resonated through my brain. Everything kept telling me to run as far away from Trent as I could, as fast as I could, but every ounce of my being wanted to be with him. I already knew that he and I weren't ever going to work out, but there was still one little piece of me that had been holding out hope. However, Shayla had just stomped out that remaining ember. I still loved him, of course, but as I watched the woman in the other room sniffling as she rummaged through drawers, I felt like I was looking into my own future. I had to let him go now so I could move on.

When Trent and Rick returned, I had a hard time pretending everything was all right. Trent noticed – I could tell from the questioning glances he was throwing my way – but he didn't ask. We collected what we needed and off we went, back to 2515.

"That went much more smoothly than expected," Trent said as he deposited his bounty onto his desk. "Well, other than landing in the wrong place inside the compound. How lucky was it that Rick found us?" Trent said with a chuckle.

"Pretty lucky," I said flatly. I removed the translator from my ear and set it on the desk. "Can I go home now?"

Trent gave me a concerned look. "Is everything all right?"

"I just want to go home."

Trent looked at his desk. "I'll have it together in a few hours, and then I can take you home."

"Good." I turned on my heel and walked out of the room.

I found my way to the kitchen and looked through the cupboards. I still wasn't hungry, but I knew I needed to eat something. I found a package of snack cakes and a tin of sardines. I decided the snack cakes were probably a safer bet. I sat down at the table and ripped open the crinkly plastic.

"Ooh! Throw me one!" I heard Trent yell from the library. He must have heard me tearing into the plastic.

I got back up and grabbed one and looked down the hall. Trent was coming up the hallway toward me. He stopped and held out his hands, so I tossed it to him.

"Thanks, love," he said as he turned and walked away.

Why did he have to say things like that? Why did he have to add little terms of endearment that weakened my resolve? I don't think he realized that that's what he was doing, but it was frustrating, nonetheless. It wasn't going to be easy to do what I had to do, but it was necessary. He could call me "love" all he wanted but it wasn't going to change the fact that I had to leave him.

I went back into the library when I was done eating and grabbed Through the Looking-Glass from the seat where I had left it earlier today. I sat down and started reading to pass the time until Trent could take me home. He tried to strike up conversation with me here and there as he worked, but I limited my responses to one-word answers. After a while, Trent seemed to get the message that I didn't want to talk, and he left me alone. I didn't want to engage with him enough to allow him to change my mind. I was leaving, and that was that. My heart would just have to deal with it.

Finally, he finished his device. "Ta-da! Look at that!" he held up the device and shouted enthusiastically. "One cloaking device for a Miss Roselyn Wolff!"

I got out of my chair and put the book back on the shelf. "Great. Let me get Cattiel and you can take me home."

I gathered up my things and the cat and met Trent in the library. I avoided his eyes as I allowed him to put his arm around me (I had no free hand for holding), letting myself inwardly enjoy that last little feeling of closeness to him. When we arrived at my home, however, I quickly ducked out from under his arm and headed to my room to put away my things. He went to work installing the cloaking device.

After several minutes, I heard him yell, "It's up and running!"

I stepped out of my room and met him in the space where the hallway, living room, and kitchen all connected.

"You are officially off the radar," Trent said with a proud smile.

"Cool. Thanks. I appreciate it."

His smile faded. "You're welcome," he replied.

We stood in silence for a few moments, with him looking at me while I looked at everything but him.

"So, I've brought you back to the night we left…after the Barry incident, of course. Someone is coming to tow the truck, so it should be out of your way before you leave for work in the morning," he said.

"Perfect. Sounds good."

"Roselyn, what's going on?"

I sighed. "It's time to just rip off the band-aid, Trent. Dragging this out isn't going to make it any better."

Trent furrowed his brow. "What are you talking about?"

"You need to go."

"Ok but—"

"And never come back."

Chapter 12

Trent looked absolutely crushed, and it killed me. "Oh. Well, all right. Ok," he said, clasping his hands together. "I…um…I guess…I guess that's it, then?"

"I guess so."

"Can I still—"

"No. Just leave me alone from now on. I appreciate your help, but I didn't sign up for all of this. I like you Trent, I really do. But there's no point to this. I can't be 'just friends' with you. If you're around, I can't move on with my life. So…I need to remove you from it." I tried to keep my voice from shaking and the tears from falling from my eyes.

"I understand," Trent said quietly. He smiled at me sadly. "I'll be on my way then, I suppose. I'll miss you, Roselyn." He opened his arms to me and approached me for a hug.

Even though it shattered my heart to do it, I held my hand up to stop him and took a step back. I then offered my hand to shake his. Trent paused and looked at me like I had just stabbed him in the heart. He took my hand and shook it briefly.

"I'm sorry…for everything. I won't bother you anymore. It was never my intention to cause you grief." Trent stepped back and smiled at me, and it was somehow the most forlorn expression I had ever seen. And then he was gone.

I crumpled to the floor. The tears flowed and my chest heaved as I sobbed. The ache in my chest I had been trying to keep at bay finally consumed me. There was nothing quite like the pain of a broken heart. No, it wasn't the end of the world – but at the moment, it felt like it. I knew it was for the best to get it over with now, though. My feelings for Trent would've only gotten stronger the longer I was with him, and it only would've hurt more if I'd waited.

I turned off all the lights and climbed into my bed. I wasn't expecting to sleep – I just wanted to bury myself in fluffy blankets and cry. I missed him already. Had I made a huge mistake? My heart kept trying to convince me that I had, but my head knew better. No, this was the right thing to do. I needed to just get it all out and get on with it. But good heavens, did I miss him. I thought about our intimate moment together. Our skin slick with sweat, our bodies sliding, pushing, grinding…his breath hot on my ear as I listened to his panting…inhaling the pleasant smell of his skin as I felt him inside of me, as close to me as another person can get…

And I would never have that with him again. I looked over at my phone on the bedside stand, wanting to call him just to hear his voice. I grabbed my phone and opened up his contact information. I stared at it for several minutes, considering the consequences. And then…I deleted it. If only it were that easy to delete him from my heart.

In the morning, I thought about calling in to work. I looked a fright and I felt even worse. However, I knew it wouldn't do me any good to sit at home and mope for the day. The gym would help distract me from my thoughts. I had a cup of coffee, hugged Cattiel, and walked out to my car. Barry's truck was gone already, as promised. I climbed into my car and headed to work, keeping the radio on the rock station to avoid any sappy love songs that might crumble my composure.

After I worked with my first client of the day, I was feeling a little less emotionally fragile. I glanced down at my watch and noticed that I had a good thirty minutes before my next client's appointment, so I decided it was time to blow off some steam. I strapped on a pair of gloves and made a beeline to the heavy bags. I trained on the heavy bag at least twice a week, but today wasn't training. Today was venting. Today was for me. I put all of my frustrations and anger and sorrow into that bag, and by the time I was done, I felt a little better. I took off the gloves and reached for my water bottle with shaky hands.

"Somebody must've pissed you off," I heard a man with a rather deep voice say. Oh great. Here we go.

I looked up and the first thing I noticed was his striking green eyes. He was incredibly tall, about 6'5", and in excellent shape – broad-shouldered and narrow-waisted. He looked to be in his late-thirties. He smiled at me, and I couldn't help but admire his lovely teeth. He had long brown hair that he wore pulled back in a manbun. He was kind of beautiful, really.

I shrugged my shoulders at him and didn't respond. I usually avoided conversation with strange men at the gym unless they approached me with a specific question or were clients. I turned away from him and went to take a drink of my water. The steadiness of my hands had been temporarily compromised from my time on the bag, and I realized that about half a second too late. The bottle fell from my hands and clattered to the floor, but not before spraying water right in my face and down my chin. I stood there, water dripping off my chin, hoping that the beautiful man hadn't seen that. I glanced over. He had. He definitely had.

He rushed over and picked up my water bottle for me. "Got the shakes, hey?" he asked as he handed it to me.

"Yeah, a little."

"I'm Sam," he said as he held his hand out to me.

"Roselyn," I said as I shook his hand. Firmly. Businesslike. I could tell from the look in his eyes that my grip startled him, and it gave me an odd satisfaction. It always did. "I'm a trainer here."

"I'm new to the area. Just moved from Kansas."

"You're a long way from Kansas, Dorothy," I mused.

"Oh, no, I'm Sam. Sam Collins," he said, the joke obviously going right over his head.

"No, it's a joke. 'Toto, I've a feeling we're not in Kansas anymore,'" I explained. Trent would've gotten it immediately, I thought to myself.

"Oh, ok," he said, still clearly not understanding.

"Well, nice to meet you Sam," I said politely. I turned and started to walk away. I had a new client coming in shortly and I needed to get things wiped down.

"Actually, I think I'm supposed to be meeting with you right now," Sam said.

You've got to be shitting me. I turned back to him. "You have an appointment for 9:00?"

"Yes, ma'am."

"Excuse me for being blunt, but you don't look like you need a trainer."

"I've always had a trainer. I just work better under supervision, I guess," he said with a laugh.

We discussed his previous workout plan and what changes, if any, he wanted to make to tweak it specifically to meet his personal goals. I ran him through a routine, but I felt like I was just there to observe rather than to train. He didn't seem to need much assistance or direction or motivation as he plowed through the workout. I wondered why he would waste the extra money on a trainer he clearly didn't need.

As he toweled off, I said, "Sam, I don't think you need a trainer."

"I just like having someone to push me," he said.

"I barely did anything," I replied.

"It's more of a mentality for me. I go harder when I know someone is expecting me to."

I couldn't fault his reasoning. "Well, then, I have a feeling you're going to be a great client," I said with a laugh.

"Actually, I don't think I want to be your client."

149

"What? Why?" I asked in surprise.

"Because I'd like to ask you out for coffee sometime, but I have a feeling that's probably against the rules between trainers and their clients."

"Oh. Yeah, that's against the rules."

He raised his eyebrows questioningly at me. "So…if I wasn't your client, would you want to?"

I sighed. Oh, what the hell. If nothing else, he'd be a good distraction to keep my mind off Trent.

"Are you married?" I asked. I wasn't about to get in the middle of anything like that.

"No. Divorced."

"I'll tell you what – I'll have you transferred to Roy, and when I get off work after 5:00, I'll stop by the coffee shop across the street. If you're there, cool. But it's not a date. Sound good?"

Sam smiled. "Sounds great."

After work, as I walked across the street, I felt strangely guilty. I felt like I was cheating. I knew it was absurd, especially since Trent and I were never "together." I wondered how he would feel if he knew what I was doing right now. Would he be jealous? No, probably not. He didn't seem like the jealous type. He was probably moving on to a new Shayla or Roselyn anyway…which made me feel instantly jealous just thinking about it.

I forced myself to quit thinking about him as I entered the coffee shop. I saw Sam straight away, standing up from a table in the corner. He waved his hand to get my attention. I held my finger up to indicate I'd be over there in a minute, but he was already approaching.

"I wasn't sure if you were serious or not," he admitted.

"Well, here I am."

I ordered a black coffee, and Sam ordered a bulletproof coffee. I had to stop myself from rolling my eyes. When we sat down, I started in on him about his beverage choice.

"You know that's all shit, right?"

"Bulletproof coffee? No way! It's great for your brain and it burns fat!"

"That is horrible for your heart health. Do you have any idea the saturated fat content in that cup? Do you think high cholesterol and clogged arteries are somehow beneficial to your health?"

"It's keto. Eat fat, burn fat."

"It's rubbish."

Sam gave me a funny look. "Rubbish? Do people really say 'rubbish'?"

Trent always said rubbish. I had to admit, it sounded weird coming from my mouth. It wasn't a word I would've used before I met Trent.

"It's garbage. It's bullshit. I mean yeah, keto works great for some people for short periods of time. But bulletproof coffee? Just…no."

"I feel like we've gotten off on the wrong foot," Sam said.

I sighed. "I'm sorry. I just…ugh, I just hate fad diets. Especially the ones with outrageous claims backed by zero evidence of effectiveness, pushed by people who have zero credentials." I paused. "You know, maybe we should talk about something else. What is it you do, Sam?"

Sam looked relieved to have a change of subject. "I'm a bartender."

"What brought you to Michigan?"

"Family. I had moved to Kansas when I got married, but now that I'm divorced, I didn't really see a reason to stay there. I figured I'd be happier if I was closer to my family and where I grew up."

"Are you? Happier, I mean."

"Yeah. I am," he said with a grin. "I don't get to see my kids as often, though, and that's kind of a bummer."

"You have kids?"

"Three daughters. Eighteen, sixteen, and thirteen years old."

"Oh god, teenage girls. I remember being one. I pity you."

"Yeah. I remember being a teenage boy. I pity me, too."

I laughed.

"Do you have any kids?" he asked.

"Me? No. I have a cat. I don't think I was really cut out for kids. I barely have this being an adult thing mastered, so I can only imagine what a disaster it would be if I were a parent."

"I know the feeling. You want to know a secret, though? Every parent thinks they're a disaster."

Sam and I sat and talked for a good half hour at the coffee shop. We exchanged numbers before we went our separate ways, though I expected nothing to ever come of it. I had been entirely too unpleasant, I was sure of it. I hadn't meant to be so disagreeable at first, but what was done was done. Besides, I didn't really care if I saw him again. He and I were a mismatch. He was attractive, for sure, but that was the only thing I found appealing about him. I needed more than a pretty face to look at. I needed witty. I needed forgiving. I needed logical. I needed funny – I really needed funny. I didn't see those things in Sam. Not yet, anyway.

That was when I realized I was comparing him to Trent. If I was using Trent as my gold standard, no one would ever be good enough, would they? There wasn't anyone else like Trent in all the world and time, of that I was certain. No one could compare to him. I needed to reevaluate my standards, it seemed.

As I climbed into my car and drove home, I felt all the feelings I had been avoiding all day. Now that I was alone, I was overwhelmed with loneliness. I let it overtake me this time, though. Rather than trying to avoid the sad songs on the radio, I sought them out. No amount of male distraction was going to remedy my broken heart. These were feelings I needed to feel.

When I got home, I took a hot shower and put on a pair of sweatpants and my most comfortable ratty sweatshirt. I turned on a sappy movie, grabbed a bottle of wine, and flopped onto the couch next to Cattiel. I was just settling in for a long night of crying when I heard my text notification tone on my phone. I glanced over at it, and was surprised to see it was from Sam. I hesitated before opening the text. What could he possibly have to say to me after our awkward engagement at the coffee shop? I sighed and snatched up the phone.

"Hey there pretty lady."

I rolled my eyes and simply responded with, "Hey." If he wanted more than that, he would have to do better than that.

He was quick to reply. "I had a good time today. Want to do it again?"

I didn't. Not really. "Not sure we really clicked."

"Maybe not yet. One more try? I swear I won't order bulletproof coffee."

I considered it. It wouldn't hurt anything, surely. And he was handsome. Ugh. "Fine. Coffee?" I looked back over my texts. God, I sounded rude. Why couldn't I stop doing that? Why couldn't I just be pleasant?

"Sounds great! Tomorrow after work?"

"Ok."

When the texts stopped, the ache in my chest returned. It was almost unbearable. I drank down a glass of wine in several gulps and poured myself another. By the time I was halfway through my movie and all the way through my bottle of Sangria, I was ready for the pain to stop. I grabbed my phone. It was unscrupulous to take advantage of someone else's interest in me in order to distract myself from my own heartache, I know, but I texted Sam anyway.

"What are you doing right now?" I asked.

"Work."

That's right - he was a bartender. "Oh ok."

"You can still text me. Slow night."

"I've been awful to you. I apologize. I'd like to make it up to you. Maybe tomorrow we can do dinner?" I offered.

"That would be fantastic, but are you sure? You didn't even seem all that into coffee a little bit ago."

"I've had time to drink."

"Time to drink?" Sam questioned.

"Think! I've had time to think! Stupid phone! Sorry. Anyway, I think dinner would be a better way to get to know you."

"LOL. Ok! I'm in."

The next day, as I stepped into the quiet restaurant where I was meeting Sam, I swore to myself that I wasn't going to allow my opinion of Sam to be influenced by my feelings for Trent. I was wiping the slate clean and starting over. I was going to be pleasant, and I was going to give the poor guy a chance. He might not be what I was looking for, but he was what I needed at the moment.

The hostess led me to a booth next to a window where he was waiting for me. When I saw him, I had to admit that my pupils may have dilated just a bit. He looked good. He flashed a smile and stood up to help me take off my coat.

"You look beautiful," he complimented me.

"Thanks. You do too. Look handsome, I mean."

He laughed as he sat back down. "Thanks for giving me a second chance. I know we were a little out of sync last time."

"It was my fault. I've just been out of sorts and more bitter than usual lately."

"Is that why you were going so hard on the heavy bag yesterday?"

I laughed and nodded. "I hope I'm not as unpleasant tonight."

The waiter came and took our orders. When he left, Sam asked, "So, what's had you out of sorts lately?"

"Oh, you don't want to hear about my problems. I'll get over it."

He gave me a knowing look. "Is it an ex-boyfriend problem?"

"He wasn't my boyfriend. Just a friend. Things got weird. That's all."

"Sorry to hear that. But not too sorry, because it means I get a chance now," Sam said with a smile.

"Mm-hmm." I was trying not to be unpleasant, but those cheesy lines just killed it for me. I looked out the window.

"So, how long have you been a trainer?" he asked.

I looked back at him. "About five years. I was going to get into physical therapy, but I found I enjoyed training better. I haven't been at this gym long, though. I moved up here after my divorce and basically had to start all over again."

"You're divorced too?"

"Sure am."

"You know, I'm kind of glad to hear that. I've tried dating women who've never been married before, and all they want to do is get married right away and have kids. They don't really get it."

"Get what?"

"What a damn nightmare marriage is. You get it though, I bet."

I looked out the window again. "Oh, I don't know. It was a nightmare for me, but I think it could be great with the right person. I'm not opposed to getting married again."

"I don't think I could go through it again. I was with my ex-wife for fourteen years, married for twelve. This December I'll have been separated from her for four years, and in that time, I still haven't found someone that could change my mind on remarrying."

"It's not for everyone, I suppose." I immediately thought of Trent, and I immediately chastised myself inwardly for it. He has no place in my head on this date.

"How long have you been divorced?" Sam wanted to know.

"Six months or so," I said.

"Oh, so it's been more recent for you."

"It's fine, though," I said. "You won't find me pining away for my ex. It was a relief to be done with him."

"I actually didn't want my divorce," Sam confided. "She was the one who filed. I'm glad for it now, but I was still in a bad place only six months after the divorce. What was the reason for your divorce, if you don't mind me asking?"

"He was abusive."

Sam looked taken aback. "I've seen the damage you can do to a heavy bag. Who would be stupid enough to lay a hand on you?"

"There are other forms of abuse. Can we talk about something else now?" I asked, feeling uncomfortable. I looked out the window again at the light snow that was starting to fall.

That was when I saw him. My heart stopped. Across the street, looking down at his watch, I saw Trent walk by.

Chapter 13

I jumped up from my chair and rushed to the entrance. I flung the door open and ran outside, adrenaline surging through my veins.

"Trent!" I yelled. I looked around, but he wasn't anywhere to be seen. "Trent!"

Sam came rushing out behind me. "What's wrong?!" he asked. "Who's Trent?" He looked around.

I craned my neck and looked around one more time, but he just wasn't there. Had he ever really been there, or had it been my imagination?

"Roselyn, are you ok?" Sam asked, touching my shoulder.

"Sorry, I just…I thought I saw someone I knew. Sorry," I apologized. I turned to walk back into the restaurant, glancing back one last time. What had I seen?

I got a lot of strange stares as I walked back to my seat with Sam. I felt idiotic. My cheeks were on fire when I sat down.

"What was that all about?" Sam asked, concerned.

"I thought I saw a friend I haven't seen in a long time. I guess I was mistaken," I said, gazing out the window.

I had a hard time giving Sam my full attention after that. I did my best to fake it, and apparently, I faked it well. On my way home, I got a text from Sam asking if he could see me again. I acquiesced.

I started seeing Sam fairly regularly after that. It wasn't love – far from it – but it was nice having someone to talk to and spend time with. The best part was that he kept my mind off Trent when he was around. He hadn't replaced Trent, because no one could do that, but he did a great job of making me forget that fact for short periods of time.

The first time I invited Sam to my house, however, we hit a major bump in the road. It was about a month after we had first met, and I had invited him over for dinner. Afterward, I was washing up the pans and loading the dishwasher as he picked out a movie to stream on the television.

I suddenly felt two big hands on my waist and hot breath on the back of my neck. Sam's lips caressed the back of my neck tenderly. I stiffened at his touch. It wasn't because I didn't like it. It wasn't because I was repulsed by him. It was because the last time I was touched so intimately, it had been by Trent's hands and Trent's lips, and this wasn't Trent. Memories flooded my mind, and I tried to get past my apprehension by allowing myself to concentrate on those memories with Trent.

Sam turned me around to face him, and he kissed me. It wasn't bad, but it wasn't great. It was almost mechanical and lacked passion. He then grabbed underneath my buttocks and lifted me up, and I wrapped my legs around his waist.

"Shall we take this to the bedroom?" he mumbled against my lips.

I nodded. What the hell – why not?

He carried me back to my room and laid me on the bed. He quickly took off his shirt and climbed onto the bed. He started kissing down my neck, and that was when it happened. With closed eyes and parted lips, the name "Trent" rolled involuntarily off my tongue.

He stopped immediately and sat back on his haunches. "What did you say?" he asked, his face angry.

"I'm so, so sorry," I apologized profusely. "It just popped out of my mouth."

"Who the hell is this Trent? Is it your ex? Jesus." Sam climbed off the bed huffily and snatched his shirt off the floor. He looked at me, waiting for an explanation.

"It's not my ex. Trent was just a friend. He's not even around anymore. I don't know why I said that. I'm sorry."

"Just a friend, hey? Why are you lying to me?" Sam slipped his shirt back on over his head. "Listen, if you can't be honest with me, I don't know what hope we have of this going any further."

"Sam, wait. Ok. Let me explain. Trent was a friend, that part is true. But we...well...had relations. Once. He was the last man I had been with. That's all."

"Where is Trent now?" Sam wanted to know.

"I have no idea. I sent him away and told him not to come back."

"How long ago was that?" When I hesitated, Sam said, "Let me guess – right before you and I met?"

I nodded.

"Christ. You know, Roselyn, I can deal with someone who is working through getting over someone. We've all been there. But I can't deal with someone who is lying to me about it. When you're ready to be open and honest with me, give me a call." Sam stormed out of my room.

I didn't follow him. I heard him putting on his coat and shoes, and I heard the front door slam. I didn't blame him for being angry. I would've been angry too if I were him. I felt bad for what had happened, but there was nothing I could do now to change it. I just sat on the bed and felt sort of...numb. I liked Sam, but it wasn't the end of the world if he didn't come back. I would be a little sad, but I wouldn't cry. There were other Sams out there. Plenty of fish in the sea, plenty of Sams in the gym.

I was just getting up to head back out to the kitchen to tidy up and finish the dishes when there was a sudden burst of blinding white light. It flooded the entire room, and I shrieked and threw my hands up over my face to protect my eyes. Just as quickly as it had appeared, however, it was gone. I blinked, my eyes still trying to adjust, and I reached for the bed behind me, intending to sit down. The bed wasn't there anymore, though, and I fell onto the floor. Startled, I rubbed my eyes, trying to force them to focus. I suddenly felt a hand grasp my upper arm and roughly lift me to my feet. My eyes were finally starting to recover, and I could tell that I was in a large room. I could see several shapes walking around – people? I didn't have much time to look, though, because I was being dragged backwards.

"What the hell is going on?!" I demanded. "Where am I?"

I received no reply.

I turned and looked at the person pulling on my arm. It was a man in a suit that resembled the ugly synsuits from SABER, but the color was more of a blue and the design was slightly different.

"Let go of me!" I shouted, yanking my arm from the man's grasp.

"Hey!" he yelled in surprise.

I started throwing punches. I felt his nose crack under my knuckles, and I followed the jab with a quick left hook. I kicked him away from me and turned to run.

I didn't make it far before I felt like someone had hit me in the back with a cattle prod. I went down hard, my body convulsing painfully. I faded in and out of consciousness for a while after that, but I remembered being dragged briefly. I woke up in some kind of tiny containment cell, about ten feet long by ten feet wide. The only furnishings in the cell with me were a small cot and a weird looking toilet. Three of the walls were solid and smooth, painted in a glossy gray color. The fourth wall was transparent, like plexiglass, and it looked out into what appeared to be a huge laboratory full of people working in matching synsuit uniforms. There was a large piece of machinery hanging from the middle of the ceiling, like a giant mechanical stalactite.

"Hey!" I shouted. I started banging on the glass. "Where am I?! Why am I here?! Somebody help me!" The people in the laboratory ignored me.

"Did you have a nice rest?" I heard an eerie effeminate male voice say. It sounded like it was coming from somewhere inside the cell.

I whirled around, but no one was there. "Who said that?"

"I did. You can't see me, silly. Wow, you primitives are daft, aren't you? It's called remote communication."

"Where am I? Who are you? Why did you take me?"

"You haven't figured that out yet? Oh, that's right. Primitive! You're in a world parallel to your own, obviously. Where is the Traveler?"

"What traveler?"

"Your companion. Where is he?"

"I have no idea what you're talking about. Why don't you tell me just who the hell you are?"

"I have no reason to tell you that."

"You have no reason not to tell me that."

"You wouldn't understand anyway. Primitives never do."

"Why did you take me?"

"Isn't it obvious? You're the cheese in the trap. The worm on the hook. The damsel in distress. He will come for you."

"Who will come for me?"

"Pay attention! The Traveler, of course!"

They must mean Trent. Am I in the place he was in when he went missing? Is this the SABER from the parallel universe? Why would they take me to get to Trent?

"I don't know who you're talking about!" I lied.

"Lying won't make a difference. We sent him a message. He knows we took you. He will come."

I forced a mocking laugh even though I was completely terrified. "No one's coming! Who's the daft one now?"

The voice stopped talking.

"So what's your plan? None of this makes any sense!"

Nothing.

I sat down on the cot and tried to sort through what I knew. I knew I was in a parallel world, likely the one that was trying to open a wormhole into my house and the one Trent was trapped in for a while. I knew they wanted Trent, and they were trying to use me to get to him. How did they know about me, though? And what the hell made them think that Trent was going to come for me? I sent him away and told him never to come back. I probably meant nothing to him by now. Dust in the wind. He was probably busy solving the man in the Jurassic mystery anyway.

"Wait," I said as I realized something. "Was it you? Were you the one I saw a hundred fifty million years ago?"

"One hundred fifty million years ago? You admit it, then?" the voice said. "You must know the Traveler."

"Obviously you have a Traveler of your own, so why do you want one from a parallel world?"

"How would you know if we have a Traveler?"

"I saw him, stupid."

"Impossible."

"I just told you I saw him in our world, during the Jurassic period."

"You are mistaken."

"I don't care if you admit it or not. I know what I saw. What do you want with Trent?"

"It matters not to you. You will die with your beloved Traveler."

"He can't die," I said insolently.

"Oh, he can die."

I felt ice shoot through my veins. "But why? What is the purpose of all of this?"

Silence.

My brain buzzed with questions. Why would they want to kill Trent? What was their goal? How did they get a "traveler" through to our world without me or Trent noticing, and why were they even bothering to deny it? What were they going to do with me when they realized Trent wasn't coming? I wasn't ever going back to my world, was I? I was going to die here, scared and alone. My family wasn't going to know what happened to me. Sam would become a suspect in my "missing person" case. Was he going to go to prison over my disappearance? And what about Cattiel? Who was going to take care of him? Was he going to end up in an animal shelter, or worse?

All of this was happening because I allowed Trent in my life. No, it wasn't as simple as that, though, was it? That wasn't it. It was happening because I kicked Trent out of my life. If he had been with me, he probably would've had this taken care of and had us home by now. Yes, I was a target because I was Trent's companion for a while, but I was a victim because I chose to walk away from him. Why couldn't I have just tried to stay friends with him? Why did I have to throw him away like that?

I lay down on the cot and stared despondently at the dotted gray ceiling of my cell. I had reached my emotional limit. I was just…numb. My thoughts stopped racing, and I started counting the tiny holes all over the ceiling that I assumed must have been there for air exchange. One, two, three, four, five…

…Two hundred thirty-two, two hundred thirty-three, two hundred thirty-four. There were two-hundred thirty-four holes in the ceiling. As I stared at them, I wondered if they were only for air exchange or if there was a more sinister purpose for those tiny, innocuous-looking holes. I sat up and looked back out at the scientists working in the laboratory. There was an abundance of computers and giant screens, large machinery, and work benches filled with lots of shiny appliances and high-tech devices – none of which I recognized as anything familiar from my world.

As my eyes scanned the room, though, I did find one familiar item. Off in the corner, at the far end of the room, there was another containment cell that looked a little like the one I was in. There were brightly colored warning stickers all over the unit. It didn't contain a prisoner, however. Through the plexiglass-like wall or door, I could see the Big Bad inside. It didn't seem nearly as scary now. It just looked like an old, run-down machine that someone had stowed away in a closet like an unused bread maker.

Did that mean that this was the room with the device that opened wormholes? Is that what the giant metallic stalactite on the ceiling was? Is this the room I had arrived in? It had been such a blur that I couldn't be sure.

Just then, something caught my eye. There was a person in the lab, walking with their back to me, who had a rather distinctive bow-legged gait. It stood out, especially in that ugly, skin-tight synsuit. It couldn't be…could it? I practically pressed my face to the glass trying to get a better look, but the individual never turned around. He continued on through the room and exited out a door at the far end of the room. I watched the room like a hawk for the next hour, but I didn't see that particular figure return. I hated to even think it – hated to even give myself that hope – but could it have been Trent?

If it had been Trent – and I wasn't saying it was – had he seen me? Did he know where I was? If it had been him – again, not saying it was – wouldn't he have rescued me? Maybe not. That's what they were expecting him to do. He wasn't stupid enough to fall into a trap. He was a lot of things, but stupid wasn't one of those things.

At the end of the day, or at least what I assumed must have been the end of the day, everyone left the lab and shut down all of the lights, leaving me there alone in the dark. I waited anxiously, feeling a tiny sliver of hope that perhaps the bow-legged man in the synsuit had been Trent, and that perhaps he was going to suddenly appear in my cell and whisk me away from this hell. I waited. And waited…and waited. I fell asleep waiting, and when I woke up, he still wasn't there. When scientists started arriving and my breakfast (a disgusting "nutrition bar") was shoved through a small slat on the floor, I knew he wasn't coming.

I felt foolish for even allowing myself to hope he was coming.

I saw that same bow-legged man walk through the lab every day for the next several days, but he always kept his face turned away from me. I noticed that he came at almost the exact same time every day, and he only showed up once each day. He followed an exact pattern. The only divergence from day to day was that he seemed to be carrying something different in his hand each time. Who was he? What was he doing? No one else in the lab seemed to follow such a stringent and unvarying schedule. No one else in the lab seemed to notice him, either. The scientists would occasionally stop and chat with each other throughout the day, but I never saw anyone ever stop to talk to him. Was that weird, or was I looking too much into this?

After about a week of imprisonment, I was feeling the effects of my solitude. I hadn't talked to anyone but myself since I had arrived. The effeminate voice that had talked to me on that first day had been completely silent ever since, despite my many attempts to strike up some kind of conversation. I had no idea what was going to happen to me, or how long I was going to be held before they got tired of waiting for Trent. I hadn't eaten anything other than nasty "nutrition bars" the entire time, and I had no source of entertainment other than the daily exercises I forced myself to do. I was starting to feel my sanity slipping, and it was the most terrifying feeling in the world.

And then, when I had lost all hope, he came.

"Well, it appears I'm late to the party," I heard a familiar voice shout out in the laboratory. It was like his voice had breathed the life back into me. I sprang up and looked out the front of my cell, and there was Trent, standing in the middle of the room under the mechanical stalactite, wearing his usual tweed suit. Everyone in the room was just standing there, looking dumbfounded. "I apologize for that, especially considering I'm the guest of honor. I hope you'll forgive me."

I rushed to the plexiglass. "Trent! Watch out! It's a trap!"

Trent smiled at me calmly and walked toward my cell. "Are you all right?"

"Been better," I said with a teary smile. "Please. Help me, Trent," I begged as I held my hand up against the plexiglass.

He held his hand up against mine on the other side of the glass. "I'm not leaving without you."

The voice boomed throughout the room. "You're right about that, Traveler. But that's because you won't be leaving."

Suddenly, several people wearing large, ornate hats and long robes materialized beneath the mechanical stalactite. There were ten of them, and they stood in a row facing Trent with their hands clasped calmly in front of them. All of the scientists quickly filed out of the room, leaving only Trent, the people in robes, and me.

"I'm so glad you could all make it," Trent said.

"You will not make a mockery of this council," I heard one of the people in the robes say. It was the same voice I had heard in my cell.

"This council is a mockery," Trent countered. "Look at you lot with your ridiculous hats and pompous attitudes, thinking you can play games with me. It's utterly laughable."

"We've trapped you, Traveler."

"Have you now? See, there's one small problem with that. You think I'm trapped in here with all of you. Unfortunately for you, it's rather the other way 'round. You all are trapped in here with me."

There were hushed whispers among the group.

"Silence!" a woman in a robe yelled. "Traveler, you are being sentenced to death for crimes against the Alliance. Do you acknowledge these charges?"

"Are these crimes I've already committed, or the ones I'm about to commit?"

"The Traveler admits to his crimes," the woman declared to the others.

"Oh yes. I've done terrible things. I don't deny it. But before you attempt to carry out the sentence, I must know – who is it? Who made the time-travel device?"

"You are in no position to ask questions."

"Oh, come now. What's it going to hurt? You're going to kill me anyway, right? Just give me some answers before I go."

The council whispered amongst themselves briefly, nodding to each other.

"Our Traveler. The one who conspired against us and compromised our mission by taking us off-course without authorization. He has been charged and his sentence has been carried out."

"You got him to develop a time traveling, inter-universal device, convinced him to spy on me, pried information out of him – and then you just killed him?"

"You are mistaken. He did not spy on you."

Trent paused. "What do you mean he didn't spy on me? Of course he did. I saw him."

"You are mistaken. He did not spy on you," the robed official repeated. "But he had served his purpose. He had paid his restitution for his treasonous acts, and he was liberated."

"Murdered."

"It is not murder. It is justice."

Trent turned to me. "See? A mockery," he said. He turned his attention back to the council. "You obviously want me out of the way so you can invade my world. I know yours has been decimated by war and depleted of its resources. You've lost most of your people and your world is a wasteland. I learned that last time I was here. But why not use the time-travel device to change the past? That is the point of having it, isn't it? Stop the war before it happens. Why bother going to the effort of invading another world? You do realize we aren't going to give it up without a fight, don't you?"

There were more whispers from the group as they looked at each other uneasily. It looked like Trent had struck a nerve.

"Oh! Oh, I see!" Trent exclaimed. "You killed him before he perfected the device, didn't you?! Or did he do something to it before you killed him? Whatever it is, you can't go where you need to go to stop the war, can you? It's basically useless to you, isn't it?"

"We do not need it," a different robed official said. "We have you. We can use your device, or we can invade your world. Once you are out of the way, it won't matter. Your world will be defenseless without you."

"Oh, did I not mention? I'm not the defense. I'm the distraction."

"Explain!" the man with the effeminate voice commanded.

Trent looked down at his watch. "I'd really love to, but it appears my time is up. I'm going to take my companion and be off now. I'd rather not be present when everything blows up in your face."

Everything happened incomprehensibly quickly after that. There were flashes of light, shaking, faint sounds of explosions, and the comforting feeling of Trent's body next to mine. And then, just like that, I was in my house, back in my bedroom, with Trent's arms squeezing me tightly. I clung to him like I was afraid to ever let him go. I knew as long as I was holding on to him, I was safe. He put one hand on the back of my head and held my cheek against his shoulder. I felt him rest his cheek on the top of my head.

"You're safe now," he said. "I'm sorry I ever let you out of my sight. I misjudged the situation and left you in harm's way. I'm a bloody imbecile."

"You came for me," I said in disbelief.

"Of course I did."

"They wanted to kill you."

"I know."

"But you came. You came for me anyway."

"Aye."

"You are a bloody imbecile."

Trent chuckled softly. "I promised to keep you safe. And I'm not entirely certain that they can kill me. Regardless, I'd rather die trying to save you than live knowing I couldn't."

He started to loosen his grip on me, intending to end the hug, but I clung more tightly to him. "Please, just a moment longer." I closed my eyes and smiled as he enveloped me in his arms in a bear hug. "Was that you I was seeing every day in the lab?" I asked, my voice muffled by his shoulder.

"It was. I wasn't sure if you had picked up on that. I'm sorry I couldn't get you out sooner, and I'm sorry I couldn't let you know what I was planning. I needed time to build the bomb, and I couldn't use my watch to teleport or time travel without them detecting it. Oh, and I needed to locate and snag this," he said as he held up a watch. "I think its time setting is malfunctioning."

"I don't understand," I said, drawing my brows together.

He pointed at the watch. "See, if they try to enter the coordinates and the universal time, it gets all wonky and—"

"No, not the watch. What bomb?"

"I built and activated a bomb in the basement of their compound. I needed to make sure the council was in that lab at that moment so they would be destroyed along with the wormhole device. I don't know if you figured it out or not, but that big machine in the center of the room was the wormhole generator. I couldn't let that continue to exist in their world, and I couldn't risk any one of the council officials escaping. The annihilation had to be complete."

"Since when can you just come and go from the parallel world?"

"Since I tweaked my watch. But I can't just come and go. I had only enough energy to make one trip there and one back. I've taken a bit of time to work on it."

"…How long? How long has it been since you saw me last?" I asked.

Trent looked down at the watch in his hands. "I don't know. Twelve years?"

It felt like I'd been punched in the gut. "Twelve years? What were you doing for twelve years?"

"Trying to save you."

I looked at him in confusion. There was so much I still didn't understand.

Trent sighed. "I never took down the alarm in your house. I had assumed the threat to us was from SABER of this world, and that the cloaking device I had installed would keep you off their radar. But I wanted to be sure you were safe, and I wanted to make sure I would be alerted if you were ever in danger. I hadn't anticipated the threat would come from the parallel world, but when I received the alert, I knew immediately what had happened. So, I got to work on a solution. It took me over twelve years of obsessive tinkering, but I finally figured it out, and I went back in time to rescue you."

"Why didn't you go back in time and stop this from happening in the first place?" I asked.

"Unfortunately, it was something that needed to happen. Some things are just unchangeable because they are the catalyst that sets other events in motion. But the important thing is that you're safe now." Trent smiled at me.

"How long was I gone?"

Trent looked down at his watch and pressed a few buttons. "I hadn't yet figured out how to time travel from the parallel world to here to bring you back to right after you were taken, so you've been gone a little over a week. Time travel between worlds is trickier than I had anticipated."

"Oh no," I started to panic. "Cattiel!"

"Oh! Hold on," Trent said. He adjusted his watch and disappeared. When he returned seconds later, he said, "There, I went back and took care of the cat. But that litter box is going to be nasty. I don't do litter boxes."

"Oh, thank god," I said with a sigh of relief.

"You're welcome."

"Wait, if you can go back in time to feed the cat, why can't you just take me back to the moment before I was taken? I get that you couldn't do it from the other world, but now that we're here, you can."

"I can't. Timelines should not be crossed, and in some situations, they can't be. This is one of them."

"I don't get it. It all seems so arbitrary," I complained.

"Just trust me. I usually know what I'm talking about."

I went out into the living room and scooped up my cat, hugging him tightly. For once, he didn't growl at me, but purred instead. He must have been lonely without me.

"See?" I said to Cattiel. "You think you hate me, but when I'm not here, you miss me. Maybe you do love me after all."

"That's not love. That's attachment," Trent pointed out.

I looked at him crossly and continued to hug the cat. "You love me," I whispered to Cattiel.

"There are things that will need to be taken care of," Trent said hesitantly.

I set the cat down and plopped onto the couch. "I don't think I can handle any of that right now. Hell, I probably don't even have a job anymore."

"It's all right! We can fix that! Where's your phone?"

"I think I left it on the counter before I disappeared."

Trent went into the kitchen and found my phone. He held his watch close to it and started pressing buttons on the watch and the phone.

After about thirty seconds, he said, "There you go. I've temporarily synced your phone with my watch. Now you can call back in time and let people know you're going out of town for the week. I'm sure you can make up something."

I sat up as he brought me my phone and handed it to me. "I don't want to do this right now. I just want to enjoy being home. I just went through a week of hell, and I thought I was going to be murdered. I think the call to work can wait."

"Is there anything I can do?" Trent asked, clasping his hands together nervously. He looked at me with concern. "What do you need?"

"I need a bath," I answered honestly.

"Did you want me to draw you one?" he asked as he jerked his thumb toward the bathroom.

"No, no. I can do it."

"Very well. I suppose I should leave you to it," he said.

"No!" I blurted as my hand shot out to him, grabbing his jacket sleeve. I rose from the couch. "Don't you dare leave me. Not ever again. You'd better still be here when I get out of the bath."

Trent smiled at me, nodding. "As you wish. I'll be right here."

I had intended for my bath to help calm me down and ease my mind. However, as much as I tried to relax in the hot, soothing water of the bathtub, I didn't linger for long. I scrubbed up quickly, realizing once I'd climbed into the tub that I was afraid Trent was going to disappear on me. I should've just taken a shower so I could get back to his side promptly.

When I was out of the tub and dressed, I hurried out into the living room. I didn't care that I didn't have on any makeup, and it didn't bother me that my towel-dried hair was a mess. I just wanted to make sure he was still there.

Trent was sitting on the couch eating a toaster pastry. I was relieved.

"You're out of pastries," he mumbled around a mouthful of food.

"All I've had to eat for the past week is 'nutrition bars' and you come into my house and eat my last toaster pastry?"

"What? It's the only normal food you keep in this house."

"It's the only junk food I keep in this house," I corrected.

"Do you feel any better?" he asked.

I nodded. "A little." I sat down on the couch across from him. "You know, there's something that's bothering me. Why did the SABER council keep denying that they had someone spying on us?"

"Because I don't think they did."

"What? Who was that man, then?"

"I don't know. While you were in the bath, I took a look at that watch. There is no way it is capable of inter-universal travel."

"Should we be worried?"

"Whoever it was, they don't seem to be trying to find us or trying to change history. I just wonder if perhaps…if it's me. Me from another time."

"Wouldn't you know?"

"Not necessarily. Whatever he was using to travel with wasn't my watch that I have now, but it doesn't mean it wasn't me."

"So, you're saying we don't need to worry about it?"

"You don't need to. I'm going to keep my ear to the ground, though."

I heard my text alert go off on my phone.

"I suppose I should make those calls now," I said with a heavy sigh.

I looked at my phone. I deleted the junk text I had just received and opened my contacts list. It had a new option in the call settings in which I could select a date and time. I chose the morning after I had disappeared, and I called work and made up an excuse about a family emergency out of town. Thankfully, I have a pretty lenient boss, and she had no problem with me taking the week off. I hung up the phone and set it down on the end table.

"That's it? Just work? What about your family?"

"It's not so unusual for me to not talk to them for a week. They won't think anything of it." Then I remembered Sam. "Oh, shoot. I should probably call Sam."

That caught Trent's attention. He gave me a questioning look. "Sam? Who's Sam?"

Chapter 14

I felt like I had been caught cheating. I knew I hadn't done anything wrong, but my heart had a guilty conscience. I needed to just be upfront and honest with him. He wasn't going to care, was he? After all, he was the one who first said that he and I would never work, wasn't he?

"Sam is the guy I've been seeing." I rose from the couch and started pacing the living room.

I saw Trent's nostrils flare as he also stood up. "Oh. You've been seeing someone? That's good. That's...good."

"Yeah."

We stood in awkward silence for a moment.

"So...where'd you meet?" Trent asked, breaking the silence.

"The gym. He's a divorcee, like me."

"The gym. He works out, then? That's cool. Cool. Is it...is it serious?" Trent asked as he picked at his fingernails a little too nonchalantly.

"I don't know. I'm not even sure if we're still dating. We kind of had a falling out right before I was kidnapped."

"Oh. Darn. Well, that's too bad."

"Maybe," I said as I pulled my phone back out.

I set the call date and time for close to the same time I called into work. I figured it would give Sam the night to cool down.

"Hello?" Sam answered after several rings.

"Hey."

There was a long silence.

"Listen," I said finally, "I'm sorry about last night. I wasn't ready to talk about it."

"Are you ready to talk about it now?" Sam asked.

"No. But I wanted to apologize for what happened, anyway."

Just then, Trent yelled to me from the kitchen, "Oh dear lord! You'll want to toss this shrimp. It's definitely turned!"

"Who is that?" Sam asked suspiciously.

"An old friend."

"The old friend?"

I hesitated. "Yes."

I heard Sam sigh heavily. "This is just too much drama for me. I'm sorry. I don't do drama."

"I understand. I don't do drama either, if I can avoid it. Unfortunately, sometimes it just happens. I'll see you around, Sam."

"That's it? That's all you have to say?"

"What else am I supposed to say?"

"I don't know. Usually people have excuses or explanations."

"Sorry, I'm not even going to try to explain all of this."

"You really don't care, do you?"

"Sure I do. But I'm not going to beg you to forgive me. I'm not going to beg for you to give us another chance. If you're done, you're done. It's ok. I get it," I said unremorsefully.

"I never said I was ready to be done," Sam said.

"You didn't? I thought you said you didn't do drama."

"I don't. I hate it. But it doesn't mean I'm ready to be done. It just means we have some things to work on."

"You seemed pretty done with things last night."

"I was upset. And rightfully so, I think. But I'm not an idiot. I know you're a woman worth working things out with."

"Oh." I didn't know what to say.

"Can I see you today?"

"Uh, no. No, I'm heading out of town today. I'm taking a little vacation to visit my brother for the week. But I'll call you when I get home."

"Oh. Really? You hadn't mentioned it before."

"It was kind of a last-minute thing. You know, after last night I realized I needed some time away to clear my head," I lied.

"I understand," Sam said. "I'll talk to you when you get back."

I hung up the phone and turned around. Trent was watching me expectantly.

"Well?" he raised his eyebrows.

"I guess we're still seeing each other," I said with a shrug.

"I see. So, when do I get to meet him?" Trent asked, crossing his arms and leaning his shoulder against the wall. "I need to make sure he is good enough for you."

"That's not your decision to make."

Trent's face became serious. "You are the most important person to me in all of the world and time. You better believe I'm going to make damn sure the man you end up with is worthy of you."

I felt my breath catch in my throat and I swallowed hard.

"Why do you have to say things like that?" I asked.

Trent's forehead creased. "Because it's true."

"I can't possibly be the most important person to you."

"Why not?"

"I'm not that important."

"No one is unimportant. And you, Roselyn, mean the most to me," he said with a smile. "I spent almost twelve years working to save you – and I would've spent a thousand if I had to. How can you think you aren't important to me?"

"Why? What does an immortal genius time traveler from the future find so important about me?"

"Have you met you?" Trent said with a chuckle. "You are my favorite person! You love hard. You live fiercely. You find the humor in life. You keep me on my toes. You forgive me even when I don't deserve it. You irritate the hell out of me and frustrate me, then you find some little thing to do or say to make me wonder why I was cross in the first place. You are never cruel. You are always so, so brave. You are everything. Everything I don't deserve...and I'll be damned if I let another man have you if he doesn't deserve you either."

I had to wipe my eye. "If you think so highly of me, how could you walk away from me so easily?"

"You thought that was easy for me? That was the hardest thing I've ever had to do! But I had to do it."

"Why? Why didn't you even try to change my mind?"

"Because that's what love is! Real love isn't trying to change each other or change each other's mind. Real love isn't clinging to someone and trying make them love you back. Real love is letting someone go if they want to go. It's letting someone have an opportunity to find happiness, even if it isn't with you, and finding happiness in their happiness. Real love isn't bitter and angry and forceful. It isn't holding on to someone at all costs to make yourself feel good. If you truly love someone, you let them do what is best for them. You let them be free to find the happiness they deserve. Real love is understanding that sometimes you just aren't what they need – and not being angry about it. I might not be perfect, and I know I've made some grievous mistakes, but I'm trying to do my best by you because you deserve the very best." Trent looked at me soulfully.

"You need to stop talking. Just stop." I said, frowning.

"What's the matter?"

"This...thing you always do!"

"What thing?" Trent said, looking bewildered.

I gestured wildly at him. "This! I convince myself, after a long internal debate, that I am indeed better off without you, and then you come swooping in with your hair and your suit and say the most eloquent, beautiful thing anyone has ever said to me and you make me fall in love with you all over again and I hate it! Hate it!"

Trent turned his head and looked out the window quietly.

"Well?" I demanded a response.

He turned to me, looked me in the eye, and said, "You're awful, your hair is messy and you smell like cabbage. And don't get me started on the damn kale."

I was flabbergasted. "Excuse me?"

"Is that better? Would you rather me say things like that?"

"I...I smell like cabbage?" I said as I took a test sniff.

Trent bit back a grin. "No, of course not. None of that is true, obviously." After he took a second to think about it, he added, "Really? That's the part you were worried about? Not the part about being awful?"

"Everybody is awful once in a while, but nobody ever wants to smell like cabbage."

"I suppose you're not wrong," he granted.

"God, it's like I can smell it now."

"You don't smell like cabbage."

"Why would you say that, anyway? I do smell like cabbage, don't I?!"

"You don't smell like cabbage."

"I feel like I need another bath now."

"You don't smell like cabbage, Roselyn."

"Ugh. I'm going to go change."

"Oh, good heavens, what have I done?" I heard Trent say in exasperation as I headed to my room.

As I changed my clothes, I remembered what we were talking about before I got distracted by the cabbage comment. How did he do that? Instant situation diffusion. Deflection. Redirection. He was like a goddamn magician.

When I returned to the living room in a fresh shirt, I found Trent kicked back on the couch again. He immediately started grilling me. "So, are we going to go hang out with Sam soon? Can I meet him?"

"I don't know how I feel about that yet," I said.

"Why not?"

"Because I don't know how I feel about Sam yet."

"Perhaps my opinion would help."

"I really don't think it will," I said. "Besides, I don't think he's going to be very excited to meet you."

"But I'm delightful!"

"He knows about…us," I said, wagging my finger between him and me and raising my eyebrows for emphasis.

"Ah, I see…but you weren't dating him then," Trent pointed out.

"I know, but…well, it's complicated."

"It's all complicated. Avoiding it isn't going to make it less so."

I sighed. "I know. But I just don't think this is the right time to put you two in the same room together."

"I'll be charming. I promise."

"No."

Trent grunted. "Fine. But you can't stop me from accidentally running into him."

"You wouldn't."

"I totally would."

"I prohibit it!"

Trent raised his eyebrows at me. "Well now you just went and made it more interesting! What is it you don't want me to know? You're definitely hiding something about him."

"I'm not hiding anything. Just leave it alone, Trent."

He leaned his head back against the back of the couch with a pouty sigh. "I get it. You're embarrassed by me."

I went over to the couch and sat down next to him. "You were bound to find out some day," I teased.

He draped his arm over my shoulder and pulled me closer to him. I rested my temple on his shoulder. "You must be tired," he remarked.

"I am. I feel like I haven't slept for more than an hour all week. Damn, I'm turning into you," I joked.

"Heaven forbid," Trent said with a short chuckle.

He was right. I was tired. I closed my eyes and just enjoyed being close to him again.

After a few minutes of relaxing silence, he mumbled, "I missed you."

Without opening my eyes, I smiled and replied, "I missed you, too. Don't let me run you off ever again, ok?"

"I was still here when you needed me," he said.

"No, you weren't. I needed you long before I was abducted by SABER."

"But you've got Sam now, though, right?"

"He isn't you. I still need you."

Trent was quiet for a while, so I let the conversation die there.

I woke up in a mild state of confusion. It was dark in the living room now, and I was lying on the couch. One of my legs was wedged between the back of the couch cushion and...someone else's leg? My body was partially on top of another warm body and my head was on his chest. I could hear a slow, steady heartbeat. It took me a moment to remember Trent was here. I lifted my head up and blinked, my eyes adjusting to the dark living room.

"Did you have a good nap?" Trent asked as he smiled at me in the dark.

"You stayed this whole time? How did we end up like this?" I asked, surprised.

"Every time I moved, you just leaned on me more. I didn't want to disturb you."

"How long was I out?"

"About three hours."

"Seriously?! You didn't turn on the TV or anything?"

He looked over and pointed at the end table about three feet out of reach. "The remote was over there."

I laughed. "I'm sorry! Weren't you bored?" I asked apologetically.

"No. Well, a little. But it was fine. Did you know you talk in your sleep? And you twitch. A lot."

"Did I say anything good?"

"Oh yes. I'm still blushing."

I laughed and laid my head on his chest again.

"You should go to bed and get some rest," he suggested.

I felt my heartbeat quicken as a question came to my lips. I opened my mouth to speak, but the words wouldn't come out at first. I had to clear my throat and try again. "Would you…would you come with me?" I felt my cheeks flush once the words were out.

Trent's silence hung in the air, weighing on my heart with every passing moment. Finally, he replied softly, "What are you asking of me, Roselyn?"

My heart was in my throat. What was I doing? There was no way he was going to go for this. "Do I really have to come out and say it?"

"I think you'd better be clear with me, yes," he said. I could hear his heartbeat accelerating in his chest. It thumped thunderously against my ear.

"I can tell by the way your heart is beating that you understand my meaning," I disclosed.

He hesitated. "We shouldn't do that again."

"But you want to, don't you?" I asked.

"Of course I want to! But that doesn't make it a good idea." He sounded conflicted, but I could feel his anticipation growing against my hip.

I lifted my head off of his chest and looked at him. It was dark, but I could see the desire burning in his eyes as he looked into mine. He just needed a little push. One tiny, little push – and he'd forget his objections. I ran my fingers gently through his hair and pressed my lips to his. That was all it took.

A soft groan rumbled in his throat as he gave in. His kiss was ravenous as he raked his fingers into my hair. I slid my leg over him and straddled his hips, feeling the hardness within his trousers between my legs. He ran his hands down to my waist as he pressed himself against me, his kiss becoming even more demanding. The heat between my legs yearned for him. God, how I needed him…

I pulled away from his mouth and sat up, looking at him beneath me. His hair was chaotic and his eyes were wild. I climbed off of him and stood up.

"Let's take this back to the bedroom," I said, my chest heaving.

Trent rose from the couch and stood in front of me. He kissed me, biting my lip gently, before smiling mischievously at me. I grabbed his tie and started to lead him back to my room, but he snatched me halfway to the bedroom and pressed my back against the wall in the hallway, his body pressed firmly against mine. He took my hand and pressed it back against the wall. His mouth devoured mine, his other hand caressing the side of my face.

When our lips parted briefly, he murmured, "Why do you do this to me?"

I just smiled against his lips. "Did you want to stop?"

He glanced down at my lips hungrily before looking up into my eyes. "You couldn't drag me away with a freight train."

I kissed him again and led him back to my room. I was already tossing my shirt aside when we crossed the threshold, but that was as far as I got before Trent overtook me. He scooped me up and dropped me onto the bed. I got up on my knees and started unbuttoning his shirt while he loosened his tie, and when he had dropped his tie and was shrugging off his shirt, I started on his trousers.

He pushed me back onto the bed once I had his pants undone, and he reached for the button on my jeans. He unzipped my pants and slid them down over my thighs. I slipped my underwear off as he tossed my jeans onto the floor. I started to scoot up to lay my head on the pillows, but Trent reached out and hooked his hand under my knee, pulling me toward him to the edge of the bed. In the darkness, I felt his mouth on my inner thigh. He trailed light kisses up my thigh until he reached my most intimate folds. His warm, soft tongue explored me gently, and I threw my head back and closed my eyes, my breath catching in my throat. As I felt my pleasure quickly growing, I stopped him. I needed all of him.

"Take me now, Trent. Please," I begged.

He kicked off his trousers and climbed onto the bed on top of me. He kissed me passionately, the taste of my desire still lingering on his tongue. He pressed himself against my wetness, and I wrapped my legs around his waist and urged him on. Feeling Trent's body pressed against mine, our bare, slick skin sliding against each other; his heavy breaths in my ear and his moans making my entire body tingle; his lips brushing against my neck; his tongue dancing with mine; my fingers in his hair; hips pushing, grinding, bucking against him – it was ecstasy. I felt my pleasure rising, and my moans grew louder as I clung more tightly to Trent and rocked my hips against his. He thrust hard and deep, sensing that I was close, and it sent me over the edge. I couldn't contain my cries of pleasure as my body was rocked by the most powerful orgasm I'd ever experienced. I buried my face in his neck and clung to him as we rode it out together.

Afterward, as we lay next to each other, catching our breath, Trent said, "We can't keep doing this."

"I know," I replied. I turned onto my side and threw my arm over his bare chest, sidling my sweaty, naked body up next to his.

"You aren't mine to do this with," Trent said guiltily. He suddenly threw his hand over his mouth and looked over at me, giving me a scandalized look. "What about Sam?! Oh, dear, I've done a very very bad thing!"

I put my hand on his cheek. "Sam isn't my boyfriend. Relax."

Trent was quiet for a moment. "Are you going to tell him?"

"No."

"Have you and him…?"

"No."

"Why does it seem like you don't fancy him all that much?"

"I don't know. I like him, I do. But…I keep holding him to impossible standards, knowing he'll never measure up. He's a perfectly all right guy, don't get me wrong. I just…I'm looking for 'wow,' and I'm not sure if he can give me that."

"You deserve 'wow,' and you shouldn't settle for less."

"I don't think I have much of a choice. It might be time to settle for 'good enough.' The great thing about 'good enough,' though, is that it doesn't hurt so badly when it doesn't work out."

"That's a terrible way to look at it," Trent admonished.

"It's the only way to look at it."

"Don't you want to be happy?"

"Of course I do. And I am happy – right now. With you. That'll do for now. You are my 'wow.'"

"You know we can't be together," Trent said quietly.

"I know. But it's nice to pretend for a while."

"I want you to have someone who gives you 'wow' every day for the rest of your life. I give you grief and trouble. I'm not your 'wow.'"

"You don't get to tell me that. You don't get to tell me how to feel."

"No, of course not. I was just observing."

"Obviously not through my eyes," I replied.

Trent gathered me up in his arms and held me tightly. "I wish I could actually be the man you see when you look at me through your eyes. I dread the day you take off those rose-colored spectacles."

"I don't think I've ever met anyone who hates himself as much as you do. What reason could you possibly have to be so hard on yourself? Why do you feel so undeserving?"

"We all have our secrets. We all have moments we aren't proud of. I have over 600 years' worth of those moments. I've had to do things no one should have to do. I've had to make decisions no one should have to make. And I've made mistakes – mistakes that cost people their lives. It didn't happen once or twice, either. This is something that happens time and time again. When you are burdened with the task I have been burdened with – when you have to keep history from being unraveled, humanity from being corrupted – the line between good and evil gets blurred. Sometimes you have to do bad things to keep others safe. Someone has to get their hands dirty...unfortunately, I'm that someone. I don't deserve your admiration, Roselyn."

"I don't know what you've done, Trent, and I'm not going to ask. Not right now, anyway. But I know that you are a good man. You have a good heart. Anything bad you've ever done had to have been done for good reason, I'm sure of it. I refuse to believe that you'd ever be malicious or evil."

"I'm not a good man. I try to do what is right, but it doesn't make me a good man. I've lived too long and fought too many battles to still be good."

"After all this time, you fight because you still care about what happens to the human race. You fight even though no one is making you. You do it because it's the right thing to do. If that isn't a good man, I don't know what is. The real evil in this world isn't in the actions of bad men, but in the indifference of otherwise good men. You refuse to be indifferent, and that tells me everything I need to know."

"You romanticize it. You make it sound noble. But you don't really understand. It's grotesque and heart-wrenching and sullying…and I write every single line of it down. Every unspeakable horror I've witnessed or had to commit, I record it. I might not have the memory of every act, but I know everything I've done or have allowed to happen. I write it down lest I ever forget who I truly am and for what purpose I am here to serve. And unfortunately, Roselyn Wolff, being your 'wow' isn't part of that purpose, as much as I wish it were."

"I don't care. I still—"

Trent interrupted me. "I had to kill someone working for SABER because they were developing technology to go back and kill Hitler. I had to protect Hitler. Do you know how that feels? Knowing that you could go back and stop the Holocaust, but you won't? You won't because it's not the way it's supposed to go? Knowing I can change something but not changing it – that kind of makes me responsible, doesn't it? If you really think about it, it does. Millions of people suffer and die horribly in an unimaginable hell because I won't allow history to change. Because I know it's how it has to go. Yes, my hands are tied, but ultimately it is my decision. And it's a horrible decision to make."

"You have no real choice, Trent. You can't blame yourself for having to let history run its course."

"I killed all of the people in that SABER compound when I came to save you. Did you realize that? That bomb was intended to take out the entire building, and everyone in it. Even the scientists. Even the cafeteria workers. The security guards. The custodians. I couldn't warn anyone, because it might've compromised my mission. I walked beside many of them every day for a week, knowing what was going to happen to them. I even learned some of their names. Some of them were good people. Hell, a lot of them were good people, just working for a corrupt authority. They're all dead now because of me. But I couldn't let them come to our world and decimate our Earth, now could I? I couldn't let them murder you. I had to destroy them before they destroyed us. Again, my hands were tied, but it was still my decision to make."

I didn't know what to say to him, so I simply said, "I'm sorry."

"That's just the tip of the iceberg. There's so, so much more…so much that I can't even tell you about. I don't think you'd ever look me in the eyes again if I tried."

"Then let's not talk about it. I didn't mean to dredge up anything."

"You didn't dredge. It's always simmering just beneath the surface. It's not something you find respite from for very long." After an extended silence, Trent looked down at me and said, "Do you still think I'm a good man?"

"I'm certain of it."

Chapter 15

I woke up in the morning still naked and tangled in my bed sheets, but Trent wasn't beside me. I looked over to see if any of his clothes were still on the floor, but they weren't. I felt a creeping anxiety rising in my chest. If he'd left, I didn't know if it was going to be for a day, a month, or forever. I didn't expect him to never leave my side, but I was terrified of him disappearing without saying goodbye and never coming back. I threw on a pair of pajama pants and a t-shirt and hurried out to the living room.

"Ah, you're up!" Trent said from the kitchen.

An overwhelming sense of relief washed over me. "Jesus, I thought you'd run out on me again," I confessed.

"We're in the wrong millennium for Jesus, aren't we? I met him once, you know. Nice chap...just don't give him a whip." Trent had his back to me, and he was busy doing something over the stove. I noticed he was wearing a different suit from yesterday.

"What are you doing?" I asked.

"Getting breakfast ready." He turned around with two plates in his hands and brought them to the table.

"Did you make omelets?" I asked, raising my eyebrows.

He nodded with a proud look on his face. "I did."

"I thought you didn't cook."

"I learned."

"When?"

"While you were sleeping."

"I see you changed your clothes, too."

He looked down at his suit. "Oh, yes. Can't take a cooking class in dirty, crumpled clothes."

"Wait, you took a whole class? To learn how to make eggs?"

"Omelets. Quit grilling me and just eat."

"Was that a cooking joke?"

Trent smirked at me. "You know it was."

I sat down at the table and looked at the large omelet in front of me. I didn't have the heart to tell him that I don't have the stomach for a big breakfast in the mornings. I was going to do my best to eat every last bite of that damn omelet, even if it was terrible. Trent brought me a cup of coffee and sat down across from me. He watched me, waiting for me to take the first bite.

"I can't eat with you watching me," I said.

"Sorry." He dropped his gaze to his own plate, but I could tell he was still observing me.

I cut off a corner of the omelet and took a bite. "Oh my god. This is actually really good!"

"I know!" he said excitedly. "I went through two cartons of eggs before I got it right, but I finally nailed it!"

"What's in it? I've never had anything like this before."

"Black truffle and robiola."

"Seriously?! Where the hell did you get black truffles around here— wait, don't answer that. Dumb question to ask a man with teleportation capabilities. What was that second thing? Rebola?"

Trent laughed. "Robiola. It's an Italian cheese."

"This is amazing. Thank you. You've ruined me for omelets now, though. Mine will taste like crap after this."

"You're welcome." Trent was beaming.

After breakfast, Trent insisted upon loading the dishwasher because I "do it wrong." I went into the living room, grabbed Cattiel off the couch, and sat down with him in my arms. I turned on the TV and channel surfed with an overfull belly and a contented heart.

"Well, I suppose I should be off now," Trent said as he dried his hands on the hand towel in the kitchen.

I dreaded those words. "You're coming back, right?"

"Well, not right back. You have your life to live, right? You have some things to talk to Sam about too, I suspect. I'll be around, though. Don't worry, I'm not disappearing forever."

I dropped the cat onto the couch and jumped up before Trent could leave. I hurried to him and threw my arms around his neck, forcing him to bend down slightly. He hugged me back tightly.

"You better not disappear forever. I'll never forgive you."

"Well, we can't have that, now can we?"

As I dropped my arms to my sides and released him, I suddenly remembered something. "Oh! Wait!" I grabbed my phone quickly and handed it to him. "I need you to put your number back in my phone."

"I thought you had my number," Trent said as he drew his brows together.

"I did. But I…erased it."

Trent entered his number and handed my phone back to me. "Why would you erase my number?"

"Because that's what you do, you know? When you try to erase someone from your life, that's the first thing you do – delete their number."

"I take it you've decided to keep me after all?"

"I'll never try to delete you again."

"I'm going to hold you to that," he teased.

"You know, there's something that's been bothering me. When you left last time, and I told you not to come back, I saw you. I was at a restaurant with Sam, and I saw you outside walking down the street. Why were you there?"

Trent gave me a doubtful look. "No, I wasn't around here. Are you sure?"

"Yes. It was you. At least I thought it was…"

Trent shrugged his shoulders. "Maybe it was me. All I can tell you is I haven't done it yet, at least."

"Oh."

"You sound disappointed."

I shook my head. "No, nothing of the sort. Anyway, I'll see you soon, right? Don't be gone too long. I'll worry."

Trent laughed. "I don't think I've ever had anyone worry about me before."

"Well, get used to it."

Trent smiled at me, and then he was gone.

I sat back down on the couch with Cattiel again. He had been right when he detected disappointment in my voice. There had been a little part of me that had secretly hoped that it had been him that day at the restaurant – that he was checking in on me to make sure I was all right. But it wasn't. What was it I had seen, then? Had it just been my imagination manufacturing a Trent that wasn't really there because I had yearned to see him so badly? It was entirely possible. It wasn't nearly as satisfying of an answer, but it was entirely possible.

After getting ready for the day, I went into the kitchen to look at what I needed to throw out and what I needed to get from the store. As I started sorting through the fridge, I pulled out my phone to call Sam. When I went to place the call, I noticed the time and date option was no longer available. My phone must no longer be synced with Trent's watch. I dialed Sam and sat in front of the fridge with the garbage can.

He answered on the third ring. "There you are," he said. "I was beginning to think you were never going to call."

"Here I am," I said. Ugh, the melon in the fridge had turned to mush. "Did you miss me?"

"I did. You didn't think I would, did you?"

"You didn't think you would." Oh my god, where did that avocado come from?

"I knew I would. So, when do I get to see you? Can I come over?" Sam asked.

"I actually need to go out. I have some grocery shopping to do today."

"Oh, perfect! Did you want to maybe meet for coffee when you get into town? I can accompany you to the store afterward if you wanted."

"Sure, that sounds good." I smelled the cottage cheese. It seemed ok, but did I trust it?

"I'll see you in, what, half an hour?" Sam asked.

I opened my vegetable drawer and saw a brown-tinted liquid covering the bottom of it. "Let's make that an hour. I've got a couple of things I need to take care of first."

Once my fridge had been purged and cleansed and exorcised, I bundled up and headed to town in the snow. It was a miserably blustery day, and as I walked from the curb to the coffee shop, I wished I had just stayed in. I'm sure I could've found something in the freezer to eat for dinner. But alas, here I was. I was just going to have to make the best of it.

I had arrived early to the coffee shop, so I got a tall black coffee and sat in the corner and waited for Sam. When he walked in the door a few minutes later, he looked out of breath. He was dressed for jogging. His face lit up when he saw me waiting for him and he waved. I grinned, despite myself, and waved back. I mean, he was cute. He got a coffee at the counter and joined me at the table. He leaned over and kissed me on the cheek before sitting down across from me.

"Sorry if I'm a little sweaty," he said. "I ran here."

"I see that. I didn't realize you were completely insane when I agreed to meet you for coffee."

Sam laughed. "It's not that bad. You warm up pretty quickly."

"You and I have very different opinions of 'not that bad.'"

Sam took a drink of his coffee. "So, how was your week at your brother's?

"Hm? Oh! Uh, yeah, that was nice. It's always good to see him."

"Did you have a chance to clear your head?"

I nodded. "A little bit, yeah."

"So…are we ok? Are we going to give this another shot?"

"Sure."

"That was a very noncommittal response."

"Yes, we are going to give this another shot," I tried again.

There was a brief pause in the conversation as we both sipped our coffee and looked at each other, waiting for the other to say something.

Sam broke the awkward pause with, "So, how's Trent?" There was a bitter tone to his voice.

My heart was instantly in my throat and I was flooded with guilt. "He's good. Things are better now."

"What does that mean for me?" he asked. "I mean, I hate to sound selfish, but is he going to be a problem for me?"

"No, he won't be a problem. He actually…well, he wants to meet you."

"So he knows about me, then?"

"Of course. He just can't wait to see me settled with someone, I think."

"…Really? Is this the same Trent…?"

"Yep. There's only one Trent. It's all good, Sam. Don't worry, I told him it probably wasn't a good idea if you two met right now."

"No, actually I'd like to meet him. Put a face to the name. It'd be nice to know what exactly I'm up against."

"It isn't a competition," I said with a sigh. "He's just a friend."

"That's not a reassuring line. 'He's just a friend.' In my experience, he's never 'just a friend.'"

"I don't know what you want me to tell you."

"The truth would be nice."

"The truth is that he and I would never work. Ok? He wants to see me with someone else."

"And what do you want?"

"'Wow.'"

Sam looked at me strangely. "Wow what?"

I sighed. "Nothing. I just want to be happy."

"What's it going to take to make you happy?" Sam wanted to know.

I looked across the room at nothing in particular. "I don't know. I'm still working that out."

"Am I wasting your time, Roselyn?" Sam asked bluntly.

I looked back at him. He looked to be on the verge of defeat. "No, you aren't wasting anybody's time. I'm sorry. I don't mean to be so cynical. I'm just trying to figure out what I want out of life, I suppose."

"I can get behind that. Hell, I'm thirty-seven and I'm still trying to figure out what I want to do when I grow up," Sam chuckled.

I smiled. "I'm still wondering when I'm going to start feeling like a grown up."

Sam laughed. "I know what you mean. I swear I'm still the same guy who was getting my old Chevy stuck in the mud somewhere out in the woods on the way to a bonfire in high school. The only thing that's changed is the truck is newer, the 'night moves' aren't as awkward, and now I'm the one kicking people out of the bar instead of the one getting kicked out."

"Did you and I go to the same high school or what?" I joked. "Man, it feels like just yesterday. I can't believe how long it's actually been. It's scary how fast the time flies by."

"Yeah. I'm creeping closer to forty now, and I'm still not sure how I feel about that."

"They say forty is the new twenty."

"Well, let's hope 'they' are right. I do what I can to turn back the clock, but when your hair is more gray than brown, it's hard to deny that time is indeed marching forward."

I looked at his brown manbun. "Your hair isn't gray."

"Oh, it is. Thankfully, though, they make this awesome product called hair dye. Could be worse, I suppose. At least I'm not going bald."

"I bet you'd look good if you let the gray show."

"You'd be wrong," Sam laughed. "The woman who used to cut my hair would laugh every time she got the clippers into it because all the gray would pop out as soon as the hair over it was trimmed. She said I looked twenty years older after my haircut. That's why I decided to grow it out."

"You grew your hair out because your hair stylist was making fun of you?" I asked.

"No, I grew it out so I wouldn't have to dye it after every cut. It looks good like this, though, right?" Sam asked with a wink.

I laughed. "It does. I can't argue with that."

Sam accompanied me to the grocery store up the road. It wasn't terribly exciting, but I was surprised by what a pleasant day it turned out to be. I noticed as we walked through the aisles, there were a couple of women who quite openly checked out Sam as we passed. He didn't seem to notice. It was kind of satisfying.

After we went through the checkout, he helped me carry my groceries to my car. "You are a very efficient shopper," he said as he put the bags in the trunk.

"How so?"

"In and out without a fuss. I like it."

"I hate grocery shopping. I like to get it over with as quickly as possible."

"You were so focused you didn't even notice the guy at the deli checking you out."

I laughed. "He did not."

"He did. Don't worry, though. I threw some shade his way." He demonstrated a stern look for me.

"Very intimidating. I'm sure you really showed him," I jested.

"I did. He was scared."

I chuckled. I looked up at the sky, watching the heavy snow starting to fall. "So, did you want a ride home?"

"Nah, I'll run it. But I would like to see you for dinner soon."

"Smooth transition," I said.

"It was, wasn't it? So what do you say?"

I nodded. "Yeah, we can do that. I think I'm pretty much open all week after work."

"Perfect. I'll text you."

Sam leaned down and kissed me casually on the lips. It was light and brief, just a peck, if you will, but it surprised me.

It surprised me because I didn't like it.

He waved as he put his earphones in and jogged off across the road. I climbed into my car and headed home. I spent the ride wondering what the hell was wrong with me. Sam looked good on paper. He was charming and handsome, was built like an athlete, made an absurd amount of money as a bartender, drove a nice vehicle, and had his own house. He seemed like a genuinely nice guy and I enjoyed myself when I was around him. Best of all, he really liked me. Why couldn't I just let myself fall for him? It shouldn't be this hard.

I just needed time. Maybe he would grow on me, like Trent did. I didn't like Trent all that much when I first met him, did I? Granted, I had warmed up to Trent immensely quicker than I was warming up to Sam, but it could happen. Trent was what I wanted, but Sam was what I needed. It was time I accepted it and quit fighting it.

The next few days were the epitome of normalcy, and it bored the hell out of me. I went back to work and made up some story about a dead grandmother to explain my week off. Well, I didn't make the story up, exactly, because my grandmother had died just as I said she did. It had just happened several years earlier. My boss and my clients were glad to have me back, though. Since I didn't really have friends, it felt good to know I was missed by someone other than just Sam.

On Friday after work, I'd made plans to get dinner with Sam. I met him at the same restaurant we had been at before. When living in a small town, variety is, unfortunately, severely lacking. When I arrived, he was waiting for me at the entrance, looking dashing in dark gray slacks and a matching suit vest. His burgundy tie was neatly tucked under the vest and contrasted nicely with his light gray oxford shirt.

He held the door open for me. "You look absolutely stunning," he said with a charming smile.

I laughed. "I feel a bit out of place in this dress." I looked around at the patrons eating dinner in their jeans and t-shirts. I was wearing a long-sleeved, somewhat form-fitting pink and black midthigh-length dress with tall black boots. I could feel the eyes on me as we were led to our seat. "I feel like everyone is staring at me," I whispered.

"There's nothing wrong with that," he replied. "I can't really blame them. You're gorgeous."

I smiled uncomfortably and sat down at the table. Compliments always made me feel awkward. "You look great, too," I said.

After we ordered our food and handed our menus back to the waiter, Sam looked me in the eye and said, "I'd like for you to meet my parents."

I almost choked on my own saliva. "What?! Why?"

He scrunched his face. "What do you mean 'why?' Isn't that what people do?"

"Yeah, but not until things get serious."

"You don't feel like this is getting serious?" Sam sounded surprised.

I didn't know how to respond. "Well, I'm not saying that, exactly...I just...I don't know, it's only been a few weeks, you know? And it hasn't all been smooth sailing, either."

Sam raised his eyebrow and leaned forward. "It's been over a month. And I've been happier with you over the past month than I've been in a long time. I know it isn't perfect all the time, but that's part of getting to know each other. Don't you feel the same? Aren't you ready to take the next step and make our relationship official?"

"You're asking me to be your girlfriend?"

Sam nodded hopefully.

I felt put on the spot. "Oh. Um. Yeah, sure. I mean yes, of course. That would be…great."

Sam looked unconvinced. "If you want to wait, that's ok, too. I'm ok with that. If we aren't both in the same place yet, I don't want to force it."

I waved my hands. "No, no, I didn't mean to sound so noncommittal. I'm ok with it. We can take the next step. I just wasn't prepared for the whole parents thing," I said with a nervous laugh.

Sam smiled. "That's ok, we can wait to meet the parents if you want." Then I saw Sam's gaze shift as his face took on a puzzled look. "Wow. And you thought you were out of place in your outfit. Get a load of that guy," Sam said as he subtly nodded in the direction behind me.

I turned and looked behind me just in time to catch eyes with Trent.

Chapter 16

Trent raised his eyebrows and smiled, raising his hand enthusiastically at me to indicate that he had found me. I gave him an embarrassed smile and turned back to Sam as Trent approached the table.

"Why is he coming toward us? Do you know him?" Sam asked, looking confused.

Before I had a chance to answer, Trent was at the table. "Hello!" he said, barely glancing at me as he focused his attention on Sam.

Sam stood up from his seat. "What do you want?" he asked curtly.

Trent held his hand out and smiled amicably. "You must be Sam. You're much...larger than I had imagined," Trent said as he looked up at Sam, who had a good six inches and at least five stones on him. Trent looked over at me with a quick frown. "You didn't tell me he was so annoyingly handsome."

Sam looked to me for an explanation, his face contorted in puzzlement.

"Sam, this is Trent. Trent, this is Sam." Dear lord, this isn't happening right now.

Sam looked at Trent's hand hesitantly before shaking it. "I've, uh...I've heard about you," Sam said.

"So I am to understand," Trent said, wringing his hands uneasily. He suddenly turned to me with his finger in the air. "Oh! Before I forget! It turns out that it was me! When you asked if I had been here and I said no – it just hadn't happened yet! I got the time wrong on my first attempt at getting here. Kind of funny, isn't it?"

"What the hell is he talking about?" Sam asked. I could tell his patience was running thin.

"Nothing, it was just some stupid thing we were talking about the other day," I said to Sam. To Trent, I asked, "What are you doing here?"

"You weren't answering your phone," Trent said.

"I shut it off because I'm on a date! It couldn't wait?"

"I seem to have misplaced a rather important item," Trent said sheepishly. "Have you seen the watch?"

I looked down at his wrist. "It's right there," I said flatly.

"Don't be daft. Obviously I'm not talking about this one. The other one."

"Oh, the faulty one? No. I don't have it."

"Bollocks," Trent said, biting his knuckle. "This never happens. How could I lose it? I don't lose things."

"Trent?" I said, trying to get his attention.

He looked at me like he suddenly remembered I was still there. "Yes?"

"Can we maybe talk about this later?"

"Oh!" Trent pointed at Sam. "Yes! Sorry! My apologies! You two have fun!" Trent winked at me as he left in as much of a whirlwind as he had arrived.

I looked at Sam apologetically. "I am so sorry about that."

"Is he always like that?" Sam asked.

"Yeah, pretty much."

"Did he call me 'annoyingly handsome'?"

I pressed my lips together and nodded. "Yes, yes he did."

"I don't...what the hell just happened?"

"Yeah, he has that effect on people. I'm so sorry."

"Are all of your friends like that?"

"No. Well, I don't really have other friends. He was actually the first friend I made after my divorce. I wasn't allowed to have friends when I was married."

"How on Earth did you become friends with that guy? I mean, that must be one hell of a story."

"He, um…he helped me find a solution for a pest problem when I first moved into my new house. We just kind of stayed friends after that."

"He's an exterminator?"

I raised my eyebrows. "I suppose you could say that. Just don't call him that to his face."

It took a while to get the date back on track after that. By the end of the night, however, Sam was at ease again. When he walked me out to my car, he lingered by my door as I unlocked it. When I opened it and turned to tell him goodnight, he slipped his hand around my waist and pulled me to him. His lips bumped against mine and his tongue invaded my mouth. I kissed him back with as much enthusiasm as I could muster, but I knew I was probably giving a lackluster performance.

When he finished the kiss, he looked down at me. "Is everything all right?"

"Yes. I'm just sorry about having our date interrupted. I feel badly about that."

"It wasn't your fault. It's not like it was ruined. Don't worry about it," Sam said reassuringly.

"I'll make sure he doesn't do that next time."

"Speaking of next time, I have tomorrow night off. I was wondering if maybe you wanted to try a do-over of the night things went a little sideways – see if we can get it right this time."

I knew this moment was going to come eventually. I nodded. "Yeah, we can do that. If you want to come to my house again, I can do up those ribeyes we picked out at the store."

"That'd be fantastic. I'll see you tomorrow, beautiful." Sam leaned down and kissed me again before we parted ways.

When I got home, I called Trent at that wonky number he had. Instead of answering, however, he just appeared in my living room.

"Did you find it?" he asked eagerly.

"No. It's not here. I don't know what you did with it. Did you check the pockets of your suits?"

"Yes! All of them! I've looked everywhere. I'm beginning to worry that perhaps I didn't just misplace it. What if someone took it?"

"Who would take it?"

"I don't know, but it wouldn't be anyone we'd want to have it," he said.

"Can't you use your watch to locate it?"

"Not unless someone uses it to time travel or teleport. I didn't have a chance to sync it with my watch."

"Well, at least you know no one is using it."

Trent tilted his head to the side. "There is that, I suppose."

"I'm sure it'll turn up."

"I don't do things like this. I can't believe this happened," Trent said, starting to pace. He looked unusually bothered.

"You said that at the restaurant. You've never misplaced anything? Surely in six hundred years you must have lost something."

"This is different. It's important. I don't lose important things."

"It's ok, Trent."

"It's not ok. What if I've forgotten? What if I did something with it and I've forgotten? What if that means I'm getting ready to change again?" Trent looked at me with panic in his eyes.

My heart stopped at the thought of him changing. "But...I thought you didn't have any warning before you changed."

"Not that I've ever noticed, but it doesn't mean there aren't subtle warning signs that I've just been missing."

"Don't panic. Please, just sit down."

"I don't want to change. I don't want to do it again," Trent said, distress etched deeply into his features. He looked at me with his eyebrows curved upwards. "I don't want to leave you yet. I'm not ready."

He was filling me with anxiety, but I put on the bravest face I could compose. I stepped up to him and put my hands on either side of his face. "Stop. Stop it right now. You aren't going anywhere. You don't have my permission to change yet."

Trent gave a short laugh and smiled at me with sad eyes. "If anyone could stop the inevitable, it would be you."

"Then stop worrying about it, ok?"

"I'm sorry. I'm ruining your night yet again, aren't I?" Trent sat down on the couch and rested his giant foot on his narrow knee, exhaling heavily.

"It's all right. Everything's fine. You know, Sam really didn't know what to think of you tonight."

"He wasn't what I was expecting, either. He's a bit older than you, isn't he?"

"...Says the six-hundred-year-old man."

"And he's big! I think he could beat me up. I don't say that often, but I'm fairly certain he could do it. And I'd probably cut my hand on that chiseled jawline if I tried to hit him back. Are you sure he isn't genetically engineered, too?"

"I know. He's uncommonly perfect, isn't he?" I said with a downward inflection.

"You make it sound like that's a bad thing."

"It's not a bad thing. I'm just having a hard time convincing myself to fall in love with him."

"Who says you have to fall in love with him? There are other men out there."

"Yeah, there are, but not a lot of good ones."

"Did you want me to steal you one from another time? Another region?" Trent teased.

I laughed. "No. I'm sure he'll do. I just need time to get used to him."

Trent looked at me hesitantly. "Can I raise a little flag of warning here?"

"What is it?"

"Falling in love is supposed to be the easy part. Staying in love is where it gets tough. If you're having a hard time with the first step, what makes you think it's going to work at all? And, I hate to be the one to say it, but…what about Sam's feelings? How would he feel if he knew how you really felt?"

"I know. Nobody wants to be the silver medal. The only thing worse than settling is finding out you were the one they settled for. I know all of this. Trust me, I've thought about it and felt guilty for it. But what am I supposed to do? When you can't be with the one you love, love the one you're with, right? Fake it 'til you make it."

Trent looked at me with disappointment. "That isn't the Roselyn I know."

I gave him a humorless smile. "We all do things we aren't proud of, don't we?"

Trent broke eye contact with me and looked down at his hands. "You're thinking that this isn't any of my business, aren't you?"

"Yes."

"I see. Well, I do wish you all the best, Roselyn. I just want you to be happy."

"I know. But maybe you should focus on finding that watch for now and let me focus on me."

Trent nodded. "Point taken. Again, I'm sorry about tonight."

"It's all right. But I should warn you that Sam is coming over for dinner and a movie tomorrow. You probably shouldn't pop in tomorrow evening…or the morning after."

Trent's jaw visibly clenched as he stood up from the couch. He avoided my eyes. "Oh. Yes, I understand. I'll stay out of your hair. I wouldn't want to…interrupt," he said with a hint of disdain.

"You want me to love someone else, Trent. You know that involves other activities too."

"Except you don't love him."

"Someday I will."

"If you say so," Trent said cynically.

"Jesus, Trent. Isn't this what you wanted?" I confronted him.

"Not this!" he shouted suddenly. "Not for you to go through the motions of love with someone that doesn't make you happy. Not for you to pretend. I want you to find the real thing."

"I did! Remember? But that didn't work out, now did it? So you don't get a say anymore!"

Trent's nostrils flared and he threw his hands in the air dramatically as he started pacing about the room. "Yes, of course, throw it in my face yet again why don't you? Everything is my fault, isn't it? I ruined you – is that it?!"

"Yes! That is exactly it!" I shouted.

Trent rubbed both hands down his face in frustration. He took a deep breath. "And what, exactly, do you think you've done to me?" he asked between clenched teeth.

I was taken aback. I stared at him with my mouth slightly agape.

"Oh, you never considered that, did you?" he continued. "Maybe if you'd pull your head out of your own perfect arse for five bloody minutes you'd realize that you aren't the only person in the world who has feelings! This isn't easy for me either! You think I enjoy the thought of another man doing the things to you that I...I can't even say it. I can't! I don't want to even think about it! But you know what? At least I'm trying. I'm doing my best for you because that's what you need me to do. So don't you dare try to tell me that I don't get a say anymore." Trent stepped in front of me, bending down slightly so that he was at eye level with me. "I gave you up, even though it kills me every second of every day, because it was the right thing to do. I will not stand here and let you act like I don't care!" he said, pointing to the ground.

I didn't know what to say. I fumbled for the words. "No, I...I never...I didn't say you didn't care. Not for one second did I ever think you didn't care. I just...I thought you were having an easier time letting me go because..." my voice trailed off.

"Because I don't feel as deeply as you do?"

"I don't know. Maybe."

"After everything we've been through? After all the times I've expressed how important you are to me? I don't know how you can possibly believe that."

"When you've spent the last several years of your life being manipulated to feel like no one could ever love you, you tend to fall back on the notion that people don't care all that much about you. It's just what I do. I don't want to feel that way. I'm not trying to use it as an excuse to be difficult. As much as I hate it, it's just who I am now."

Trent grasped his chin, resting his elbow on the wrist of his other folded arm. "You know, you and I are like sodium and water. Put us together and boom!" Trent threw his arms around wildly to imitate an explosion. "Instant, intense reaction! Sometimes it's a good intense, sometimes a not so good intense. It's both exhilarating and exhausting."

I couldn't deny it was true. In an effort to slow the current "reaction," I said, "So, I guess the real question is: which one of us is the sodium?"

Trent looked at me and grinned, and the tension in the room was instantly lifted. "If only we had a little chlorine, we could have the solution," he joked.

"Let's try not to be so salty," I laughed.

Trent clapped his hands together and pointed at me with a chuckle. "Nice."

If there was one thing I could say for Trent and me, it was that we didn't stay angry with each other for long. We always found a way out of it. One of us always relented. We knew when the flash of anger had run its course, and we let it die before too many hurtful things were said. It was why we could still be friends despite all the tension that had built up between us. And to be honest, I think we both kind of enjoyed the occasional explosion.

"Well, I should probably go before we find something else to argue about," Trent said. I saw his eyes quickly look me up and down. "You look fetching tonight, by the way. I couldn't tell you that earlier because Sam probably would've punched me, but I wanted to."

I felt my cheeks getting hot. "Thank you. I don't think you've ever seen me in a dress."

"I haven't. It's quite breathtaking," he said with a warm smile.

I blushed so hard my ears were on fire.

"Sorry, I didn't mean to embarrass you," Trent said. "I'll be off, now. See you in a while, Roselyn."

I gave him a little wave as he teleported out of the house. I didn't see him again before my date with Sam the following night.

When Sam showed up at my house for dinner, he was dressed a little more casually than he had been the night before. I was glad for that, because I was, too. But he looked handsome in his jeans and black polo shirt. He handed me a bouquet of red roses as I invited him into the house, and he kissed me lightly on the lips as he stepped inside. I turned away to go get a vase for the roses he'd brought while he was slipping his shoes off. As I turned, I unconsciously ran the back of my hand over my mouth.

"Did you just wipe off my kiss?" Sam asked.

"What? No. Did I? I didn't mean to!"

"Relax, I'm just kidding," Sam said.

I laughed uncomfortably. We weren't off to a great start.

"The steaks are ready," I said as I looked at the clock on the stove. "Your timing couldn't have been more perfect." I reached up into the cupboard above the fridge to grab a vase, but I couldn't quite reach it. As I started to climb onto the counter, I heard Sam laugh behind me.

"What are you doing?" he asked.

"I was getting a vase."

"Here, let me," he said, still chuckling. He reached up and easily grabbed the vase from the cupboard as I slid back down off the counter. He handed it to me with an amused grin.

"I could've gotten it," I said matter-of-factly as I filled it with water.

"I don't doubt it for a second. You're quite acrobatic."

"Um, thanks?" I said as I crinkled my nose. "Have a seat. Let's eat," I ordered.

I put the roses in the vase and set it on the table between our place settings. I then fixed a plate for Sam and brought it to him. I sat down with my plate and looked across the table at him – and all I saw were the roses.

Sam leaned over and peeked around the roses at me. "Mind if I slide these aside?" he asked with a chuckle. He moved the vase to the edge of the table. "There you are," he smiled.

"I hope you like your steak medium rare. It's the only way to eat a ribeye, if you ask me."

"That'll be perfect. It smells great."

I smiled politely and started to cut into my steak. Unfortunately, the sawing motion of our steak knives jostled my small table enough to shake the vase right off the edge. It crashed to the floor, shattering, and water splattered across the kitchen. I just stared at the mess in disbelief.

"I'm so sorry, that was my fault," Sam said as he jumped up to clean up the disaster.

"It's nobody's fault," I said. I grabbed a roll of paper towels and the garbage can and got down on my knees to help him carefully pick up shards of glass.

"No, you go ahead and eat," Sam said as he took the roll of paper towels from me. "Enjoy your steak while it's hot."

"If I help you, we'll get it cleaned up faster and we can both enjoy our steak while it's still hot."

"It's ok, I can get it."

I ignored him and kept cleaning. "I'm not about to let my guest clean up a mess while I sit and eat and watch. Don't be silly."

We went back and forth like that until all the glass was collected and the water had been sopped up. When we sat back down to eat, the steaks weren't quite as warm as I had hoped they'd be. Tonight was turning out to be a total catastrophe.

When we finished eating, I put our plates in the sink and looked at the roses I had tossed in the other side of the sink. There were tiny shards of glass interspersed throughout the foliage, so I had figured I'd take care of them later. The way they sat there, though, looking so cast aside, it was a feeling all too familiar. They were so beautiful and elegant, but all it had taken was one little mishap and they'd wound up tossed carelessly in the damn sink. I left the dishes and the roses in the sink and went into the living room to pick out a movie with Sam.

As Sam and I sat next to each other on the couch, with Cattiel sitting on the couch opposite us, giving us the evil eye, I was keenly aware of Sam's hand on my thigh. Every time he moved, I tensed up. I wasn't even paying much attention to the superhero movie we were watching because I was too worried about what was coming next. I knew what was going to happen tonight. Sam knew what was going to happen tonight. I was just waiting nervously for it to begin. I had tried to prepare myself for it by thinking about it all day, but it hadn't helped at all. I hoped that I would be more into it when it actually happened. Sam was a devastatingly handsome man, and there was no reason I shouldn't be able to enjoy a night with him, right? I just had to relax and not think about Trent.

Except now I was thinking about Trent.

And then it happened. I got up to use the bathroom, and when I came out, Sam was leaned against the back side of the couch waiting for me near the hallway. I froze in the hallway, not sure what to do. Was I ready? He sauntered up to me and pulled me to him, kissing me softly.

"I'm not really into this movie anymore. What about you?" Sam whispered into my ear, then ran the tip of his tongue along the edge of my ear lobe.

I wrapped my arms around his thick neck. "I wasn't really into it from the beginning," I said. I was going for it. It was going to be great, and it was going to change everything. It had to. I just had to ignore the mildly empty feeling in the pit of my stomach.

Sam scooped me up in his arms and carried me back to my room. He reached over and flicked on the light switch as soon as he crossed the threshold. I reached back over and swiped the switch off.

"No lights?" Sam asked.

I didn't think I could handle lights tonight. Not yet. I was nervous enough as it was, and lights just made it worse. "No lights."

"Why?" he asked as he lowered my feet to the floor beside the bed.

"It's too distracting," I said. It wasn't entirely untrue.

"Fine. But next time, I want lights," Sam bargained.

Next time? He was already thinking about next time? "Deal," I said.

Sam leaned into me, and I backed up onto the bed. He climbed over top of me and kissed me. It wasn't the way Trent kissed me. It wasn't urgent, or hungry, or passionate. It was…mechanical. His technique was adequate, but there wasn't any fire behind it. He pulled away from me briefly to take his shirt off, so I took that opportunity to slip mine off as well. When he returned to me, he kissed me once, then wrapped his arm around me and rolled onto his back, pulling me on top of him.

I didn't want to be on top, but I tried to go along with it. I straddled his hips and kissed him again. I felt him pushing me away gently, so I sat back, trying to figure out what he wanted me to do.

"Let me look at you," he whispered. He reached up and lifted my bra, pushing it up awkwardly toward my neck. I quickly reached up and unhooked it, slipping it off. He ran his hand from the center of my chest all the way down my stomach to the waistband of my jeans. "God, your body is so tight. Look at those abs," he admired.

"Oh. Uh, thanks. It is kind of my job," I said with a forced giggle.

Sam unbuttoned my jeans, then sat up. He flipped me around onto my back again. I wasn't used to being moved around like this. It wasn't bad, it was just…different. He slipped my jeans off me and lowered his – but he didn't take them off all the way. He just pulled them down to his thighs. I heard him opening a wrapper, and I waited for him to roll on the prophylactic.

When he climbed on top of me again, I felt his manhood press against me – and it felt so wrong that it made my stomach turn.

"No, wait. No. Jesus, I'm so sorry. I can't do it," I cried as I scooted out from under him. I felt tears welling up in my eyes. Oh god, don't cry. Don't cry. Don't cry.

"What? Seriously? What's wrong?" Sam asked, flabbergasted.

"I'm not ready. I'm not ready for this yet. I'm so, so sorry," I apologized profusely.

Sam sighed as he pulled his pants up. "It's him, isn't it?" he asked knowingly. "The skinny weirdo in the hipster suit with the stupid hair. Trent," he said mockingly.

"I'm just not ready yet."

"I don't get it, Roselyn. What does he have that I don't? I seriously do not get it."

"I just need some time, Sam. I'll get there, I promise."

"No, you won't. As long as he's around, you won't."

Sam got up and stood next to the bed. He bent down and grabbed my jeans and underwear off the floor and handed them to me. I thanked him quietly and pulled them on.

"I'm trying, Sam," I said.

"You shouldn't have to try this hard," he replied sourly. "I never had a chance, did I?"

I chose not to answer him. I climbed off the bed on the opposite side from him and picked up his shirt from the floor. I tossed it across the bed to him and started searching for my bra.

"Hey, is my bra over there?" I asked embarrassedly when I couldn't find it on my side.

"I didn't see it. Get the light. I'll check under the bed over here."

I stepped over to the light switch and flicked it on, then crossed my arms self-consciously over my bare breasts.

"Oh, here it is," I heard Sam say from under the bed. Then, "What the heck is this?"

"What?"

Sam stood up, holding my bra in one hand, and a watch in the other. A look of realization crossed his features. He gave me a knowing look. "This is the watch he was looking for, isn't it? Hm, I wonder how it ended up under your bed," Sam said accusingly. He looked down at it, still holding my bra in his other hand, and wiped his finger over the face of it.

And then he disappeared – with my bra.

Chapter 17

"Sam!" I shrieked. Oh shit oh shit oh shit oh shit—

I heard my phone going off in the other room. I didn't even grab a shirt before I ran out to answer it. It was Trent.

"He disappeared!" I shouted into the phone frantically. "He found the watch, and it took him!"

Trent was in my living room instantly. He looked at me, looked down, and slapped his hands over his eyes. "Ah! Sorry! I didn't know you weren't decent!"

I grabbed his hands and pulled them down, all sense of modesty gone out the window. "Forget that! The watch took Sam! He's gone! We need to find him!"

"Yes, I got that! I saw the signal on my watch. Now please, go put a shirt on! I'll find him." Trent looked down at his watch, then back up at me. "I'm kind of relieved, to be honest. I was really starting to worry about what had happened to that wa—"

"You can be relieved after we get him back home!" I shouted down the hall as I ran quickly to my room to snatch my shirt.

"'We'?"

I threw my shirt over my head, running back down the hall while still putting it on, and I bumped blindly into Trent. I grabbed his arms. "Yes, 'we'! Let's go!"

"Hold on a tick! Who said you were going?"

"I did. You're wasting time, come on!"

"I'm not going to talk you out of this, am I?"

"No."

Trent sighed heavily as he walked past me down the hall to the bedroom. I saw him take a sideways glance at the rumpled bedding when he entered the room, but he didn't say anything. He looked down at his watch and moved around the room, like he was following a compass. He walked over to where Sam had disappeared and stopped.

"The trail's still fresh. Come on, we can follow him."

I threw my arms around Trent's torso, and we were teleported to – a familiar savannah-like landscape.

"Are...Are we in the Jurassic again?"

"We are," Trent said, looking down at his watch. "That's odd. This is almost exactly the time that we—OH!" Trent pointed at me with wide eyes.

"Wha—OH! Oh!" I threw my hand over my mouth as I put it together. "It was him! Sam was the man in the Jurassic!"

Trent laughed and threw his hands up. "Mystery solved!"

I looked around. "But...where'd he go?"

Trent looked down at his watch. "He teleported again. From over there," Trent said as he pointed off to his right. "We just missed him."

I followed him to the location Sam had teleported from, and I found my bra sitting on the ground.

"Oh, thank god. It was my favorite one," I said as I picked it up and shook it off. I then proceeded to put it on under my shirt while Trent looked on with one raised eyebrow. "What?" I asked defensively.

"Nothing. I'm not saying anything," he said, holding his palms up to me.

Trent and I followed Sam's trail and tracked him to a busy sidewalk. A woman wearing a weirdly baggy, pink sweater stopped abruptly and gasped as she almost ran into us.

"Sorry!" Trent said, looking up. "That was a farther drop than I thought it would be!" Trent ushered me away quickly while the woman looked up to where Trent had been looking, trying to figure out where we had jumped from.

"Is that how you explain it when you land in busy places?" I asked as we rounded the street corner.

"Sometimes. Sometimes I just act like it's a part of a magic trick. And sometimes I just run. Why do you think I'm such a matchstick? All the running!"

"Where are we going?" I asked. "Where did we end up?" I noticed everybody was wearing ugly baggy clothing, and a lot of women had shaved heads.

"We are in Germany, 2462. I'm not getting a signal. I don't think Sam has transported out of here yet, but I have no idea where he is. We'll have to find him the good old-fashioned way, I guess."

"He couldn't have gone too far," I reasoned.

"Well, he probably had about a thirty-minute head-start on us."

"Oh. Well, shit."

"Where would he go?" Trent asked me.

"How the hell should I know?"

"You know him."

"Yeah, but not that well. Not well enough to be able to guess where he would go."

"Well, you know him well enough to let him carry your bra around."

"Shut it," I said, jutting a finger at him.

"Maybe we should check out the nearest gyms. When people panic, they head for familiar territory," Trent said, half-joking.

"Oh! A bar! Maybe he'd go to a bar!" I suggested.

"Really? A bar is familiar territory for him?"

"He's a bartender! Hell, I think anyone would seek out a place to drink in this situation."

"Oh wait! He's moved again," Trent said, looking down at his watch and holding his finger up to halt me. "Oh, bugger. We'd better hurry. The trail is across town."

With all this running, I was glad I had found my bra.

When we made it to the next trail, Trent said, "It's growing faint. If we fall too far behind him, we'll lose him. Just imagine the kind of damage he could do to Earth's timeline bumbling around with a device he doesn't understand. We need to hurry."

When we teleported this time, we landed in what appeared to be a big aquarium. I looked at the tanks around us, and while there were some familiar creatures, such as sharks and octopi, there were also creatures I had never seen before. Creatures that didn't look of this world. As I turned around to see the tanks behind me, I saw a sight I never thought I would see outside of a movie theater. There was a family admiring the sharks in a tank – but it wasn't an ordinary family. They weren't people. They were anthropomorphic, but they weren't human. They appeared to be…alien. They were quite short, only about four feet tall, and they had blueish colored skin. They had freakishly large, gold-colored eyes, and when they turned those eyes toward me, I quickly looked over at Trent. He was staring at them also, his eyes wide.

I elbowed him. He looked at me and a huge grin spread across his face. "Something new!" he whispered in wonderment. "I love new things!"

"Where the hell are we?!" I asked. "Are we still on Earth?!"

"Yes!" He looked down at his watch. "But we are way beyond where I have ever been. This is 5211!" He rubbed his fingers together and looked around eagerly, as though he were trying to decide what to investigate first.

"Focus, Trent! We need to find Sam. He's probably freaking the hell out right about now."

"Oh! Right!" Trent looked down at his watch again. "Well, he hasn't left yet."

"Why would he stay here? Why wouldn't he have tried to teleport out of here right away?"

"He's probably getting scared he's going to end up somewhere even weirder. There are two kinds of panic, Roselyn. The frantic kind, and the shut-down kind. It looks like Sammy may be experiencing the shut-down kind."

"Is that a good thing or a bad thing?"

"That's a good thing. If he starts mashing buttons on that watch in a frantic panic, who knows what will happen. If he just stops and freezes up, we've got a much better chance of finding him. Now, come on. Let's explore – carefully. He might still be in here."

I hooked my arm through Trent's and walked alongside him through the aquarium. I marveled at the strange creatures in the tanks and the even stranger creatures walking around the aquarium with us. There were plenty of people in the aquarium too, but they weren't like the people I was used to seeing. Everyone was unusually similar and unusually perfect. Everyone had skin the color of caramel, and everyone had short hair. Men and women both wore similarly styled, extremely form-fitting clothing. They reminded me of the synsuits from Trent's time, except they didn't cover from head to toe, they were more colorful, and made of a thinner material. Trent and I stood out like a sore thumb, and we got a lot of strange looks.

There were almost as many of the little blue people with the gold eyes as there were humans. They dressed like the people did, apparently sharing the same fashion preferences. I wondered how much of the culture was shared between the humans and the little people. I wondered where these little creatures had come from. Were they alien? Were they a species of Earth? Were they some other kind of creation entirely? I wanted to query Trent for his thoughts on the subject, but I noticed that no one in the building was talking. I heard a giggle or a sneeze or a cough here and there, but no one was talking. I would catch people nodding and smiling at each other, as though they were having some kind of private conversation, but no words were passing their lips.

Once we made it all the way through the aquarium and determined that Sam wasn't in the building, Trent was ready to see the world outside. He had spent a lot of his time in the aquarium staring at his watch rather than looking at the exhibits and the animals, and he seemed eager to share something with me. When we walked outside, though, we found it to be eerily silent out there, too. Birds weren't singing. People weren't talking. The streets were filled with small, pod-like vehicles that were quietly floating a few inches off the ground on some kind of track. Life was bustling all around us, but it sounded like we were in a monestary. I looked up at Trent for answers.

He raised his eyebrow at me and smiled. He pulled a device out of his pocket, and I recognized it as the translator he had given me when we had gone to his time. He took my hand and opened my palm. He set the device in my hand and then used the watch on it the same way he had used the watch on my phone when he programmed it to call the past. When he was done, he gestured for me to put it in my ear. I placed it in my ear and Trent reached over and tapped it.

My world was suddenly filled with sound. Advertisements blared at me from unseen solicitors while music played in the background, and I could hear a robotic woman's voice notifying me that I had message requests. I looked at Trent with wide eyes. I pulled the device out of my ear, overwhelmed by the sudden sensory overload. Trent took the translator from my hand and stuck it in his own ear. He listened for a moment, then held his watch up to his ear, apparently making programming adjustments.

When he was done, he grinned and whispered, "This is really quite brilliant, but it's only half of the sensory unit. You need the eyepiece, too."

"How do you know all this? Have you been here before?" I asked.

"No. I've been collecting data," Trent answered.

He slipped on his glasses and activated the holographic display on his watch. It showed a screen similar to what you'd see on an internet browser – several tabs open to messenger-like applications, advertisements, sound options, and captions and links displayed over everything we could see through the hologram. It was real-time internet and social media, basically.

I leaned closer to Trent, noticing the people staring at us. It was probably unusual for them to see people actually talking to each other. I whispered as quietly and discreetly as I could, "Sam isn't going to have any idea what the hell is going on. He's going to look like a crazy person to these people."

"All the easier for us to find him, then," Trent said. He tapped the device in his ear and started manipulating the display on his watch.

"What are you doing?" I asked.

"Searching."

Trent started walking down the absurdly clean and smooth sidewalk, still focused on his watch. I walked alongside him and tried to keep him from running into the little people that were below his line of vision.

"Aha!" he shouted suddenly.

Everyone around us turned and looked at him. He cringed and held his hand up with an apologetic smile. When everyone turned away again, he took off across the street at a rapid pace, and I had a hard time keeping up with him without running. He weaved through the people on the sidewalk, his eyes darting from his watch display to his surroundings and back again. He reminded me of a bloodhound hot on the trail of a wanted criminal.

Finally, he stopped. So abruptly, in fact, that I ran right into him. I looked up at him, and saw he was pointing. I followed the direction of his finger with my eyes and saw Sam standing among a group of people, trying to talk to them. He waved his hands around, gesturing wildly, apparently assuming that they either couldn't hear him or didn't understand him. They all looked at him curiously, but no one was speaking to him. They just stared. Some of them were smiling in amusement at his behavior. Trent grabbed my hand and we rushed to Sam.

When he saw us approaching, he looked briefly relieved, then angry. "What the hell is going on?!" he demanded.

Trent shushed him as he deactivated the holographic display on his watch. He then snatched up Sam's arm and inspected his wrist, and I saw that Sam was wearing the watch he had found under my bed. He quickly unhooked it and pulled it off Sam's wrist.

"Don't shush me! What are you doing?!"

Without responding, Trent grabbed Sam and me and pulled us in close to him, as though we were going in for a huddle. We were instantly back in my bedroom. Trent turned and walked out of the room without a word, looking down at his watch and the watch he had taken from Sam.

I looked over at Sam hesitantly. "So...the dinosaurs were cool, hey?"

Sam stared at me like I had lost my damn mind. "What was that?! Where was I? What the hell did that watch do?!"

"Ok, calm down. I'll explain. Um...ok...where do I begin? You were time traveling. You went to the Jurassic. You saw Trent and me there, actually. Well, not us from right now, but us from a few weeks ago. It was me before you met me. But that's a whole different story for another time. Anyway, you then went into the future. The last place we were in was...what, like three thousand years from now I think? I don't remember. It was something like that."

"...What?!"

"The watch is a time-travel device. Trent has one that he created a long time ago – well, in the future, but a long time ago to him – oh! And it's also a teleportation device. He can go anywhere or anywhen."

"Anywhen isn't a word!" Sam shouted, extending his arms dramatically. "None of this makes any sense!"

"Anywhen most certainly is a word," Trent said from the doorway. I turned and saw him leaning casually against the door jamb. He slid his glasses off and stuck them in his breast pocket. "And it all makes perfect sense."

"You just aren't quite there yet," I added.

Sam pointed at Trent and me. "You're both completely insane. I don't want any part of this!" He brushed past me and bumped Trent's shoulder roughly on his way out of the bedroom.

"Wait!" I shouted, following after him. "Don't you have questions?"

Sam stopped and turned. "Yeah, I do have a question: can I leave now?!"

I knitted my brow. "That's it? Really? You aren't even the slightest bit curious about what just happened?"

"I don't need to know! I just want to forget it, ok? And I never want to see you again. This has been the absolute worst day I've ever had, and that's saying a lot. Goodbye, Roselyn."

"Sam!" I said, reaching for him.

Trent grabbed my arm and stopped me. "Let him go," he said calmly.

Sam looked at us. "Yeah, listen to your boyfriend," he said snidely. He slipped his coat on, and as he walked out the door into the night, he added, "And lose my number."

I couldn't say I blamed him. I didn't understand how he couldn't be curious about what he'd just experienced, but I couldn't blame him for not wanting to have any part of it. I couldn't blame him for not wanting to see me again, especially after what had happened between us before he had found the watch under the bed. I wouldn't want to see me again either. I wasn't particularly upset about it, but I would be lying if I said it didn't hurt my feelings just a little bit. Sam wasn't a bad guy. He just wasn't the right guy for me, and that was now more obvious than ever. I couldn't be with someone who lacked imagination and curiosity. I couldn't be with someone who wouldn't be able to eventually accept that my life was a little bit...exciting.

"I'm sorry," Trent said softly.

"Sorry for what? You didn't do anything."

"I was careless. If I hadn't lost the watch under the bed, none of this would've happened."

"Yeah, well, the watch wouldn't have gotten lost under the bed if I hadn't invited you into my room that night, but I don't regret doing that."

"So…did Sam find the watch in the same manner that I lost it?" Trent asked.

"Um…"

"Sorry, that's none of my business," Trent said, holding a palm up to stop me from responding.

"It didn't happen," I blurted.

"Beg pardon?"

"I didn't…I didn't go through with it. I couldn't do it."

"Oh." Trent sounded almost pleased.

"It just didn't feel right. I'm beginning to think that maybe you have ruined me," I said, trying to make it sound like a joke, but finding a great deal of truth in those words.

Trent didn't laugh. He smiled dryly and said, "You'll find someone. He just wasn't right for you."

"Evidently. If he can't handle a little bit of unexpected time travel, then obviously he just can't hang with us."

"Am I a problem, Roselyn?" Trent asked suddenly.

"What do you mean?"

"Am I screwing up your life?"

I scowled at him. "Don't you dare. Don't even think about it. If you care about me, you won't even think about leaving again."

"Just because you care about someone doesn't mean you should stick around and screw up their life."

"Too late for that. That ship has sailed. I can't go back to a time before you shattered my narrow view of the world. I can't go back to a time before you showed me what real passion felt like. You've already destroyed any chance I have at being happy with a normal life. You have already planted yourself firmly in my heart, whether either of us intended for it to happen or not. So, yeah, if you care about me, you will stick around and continue to screw up my life – because I kind of love it."

Trent laughed softly.

"Ok?" I asked, looking for an indication that he understood me.

"Ok," he said with a smile.

"Guess what?" I asked in a playful tone, trying to lighten the mood.

"What?"

"I bought toaster pastries," I said with a big grin as I rushed into the kitchen and threw open the cupboard. I pulled out one of the noisy, crinkly packages and tossed it to Trent. "And wine! But that's for me," I added as I grabbed a goblet. When I passed the sink on the way to the fridge, I noticed the dirty dishes I had left in the sink. Then I saw the roses still sitting there. Tossed aside. Abandoned. Forgotten. All of this before they had even begun to wilt.

Like Sam.

I felt immediately guilty. I should be more upset about losing him, but all I felt was relief. I had thought I could make it work with him, but as soon as he had walked out that door, all I could think about was how much more time I could spend with Trent now. I knew I'd have to find someone eventually, but…not just yet. That could wait. I grabbed the roses and tossed them into the trash.

I poured myself a huge, brimming goblet of wine and sat down on the couch across from the chair where Trent was sitting with his toaster pastries. I brought the bottle with me.

"That place we visited – the one way into the future – that was absolutely wild," I said.

Trent raised his eyebrows. "I know!" he exclaimed, a few crumbs of pastry flying from his mouth in his enthusiasm.

"What were those little blue people?" I asked.

"I don't know! They weren't like anything I've ever seen before! I tried to scan one of them discreetly when we were in the aquarium, but they were far too wary of us. All I was able to pick up was that they aren't DNA-based life forms. Whether they were synthetically created life or alien life is still unclear."

"Why did all the human people look the way they did? Why was everybody so…similar?"

"I'm not sure. People don't look like that in my time. I'm guessing maybe they've created synthetic bodies and that just happens to be the 'style' they chose. In my time, they regrow tissue that becomes damaged or old, but maybe they've replaced that system with synthetic bodies. They would be much more durable, I imagine, and it would make it easier to link them all together through a common network."

"It was like they were living in Facebook."

"Basically, yes."

I took a big gulp of wine and looked at the smile on Trent's face. "You had fun in the future, didn't you?"

"It was wildly exciting!"

"Are you going to go back?"

"Oh, no, I can't do that. I had to go to retrieve Sam, and that was the only reason I went."

"The world didn't fall into chaos. Don't you think you could venture into the future just a little bit? Just occasionally?"

"It's a bad idea. We've discussed this."

"I know. But some of the best ideas are bad ones," I said. "You've obviously never been a rebellious teenager."

"No, not really. Not in the way you were. But I do know plenty about rebellion and bad ideas – I'd even venture to say I've had more experience with bad ideas than you have."

"Oh yeah?" I challenged. I finished my glass of wine and poured another while Trent looked on.

"Yeah. And hanging out with you is on the top of that list," Trent teased.

I laughed. "If you're waiting for me to contradict you, you're going to be waiting a while." I took a drink. "But you like it."

"Yeah, I kind of do," he admitted with a grin.

"Seriously, though, Trent. You should really start thinking about the future."

He laughed out loud. "I feel like you're about to give me a talk about savings accounts."

I laughed. "I'm just trying to point out that you've already been to the year 5000-something, so you already know what's going to happen then. What's wrong with going back and sight-seeing?"

"I don't know what happens. I just got a small snippet of it. There's still a whole lot of damage that could be done if I went back."

"If you do, then change it! If you have to actively stop SABER from going back in time and changing things, then obviously it's something that can be done. The past can be changed, and so can the future."

"Yes, it can be changed. But you never know what you are changing. You never know what the outcome will be…and I shouldn't be the one to decide what to change."

"You decide to stop SABER. Doesn't the very act of stopping them from changing things change things?"

"Yes, in a way, but it's a corrective change – like if someone nudges a steering wheel and you nudge it back. I'm not actively picking out the route."

"Then who is?"

"Humankind. Not SABER, and certainly not Trent Morgan," he said. "No one person should have that power. I think that's what scares me most – seeing a future that I want to change, knowing I have the capability to change it, but also knowing that I shouldn't. It's hard enough wrestling with the moral ambiguity of keeping the past unchanged. I don't need to have the future on my conscience, too."

"You're kind of like a god," I said.

"No, I'm not. I don't want to be a god."

"I want to be a god."

"I think you should slow down on the wine."

"…I think you're right."

Chapter 18

Trent got up and coaxed the glass from my hand, but not before I downed the rest of its contents. He grabbed the bottle off the floor next to the couch and took it into the kitchen.

"This bottle is almost empty," he chided.

"I only had two glasses," I said defensively.

"Two fish bowls is more like it," he mumbled.

A few moments later I heard dishes clanking. I craned my neck and looked over into the kitchen.

"What are you doing?"

"Nothing." I could see him putting dishes in the dishwasher.

"I was going to do that," I said.

"You do it wrong. How do you always do this wrong?" He was pulling things out and rearranging everything I had in the dishwasher.

"Dude, just leave it," I said.

He stopped and looked at me indignantly. "Did you just call me dude?!"

I laughed. "Sorry. Kind sir, please leave it."

Trent nodded his head approvingly. "That's better. But no. I must remedy this atrocity."

"You're cleaning up dishes I dirtied while having a date with someone else. Doesn't that bother you? Even a little?"

"I'm not your boyfriend."

"I know, but...don't you ever think about it? What it would be like if you were my boyfriend?" I leaned my head back against the couch and closed my eyes as I talked. My eyelids were suddenly heavy.

"I try not to."

"Why?"

"There's no point to it. It isn't going to happen, so why think about it?"

"You know what I think? I think it would be a lot like it already is. I think you and I are already bound to each other. It masquerades as friendship, but we both know what it really is. We're just trying to put off the inevitable."

The silence in the kitchen lasted so long that I had actually started to drift off to sleep. I was startled awake when I heard Trent say, "When you find someone, it won't feel this way anymore."

"Hm? Feel what way?" I was trying to remember what we had been talking about before I fell asleep. The wine was fogging my memory.

I heard Trent sigh. "Never mind. You should go to bed."

"I should."

Trent came into the living room and handed me a large glass of water. "Drink this first, though."

"Why?"

"It'll keep you from getting dehydrated and having a headache in the morning."

"I'm not going to get a hangover from two glasses of wine."

"Just drink it. Doctor's orders."

I grabbed the glass from him and chugged it. I wiped my mouth on my sleeve and handed him back the empty glass. "Happy?"

"You can thank me later," he said as he took the glass back to the kitchen.

I stood up and stretched my arms, yawning. "I'm going to bed. I'm beat."

"Goodnight," Trent said as he shut off the lights in the kitchen and stepped back into the living room. He stood there with his hands in his pockets, looking at me. I could tell something was on his mind.

"Did I say something?" I asked. "You look like I killed your kitten."

"Eh, don't worry about it. I'll check in tomorrow and maybe we'll talk then."

I felt a sudden tightness in my chest. "What do you mean we'll talk then? Is there something we need to talk about?"

Trent looked down at the floor instead of at me. "I think maybe. But this isn't the time."

"No, don't do that. Don't do that shit," I said angrily. "Now I'm worried and I won't be able to sleep and I'll sit up all night fretting over what you want to talk about with me. You might as well just spill it now."

"I can't yet."

"Why?"

"Because I'm not sure what it is I want to say yet."

"Give me something, Trent," I begged with watery eyes.

"I'd rather have this conversation when you have a clear head. I'll see you tomorrow. Goodnight." Trent held up his watch.

"Trent, wait!"

It was too late, though. He was already gone.

"Damn it!" I shouted. "Goddamn it, Trent!"

I lay awake in bed for what felt like hours, my mind coming up with all kinds of heartbreaking scenarios. He was going to leave me, wasn't he? That had to be it. What else could it be? What had I said to him that had changed his demeanor so drastically tonight? I couldn't remember. It couldn't have been that bad, could it? If I'd said anything too outrageous it seems like I would've remembered it, even if I had been tired and tipsy. But obviously something had struck a nerve.

I spent my entire Sunday morning waiting. Every time the floor creaked or the cat jumped off the furniture, my heart leapt into my throat and I whirled around, expecting to see him standing there. But he didn't come. By lunchtime, I was starting worry. Was he coming at all today? I tried to call him, but he didn't answer. He was a time traveler – he had no excuse to keep me waiting. But I waited, and he didn't come. I ate dinner and paced around the house all evening. But he didn't come. I watched the clock on the wall tick over to midnight. He was officially a day late. Something was wrong. Something had to be wrong.

I hardly slept at all that night, and I went into work on Monday morning looking like a train wreck. I was distracted all day by my own thoughts, and I had a hard time focusing on my clients. Where was he? Why hadn't he shown up? Why wasn't he answering his phone? What had happened to him?

On the ride home, a terrible thought occurred to me. What if he'd changed after he left me Saturday night? What if that's where he was – lying on a floor somewhere, unconscious, changing. What if I had lost the Trent I loved? What if he had forgotten me, and I was never going to see him again? Then again, what if he didn't forget me, but he didn't want to come back? What if he thought I wouldn't love him the same? Would he really just leave me out on a ledge like this? Would he deny me closure? Would he deny me the opportunity to try to love the new him? I couldn't bear to think about it.

After my shower, I went into my room to get dressed, but instead I climbed into bed. I was exhausted, and I was a nervous wreck. I just wanted to close my eyes and enjoy the numbing relief sleep provided. I pulled my blankets up over my head to shut out the evening light filtering in through my curtains. I must've been more worn out than I had realized, because it wasn't long before I was teetering on the edge of sleep, my mind halfway dipped into a dream.

I suddenly felt the blankets being pulled down off of my face, and my eyes opened slightly. When I saw a face looking down at me, my fist reflexively shot out at it before I registered who it was that was looking down at me. I punched Trent right between the eyes.

He leapt back with his hands over his face. "Bloody hell!"

I sat up in bed, but quickly remembered that I never did get dressed after my shower. I pulled my covers up over my bare breasts.

"Jesus, Trent! Are you ok?!"

"Damn. I'm usually pretty quick, but you still got me." He walked over and looked in the mirror. "Well, at least there isn't any blood."

"Are you going to have a black eye?"

"No, I don't get black eyes. I heal much more rapidly than the average person." He turned back to me and approached my bedside. "What are you doing in here? You never go to bed this early. Are you feeling all right?"

I ignored his questions. "Where the hell have you been?!" I demanded angrily. I had been so worried about him that now that he was here, it manifested as anger.

"What do you mean? I was only gone for a couple of days."

"You didn't answer when I called!"

"I was busy."

"So busy you couldn't let me know everything was ok?"

"Why are you so cross with me?" Trent asked, bewildered.

"I thought you'd left me!" I cried, my eyes reddening.

"Why would you think that? It was only a couple of days!"

"A couple of days means a lot more to me than it does to you! I think you forget that! I only have so many days – I don't get an endless supply like you do. And I don't want any more of them wasted without you in them, you jerk!"

Trent's expression softened. He reached out and used his thumb to wipe away the tear that had started to roll down my cheek.

"I'm sorry. I didn't realize."

"It didn't help that you left me the other night saying we needed to talk, and everybody knows that 'we need to talk' is never a good thing. So, I've been a jumble of nerves worried about you and worried about us and I haven't been sleeping well and—"

Trent's lips were suddenly against mine, silencing me. I could feel my anger and anxiety melting away. God, how I had missed those lips. I threw my arms around his neck, dropping the covers I had been holding up around me.

When the kiss concluded, Trent glanced down. "You're naked!"

"Don't act so scandalized. It's nothing you haven't seen before." I reached out and tugged gently on his tie, encouraging him to join me on the bed. He sat down on the side of the bed and turned toward me with one foot still on the floor.

He looked down at the bed. "Is it terrible that knowing that I wasn't the last man in this bed fills me with jealousy?"

"No. But don't let it bother you too much. You might not have been the last one to be in this bed, but you were the last man for everything else."

Trent looked down at his hands. "Is it terrible that I wish I could be the only man?"

I felt my heart flutter.

"I thought you wanted me to find someone else?" I said questioningly.

"I thought I did, too."

I paused. "Trent, what are you saying?"

"I've been thinking about what you said. You were right. The way we're going on right now...there's really no point in denying it, is there?"

"...What did I say?"

Trent gave me a puzzled look. "When you said we were bound to each other, and our friendship isn't really just friendship. You don't remember that?"

"Oh, yes. That. Of course." I didn't remember saying that. I had felt that way for a long time, but I never meant to say it.

"You were right."

"Wait, what are you saying, exactly?"

Trent reached over and took my hand in his, looking at me with soulful eyes. "Roselyn Wolff, I love you. I love you like I've never loved anyone. I've loved you since I first met you two hundred years ago, and you've stuck in my heart through every change ever since. I waited all that time, knowing I would get to be with you again – knowing that someday perhaps you would fall in love with me, when I bore a different face. I never told you this, but as time passed, I checked in on you. I wasn't trying to be creepy. I wasn't stalking you, and I only did it a handful of times. I just...needed to see you. You never noticed me, and that was the way I wanted it to be. I knew eventually I would be called to you and you would notice me this time. But the more I thought about it – the older I got, and the more jaded I became – I began to realize that I wasn't what you needed. I decided that if I loved you, I needed to let you go. And I tried to. I really did. But, dammit, my heart has just refused to let you go completely. So now I put it in your hands. What do you want, Roselyn? What do you need from me? Is this a life you can live with? Do you want more? Do you want less? What do you want?"

I was speechless. I'd heard Trent talk about love in regard to me before, but this was the first time he'd ever explicitly told me he loved me. I looked away and wiped my eyes.

"If this isn't what you want, I understand," Trent said dejectedly.

I turned back to him. "Haven't you been paying even the slightest attention? Jesus, Trent. Yes, this is a life I can live with. I want more. I want everything you have to offer, the good and the bad. I want it all! That's what I've been asking for this entire time!" I leaned over and kissed him. "It's about time you finally asked me what I wanted."

Trent smiled against my lips. "Then I guess there's just one more thing to ask you then." He pulled the watch that he had stolen from the parallel world out of his pocket – the one that had caused all the ruckus with Sam. He held it out to me. "Roselyn...run away with me."

I threw my hand over my mouth. "You...you're giving it to me?"

"I am giving you everything I have. All of time and all of me. Now you will always be able to find me no matter where or when I am. No force on Earth will be able to keep us apart."

"But...what if I screw something up?"

230

"Don't worry. I've repaired it and reprogrammed it. It's basically got 'training wheels' programmed into it right now, and I'll work with you on it."

I gently took the watch from him. "I don't know what to say."

"Say yes."

My heart soared. I touched my forehead to his and nodded. "Yes. Of course, yes."

Trent grinned happily at me. "So, is there anywhere or anywhen you want to go first?"

I started to unknot his tie. "I just want to be right here, right now – with you."

As Trent leaned over me and kissed me, his hands exploring the body that now belonged to him and him alone, the watch he had given me slipped unnoticed from my hand and clattered under the bed.

I've never looked back.

Book 2

A Change of Face

Chapter 1

Life was never the same after Trent Morgan. From the moment
he showed up on my doorstep, everything changed. He'd loved me
in a way no one else ever had – unselfishly and unconditionally. And
now I realized just how much he not only loved me, but how much
he trusted me, too. He had bequeathed me with a power that he alone
had possessed, and though it was a colossal responsibility to bear, I
wanted to do my best to prove to him that I could be trusted to share
his burden.

"I'm afraid I'm going to break the world," I said as I looked down
at the time-warping watch Trent was strapping to my wrist.

"You won't break the world. I'm not giving you free reign of
time. Like I said, I've put safeties in place. You can't go anywhere

too important." Trent looked at me and smiled. "And I'll be right there by your side."

"So where am I going?"

"Any requests?" Trent asked.

"Well, I've always been curious about what early humans were like."

He gave me a hesitant look. "Let's start small, shall we?"

"Ok. Hmm…can I go see the hanging gardens of Babylon?"

Trent rubbed his chin. "Yes, that should do nicely." He held a finger in the air and added, "Fun fact: they aren't actually in Babylon. They were in Nineveh, about three hundred miles north of Babylon. The confusion arose later on when the Greeks and Romans wrote about them because Nineveh was referred to as New Babylon after Babylon was conquered by the Assyrian empire."

"…Yeah, ok. So how do I do this?"

"There are historians who would be drooling over definitive proof of this. Your lack of reverence concerns me," Trent said with a raised eyebrow.

"Sorry. History was never really my thing."

"Well, it had better become your thing if you're going to be using this device."

"I'd really rather see the far future, but you won't let me do that."

"You'll be able to explore some of the future, in due time. We'll get there. Baby steps."

I changed out of my jeans and t-shirt into a dress I had in my closet that Trent assured me was a little more appropriate for the time. It wasn't perfect, but he said it would garner me fewer strange looks. Then Trent showed me how to manipulate the watch to change the time and location. He demonstrated how to adjust the other settings, such as conditional, if/then programming (if the destination is underwater, then the landing location should be moved to the nearest place above the water, etc), and he showed me the settings I was never to change (if the destination falls half within and half outside of a building, then the landing location will be slightly adjusted so I don't end up stuck in a wall – things like that).

"Are you ready?" he asked with his hand on my shoulder.

"Are you?" I replied. "You look more nervous than I do."

"I probably am. But I'm ready."

I looked down at the watch, my finger hovering above the button that would send me to 590 BC. I took a deep breath and looked up at Trent. "See you on the flip side!"

I pressed the button and watched my surroundings change in the blink of an eye. I was standing in an enormous shadow next to a huge column. An overpowering floral scent filled my nostrils. It was so strong it was almost nauseating. My view of the busy stone street was obscured by the column, so I stepped around out from behind it. No one seemed to notice that I had popped out of nowhere, and no one really paid much attention to me. I looked up and realized I was under a massive structure of stone and...roots? I slowly backed out of the shadow of the structure and into the street, and my mouth dropped open.

There they were. Rising into the sky before me were the hanging gardens of...Nineveh? It was like standing at the foot of a lush, green mountain. There were trees and shrubs and flowers in abundance and variety that were unlike anything I had ever seen. It was as overwhelming for the eyes as it was for the olfactory nerves.

"Brilliant, isn't it?" I heard Trent say from behind me.

I turned to him. "It's so much...more than I imagined."

"There's the awe I was looking for. So what do you think? You think history might become your 'thing' after all?"

I grabbed his arms excitedly. "I want to see ancient Egypt! I want to see the Colosseum! I want to see how they built Stonehenge! I want—"

Trent put a finger over my lips to shush me, chuckling. "I'm glad to see your enthusiasm, but one thing at a time. Remember, we can have our little adventures, but I don't want you gallivanting around just anywhen without me. I gave you the watch to give you full access to me – my homes, my life, my world – but it doesn't mean you can use it frivolously. You still need to be exceedingly careful."

I turned away from him and looked back up at the marvel before me. "Yes, sir," I said sarcastically under my breath.

"I heard that."

"I meant for you to."

We walked the perimeter and gazed at the gardens for almost half an hour. I saw a couple of people look askance at us as they passed by, but no one bothered us. When I had seen enough, Trent and I walked around to a relatively quiet space under the gardens. I demonstrated for him that I knew how to adjust the time setting on the watch, setting it for one minute past the time we had left. When he was satisfied that I had done it correctly, he stepped back and gave one last look around to ensure no one was watching.

"See you at home," I said as I pressed the button to send myself back to my own time.

I headed for my bedroom as soon as I was back in my own house so I could change into my regular clothes. I was just slipping off my dress when Trent walked into the room.

"Don't you ever knock?" I asked as I tossed the dress into the closet.

Trent's eyes observed me with a sudden keenness as I walked across the room in my underwear. I grabbed my shirt off of the bed where I had left it.

"I didn't realize I needed to," Trent said as he strode up to me and snatched the shirt from my hands. He leaned close to me. "Are you afraid I might see you naked?" he whispered teasingly into my ear.

His lips brushing the outer ridge of my ear sent pleasant tingles through my entire body. He kissed the side of my neck tenderly as his hands slid down to my waist, pulling me against him.

"As much as I want to, we can't do this right now," I said as I grabbed his hands and lifted them off of my hips.

"Why not?" Trent asked, looking injured.

"My parents are coming today, remember? I still have to clean the bathrooms and vacuum the furniture. And you need to skedaddle."

"Come again? You mean you aren't going to let me meet them?" Trent frowned at me.

"I don't know if they're ready for you yet."

"You still haven't told them about me, have you?" Trent said disappointedly.

"...No."

"Why? Are you...are you embarrassed by me?"

"No! Of course not! It's just that...well...I don't know how to explain you to them."

"What's to explain?"

I gave him an incredulous look. "How about where you're from? What you do for a living? How did we meet? Where do you live? How old are you? Seriously, Trent. These are basic questions, and I have no idea what kind of answer I would give my parents to any of them."

"Just tell them I'm from the UK, I'm a stock broker, and I live in...oh I don't know, any of the neighboring cities around here. Munising. Escanaba. The other end of town. Take your pick."

"How did we meet?"

"At the gym."

"How old are you?"

"How old do I look?" he asked.

I scrutinized him. "I don't know. Thirty-something?"

"Thirty-four? Does that work?"

"I'd believe it."

"Well there. It's settled, then. I'm meeting your parents," he said as he handed me my shirt. He gave me a quick kiss on the forehead and was dashing from the room before I had a moment to think.

"Wait! Where are you going?" I shouted after him. I threw my shirt on and stuck my head out the door. "I didn't agree to that!"

I heard the vacuum roar to life in the living room before I had even finished my last sentence and Cattiel came barreling down the hallway, seeking safety beneath my bed. From the doorway I could see Trent running the vacuum over the couch – the whole vacuum, not just the hose. Well…bless his heart for trying. I slipped my jeans on and went to work cleaning the bathrooms.

I heard the vacuum stop long before I was done with the bathrooms, but Trent never came looking for me. When I had finished the upstairs bathroom, which didn't take long considering it was rarely utilized, I went downstairs to see what Trent was up to. I was surprised to find that the living room and kitchen were spotless and organized. The coffee maker had even been scrubbed. But Trent was nowhere to be found.

"Trent?" I called out. Nothing.

I sighed and put away my cleaning supplies in the hall closet, and as I returned to the kitchen to put together a snack tray for when my parents arrived, Trent suddenly appeared in front of me.

I gasped in surprise and jumped back. "Ugh! I hate it when you do that!" I admonished.

"Rubbish. I keep life exciting," he replied with a smirk.

I noticed he must have left so he could change. He was wearing a suit I'd never seen him in. He usually wore various shades of browns, or an occasional black suit, but today he wore a new gray suit with a black bowtie and shiny black oxfords. It appeared he had also gotten a haircut – it wasn't a lot shorter, and it was still parted on the left side, but it was slicked off to the side and back instead of his bangs hanging down over the right side of his face. He looked sleek and professional rather than eccentric. It wasn't the way I was used to him looking, but I couldn't deny that he looked good. He smiled at me, and it made my heart flutter.

"What do you think?" he asked, extending his arms out away from his sides.

I raised my eyebrows at him. "I think I feel incredibly underdressed now. Why did you do all of this?" I asked as I gestured to his hair and outfit.

"I want to make a good impression with your parents. I've been told I'm not exceedingly skilled at first impressions, and I was hoping this would help."

"Yeah…I was the one who told you that, and I hate to say it, but your clothes were never the culprit."

"You don't like it?" he asked, deflated.

"Oh, I like it. I love it! You look…mmm," I wiggled my eyebrows and grunted rather than using words to describe his new look.

Trent appeared mildly troubled. "I was going for 'respectable,' not 'mmm.'"

I laughed. "Can't it be both?" I asked as I walked past him and opened the fridge. "Besides, I don't remember agreeing to let you meet my parents."

"Oh, come now!" he complained. "How long do you plan to keep me a secret?"

"I'm not keeping you a secret. I just think maybe we should wait a little while, you know? To make sure," I said as I carried several blocks of cheese to the cutting board on the counter.

Trent gave me a suspicious look. "Make sure of what?"

"Well, you know…to make sure this is…going somewhere," I said hesitantly.

Trent scowled. "Are you uncertain of me?"

"I'm not saying that, exactly. I'm just…I mean, what if you change your mind about me?"

"I've loved you for more than two hundred years. Why would I change my mind now?"

"Because now you have me. Sometimes the idea of someone is more appealing than the reality of them."

Trent's scowl deepened. "Is that how you are feeling about me?"

"No! No, of course not! It's not my affections I'm worried about. I just worry that you might, I don't know, get…bored." I turned away from him and reached up into the cupboard to get crackers.

"I would rather be bored and have you than in the midst of chaos without you."

"You say that now, but—"

Trent whirled me around and pulled me to him. He planted his lips firmly on mine, effectively stealing my words away. All I could manage was a feeble whimper.

Suddenly, the front door burst open.

"We're here!" I heard my mother exclaim.

Trent took a quick step away from me, looking at me like a dog who has just been caught stealing food from the table.

I cleared my throat and ran my hand through my long hair. "Hey! You made it! How was the ride?" I asked casually as I went over and gave my parents a hug.

My mother leaned to the side, looking past me at Trent. "Oh, hello!" she said to him. She looked at me again. "I didn't know you were going to have a guest."

"Mom, Dad, this is Trent Morgan. Trent, these are my parents, Nadine and Roger Wolff."

Trent smiled and raised his hand awkwardly in greeting. His appearance said "businessman," but his demeanor still said "madman in a suit." He hurried over and shook both of my parents' hands enthusiastically.

"It's lovely to meet you, Mr. and Mrs. Wolff. I have heard very little about you, but I look forward to getting to know you," he said with a wide smile.

"Oh, well, all right then," my mother said, giving me a questioning look.

"He's kidding," I said with a forced laugh. "Of course I've told him about you."

Trent turned to me. "No, you really haven't," he said innocently.

I grabbed his arm. "Hey, could I get you to go finish that snack tray I was working on?"

"Oh! Yes, I can do that. You want me to slice the cheese, too?" he asked.

"That's probably better than cutting it," my dad joked as he was taking off his shoes.

I closed my eyes and tried not to laugh. "Yes. Off you pop," I said to Trent as I pushed him toward the kitchen.

I helped my parents carry their luggage up to the spare bedroom across from the one Trent had stayed in. As soon as I had put the suitcase down, my mom started in with the questions.

"So, who is Trent? You've never mentioned him. Is he a new boyfriend?"

"Yeah, you could say that."

"Does he live here?"

"No. He lives, um…over in Harvey."

"Where is his car?" my dad asked.

"What?"

"There aren't any other vehicles in the drive," my dad persisted.

"Oh. Yeah. Um…I picked him up. His car is in the shop." My ears were starting to burn. I hated lying.

"Where is he from? You don't usually hear a British accent in the U.P.," my mom wanted to know.

"He's from the UK."

"What brought him to the U.P.?" she asked.

I could feel my palms starting to sweat. "Work. He's a stock broker. Say, maybe we should get back downstairs. I don't want Trent to know we're sitting up here talking about him."

As we headed out the door, my dad pulled me aside briefly. "I just have one more question. Is he kind to you?"

I smiled and nodded. "He's a good man, Dad. He might be awkward and say weird things, but he is always kind to me."

My dad smiled and patted my shoulder. "Good."

I went into the kitchen to see what kind of progress Trent was making with the snack tray. He was just pulling the cracker sleeves from the box. I stood next to him and started rearranging the cheese slices on the porcelain platter.

"What are you doing?" he asked.

"Making it pretty."

"I've already arranged them."

"But they'll look better this way."

"But, see, if you do it that way, then if you want this piece of cheese, you have to dig it out from under that piece of cheese. It should be organized by types of cheese, not all jumbled together," Trent said, holding his hands up and wiggling his fingers to demonstrate "jumbled."

"It looks boring like that, though," I argued.

"It's utter chaos if you do it the other way," he countered.

"Hey, I let you rearrange the dishwasher. Let me rearrange the cheese."

"That's because you pack the dishwasher like a lunatic, just like you're arranging this cheese like a lunatic."

"Just let me do it!"

Trent sighed. "Fine. I hope you enjoy your chaotic cheese," he relented. "Can I at least do the crackers?"

"I don't know. What were you planning to do with them?"

"Never mind. You can do the crackers, too. Is there something else you'd like me to do?"

"Put some coffee on. Please."

I glanced over at Trent as he measured out coffee to put in the coffee maker. Whether we were walking through the Hanging Gardens of Babylon or making snacks in the kitchen, everything was just so comfortable with him. Even when he was being weird and embarrassing me, or when we were bickering over something silly, I still felt at home around him. I smiled to myself thinking about how hard I had fallen for my lanky, eccentric time traveler.

As he closed the lid on the coffee maker and turned it on, his eyes turned to me. He gave me that smile that seemed to shine right into my soul.

My mother walked into the kitchen. "Is there something I can help with?"

I handed her the snack tray. "You can bring these out to the living room."

She looked down and noticed the watch on my wrist. "Oh, is that one of those fitness trackers?"

I glanced down at it. "My Trent tracker?"

"What?" my mom gave me a puzzled look.

"What?" I raised my eyebrows, realizing that what I'd just said would've sounded incredibly strange to her.

My mom gave me an odd look, but didn't press the issue. She headed back out to the living room while I climbed up onto the counter. Trent watched me as I opened the cupboard and reached up onto the top shelf to pull out the porcelain serving dishes that matched my snack tray. I held them out toward him, indicating that he should come and take them from me so I could climb down.

"You know, they make step ladders for things like that," he said as he took the dishes from me.

"This is much more exciting," I replied.

Trent and I brought the serving dishes and cups of coffee out to the living room and sat down next to each other on the couch across from my parents. I saw that my dad had already turned on the television and was watching a documentary on ancient Egypt.

Trent caught a brief snippet of the narrator talking about Hatshepsut, and he mused, "Oh, if only they knew…"

My dad turned to him. "If only they knew what?"

Trent raised his eyebrows at him. "Hm? Oh! If only they knew more about Hatshepsut. That would be great, wouldn't it?"

"At least we aren't watching that silly show about the alien theories. That one kills me," I said.

"What show is that?" Trent asked.

"The one that tries to tie every single aspect of history to some kind of alien involvement," I replied.

Trent frowned. "Do people really have such little confidence in the knowledge and skills of our ancestors?"

"Yes. It's because people these days don't understand what it means to put in hard work and effort to achieve something," my dad grumbled. "They think nothing can be done without computers and heavy machinery."

Trent agreed, "That's true. You'd be surprised at the things that can be accomplished with a whole lot of man power and a few simple fulcrums and levers."

"It wouldn't surprise me one bit. I grew up on a farm. I know what a group of hard-working people can accomplish when they set their mind to it," my dad said.

"Speaking of hard work, Trent," my mom chimed in, "Roselyn tells us that you're a stock broker? How long have you been doing that?"

Trent turned his eyes upward as he fabricated an answer. "Well, I suppose it's been about ten years, now."

"What made you want to get into that?"

"The money, of course."

I laughed uneasily. "Well, at least he's honest," I said ironically.

Trent turned to me. "Isn't that the purpose of a job? For money?"

"Yes, I suppose it is. But sometimes people choose a job because it's what they enjoy doing. Like me, for instance. I love working in physical fitness. I probably could do things that pay more, but I wouldn't be as happy doing it."

"Well, it's a good thing I have a rewarding hobby," Trent said, winking at me.

"And what would that be?" my mom inquired.

"I, uh…I like to travel."

"Oh, that's exciting! Where have you been?"

Trent pressed his lips together and tilted his head slightly. "Pretty much everywhere."

"Have you ever been to Egypt to see the pyramids?" my dad asked.

"Well, yes, but, um," Trent cleared his throat, "not recently."

Trent somehow managed to make it unscathed through the interrogation my parents gave him. As afternoon shifted to evening, my mother and I went to the kitchen to prepare dinner, leaving the men in the living room to watch historical documentaries. It seemed that my father had finally found someone who actually enjoyed talking about history with him.

I stood at the stove and rolled out the dough for flatbread while my mother was at the counter next to me preparing the tzatziki sauce for gyros.

"I like him," my mom whispered to me. "But I must say, I'm a little surprised. He doesn't seem like your type at all."

"Obviously my type wasn't working so great for me."

"You know what I mean. He's...well, he's the exact opposite of what you usually go for. I'm not complaining about that, I'm just wondering what brought you two together."

"I met him at the gym."

My mom gave me a surprised look. "He doesn't look like a gym rat."

"He's not. He just likes to run. He comes for the treadmills sometimes."

"How long have you two been dating?"

"Not terribly long."

"You guys are awfully in sync for two people who haven't been dating long," my mom said, giving me a questioning sideways glance.

"Well, we started off as friends when I first moved here, so it's not like we're total strangers or anything."

"Why didn't you ever mention him?"

"I don't know. I didn't know how long he was going to be around."

"Why? Was he going somewhere?"

"He travels a lot."

"Yeah, he mentioned that. Is that something that's going to be a problem later on down the road?"

"I'm not really too worried about later on down the road yet, Mom," I said in mild annoyance.

"Well, I am. I would like some grandbabies someday, you know."

"You might have to look to Jack for that," I said, referring to my brother. "I'm thinking kids probably won't be in the cards for me."

"Oh, you'll change your mind."

"I don't know about that."

"Does Trent want kids?"

"Mom!"

My mom held her hands up apologetically. "Sorry. I was just asking."

"Well, stop." I started preparing the bacon mushrooms and cayenne chickpeas while my mom cut up the vegetables.

After a few minutes of silence, my mom said, "He obviously thinks the world of you."

"What?"

"Your Trent. I can see it on his face when he looks at you. That boy is smitten."

I laughed. It was amusing to think of six hundred-year-old Trent as a "boy." I turned and looked at him in the living room. He was sitting on the couch with one leg crossed over his other knee, gesturing enthusiastically as he conversed with my dad while Cattiel lay on the cushion next to him. It was such an odd scene to behold. It seemed so...normal. I caught eyes with Trent, and he shot me a quick smile before he continued his conversation with my dad.

Yeah...I was smitten, too.

Chapter 2

That night, as my parents were heading to bed after inflating the air mattress they had brought with them, my mom asked me if I was going to drive Trent home. I had completely forgotten about that particular fabrication, and Trent gave me a questioning look.

"Oh, yeah. I'll have to take him home in a little bit," I said.

"How far away is Harvey?" my mom asked.

"Not far. Only like ten or fifteen minutes."

My parents said goodnight to us and I heard the bedroom door close upstairs.

"What was that about?" Trent whispered.

"They wanted to know where your car was, so I said it was in the shop and I had to pick you up. So now I have to take you home, I suppose."

"Do we really have to get into the car and drive somewhere?" he asked.

"If you want to sell a lie, you have to commit to it," I said.

"Are you the lie expert?" Trent teased. "Can't you just tell them you brought me home later, while they were sleeping?"

"Why don't you want to get in the car with me?" I asked suspiciously.

Trent looked worried. "I've seen the way you drive."

"Hey! That's not fair!" I knew he was referring to the night he showed up at my house when I was in my car after hearing the voices. "What you saw wasn't 'driving.' That was panic and anger!"

"I would hate to see you in a tailback."

"A what?"

"Tailback."

"What the hell is that?"

"You know, when the cars are all backed up on the road."

"You mean a traffic jam."

"Tailback. Traffic jam. Same thing."

"There aren't going to be any traffic jams at ten o'clock at night."

"I didn't say there were."

I sighed. "Fine. You can teleport to wherever you choose. But I still need to get in the car and leave for a bit to make it seem like I'm taking you home. I was just hoping to have some company."

"This all seems very unnecessary," Trent said in exasperation. "Can't I just stay here?"

"No! I don't want my parents thinking you live with me."

"But I did live with you for a while."

"We weren't dating then. It was different."

"Do you think they would disapprove?"

"Yeah, I do."

"Why?"

"Because it's too soon for living together."

"But it wasn't when we were basically strangers?" Trent pointed out.

"You were a roommate then. You had your own room. You paid rent. It was different."

"I don't see how."

"I know you don't. It's just the way things are, ok? You can't stay here while my parents are here."

"I'm beginning to think just telling them the truth would be easier," Trent sighed, running his hands through his hair and messing up the perfectly slicked back style he had maintained all day.

"Absolutely not!" I warned.

He gave me a defeated look, and a small section of his bangs dangled down near the corner of his right eye. God, he was handsome. I leaned over and put my hand on the side of his neck and kissed his lips.

"So...have you ever been 'parking,' Trent?" I whispered into his ear.

He gave me a sly grin. "Are you suggesting we try it?"

"I'm game if you are."

"Get your keys," Trent said as he leapt up and vaulted over the back of the couch.

I drove up the road a short distance to the two-track trail that winds through the woods to the north. I didn't go too far up the trail, though, because it appeared that no one had been back there in a long time and I couldn't tell how deep the snow was in the dark. I put the car in park and climbed into the back seat with Trent.

When we had finished making love, I draped my arms around his neck and leaned my body lazily against his, my face buried in his neck.

"I love you," Trent said softly as he kissed my shoulder.

I smiled blissfully. "I love you, too."

After I got dressed, I sat in the backseat with Trent a little while longer.

"I think my parents liked you," I told him.

"Are you admitting that I actually made a good first impression?"

I laughed. "Yeah, I guess I am. My mom thought it was odd that we were so 'in sync' for having been dating only a short time. If only she knew the things we'd been through together, she'd understand."

"No, if she knew, she'd probably wonder why you haven't run far, far away from me yet."

"Eh, you're probably right." I agreed.

"Am I going to be able to see you tomorrow?" Trent wanted to know.

I gave him an apologetic look. "I should probably spend some time with my parents tomorrow. But I'll see you on Sunday, though."

"That's all right. I can just skip Saturday and go straight to Sunday – the perks of being a time traveler," he said with a grin.

"Or, more likely, you'll spend a week of your time on some kind of side adventure between now and Sunday," I said knowingly.

"That is always a possibility."

Trent kissed me goodbye and opened the door.

"Why are you getting out?" I asked. "Can't you just teleport from here?"

"It's rather awkward to teleport in a sitting position. The landing isn't very graceful. I'm sure you'll make that mistake once or twice."

I grabbed Trent's hand and stopped him from getting out of the car. When he turned to look at me, I put my hand on the nape of his neck and pulled him to me for another kiss. I wished I didn't have to let him out of my sight.

"Don't go getting yourself in trouble, young man," I warned him before releasing him.

Trent laughed. "Now what's the fun in that?" He gave me one last little peck on the lips before stepping out of the car into the snow. "Goodnight, love." He smiled and disappeared.

As I climbed into bed that night, I wondered where he had gone tonight when he teleported. Did he go to the future? The past? I knew that if I really wanted to know, all I had to do was set my watch to sync with his and press a button, and it would take me to his side. But I was still afraid of that watch. I didn't trust myself with it. I wasn't sure if I would ever be comfortable using it, but it was reassuring to know that it was an option if I had to use it.

I was startled from my sleep by what seemed like a bright camera flash in my face. I sprang up in bed and snatched the .45 from my bedside stand before my eyes had a moment to focus. I saw a dark figure standing in the middle of my room, but I couldn't make out who it was. It wasn't a familiar form. I racked a bullet into the chamber and raised my gun, keeping the safety on and finger off the trigger.

"Who is that?! What are you doing in my room?!" I demanded.

As my eyes focused more clearly on the figure, I saw that he was also holding a gun – and it was pointed at me.

"Put the gun down!" A deep, male voice said. A deep, male, English-like voice. "I don't want to hurt you!"

"You put your gun down! You're in my house!" I said firmly. I didn't want to call out to my parents or shout too loudly and wake them. I didn't know what kind of situation this was, and I didn't want to get them involved.

"Are you Roselyn?" the man asked.

"Who's asking?"

Suddenly, Trent burst into the room and threw the light on. I shielded my eyes from the harsh light, but I kept my gun pointed at the other man in the room.

"Roselyn!" Trent shouted, throwing his arm across in front of me, essentially turning himself into a human shield. There was a tense moment of silence as my eyes adjusted to the light. Then I heard Trent say, "Jaeger?"

The man quickly holstered his weapon. "Trent! How the bloody hell are you, mate?"

I blinked in confusion as Trent put his hand on top of my raised gun and guided it into a lowered position.

"It's all right, Roselyn," Trent assured me.

"Who is he?!" I demanded.

"This is Jaeger Novak."

"The 'you' from the parallel world?" I asked in disbelief.

"The very same."

Jaeger gave me a little wave and a crooked smile. He didn't look anything like Trent. He was taller, around 6'1", and he was bulkier – more broad-shouldered. His light brown hair was shorter than Trent's and styled in a mildly spikey manner – a lot like the past version of Trent that I had met when my Trent was trapped in Jaeger's world. His eyes were almost the same hazel-green as Trent's, but his face was completely different. It was a ruggedly handsome face, with a straight nose, symmetrical features, and unusually perfect lips. When he smiled, the corners of his eyes crinkled in a way that made him look incredibly friendly, despite his dusty shirt jacket and torn jeans, five o'clock shadow, and gun strapped to his hip. I didn't know what to make of him – and that made me wary.

"Why doesn't he look like you?" I asked.

"He does, actually. That was what I looked like the first time 'round. He doesn't change, remember?" Trent turned to Jaeger. "How are you here? I mean…at the risk of sounding indelicate…I thought you were dead."

"Except we don't die, do we?" Jaeger said with a grin. "Well, I suppose we could. They thought they'd killed me, and they probably almost did. They injected me with euthanizing chemicals to stop my breathing and stop my heart. It felt like I was dying, and I eventually lost consciousness. I woke up as I was being thrown through the air from an explosion. Oh, and I was on fire."

"Jesus," I said in horror.

"I should thank you for that, Trent." Jaeger said gratefully. "If it hadn't been for your explosives, they probably would've finished the job eventually."

"You were still in the building when Trent set off the bomb?" I asked. "They said they'd killed you. Why would they keep your body around?"

"Maybe they were going to incinerate me. Maybe they wanted to experiment on me. Maybe they needed something from my DNA. Who knows. All I know is I'm glad they did keep me around."

"You were able to recover from that degree of injury?" Trent asked interestedly. "I've been shot, poisoned, and stabbed, but never anything quite that extreme."

"It took a while, and it hurt like bloody hell, but I recovered completely." A smile suddenly crept onto Jaeger's face. "Say, do you realize that if I had set that bomb to blow up the SABER compound, it would've been called a Jaeger Bomb?" he looked at us with an expectant grin.

I looked at Trent with a raised eyebrow. "You know, I think I see the similarities now."

Trent didn't seem amused. "Where did you hear that term?" he asked Jaeger seriously.

"It's a drink from the 20th century. It's—"

Trent cut him off. "I know what it is. Did you learn that in your own world or this one?"

Jaeger furrowed his brow. "Mine. I couldn't even get to this world until just now."

Relief washed over Trent's face. "Good." He clasped his hands together with his index fingers extended and pressed together. He then pointed his index fingers at Jaeger. "So...you must have a device. I know it can't be the same device you had, because I nicked that from the compound."

Jaeger rolled back the sleeve of his grungy green shirt jacket to reveal a clunky-looking contraption on his wrist. "I made a new one. Trust me, it was no easy task to come up with the parts in my world after SABER was dismantled. I made a lot of questionable deals with a lot of shady people to get what I needed to cobble this."

Trent looked at the device with obvious distaste. "Yes...I can see that. Jaeger, how long has it been for you? Last time I saw you, you looked considerably less...weathered."

Jaeger looked down at himself. "Oi! I'd like to see you try to look this good after a hundred years on a war-ravaged planet!"

"A hundred years?" I asked in astonishment. I turned to Trent. "How could it be a hundred years for him? It wasn't that long ago when you blew up the SABER compound."

"I've been traveling," Jaeger answered. "I've been trying to fix everything – to prevent the war from happening and the planet from becoming a wasteland. I've tried everything, but there's always some new variable I hadn't accounted for that starts humanity down a new path of destruction. Every time I put the hamster back on the wheel, it falls off again. That's the reason I'm here, actually. I was hoping you could help me," Jaeger said, pointing to Trent.

Trent held up his hands and took a step backward. "Oh no. No. Absolutely not. I do not meddle. That is rule number one. Humanity in your world made their choice, and it is the choice they must live or die with."

Jaeger's face filled with disbelief. "Why? Their choice was wrong, and I have the power to fix it. I have the power to save everyone."

"How many lives have you ended in your quest to save your world, Jaeger?" Trent asked.

Jaeger shrugged. "I don't know. They were sacrifices that had to be made."

"Were they? Did it help? Did you fix the world?"

"Not yet. I'll figure it out, though. If you help me, we can get it right."

"No, we can't!" Trent exclaimed. "All you'll do is further tangle time until your world is completely unrecognizable!"

I heard footsteps upstairs.

"Shit!" I grumbled.

Jaeger drew his gun, which I now noticed was a rather strange looking firearm. It was dark blue with rounded edges and three "barrels."

"Put that away!" I ordered in an angry whisper as I threw my blankets aside and clambered out of bed. "And you two shut up!"

I stepped out into the hall and padded barefoot toward the living room. I could hear my mother coming down the stairs – I could tell by the lightness of her footsteps that it was her and not my father. I walked into the kitchen, as though I were just getting a drink of water.

"Roselyn, is someone here?" my mom asked me as she walked out into the living room. "I thought I heard voices."

I turned and looked at her, trying to look confused. "Voices? In the house?"

"It sounded like a man."

"Oh, you know what? It was probably just my tv. I'll turn it down when I get back to my room. Sorry I woke you!" I apologized.

She seemed to buy it, and I made sure she headed back upstairs before I returned to my room. When I opened my bedroom door, however, I found that Trent and Jaeger had disappeared.

"Oh no you don't. You are not excluding me from this," I said to myself as I looked down at my watch. I nervously pressed the button that brought up the holographic display and selected the option to sync my watch with his. My "Trent tracker" showed that it was locked onto his location in August of 2255. I glanced down at my sweatpants and t-shirt, briefly considered changing, but shrugged and executed the command to commence with the teleport anyway.

I arrived in a large, brightly lit home library – right in the middle of an argument.

"Do as you please in your own world!" Trent yelled. "It's none of my business what you do there! But I will not assist you in such folly! And if you take one step out of line in our world, I'll—"

Jaeger cut him off and stepped up to Trent. "You'll what? What are you going to do? Nothing! As far as I can tell, all you do is nothing!"

I threw myself between them and pressed my hand firmly against Jaeger's chest, pushing him away from Trent. "Woah, woah, woah! Everybody step back and take a deep breath," I commanded sternly.

Jaeger gave me a startled look. "Where'd you come from?!"

I held my wrist up, showing him the watch. "My Trent tracker. Compliments of you, I believe."

"I repaired it," Trent added. "It was a bit of a mess when I acquired it."

"I hadn't had time to perfect it yet," Jaeger defended. He looked at me curiously. "I never imagined a primitive wielding it."

"Excuse me?" I asked, bristling.

"Well, I don't mean any offense by it. It's just a fact," Jaeger said flatly.

"That's funny…I'm the 'primitive,' yet here you are acting like a foolish child with a Lego set and no instructions, thinking you have everything all figured out when you know absolutely nothing."

"You're, what, 25? 30? I've lived your life twelve times over! Don't blather on to me about what I know and what I don't know!" Jaeger spat.

Trent interjected calmly, "And I've lived your life almost twice over, Jaeger. If you're going to use age to gauge wisdom, then you should be listening to me instead of fighting with me."

"If all the wisdom you have to offer is to do nothing, to let my Earth waste away and watch all of humanity die, then no, I shouldn't be listening. I've seen what happens to them. I've visited the future, only to find that there is no future. Everyone is gone by 3416. Allowing that future to remain as reality is a travesty, not a solution."

"You've seen it, Jaeger. When you alter the past, does that hopeless future ever change?" Trent asked.

Jaeger shot him a scowl, but didn't reply.

"Have you considered that maybe it's because it isn't something that is changeable?" Trent continued.

"Everything is changeable."

"Maybe it isn't. Maybe you can't make it better. Or maybe you were the one who started the whole mess in the first place by trying to change the past. 'A person often meets his destiny on the road he took to avoid it.'"

Jaeger put one hand on his hip and rubbed his temples with the other hand. "This isn't my fault. I didn't do this. It was them. I was just trying to save them."

"Some things can't be saved," Trent said softly.

Jaeger suddenly shouted, "I refuse to believe that!" He turned to me. "What would you do? Do you lack such compassion as your companion so clearly does?"

"It isn't a lack of compassion," I replied. "It's just an understanding that some things aren't up to a single individual to decide."

"Rubbish! Plenty of history-making decisions are left up to single individuals to make!"

"Yes, but with the support of others in some form or another. It isn't the same as what you've been doing," I pointed out.

"But I have a serious advantage over them. I have knowledge they didn't have when they made their choices."

Trent chimed in. "But when you change things, you lose that advantage. You have no idea what the outcome will be when you change something."

"Yes, but I can find out what the outcome is and adjust things as needed. With enough patience, I could craft the perfect history and create the perfect future for my people," Jaeger said, his eyes full of hope.

Trent sighed. "If you were able to do that, don't you think you would've seen it already?"

Jaeger waved his hand dismissively. "You don't know everything. You're clever, as am I, but there are still mysteries even we don't fully understand. There are still phenomena that defy even our advanced logic."

"You aren't wrong," Trent conceded. "But that doesn't change the fact that the fate of humanity shouldn't rest solely in your hands."

"Then help me!" Jaeger begged as he stepped toward Trent. "We can do it together! We could create an entire world to fit our own vision of perfection!"

Those words from Jaeger sent a chill down my spine. "Jaeger, are you trying to save humankind or are you trying to be a god?" I asked warily.

Jaeger looked at me and raised his eyebrows. "Can't it be both? If I saved humankind, I would be a god. Isn't that what a god is? Someone with the power to watch over and decide the fate of an entire world? You know, it's interesting – all along people have been arguing over whether God created humankind or if humankind created God. Turns out humankind did create God, just not in the way they thought. He was engineered, not just imagined."

Trent and I looked at each other in alarm.

Chapter 3

"Jaeger, you are not a god," Trent said firmly.

"Well, maybe not in the omnipotent sense. I admit that I'm fallible. But you and I both know we are more than just humans. Maybe we wouldn't be gods to more advanced civilizations on other planets, but on this planet, to these creatures, we are," Jaeger said confidently.

"These creatures?!" I snapped angrily. I jabbed my finger toward Jaeger's face. "You arrogant, egotistical asshole! You know, I was touched by your mission to save your people, but now I see what this really is. I see that you just need to have someone around to be impressed by you. Well guess what? I'm not impressed. You're ridiculous. You're so human it's hilarious. The only thing that makes you special is your proficiency with technology. And guess what? I have the same power you have!" I held up my wrist to show him my watch again. "I suppose I'm a god, too? Let me assure you, if I were a god, I'd smite your smug ass!"

Jaeger was leaned away from me, looking at me like I'd just thrown cold water in his face. I felt Trent's hand on my shoulder as he gently pulled me back, closer to him.

"Well, I suppose it's a good thing none of us are gods, eh?" Trent quipped.

As I watched Jaeger turn away from us and start pacing, I noticed he was as bowlegged as Trent. It irritated me to see any similarities between the two, as I had already made my mind up that I severely disliked Jaeger. I didn't want to be reminded that at one point in time, Trent wore a face just like that. Was it possible that Trent had been as foolhardy as Jaeger at one time, too?

"Were you ever like this?" I whispered to Trent while Jaeger had his back turned.

Trent glanced at me, but quickly looked away with a look of shame on his face. "Maybe a little. I always fought the urge to change the past...but I haven't always been the man you know today. Let's just say more than my face has changed over the years."

I sighed. "Well...I guess that just means there's still hope for him yet."

Jaeger turned to us and folded his arms across his broad chest. "If you won't help me, then at least let me study your world," he suggested.

"I beg your pardon?" Trent asked with raised eyebrows.

"It's quite simple. I travel around your world and see how history has played out, and how it has affected future events."

"Why would you do that?" I asked.

"I might want to replicate it. Even if I don't, though, it would be nice to have an outside source for reference."

I looked at Trent, wondering if his distrust of Jaeger ran as deeply as mine. From the concern etched on his face, it appeared so. Jaeger saw it, too.

"I won't muck up your time," Jaeger assured Trent. "You have my word."

"Forgive me if I question how much weight your word carries," Trent replied. "If I am to understand correctly, you guaranteed me your silence regarding myself and our world, yet it was your betrayal of that promise that led to SABER capturing and threatening my Roselyn."

"It wasn't as though I offered that information freely," Jaeger defended. "It all worked out, though, didn't it? As I said before, if you hadn't blown up the SABER compound, I might not be here today."

"I'm not sure I'm grateful that you are," I said derisively.

Jaeger turned to me. "What is your qualm with me?" he asked in frustration. "Is it because I pointed a gun at you? If you'll recall, you were pointing one right back at me. If it's because I told SABER about you, it was only because I didn't think it would matter. I didn't imagine they were going to come after you. I didn't know what they were planning. Trust me when I say I have no desire to be your enemy."

"I'm surprised you care at all, considering I'm just a 'primitive creature.'"

Jaeger exhaled loudly. "You misunderstand me. It was never my intention to insult you. You obviously have captured Trent's mind and affections, so far be it from me to insinuate that you aren't on par with current company."

"You can backpedal all you want. It isn't going to make me trust you," I said.

"Well, perhaps you can accompany me, then. I can learn what I wish to learn, and you can monitor me to ensure I don't make any blunders."

Before I could answer, Trent stepped in. "I will go with you."

Jaeger raised one corner of his mouth in a lopsided, tight-lipped grin. "All right, then. Let's go!"

Trent held up his index finger. "But I want to set some rules straight away. First off, I'm in charge. If I say we leave, we leave. If I say run, run. If I say shut up, shut up."

"If you say jump, I say how high," Jaeger added.

Trent scrunched his face at him. "No, if I say jump, you bloody jump! Second rule: If I detect something amiss, that takes precedence over your little holiday."

"That still kind of falls under the first rule, if you think about it," Jaeger pointed out.

Trent ignored him and continued, "Third rule: the moment I feel even an inkling that you are up to something, we're done and you go back home and never return."

"Is that all? Great. Now that I've heard the 'Trent Commandments,' we can go."

"Not so fast!" I interjected. I looked at Trent. "You'd better stop in and see me, you know. I don't want to find out you're ten years older the next time I see you."

Trent pulled me to him and hugged me tightly. "You've nothing to worry about. I don't think I could endure more than a day or two without seeing you."

"Be careful," I whispered in his ear. "I don't trust him."

He gently lifted my chin and looked me in the eyes. "There was a time when you didn't trust me either, remember? I'll be fine. I always am." He pressed his lips to mine and it made my heart swell. "I'll be back before you even notice I'm gone."

I returned to my own time while Trent and Jaeger took off to the deep past. I climbed into my bed and lay awake, worrying. I just didn't know what to make of Jaeger, and I didn't like the idea of him and Trent alone. It was obvious that killing wasn't something that weighed heavily on his conscience if he felt it served a greater purpose. Did he have any reason to try to kill Trent? I didn't know. He didn't seem to have any desire to take over this world. He was more concerned about turning his world into his own perfect paradise than he was about what ours had to offer him. But what if he liked what he saw? Would he try to get Trent out of the way? I wouldn't put it past him. There was something dark about Jaeger. Perhaps his intentions were good, but it was also apparent that he was of the mindset that the ends justify the means – and that always had the potential to be dangerous.

I woke up the next morning to the aroma of fresh coffee wafting into my room. I could hear the television in the living room and the clang of pots and pans in the kitchen. I rolled out of bed and shuffled out to the kitchen a good hour before I normally would have on a Saturday simply because I knew my mother was out there working on getting breakfast started. There was no way I was missing out on morning pancakes.

"Good morning," my mom greeted me cheerily.

"Mmhmm," I mumbled as I poured myself a cup of coffee.

"What time did you bring Trent home last night?"

"I don't know. Not long after you went to bed."

"It's just so weird…I could have sworn I heard him talking last night."

"I told you, it was probably just my tv."

"You know, if he's been staying the night with you, you don't need to lie to me about it. I know you are a grown woman who can make your own decisions."

I sat down at the kitchen table and glanced at my father who was sitting on the couch watching television. He seemed completely focused on his show, oblivious to the conversation taking place.

"Mom, I can assure you he didn't stay the night."

My mother poured pancake batter onto the hot griddle on the counter as she replied, "Ok. That's fine. I'm just saying that I would understand." She dug out a spatula from the drawer and stood over the griddle with her back to me. She was quiet for a few minutes before blurting, "He has such a delightful accent, doesn't he?"

I smiled. "Yeah, he does. He might say the most ridiculous things, but at least he sounds great saying them."

"It's just that I swear I heard that same accent last night. What were you watching?"

My smile was quickly replaced by a frown. I felt like an angsty teenager all over again. "Mom! Stop! Are you sure you aren't just getting senile? Why won't you just leave it alone?"

My mom turned to face me. "Because I feel like there's something more going on here, and I wish you could be honest with me. Does he live here? Is that what it is?"

I scowled at her. "No! He doesn't live here! You know, this is why I don't tell you things. You start jumping to conclusions and assuming things. Why can't you just say, 'That's nice, dear,' and be happy for me and leave it at that?"

"Because when you found yourself in an abusive relationship, you lied to us constantly about it. You hid things from us. You pretended things were fine when they weren't. So excuse me if I've become a little paranoid. When something seems fishy, I'm going to trust my gut this time. And something seems fishy."

I couldn't fault her for her paranoia. I was lying to her, after all, so it was silly of me to be angry with her for calling me out on it. But I still couldn't let her know the truth. Not yet.

I sighed heavily. "Ok. I understand where you're coming from. I get it. And you aren't wrong. There are things about Trent that I haven't been entirely truthful about, but I can assure you that it isn't because he's mistreating me or up to no good. It's just...there are things that aren't my place to tell you. I'm sure eventually you'll be in the know, but for now, just trust that I'm happy, Trent is an amazing man, and there isn't anything to worry about."

My dad must have turned his attention to our conversation at some point because he chimed in with, "Well, it's kind of hard not to worry now. Is he into something illegal?"

"No, nothing like that! It's more like...classified information."

"Like James Bond?" my mom asked. "Oh, I don't like that one bit."

"No, not like James Bond. More like—"

As if on cue, Trent and Jaeger appeared in the living room. My dad sat back in his chair, eyes wide with surprise, and my mom gave a short, startled yelp.

"—well, like that," I said flatly as I gestured toward Trent and Jaeger.

Trent glanced around, and as soon as he realized my parents were there, his eyebrows jumped up while his mouth made an "O" shape as though to say "oops." Jaeger just stood there looking unsure of what to do.

"Oh…blimey," Trent said. He looked to me for help.

I stood up. "You forgot they were here, didn't you?"

Trent grimaced and nodded. "Yeah." He held his forefinger and thumb close together and added, "A little bit." He looked at my dad, who was still frozen in shock. "Sorry to just drop in on you like that. Um…this is my friend, Jaeger. Jaeger, this is Roselyn's father, Roger." Trent then gestured toward my mom in the kitchen. "And that is Roselyn's mum, Nadine."

"…Hi," Jaeger said uncomfortably.

Trent headed into the kitchen, leaving Jaeger to stand awkwardly in the living room. "I hope you bought more toaster pastries. I'm famished!" he declared as he flung open the cupboard. He pulled out the box and tossed a package to Jaeger.

"My mom is making pancakes," I pointed out.

"Ah, so she is!" Trent leaned closer and looked at the griddle while my mom still stared at him, dumbfounded. "Um, Nadine, I hate to tell you how to do your job, but I can't help but notice you may want to flip those. I think they're starting to burn," he said as he took a huge bite of his toaster pastry.

My mom blinked and furrowed her brow. She started to flip a pancake, then turned back to Trent. "How…? What…what is going on?! Where did you come from? How did you do that?!"

Trent looked at me, obviously hoping I would answer for him.

"Yes, pray tell, how did you do that?" I asked as I sat back down in my chair and leisurely sipped my coffee.

Trent narrowed his eyes at me, then turned to my mother. "Well, you see, I, um…I have a thing that does a thing."

"A what that does what?" my dad asked in confusion from the living room.

"I have a device that takes me from here to there in an instant. It's not on the market yet, but someday…I wouldn't hold my breath though. It'll be a while."

My mom looked at me blankly.

"He has a teleporter," I said simply. "But don't tell anyone."

"I doubt anyone would believe us if we did," my dad said.

"I'm not sure I believe it myself," my mom commented. She looked at my watch. "That isn't a fitness tracker, is it?" she asked.

"Hm? Oh." I looked down at my watch. Shit. "This one…this just helps me find Trent."

"And who is that? He has one too?" she asked, nodding toward Jaeger.

"Jaeger is a friend of Trent's. He's just visiting from…out of town."

Jaeger lifted his hand. "Hi," he said again. For a "god," he sure was timid all of a sudden.

I got up and took the spatula from my mom and told her to go sit down. Trent was right – the pancakes were starting to burn. I flipped the entire batch right into the garbage and poured some fresh batter onto the griddle.

"Is this a prank?" my mom asked after sitting down at the table.

"It's not a prank," Trent assured her. "I can show you."

"Oh, no, no," my mother said, waving her hands in front of her. "I want no part of that!"

"It's not that bad, Mom. You don't feel a thing."

"I'd like to try it," my dad said, rising from his chair.

"Brilliant!" Trent exclaimed. He fiddled with his watch as he walked over to my dad. He put his hand on my dad's shoulder and held out his watch. "Press that top blue button," Trent instructed.

My father pressed the button and the two disappeared. My mom gasped and covered her mouth with her hand. Jaeger looked over at me with an expression of boredom.

"Have a seat, Jaeger. You might be here a while," I said.

"Is that even safe?" my mom asked, sounding mildly horrified as she continued to stare at the empty space where Dad and Trent had been standing.

"Don't worry, Trent knows what he's doing," I replied.

"What about radiation? Or what if they get mixed up when they rematerialize?!"

"This isn't 'The Fly,' Mom. Dad will be just fine."

Trent and my father reappeared in the living room. My dad looked delighted.

"Wow! That's truly amazing!" he marveled.

"Where did you go?" I asked, giving Trent a suspicious look.

"I just took him down the road a bit to show him how it worked," Trent replied.

"How far can you go with that thing?" my dad asked.

"Anywhere on Earth."

"Wow. Now I see why you travel so much. I would, too, if I had one of those gadgets!"

I smiled to myself as I flipped the pancakes. "You should take him to the pyramids next," I chimed in.

"No, he's not going anywhere else using that thing," my mom cut in. "Has it even been tested for safety, Trent?" she asked accusingly.

"It's perfectly safe."

"And what do other people say when you just appear out of thin air?" she wanted to know.

"You'd be surprised at how little people pay attention to their surroundings, but I usually try to avoid landing in places with people around. It isn't usually much of an issue."

"I don't know. The whole thing seems incredibly dangerous and unnatural to me."

"Oh, it's perfectly natural. I take it you aren't familiar with quantum mechanics?" Trent asked.

My mom scoffed. "Who the hell is?"

"Well, I am. So is he," Trent said, pointing to Jaeger.

Jaeger waved from the couch, where Cattiel was allowing him to pet him. "Hi."

"You can stop doing that," Trent said to Jaeger. He returned his attention to my mother. "My point is, I know what I'm doing. I'm very clever. And I can tell you it is safe, and you needn't worry."

My mom turned to me. "So, the whole business about his car being in the shop and you having to drive him home was a lie, wasn't it? And it was his voice I heard last night, wasn't it?"

I felt my cheeks redden. "Well, you have to admit my hands were kind of tied, don't you think? I couldn't just say, 'Oh, he doesn't have a car because he teleports everywhere.' But I didn't lie about him spending the night. He did not spend the night. He just stopped in for a minute to check on something."

"What else is a lie?" my mother wanted to know.

Jaeger stood up from the couch. "Does any of this matter? I fail to see why anyone needs to explain themselves to you. You hold no special rank or status."

Trent and I looked at each other with wide eyes. Oh, shit.

"Oh, dear." Trent immediately apologized to my stunned mother. "You'll have to forgive his manners. He lacks the capacity to properly interpret social situations."

My mom's expression softened slightly. "Oh! He's on the spectrum, then?"

Trent threw me a questioning glance.

"He's not autistic," I said. "He's just an asshole."

Jaeger looked taken aback. "I'm not an asshole! I'm impatient. There's a difference."

I feigned a thoughtful look. "Hmm...no, no there isn't. Not in this case." I turned my back to him and grabbed some plates from the cupboard. I served up a short stack on each of two plates and brought them to the table. "Here, Trent. You and Jaeger can eat now so you can get him out of here."

"Oh, I can leave right now if you want me to," Jaeger snapped.

"No, you can't," Trent said sternly. "We had a deal. Now, sit down and eat."

Jaeger huffily plopped himself down into a chair and started shoveling pancakes into his mouth as though he were trying to win an award for "Most Attitude While Eating."

I poured another batch of pancakes onto the griddle as the kitchen filled with uncomfortable silence. I looked around. Trent was watching Jaeger warily while Jaeger kept his eyes cast downward to his own plate. My mother was looking bewildered at me and my dad, and my dad was staring off into space dreamily, likely thinking of all the places he would go if he had a teleporter.

I decided to break the silence. "So, what did you want to do today?" I asked my parents casually. "There are some movies playing at the cinema I was interested in seeing. Or we could hit up a museum. Or we could go check out the ice caves. Any thoughts?" I asked.

My mother looked at me like I had a hole in my head. "Or maybe we could have a nice, long conversation about all of this," she said as though it were the obvious choice.

"I'd rather not waste our day on something as boring as that," I replied. "Besides, I'm not sure what else there is to talk about regarding the matter. I think we pretty much covered it."

"I would love to go see the ice caves," my dad said.

"Perfect. Sounds like a plan," I responded.

"And we can talk in the car," my mom added.

"Oh, goody," I said sarcastically.

When Trent and Jaeger had finished their breakfast, Trent took me aside for a private word.

"What possessed you to pop up in the middle of my living room when my parents were here?" I asked him as soon as I had him alone in my room.

"I forgot! I'm not used to you having company!"

"What did you want?"

"I just stopped in to see you. I'd been running all over time with Jaeger for two days and I thought it was time to check in."

"How's it going with him, anyway? Is he behaving?"

"He's been fine. Well, he did instigate a fight in Mesopotamia, but other than that he's been fine. He seems to like you," Trent said.

"What? You were talking about me? Why the hell would he like me?"

"I always talk about you. How do you think he knew about you in the first place? He thinks you're a strong woman. He respects you."

"Oh. Well, that's kind of nice. But I still don't like him."

Trent laughed. "He's not so bad once you get used to him. He's gotten a little rough around the edges from living in his desecrated world for so long, I will give you that. And obviously he's not as delightful as I am...but he's not terrible."

"I'm not sure how I feel about him taking you away from me to do these little field trips. Can't he just read some history books?"

"The problem with history books is that they were written by people. People with biases. People who won. People who survived. History books from different regions tell vastly different tales depending on who wrote it. No, history books tell incomplete and often inaccurate stories. If Jaeger truly wants to understand our history and how our global society develops, then he needs to see it and experience it."

"I suppose. Well, when my parents head home, you should let me accompany you guys for a while so I can spend some time with you."

"You would have to be around Jaeger," Trent pointed out.

"I can deal with that if it means I get to spend more time with you."

"Well, I can't say no to that." Trent cupped my face with his hands and kissed me tenderly. "I've missed you."

I put my hands over his. "Good. As long as you miss me, you won't stay away for long."

"This will all be over and Jaeger will be back in his own world before you know it, and then things will go back to normal."

I chuckled.

"What?" Trent asked.

"It's just funny to think of any of this as 'normal.'"

"Well, ordinary normal is rather boring. I think our normal suits us much better." Trent smiled.

I raised myself up on my toes and kissed his smile.

Out of the corner of my eye, I noticed Jaeger standing in the bedroom doorway, watching us kiss. I wasn't sure if it was my imagination, but it seemed that he was perhaps watching us a little too keenly.

Chapter 4

"Yeah, that's not creepy at all," I said sarcastically to Jaeger as I pulled away from Trent.

Jaeger scowled at me. "What? I wasn't trying to be creepy. Are you done snogging so we can go now?"

I looked at Trent. "You let him run around with you dressed like that?" I asked, referring to Jaeger's dirty shirt jacket and ripped blue jeans.

Jaeger looked down at his clothes. "What? I fit in better with primitives from the past in these dirty clothes than your boytoy does in his fancy suit."

"He's not wrong," Trent agreed.

I shrugged my shoulders. "Whatever. You don't have to look like a bum all the time, you know."

"I don't look like a bum!" Jaeger exclaimed defensively. He rolled his shoulders. "I look...rugged."

I ignored him and turned my attention to Trent. "Be careful. If I don't see you tomorrow after my parents leave, I'm tracking you down. I'm serious about joining you for a while."

"I never doubted that you were. I'll be here. It's a date," Trent promised.

I kissed him once more and bid him farewell, and he and Jaeger disappeared.

The car ride with my parents to the ice caves was almost as pleasant as I had imagined it would be – and by pleasant, I mean not at all pleasant. My mother drilled me with questions and hammered me with criticisms of Trent. It was that special kind of torture only mothers know how to dole out.

"How long have you known about this? Why does he have a device like that?" my mom demanded from the passenger seat of her car almost as soon as my dad pulled out of the driveway.

"I've known since before we started dating. He invented it," I said from the backseat.

"I don't think I like this. It seems dangerous to me."

"You may have mentioned that once or twice already."

"I don't want you using that thing. I don't know how I feel about you dating someone like that."

"What do you mean 'someone like that'? A genius? You don't know how you feel about me dating a genius?"

"He's reckless."

"Only occasionally."

"What does he really do for a living? He definitely isn't a stock broker."

"How would you know?" I asked defiantly.

She rolled her eyes at me. "What else is a complete fabrication?"

"You need to just let it go. As I recall, you said this morning that I was a grown woman capable of making my own decisions. And I am. You don't need to know every little detail of our relationship."

"I'm worried about you! What have you gotten yourself into?!"

"Nothing! It's not like I'm dating some kind of international criminal drug lord. He's a genius who invented a teleporter. Most mothers would be supportive of their daughter dating a genius."

"Genius, maybe. But this is something else. And what was with the guy that was with Trent? He looked like a thug."

I laughed. "A thug? Really? More like a bum."

"I didn't like him at all."

"I don't like him either. We should start a club."

"This is no joking matter, Roselyn."

"It's not the catastrophe you seem to think it is, either."

"I'm not so sure about that."

"Listen. Trent is a good man. A very, very good man. And he is very good to me. You have no reason to be so confrontational. It isn't like we're getting married."

My mom sighed and her tone softened slightly. "I have no doubt that he's a nice guy. I'm not saying he isn't. He seems lovely. But when you look at the bigger picture here, you have to admit that maybe he isn't a great fit for you. I have a feeling you're in over your head with him. Why can't you just date a normal guy?"

"Because I don't want 'normal.' I want 'wow.' And he is every bit of 'wow' and more."

"'Wow' isn't what makes a relationship last, sweetie," my mom said. "Let's be practical here. He's obviously got a lot going for him, but how well are you going to fit into his life? Maybe it works for now, but how long will that last? Let's face it: he's going to outgrow you. Men like that don't settle down with average women."

It felt like she'd just stabbed me in the heart. "I can't believe you just said that."

"I'm not trying to hurt your feelings. I'm just being honest with you. I don't want to see you get hurt again."

"You know nothing about him or my relationship with him."

"Because you refuse to tell me the truth about him, and that's the biggest red flag of all."

I had to blot a tear from my eye with my jacket sleeve. "I get why you think what you think, but you're wrong about him, and I don't want to hear another word about it."

"Fine. I've said my piece."

My dad drove on silently.

I tried to enjoy my time at the ice caves with my parents, but my day was overshadowed by the unpleasantness of earlier. I kept thinking about what my mom had said – that men like Trent don't settle down with average women. Maybe she didn't know much about him, but perhaps she had hit the nail right on the head with that assessment. In six hundred years, had Trent ever been married? I knew he'd had at least one intimate acquaintance, but there must have been more. How many more? How many women had he left in his wake? How many had been just like me? Was I really as special as he would have me believe? It wasn't that I doubted his sincerity. I knew he loved me. But someday he would forget me. It wasn't a matter of if, but of when. He would forget me. Someday, I would be nothing to him. I tried to push the thought from my head, but it lingered, lurking in the back of my mind all day.

By some miracle, my mom didn't bring up Trent for the rest of her stay. I could tell that my dad had things he wanted to say on the matter, too, but he kept his thoughts to himself. If I had to guess, I would say he was more in favor of my relationship with Trent than my mother was, but I think he had his reservations as well. Ultimately, though, it was my life, and, while I took their opinions into consideration, it was my choice. And as soon as they left on Sunday morning, I called Trent.

As soon as he answered, I said, "I'm free to roam! Are you coming?"

"Brilliant! We'll be there shortly. I need to snag Jaeger from these Norsemen. He is having entirely too much fun here. I suspect Jaeger may be the inspiration for the Norse god Loki."

"I thought he was only supposed to be observing, not interacting."

"Ideally, yes," Trent said hesitantly.

"Never mind. I'll just come to you."

"Are you sure?"

"It's probably easier."

"Give me a minute to get somewhere more private. We don't need to draw any more attention than we already have. Oh, and make sure you wear something drab. No sweatpants. I don't care how bootylicious they are."

"What season is it there? Should I dress warm?"

"Bring a sweater."

I hung up and changed into a long, flowing khaki skirt and a gray wool cable knit sweater. I quickly filled an extra bowl of food and water for Cattiel, just in case, and then looked up Trent on my Trent tracker. I locked onto his location and sent myself to northern Scandinavia in the 9th century AD – or what would someday become Norway. I found myself standing outside, facing an oddly long, grassy building at twilight.

"There you are," I heard Trent say behind me.

I turned and looked at him. He wasn't wearing his usual suit. Instead, he had on old brown boots, dirty tan slacks, and an oversized rusty-colored flannel. His hair was a disaster.

"What the hell happened to you?!"

"When in Rome…well, Scandinavia," he said, holding his arms outward.

"I don't think I like you hanging out with Jaeger," I said as I looked him up and down with furrowed brows.

"What, don't I look rugged?"

"You look…what's the word you used? Weathered?"

Trent laughed. "It's been a long day. And I somehow need to get that wanker away from his new friends and get out of here," Trent said as he pointed at the grassy building next to us.

"I'll get him out of there," I said as I started around the building to find the door. It sounded like there was a raucous party going on inside.

Trent grabbed my arm. "Wait. You haven't even greeted me properly yet." He grinned mischievously at me.

He backed me against the side of the building and pressed his body against mine, his mouth descending upon mine with such urgency that it felt as though he hadn't seen me in years. He grabbed my thigh and raised my leg up, hitching my knee over his hip. He ran his hand up my leg and under my skirt, grabbing a handful of my round buttocks. I reached one hand up and splayed my fingers into the hair at the nape of his neck, and the fingers of my other hand dug into his back while I tilted my pelvis and pressed it against him.

We were so focused on each other that we didn't hear the footsteps approaching. It wasn't until I heard what sounded like water being poured onto the ground that I opened my eyes and looked around. Someone was standing about ten feet away from us with his back to us.

"Trent!" I whispered as I pushed him away and pointed at the man with his back to us.

Trent turned and looked. "Jaeger?"

"Aye, mate," he replied without turning around.

I squinted at him. "Are you...are you pissing?"

"Indeed I am."

"Why are you going back here?!" Trent asked in disgust.

"Their bathrooms are disgusting and smell bloody awful. Besides, I figured you were back here. I know you've been itching to get out of here. I think I'm ready now," Jaeger said as he finished up and turned to us.

Trent grunted with irritation. "Brilliant timing."

"I noticed." Jaeger smiled smugly as he approached us. "So, where are we headed now?"

Trent looked at me. "Any requests?"

"Am I limited to a certain timeframe? Does Jaeger have some kind of itinerary we need to follow?"

Jaeger shook his head. "I'll go wherever you want to go."

"Oh. Ok. Well, I've always wondered what ancient Egypt was like."

"Any particular time period in ancient Egypt?" Trent asked.

"What about when Nefertiti was queen?"

"You're just curious about Akhenaten, aren't you?" he said knowingly.

I shrugged. "Can you blame me?"

"Not really. He was an odd fellow. I will warn you, though, that there'll be some more social tensions at that time, so just be careful. Try not to interact too much. You got that, Jaeger?" Trent asked as he clapped a hand on Jaeger's shoulder.

Jaeger clicked his tongue and winked at Trent in affirmation.

"What are you wearing under that sweater?" Trent asked me.

"A white tank top. Why?"

"That should do. You're probably not going to need your sweater," Trent said as he unbuttoned his flannel. "Now, we're going to stick out a little, but as long as we keep to ourselves, it should be fine. Oh, wait!" Trent said as he raised his eyebrows and held up his forefinger. "Be right back." He fiddled with his watch briefly and then disappeared.

Jaeger and I looked at each other in confusion, but as soon as I opened my mouth to ask if Jaeger knew where he had gone, Trent reappeared.

"Translator," Trent said as he handed me the little device for my ear. "That'll make things easier."

Trent started to coordinate his watch settings with Jaeger.

"What about me?" I asked.

"You can travel with me," he replied absently.

"No," I said. Trent stopped and looked at me in surprise. "I need to learn this. I want to do it on my own," I explained.

He nodded. "Very well, then. I suppose you're right."

We all set our watches to 1341 BC, and Trent recited the location coordinates we were to enter. When we were all sure that we were ready, we all teleported at the same time. In an instant, I was standing in a stone street near some stone and mudbrick buildings. They looked to still be under construction. I looked around for Trent and Jaeger, but they weren't next to me. The sun was beating down, as it must have been about midday, so I removed my sweater and folded it over my arm while I walked to the corner of the building. I swiped my hair out of my face as I looked down the street to my right. There, some distance up the path, I saw Trent looking down at his watch while Jaeger looked around. I waved my arms and caught Jaeger's attention. I saw him nudge Trent, and I started toward them.

As I hurried down the street, I didn't notice the group of men rounding the corner from my left, and I ran straight into them, knocking one of them off balance.

"Oh, sorry!" I apologized as I reached out to steady him.

The four men looked at me curiously and then at each other. One of them smiled, but it wasn't a pleasant smile. It was menacing.

The smiling one looked me up and down. "Not from around here, are you? What language is that?" I started to back away, but he snatched my wrist and pulled me to him roughly. "You have a pretty face. Let's see what the rest of you looks like." He clawed at the neckline of my tank top.

I snaked my hand around his wrist, twisting my arm free, and immediately followed up with a right hook to his jaw and a knee to his groin. As he collapsed to his knees, Jaeger suddenly rushed in and planted himself between me and the group of men, his gun drawn, while Trent swooped in behind him and quickly assessed my condition.

"She'd better not have a scratch," I heard Jaeger say.

"Are you all right?!" Trent asked, worry lining his features.

"I'm fine. More than I can say for him," I pointed out, nodding toward the guy on his knees, cupping his crotch. I reached down and picked up the sweater I had dropped.

Jaeger lowered his gun and forcefully kicked my assailant in the face, sending him sprawling backwards. He then spread his arms wide, puffed up his chest, and stepped toward the other three men in the group, an obvious challenge in any culture. Jaeger had a good six inches and three stones on them, and the way they looked up at him fearfully was absolutely satisfying. They left their comrade and ran back up the street from whence they came. Jaeger looked down at the guy lying in the street and kicked him in the head again. Hard.

"Jaeger, I think that's enough," Trent said, still holding me close.

Jaeger turned to him, a look of rage on his face. "Men like that don't deserve to be breathing."

"I agree, but we need to be careful. We can't stir things up too much. We need to move along."

Jaeger ignored Trent and looked at me. "Do you want me to kill him?"

I was caught off-guard. "What? No! No, I don't want you to kill anyone! He got what he had coming to him," I said.

Jaeger grunted and holstered his gun. He spat on the unconscious pervert and walked on ahead, and Trent and I followed.

"I'm sorry we got separated," Trent said. "We'll have to be more careful about entering coordinates next time."

"You mean I'll need to be more careful about entering coordinates next time," I corrected him.

"Well, I didn't want to say that. But yes. That could've been a lot worse than it was."

I looked at the buildings around us. "Where are we, exactly? Why does it look like this place is under major construction?"

"We're in Akhetaten."

"I thought that was the pharaoh."

"Akhenaten is the pharaoh. This is the city he is having constructed, called Akhetaten. It means 'the horizon of the Aten.' You may have heard of it referred to as Tell el-Amarna."

"Never heard of it."

"Well, it's been under construction for about nine years. It's quite amazing how quickly it has grown. The most interesting fact, I think, is that this will all be abandoned in a little over ten years from now."

"They built a whole city, then just left it?"

"After Akhenaten, the Egyptians revert back to their polytheistic religion and demolish a lot of what Akhenaten had established in honor of his monotheistic religion. They do their best to erase him once he's gone, basically."

I scanned what I could see of the horizon. "Where are the pyramids?" I asked. "I thought I'd be able to see them."

"You're about three hundred kilometers too far south."

"Well, shit," I said disappointedly as we rounded a corner to our left.

"How about we go see Akhenaten and Nefertiti instead?"

Jaeger stopped in front of us and Trent and I walked up and stood next to him. I noticed there seemed to be a gathering around us, and everyone was looking up at a big, enclosed bridge that arched over a wide roadway. There was a big opening at the center, and I watched as two people adorned with gold jewelry and extravagant clothing stepped out into the opening to greet the people gathered in the street. Everyone started cheering. It was Akhenaten and Nefertiti.

I felt a lump in my throat. I was overwhelmed with the significance of what I was experiencing. I was the only person on Earth from my time that would ever see this infamous couple in living flesh. I was the only person from my time who could see with my own eyes that Akhenaten was just as strange looking in person as he was in his depictions. He had wide hips and rounded shoulders – one couldn't be blamed if they mistook him for a woman. I was surprised, however, at Nefertiti. She wasn't the great beauty I had expected. If it weren't for her fancy clothing, she wouldn't have caught my attention if I'd passed her on the street. It was overwhelming to be privy to such knowledge, but it was almost vexing to know there wasn't anyone with whom I could share such information.

The royal couple soon moved along, out of sight, and the crowd began to disperse. Jaeger elbowed Trent and tipped his head to the right. My eyes followed the direction Jaeger had indicated, and there were the three men that had run from us earlier. They were talking to some rather official looking fellows and pointing our way.

"It appears we've attracted some attention," Jaeger said.

"So it does. Come on," Trent said as he led us back up the street in the opposite direction of the three men. He fiddled with his watch while he weaved through people. "Let's go to the Glasgow flat," he said to Jaeger. "Roselyn, you're with me this time."

We quickly ducked around a corner that was out of sight of the street and teleported out of danger. I looked around and realized we were in the same place we had been when I had interrupted Trent and Jaeger's argument that first night he had shown up. It was one of Trent's homes that I hadn't seen before that. We must have been somewhere in the vicinity of the year 2255.

"Is anybody else hungry?" Trent asked. "That Norse food was completely unpalatable. I'm ordering takeaway."

"I'm fine," I said as I took my translator out of my ear. I tucked it into my sweater and set it on Trent's desk, then flopped down in an oversized green chair with velvety-textured upholstery. I swung my legs over one arm of the chair and leaned my head back against the other arm. "I ate before I left home."

"A terrible kale salad, I'm sure," Trent teased. "I can order you some real food if you'd like."

"I don't know how many times I have to tell you I hate kale."

"Lies."

I rolled my eyes.

Trent turned to Jaeger. "Jaeger?"

"I'll have whatever you're having," Jaeger answered.

Trent walked out of the room. I glanced over at Jaeger, who was standing in the middle of the room with his hands hanging at his sides. He looked troubled. He gave me a furtive glance, and it felt like such uncharacteristic behavior from him.

"Is everything all right?" I asked him.

"I should be asking you that," he said.

"What? That guy? I'm fine. We dealt with it."

Jaeger looked down at his feet. "You handle yourself well."

I gave him an odd look. "Oh. Um…thanks."

One corner of his mouth lifted and he looked over at me. "You and I would make a formidable team."

"I'd say the three of us are quite a formidable team," I said, making sure to include Trent.

"I'm sorry Trent failed you today," Jaeger commented.

I frowned. "What are you talking about?"

"He should've been more worried about defending you than about trying not to make a scene. You deserve better than that."

I sat up. "What makes you think I need someone to defend me? I had it under control. I'm not helpless."

I saw Jaeger's eyes suddenly dart to the doorway. I glanced over and saw Trent standing there, glaring at him.

Chapter 5

"The moment I leave the room, you take the opportunity to disparage me?" Trent accused Jaeger.

"No. Just calling it like it is," Jaeger replied.

"If you have a problem with me, perhaps next time you should confront me directly about it rather than mumbling about me behind my back…with my companion, no less. I know what you are doing, and I'd advise you cease and desist at once."

"Well, perhaps you should take better care of what's yours before you find it's no longer yours."

"She doesn't need to be taken care of. She's my partner, not my ward. Do you really believe her to be so fragile? Yes, she is under my protection if she needs it, but she's not the type of person who requires someone to run around defending her honor."

I scowled. "She's also right here and would appreciate it if you quit talking about her like she isn't in the room."

"My apologies, Roselyn," Trent said, still glaring at Jaeger.

Jaeger turned to me. "I meant you no disrespect."

"In case anyone was wondering, I'm completely fine. You think that's the first time I've ever had something like that happen? Times may have changed, but not as much as one might hope. I'm not saying I won't accept help, and I appreciate you stepping in, but you don't need to act like you rode in on a white horse and rescued me, Jaeger. And don't you dare try to put any fault on Trent. He came just as quickly as you did. Just because he didn't run in waving a gun around doesn't mean he did any less to assist me than you did. So don't for one minute think that you are somehow better than him."

Jaeger grunted with irritation and crossed his arms, turning his head away from me.

Trent approached Jaeger and shoved his food container toward him. "The lady has spoken. Now let's eat."

Jaeger snatched the food container from him begrudgingly and took a seat at Trent's desk. Trent came over to me and gestured for me to make room for him to sit. I turned onto my side to give him room to sit on the chair cushion in front of me, essentially turning myself into a living back support pillow. I watched Trent open the lid on his food container and the savory aroma wafted to my nostrils.

"Whatchya got there?" I asked.

He gave me a sideways glance. "I thought you 'weren't hungry,'" he said, raising the pitch of his voice to try to imitate mine.

"I wasn't….but that smells good."

Trent took a big bite of what appeared to be a Chinese dish with chicken and ramen noodles and an assortment of colorful vegetables. He groaned obnoxiously.

"Mmm…it tastes good, too."

"I want some."

"No."

"Come on, don't be stingy."

He took another bite. "You should've asked before I ordered."

"Give me a bite or I'll start sneaking kale into your food," I threatened.

Trent gave me a look of outrage. "You wouldn't!"

I nodded. "I so would."

"Blimey, just give her a bloody bite," Jaeger said with annoyance.

"He has the same thing I have," Trent said to me, pointing his chopsticks toward Jaeger. "Go take his."

"Hey, now, wait a minute," Jaeger said, shaking his head in protest.

"Fine. Whatever. You just wait, Trent. Maybe I'll do something to your toaster pastries."

"Leave them out of this! They didn't do anything to you!"

I laughed. "Collateral damage."

"You can have what's left when I'm done," Trent offered.

"Oh, gee, thanks, but no. Too little, too late."

I watched as Trent ate every last bit of his food. He even tipped up the container and used the chopsticks to scoop the noodle bits at the bottom into his mouth. He then looked at me with a raised eyebrow.

"You're an ass," I said, laughing despite myself.

"I figured it might be my last meal, so I thought I'd better enjoy it," he said with a playful wink.

I sat up and wrapped my arms around Trent's chest, resting my head on his back. "Eh, I don't think trying to kill you would do me any good," I teased. I sniffed his ugly flannel shirt. "You need a shower. You smell as dirty as you look."

"I know. But to be fair, so did everyone else in Scandinavia and Egypt. I fit right in."

"Cool story. Take a shower."

"Hey, I was just committing to the part."

"So what's his excuse?" I asked, hooking my thumb toward Jaeger.

Jaeger frowned at me, then took a tentative sniff of his shirt. "Whatever. I smell like a man."

"You need some new clothes," I said to Jaeger. "Trent, can't you loan him something…anything?"

"He's not going to fit in anything of mine."

"Oh, does that mean we get to go shopping?" I asked.

"Get to, have to…all a matter of perspective," Jaeger said. "Can't I just wash these?"

"What are you going to wear while they're in the wash?"

Jaeger wiggled his eyebrows at me.

"Oh, good lord," Trent said in disgust as he stood up. "We'll go shopping as soon as I get out of the shower." As he walked out of the room, he stopped and turned around. "And I better not find out you were being a wanker while I was out of the room," he warned as he pointed at Jaeger. "You keep him in line, Roselyn."

"We'll be fine," I said.

The room was awkwardly silent for a while after Trent walked out. It was strange how uncomfortable I was when I was alone with Jaeger. I couldn't place what exactly it was about him that made me uneasy, but we didn't click at all. It was hard to believe that he was a parallel version of Trent.

I watched him lean back in Trent's chair and kick his dirty boots up on his desk. He looked over at me.

I tried to think of something to say to break the tension. "So…is our history anything like yours? Your world, I mean."

"From what I've seen so far, yes. I haven't yet found the divergence."

"You think there was one thing that set your world on a different path from ours?"

"Either one big thing or a series of small things in quick succession. You don't think of small incidents as making much of a difference in the grand scheme of things, but sometimes that's all the catalyst needed to change an entire world."

"Do you think you'll be able to get your world back on track? It sounded like you already changed a lot of things, and, well, it isn't like there's a big reset button."

Jaeger sighed. "You aren't wrong. But I can try to get it back. Maybe I'll go back and stop myself from changing things. I don't know if I can do that, but it's worth a shot."

"Or maybe that's all the more reason to just leave everything the hell alone. The more you meddle, the more you potentially mess up."

"It's already a mess. I can't leave it like that."

"What if you stop SABER from coming into existence? Wouldn't you disappear?"

"I can't. If I'm the one changing things, I have to exist. I'm a set point in time that cannot be erased."

"Well, how convenient for you."

"Why don't you like me?" Jaeger asked suddenly.

"What?" I asked, unsure of how to answer a question like that.

"I know you don't like me. It's obvious. You look at me like you wish I would disappear. You have to force conversation with me. You avoid standing anywhere near me. I just want to know why."

"Honestly, Jaeger...I don't trust you. And I think you already knew that."

"What reason do you have to still distrust me?!" he asked, offended.

"What reason have you given me to trust you?" I countered.

"I saved you from those men, for one," he argued.

"No, you didn't 'save' me from them. I saved myself and you popped in afterward."

"You know it wouldn't have ended that simply if I hadn't been there."

"Do you think I should feel indebted to you or something? Because I disagree."

"No. I'm just trying to make a point that I intervened in a situation to ensure your safety, and I feel that warrants a certain level of trust."

"I'll decide what warrants my trust and what doesn't."

"I don't want you to dislike me, Roselyn."

"Why? What does it matter? You're only going to be here a little while, and then you're going back to your own world."

"True, but I'll still have access to this world. I was hoping we could be friends."

"What do you need friends for? I thought you were a 'god.'"

"It doesn't mean I enjoy being alone," Jaeger said as he looked down at his hands in his lap.

I was surprised by his answer. "What do you mean 'alone'? You don't have any friends in your world?"

He gave a short, sarcastic laugh. "I was always an outcast at SABER, and then after they tried to kill me and Trent blew everything up, there was no one left who even knew who I was. After that, I spent my time traveling and trying to change things, which did involve interacting with a lot of people, but I wasn't there to make friends. I didn't have a companion. It wasn't like it has been here. I…I kind of like this. It's funny, you know? You don't even realize how lonely you are until you suddenly aren't." Jaeger said, finally looking up at me again.

"I'm sorry, but that doesn't change anything. Not yet."

"What made you trust Trent so fully?" he asked.

"He earned it. He proved himself to be trustworthy." I narrowed my eyes at Jaeger. "Why is this so important to you? I heard the sob story, yeah, but really…there are plenty of other people to make friends with."

"Nobody who understands this life like you and Trent do."

"I only understand it because Trent showed it to me. It could've been anyone. It didn't have to be me. You could do the same with someone else."

Jaeger made a face that indicated he didn't approve of that idea. "I'm not great with people. I don't like them overmuch."

I grunted. "Yet you want friends. Maybe you should get a cat."

I suddenly heard Trent calling for me from another room.

"What?" I yelled.

"I'm not going to shout a conversation with you across the whole flat! Just come here!"

I excused myself and walked out of the room, relieved to have an excuse to get out of this conversation with Jaeger. I walked up the narrow hallway and saw a closed door at the end with a sliver of light shining through the gap at the bottom.

I knocked. "Trent?"

Trent opened the door slightly and pulled me into the bathroom, the room still steamy from his shower. My eyes instantly fixed on his half naked body. He had a white towel wrapped loosely around his waist, sitting just below his hip bones and the lower portion of his external abdominal obliques. He was thin, but he wasn't scrawny. His muscles were long and lean, but they were well-toned.

He wrapped his arm around my waist and pulled me against him. He looked down at me, his damp, messy hair dangling over his forehead, and I reached up and swiped his hair out of his eyes. I recognized the needful way he was gazing at me, and it made my thighs tingly.

"No, not right now," I said before he even had a chance to say a word.

He grinned as his hand slid up under my tank top. "Why not?"

"First off, Jaeger is just in the other room, unsupervised. Second, you wouldn't share your food with me, so why should I share my goods with you?" I sassed. I put my hand firmly over his as he started to fondle my breasts.

Trent laughed. "Oh, is that how it's going to be? There's one problem with that reasoning."

"And what's that?"

"I didn't want to share. You do."

"You seem awfully sure of yourself, Mr. Morgan."

Trent pressed his lips to mine and my tongue immediately sought out his, betraying my ruse. When our kiss concluded, I was breathless. He had awakened my need so quickly it made my head spin.

"Well, if you insist that you don't want to…" Trent said as he pretended to pull away from me.

I clung to him. "Oh, I don't think so. You'd better finish what you started," I warned.

Trent smiled. "I fully intend to." He pushed me back against the sink and knelt down. He lifted up my skirt and slid my underwear down to my ankles. When I felt his mouth on me, I inhaled sharply. With every wiggle and flick of his tongue, my legs grew shakier and I leaned back against the sink for support. As I felt myself approaching the brink, I bit my lip and thrust my fingers into Trent's hair. I tried to keep the volume of my moans under control as he brought me over the edge, but the bathroom walls echoed and amplified every little sound I made. When Trent rose from his knees, he dropped his towel and lifted me up effortlessly, perching me atop his awaiting hardness. I threw my arms around his neck and wrapped my legs around his waist, and he carried me over to wall next to the shower, pinning my back up against it. I was already slick and ready for him, so it wasn't long before he was buried inside me. His thrusts were hard and deep, and when he came, I latched my lips onto his and kissed him, effectively muffling his moans.

When we were finished, I put my underwear back on and straightened my long skirt over my tired, shaky legs. "I hope I wasn't too loud," I whispered as I watched Trent dress. "I don't know how well sound carries through these bathroom walls."

"Are you embarrassed?"

"I would be if I knew Jaeger could hear it."

"Who cares if he hears it? I like the sounds you make. I'm rather proud of them. It gives me great pleasure to know I'm the one coaxing those kinds of sounds from you."

"That's fine in private, but nobody else needs to hear them," I said, my cheeks starting to redden.

"Oh, I don't know. I wonder if maybe he does. I'm beginning to think he needs a reminder that you're with me," Trent said possessively as he buttoned his white shirt in the mirror.

"What are you talking about?"

Trent looked at me in the mirror. "You didn't notice what he said earlier? That thing about how I should take better care of what's mine before I find it isn't mine anymore? You do know he was talking about you, right? He was threatening me."

"What business is it of his how we get along together?"

"Because he wants to get along with you, obviously," Trent said as he draped his tie around his neck.

I crinkled my nose. "No, I think you're mistaken."

Trent tipped his head to the side. "Maybe. But it isn't often that I'm wrong."

I crossed my arms. "As if I wasn't already uneasy enough around him, you go and tell me something like that."

"Eh, don't fret too much about it. He'll be gone before long."

"He told me he wants to still be able to visit us," I informed him.

Trent turned to look at me, a concerned expression on his face. "He did? When did he say that?"

"While you were in the shower."

He slipped on his suit jacket. "I don't know how I feel about that. I'd rather him stay in his own lane and we stay in ours, to be honest."

"He said he wants us to be his friends."

"Hm," Trent grunted, but he didn't say any more about it. He grabbed his watch and slipped it on his wrist. As he started to turn toward the door, he stopped and looked back down at his watch with a puzzled expression. "Bollocks," he mumbled, dashing from the bathroom.

"What? What is it?" I called after him, following on his heels.

He went into a room off to the left and grabbed a pair of glasses from the nightstand without answering me. He quickly slipped them on and brought up the holographic projection on his watch. He scowled as he scrolled through the nonsensical display of symbols and numbers.

"Something's not right," he said forebodingly.

"What isn't right?"

"Someone's messed with time."

"Jaeger?!" I suggested accusingly.

"No, he hasn't used his teleporter. My watch would have notified me immediately if he had. It isn't him…or at least it isn't him from right now."

"What's off? What's different? Can you fix it?" I asked.

Trent crinkled his forehead as he looked at me, his eyebrows curling upward. "I don't know yet." He brushed past me and hurried down the hall to the library where Jaeger was waiting. "We have a slight change of plans, Jaeger. Roselyn will take you to get some clothes. I have more pressing matters I must attend to."

"What's going on? I can help," Jaeger offered.

"No. Well, maybe in a while. I need to get a better idea of what I'm working with first. I'll check in soon."

Without further instruction or direction, Trent teleported from the apartment. Jaeger and I looked at each other blankly.

"So…where are we supposed to get money to buy your clothes?" I wondered aloud.

"He must have some kind of cash or cards or something stowed away in here," Jaeger said as he started rummaging through Trent's desk drawers.

"No, stop," I said. "Let me look. I'm not sure how comfortable he would be with you digging through his things."

"I'm not going to take anything," Jaeger said defensively.

"I'm not suggesting that you would."

I spent a good twenty minutes turning his apartment upside down before I found a stash of cash in his sock drawer. "I hope he wasn't saving this for a rainy day," I said as I snatched it up. I handed it to Jaeger, who had felt it necessary to follow me around while I conducted my search.

"You wouldn't let me help you look, but you're giving me the money now that you've found it?"

"It's to buy clothes for you, and I don't have pockets." I looked down at my attire. "Ugh, I wish I could change my clothes. I'm dressed for the past, not the future."

Jaeger raised his eyebrows and pointed toward Trent's closet. Trent had left the doors open on one side, and I could see the bottom of a dress hanging down, crammed to the end of the hanging rack. I felt a twist of jealousy in my chest.

"What about that?" he asked.

I furrowed my brow. "Why does he have a dress in here?"

"Maybe he likes to feel pretty," Jaeger jested.

I slid Trent's suits aside and looked at the light blue maxi-style dress. It was my size, but whose was it? I didn't want to wear one of his exes' dresses. Why would he keep this around? I'd have to ask him about it when I next saw him.

I closed the closet door. "We should go."

"Maybe you aren't the only one he's been entertaining in the shower," Jaeger said.

I turned on him wrathfully as rage roared through my veins. I clutched the front of his shirt in my fist and pulled him down to my level.

"Don't you ever say anything like that to me again, or you won't live long enough to finish the sentence."

"Sorry. I was just thinking aloud," Jaeger said, holding his hands up defensively. "Obviously he would have to be an idiot to—"

"Don't. Just don't."

I released Jaeger and turned on my heel, storming from the bedroom. He'd managed to ruin my day with one misguided musing. Not only had he insinuated that Trent was cheating on me, but it also meant that he knew what Trent and I had been doing in the bathroom, which embarrassed me. My cheeks were on fire. As I grabbed my sweater and my translator off Trent's desk, I tried to ignore the pit that Jaeger had opened up in my stomach.

We found our way out of the apartment and wandered down the sidewalk toward what appeared to be a bustling shopping district. Jaeger walked slightly behind me rather than next to me, and it made me feel like he was on guard duty. I slowed my pace, and he slowed his. I stopped and turned around.

"Why are you walking behind me?"

"You seemed to know where you were going."

"I don't like you following me like a creepy bodyguard."

"What am I supposed to do? You want me to go across the street? You want to go back to the flat while I do my own shopping? What do you want from me?!" he asked in frustration.

"Just…walk next to me, not behind me. I hate feeling like you're watching me."

"You're giving me a complex," Jaeger said with a heavy sigh.

"I could say the same about you," I mumbled as we started walking together.

"What was it that Trent took off to investigate?" Jaeger asked, changing the subject.

"His watch detected something was off. He didn't really elaborate."

"He should've taken us with him. He could be in danger, and we're out clothes shopping. This is rubbish," Jaeger said, stopping. "Your watch can track him, right? Take us to him."

"No. He wanted to look into it himself, so that's what we're going to let him do. Come on." I grabbed Jaeger's dirty sleeve and dragged him along with me. "We'll get you a suit, get back to the apartment, and wait."

Jaeger grunted. "Get me a suit? No. Hell no."

"What are you going to get, then?"

"A shirt and jeans. And pants. And socks."

"Well, that's boring."

"It's practical."

"And boring."

"Lucky for me, I don't care."

"What about underwear?" I asked.

"Yeah, I said that. Pants."

"Oh. I thought you meant pants pants. Like trousers."

"If I meant trousers, I would've said trousers."

"Well, excuse me," I said sarcastically with raised eyebrows.

After a few blocks, we found a men's clothing store. Jaeger walked straight to the jeans and grabbed the first pair he found in his size. He started to head toward the shirts before I stopped him.

"Aren't you even going to look at the styles?" I asked. "Let me see those." I grabbed the jeans from him and held them out at arm's length. "These are like weird man capris," I said with a grimace.

Jaeger frowned. "Oh. No. I don't want that."

"Yeah, didn't think so. You need to look before you just grab things."

After a bit of searching, I found a style that better suited him. We moved on to shirts, and he refused to get anything other than plain black or white t-shirts. When it came to the underwear and socks, I let him pick those out on his own. When he was satisfied with what we'd selected, we paid and left.

"I think that cashier was surprised to see you actually had enough money," I joked as we headed back toward the apartment building.

"That happens when you look like two hobos."

"I don't look like a hobo! You do!"

Jaeger looked me up and down. "Yeah, ok," he sneered. He looked down at his watch and ducked into an alleyway.

"What are you doing?" I asked, following him.

"Teleporting back to the flat."

"Oh."

"What's with that look? Is there something wrong with that?"

"No. It's just that…I don't know how to do that without knowing the exact coordinates. I haven't learned that yet."

"You can travel with me, then," he said, holding his hand out to me.

"No, that's ok," I said as I took a step back. "I'll just walk."

"What's the big deal? You do it with Trent."

"That's different."

"Roselyn, I don't bite. Come on."

I turned and walked away from him. I heard Jaeger give an exasperated sigh behind me and he jogged to catch up with me.

"Fine, I'll walk, too," he said.

"I didn't ask you to."

"Well, I can't very well run off without you when you're supposed to be keeping an eye on me, now can I?"

I didn't respond. I didn't like how comfortable he was getting with me, and I really didn't like how comfortable I was getting with him.

When we found our way back to the apartment door, I ran into a snag. I had no key to open the door. How could I have forgotten such a simple little detail?

"I'll just pop in and let you in," Jaeger offered.

"Ok. Thanks," I said begrudgingly, feeling foolish.

In a matter of seconds, Jaeger was in the apartment, holding the door open for me. I walked in and headed toward the kitchen, intending to see if Trent had any snacks in his cupboards. As I checked empty cupboard after empty cupboard, I heard Jaeger's voice from across the apartment.

"...Bloody hell?"

I stopped and listened.

"Roselyn! Something's wrong!" he called to me.

I ran to the library where he was yelling from, and as I rounded the corner, the scene I saw made my heart stop. Trent was lying unconscious on the floor behind his desk, his chair tipped onto its side and a Bible tossed haphazardly a few feet away from him.

Chapter 6

"Oh my god," I cried as I rushed to his side. "Trent? Trent! Wake up, Trent!" I put my fingers on his neck. He still had a pulse. He seemed to still be breathing. I lifted his eyelids, and his pupils contracted slightly and appeared to be even. But he was completely unconscious. My heart shattered into a million pieces. I knew what this was.

"What's wrong with him?" Jaeger asked, hovering over my shoulder.

I couldn't control the tears that welled up in my eyes. With a cracking voice, I replied, "He's changing." I sat cross-legged on the floor and gently laid Trent's head in my lap. "He's leaving me." I stroked his hair and cradled his cheek. I bent down and kissed his forehead. "This wasn't supposed to happen yet," I managed to say before I completely lost my composure.

Jaeger walked around me. He knelt down and started to attempt to move Trent's body.

"Don't touch him!" I shouted angrily, trying to shove him away. It was like trying to shove a brick wall.

"We should put him somewhere more comfortable," Jaeger reasoned calmly.

"Just leave him alone!" I threw my arms over Trent protectively.

"Roselyn, I'm trying to help. I'm not going to hurt him. We can't leave him on the floor."

"I know that! I just…I…please, don't take him from me just yet," I pleaded.

"I'm not taking him away. I'm just moving him. Come on, it'll only take a moment," Jaeger said as he carefully scooped Trent's limp body up into his arms.

"Be careful," I fretted.

As I followed Jaeger down the hall to Trent's bedroom, all I could focus on was the lifeless way in which Trent's arm dangled while Jaeger carried him. Seeing Trent so completely helpless broke something in me. I'd never imagined he could exist in such a state. With his boundless energy and lively personality, it seemed something of which he would be incapable. He was supposed to be indestructible, yet here he was, looking hopelessly fragile.

Jaeger laid him on the bed. He started to unknot Trent's tie.

"What are you doing?" I asked.

"If he's changing, we should be careful about anything constricting around his neck. If he changes into someone of my size, that tie could choke him."

Jaeger helped me get Trent out of his suit, leaving him in only his boxers and undershirt. I pulled the bedcovers up around him.

"Did he tell you anything about what happens when he changes?" I asked Jaeger.

"He only told me he wakes up as a different person, and he forgets things sometimes."

"I wonder if we're going to have to take care of him the same way as someone who is in a coma. His body is changing, but is it still processing the same way as normal? Does he still need to eat and use the bathroom?" I wondered.

"He's done this on his own countless times, hasn't he? I think his body just goes dormant while it happens – like suspended animation. I think we just need to keep watch over him."

I looked at the peaceful expression on Trent's face. That was when I realized that it didn't look quite the same. To the average person, he probably still looked the same, but I'd spent a lot of time looking at that face – I loved that face – and it wasn't the same. I couldn't place exactly what was different, but something was off. It was at that moment it truly hit me that I would never see his face the way it had been ever again. I choked out a sob.

"Hey, it's ok," Jaeger tried to console me. "It's not like he's dying. He'll wake up again."

"He is dying," I cried. "This Trent, the one that I fell in love with, is dead. I'll never see him again. Ever. He's going to wake up as someone else, and he's not going to know who I am, and it's going to kill me. It's going to absolutely kill me," I sobbed. I laid my head on Trent's chest and threw my arm over him, curling my body up next to him as closely as I could. I could hear his heart beating slowly. "This heart isn't going to beat just for me anymore."

"You don't know that," Jaeger said. "He told me he always remembered you. What makes you think this is going to be any different?"

"Because that's just how life works," I said cynically. "When you finally find something great, something worth living for, it gets stolen away. Nothing beautiful ever lasts. Happiness is always temporary. I just…I had hoped I had more time."

"Are you afraid that he isn't going to love you when he wakes up…or are you afraid you aren't going to love him?"

It stabbed me in the heart to even entertain the thought. I glowered at Jaeger. "The only way I would ever have a hard time loving him is if he woke up acting like you."

Jaeger glared at me. "I know you say that to wound me, but let me remind you that he was like me once. You're basically looking at his original packaging." With that, he turned and walked out of the room.

I hadn't meant to lash out quite so viciously, but Jaeger had hit a sore spot with his probing. The truth was, I was afraid of what Trent would turn into. I loved the man he had been. I had met one of his previous incarnations, and I wasn't able to see him as the same person. He and his past self were two different people in my eyes. I probably could have grown to love his past self, but I didn't know if I could have felt the same way about him that I felt about my Trent. The way he was now – or, the way he was recently – was perfect to me. I could have happily spent the rest of my life with that Trent. I never would have needed more than that. Who was he going to be now? Would he be as witty as my Trent? Would he be as charming? Would he be able to make me laugh? Would he be as handsome? Would he have a temper? Would he be arrogant? There was no way of knowing who he would be until he woke up. Until then, my heart was left hanging in the balance.

After a couple of hours, Jaeger came back to the room and turned the light on, as it was starting to get dark. I opened my eyes, not even realizing that I had closed them. I was still curled up next to Trent, desperately clinging to a man whom I had already lost, afraid to let go.

"We need to eat," Jaeger said. I noticed he had showered sometime while I was lying with Trent, and he was wearing his new blue jeans and black t-shirt. He cleaned up well, even if he hadn't shaved his stubbly five o'clock shadow.

"I'm not hungry," I replied.

"That may be, but you still need to eat."

"Go get something, then."

"I don't have any money. We spent it on clothes, remember?"

I sat up. "Well, shit."

303

"Do you think we should we take him back to your house? It might be better that way since neither of us know anything about this area or time period. And you have food and money."

He had a point. "Fine. I can order you a pizza or something," I said impassively.

I turned and looked at Trent as Jaeger lifted him off the bed into his arms, and I could see the changes had become more noticeable. I clenched my eyes closed, irrationally afraid that looking at his changing face for too long was going to make me forget the way he had looked before. I didn't want to forget. I didn't even have a photograph of him. I had no recording of his voice. It was like he was being slowly erased, and I was afraid that soon it would be like my Trent had never existed at all.

I entered my home coordinates into my watch – Trent had helped me to save them in my watch – and selected to return to the time right after I had left on Sunday morning. I put my hand on Jaeger's shoulder and teleported all of us back to my living room. I followed Jaeger to my room and watched him carefully lay Trent on my bed.

"He already doesn't look the same," Jaeger commented as he looked down at him. "It's so weird."

It wasn't just weird – it was heartbreaking. I turned away from him and walked out of the room. I couldn't bear to look at Trent right now.

Jaeger followed me down the hallway. "You knew this was going to happen someday," he said bluntly.

"Yeah, but 'someday' came sooner than I expected."

"It always does. It's not an excuse to not be prepared."

I whirled around. "And how the hell was I supposed to prepare for this? Hm? Do you even have feelings? Is it so impossible for you to understand that there are some things you just can't prepare for? Things you can't steel yourself against? I know everyone I love will die someday, but does that mean I need to spend every day prepared for someone to die?"

"People die. That's what people do. But that's not what Trent is doing. If you truly love him as you say you do, should it matter what he's like when he wakes up? At least he isn't dead, right?"

"You don't understand how I feel. You don't understand any of this."

"You're right. I don't. But I think you're being petty."

"I don't give a shit what you think," I spat as I walked away from him.

"I'm trying to make a point, Roselyn," he said as he continued to follow me to the kitchen.

"I'm not interested in hearing it."

"You don't love him."

I skidded to a halt so quickly that I almost tripped over my own feet. "If you value your face, you shouldn't say another word."

"No, I get that you think you love him. But do you really? If this is all it takes to make you doubt your future with him, did you really have a future to begin with?"

"Why are you doing this? What are you getting out of infuriating me? Does it make you feel better about yourself when you make everyone around you as miserable as you are?"

"I'm not trying to make you miserable. I'm just calling it like I see it."

"Well, you're a goddamn idiot, and you can shut your trap from now on, Jaeger, because you know nothing."

"An ad hominem argument usually indicates you have no valid argument against what the other person is saying."

"I don't need to defend myself against you or prove myself to you!"

"This isn't about me. It's about you still trying to convince yourself of something you know isn't real."

I grabbed a mug off the counter and whipped it at Jaeger's face. He reflexively put his hand up and caught it two inches from his nose. Goddamn his reflexes.

I turned away from him and rested my hands on the counter, taking a deep breath. "Go home, Jaeger. I don't want you here."

"You need me here."

"Why the hell would I have any need for you?"

"Because I think I know what Trent was looking into before he passed out."

"What are you talking about?" I asked as I turned to look at him.

"He was investigating some kind of anomaly, remember? While you were lying around feeling bad for yourself, I took it upon myself to take a look at the books on Trent's desk. He was reading about an incident involving two cities, Sodom and Gomorrah."

"Like the stories from the Bible? The cities that were destroyed with fire from the sky?"

"The very same. Whatever is wrong, that must be where it's centered. What did he tell you before he took off?" Jaeger wanted to know.

"He noticed something with his watch, but I couldn't decipher what any of it meant as he scrolled through it. He told me that someone had messed with time, but that was all I got from him."

"I need to look at his watch," Jaeger said as he started to walk back to the hallway.

"No, absolutely not," I said.

Jaeger stopped and turned around. "What? What do you mean 'no'?"

"We will discuss it with him when he wakes up. We don't even know what we're up against."

"If you let me look at his watch, I can tell you what we're up against."

"It isn't your problem, Jaeger."

"Yeah, it kind of is. I want to see the history of this world as it was meant to unfold, but that's a bit pointless if someone is running around changing it as we speak."

"It isn't your place to interfere," I pointed out. "We're waiting for Trent."

Jaeger looked at me like I was the stupidest person in the world. "This is absurd. Maybe it isn't my place to interfere, but it sure as hell is yours. Trent didn't give you my watch so you could squander its capabilities. Like it or not, you're now a caretaker of this world's history. This is your responsibility. You don't want someone turning your world into something like the mess I have back home."

"And what if we do go, and we try to figure it out and fix it, but we end up making it worse? No, we're waiting."

Jaeger tried to argue with me, but I turned around, grabbed my phone and earbuds off the counter, and plugged the earbuds into the phone. I stared defiantly at Jaeger as I stuck the earbuds in my ears and turned on the radio on my phone. His mouth stopped moving and he clenched his jaw and gave me a look of complete disgust.

"If you're hungry, you can make yourself something," I said curtly as I walked past him, scooped up Cattiel from the couch, and went back to my room, closing the door behind me. I leaned my back against the door and squeezed the fluffy cat while obnoxious techno music blasted through my earbuds. After a few minutes, I deposited the squirmy Cattiel onto the floor. I shut off my radio, set my phone on the nightstand, and looked over at Trent. He'd changed enough to look like someone who could be related to Trent, but he didn't look like Trent anymore. It brought tears to my eyes and broke my heart all over again. Is this how it was going to be every time I looked at him? I lay down on my side near him, my hands tucked close to my chest. I gazed at him, studying every feature that had changed. His nose was narrower. His chin had shrunk. His eyes seemed bigger. I reached over timidly and lifted his eyelid. I gasped and quickly snatched my hand away. His eyes weren't hazel-green anymore. They were turning brown.

"Who are you?" I whispered, tears running down onto my pillow. I closed my eyes. I pleaded quietly, "Please, Trent. Please leave enough of him for me to still recognize you. Don't erase him. Don't become someone else. We all change in some way – I know that. I've changed since I met you, and I'm a better person for having known and loved you. But I'm still me. Please…if you can…when you wake up, could you…still be you? Could you do that for me? I don't care what you look like on the outside – that's not what I'm talking about. I don't care if you have brown eyes. I don't care if you are taller or shorter. All I ask is that you don't change on the inside. Keep your sense of humor. Don't lose your wit. Gesture wildly when you talk. Smile at me like I'm the only other person in the world that matters to you. Be kind. And most of all...remember me. Please...when you wake up...love me."

I sat up and wiped the tears from my eyes. I climbed off the bed and shuffled to my closet to find some clean clothes. I needed to take a long, hot shower and have a private, ugly cry. I grabbed a pair of skinny jeans and an old sweatshirt and walked out of the room. I hesitated at the bathroom door, wondering if I should check on Jaeger. I shouldn't keep leaving him unsupervised, but he hadn't tried running off yet, so why would he try to now? I could hear him moving around in the kitchen, probably trying to make himself something to eat. I decided to let him be, and I closed and locked the bathroom door behind me.

As I stood in the shower, hot water running down my back, I realized that this was the first time I'd had a moment to myself since before Scandinavia. It was the first time I'd been in a room alone since we'd discovered Trent lying on the floor. I finally was free to let the tears flow without fear of judgement or interruption. I rested my forehead against the shower wall and sobbed so hard that no sound came out.

When I finally emerged from the bathroom with puffy, red eyes and a stuffy nose, I expected Jaeger to be there to ridicule or pester me. But he wasn't. I checked the living room and kitchen, and he wasn't there either.

"Jaeger?" I called, but there was no reply. I felt panic grip my chest as I dashed to my room. As soon as I laid eyes on Trent, I knew what Jaeger had done.

Trent's watch was missing

"You little shit!" I roared. I ran to my closet and threw on a pair of boots. I checked my Trent tracker to see if I could get a link to the location of Trent's watch. "Bingo," I said as it locked on. I looked over at Trent, my finger hovering over the button to teleport. I couldn't leave him here all by himself, completely defenseless, could

I? But I couldn't let Jaeger mess with our past, either. I closed my eyes. "I'm sorry, Trent. I won't be long, I promise." I pressed the button.

Before me was a smoldering city of rubble. Smoke and embers rose into the sky as though they were trying to escape the flames as urgently as the people who fled into the surrounding plain. It took me a moment to tear my eyes away from the horror in front of me. I looked over at Jaeger, who stood to my right. He was staring at the decimated city with a look not of horror, but of regret.

"This looks like my world," he said.

"You shouldn't be here," I replied. "You need to come back with me and return Trent's watch. That was a bullshit move."

He turned his head toward me. "Someone did this to get our attention. This is one great big, terrible calling card. We couldn't not answer."

"Jaeger, we need to go before we screw something up."

Jaeger raised his arms and held them wide. "This is already screwed up! This city isn't supposed to burn today. Neither is that one," Jaeger said, pointing to a patch of smoke rising in the distance. "According to Trent's watch, this is an anomaly."

"They are supposed to burn. Everyone knows the story of Sodom and Gomorrah. They both burned."

"Yes, but they aren't supposed to burn today. It's a day too early. There's supposed to be a cosmic airburst event – a huge meteor is supposed to explode in the atmosphere above this place and rain fire down on both cities tomorrow."

"That's what Trent's watch told you?"

"That's what it showed."

"So what do you propose we do?"

"We find out who wanted to get our attention so badly that they had to burn down a city to do it."

A woman suddenly stepped up behind us. "That would be me."

Chapter 7

Jaeger and I spun around to face the stranger. She was tall, probably close to six feet, and had an athletic build. Her long dark hair was slicked back in a tight ponytail. Her almond-shaped brown eyes gazed at us with a sinister sparkle, and a smug smirk danced on the corner of her lips. She wore a burgundy scarf under a black leather jacket with tight black pants and black boots. I wanted to ask her how she wasn't sweating her ass off in all that black leather, but the huge rocket launcher she had slung over her shoulder persuaded me to keep my mouth shut.

"The ever-elusive Trent Morgan," she said, looking at Jaeger. She sized him up. "Looking good."

"Who the—" I started to say before I suddenly found the point of a knife touching the tip of my nose. I didn't even see her draw it.

"You will speak when spoken to," the woman informed me with an annoyed expression. She lowered the knife and returned her attention to Jaeger. "I knew you couldn't miss my message. The best way to find a vigilante is to make a scene and wait. One rocket launcher and a stockpile of explosives - it was almost too easy."

"Who are you and what do you want?" Jaeger demanded firmly.

"Straight to the point. I like it. I'm Megan. And you'll be coming with me."

"He's not—" I began.

There was a brief flurry of movement right in front of my face, and it took me a moment to realize that Megan had chucked her knife at my face – and Jaeger had flung his hand out to block the path of the blade. It had pierced all the way through and was protruding out the back of his hand, the tip of the blade only about an inch from my face, covered in Jaeger's blood.

"Fuck!" I cried in shock.

"Oh, dear," Megan said with a fake pout. "Well, that was very chivalrous of you to offer a helping…hand. A bit over the top, if you ask me, but to each his own. I wonder if you can stop this?" Megan propped the rocket launcher up on her shoulder and aimed it at me.

"Jesus Christ!" I shouted and cowered with my hands over my head.

Jaeger pulled the knife from his hand and stepped between Megan and me. "Relax, Roselyn. It isn't loaded," he said.

"Don't fucking tell me to relax! She just threw a knife at my face! She stabbed you in the hand!"

"What do you want me for?" Jaeger asked Megan.

"It's time for you to come home. You've had your fun, but you need to come back to SABER. Playtime's over. Say goodbye to your trollop and let's go."

I had so many things I wanted to say, but I didn't dare open my mouth. That was a first.

"I hate to disappoint you, Megan, but you've wasted your time. I'm not going anywhere with you."

Megan gave a humorless laugh. "Oh, darn. Boo. I guess I'll just go home, then. You sure told me. Shucks. Too bad. But before I go, how about I ask you just one more time, and this time in a way that might persuade you. Come with me, please, and if you do, I won't follow your bitch home and murder her and everyone she's ever talked to."

"I'm not the kind of person you want to threaten," Jaeger said in a disturbingly calm voice.

"I'm not threatening you. I'm threatening her. I'm persuading you."

"What makes you think I'm Trent?"

Megan pulled a crumpled up paper from her jacket and held it out for Jaeger to see. It had pictures of two men on it. "Oh, aren't you? I suppose she must be Trent, then," Megan said sarcastically as she nodded toward me. "Oh, wait—" Megan turned the paper so she could take an exaggerated look at it. "Who is that guy right there?" she asked, pointing to the photo that looked exactly like Jaeger. "Funny...gosh, that guy looks familiar. Who does that look like to you?"

"If you know Trent, you know he changed and doesn't look like that anymore."

"So they say. Then who could you be, I wonder?" Megan shoved the paper back into her jacket. "A clone? A doppelganger? A long lost evil twin no one knew existed? Cut the shit. I don't know how you managed to revert back, but I don't care. The longer you stall, the more likely it is that I'm going to kill this...Roselyn, was it? If you care about her at all, you'll comply."

Jaeger looked back at me. I was expecting a contemplative expression, but all I saw was resignation in his eyes. He'd already made up his mind.

"Fine," he said. "I'll go with you, but I want a moment to say goodbye."

"Ugh. Ew. Whatever. No funny business, though, or you know what'll happen. Don't even think about trying to teleport out of here because I'll just track your jumps. And then she'll die. Make it quick."

"No funny business," Jaeger agreed.

I looked at Jaeger with wide, fearful eyes as he turned around and wrapped me in his arms. I stood there with my arms hanging at my sides, unsure of what to do while he squeezed me tightly against his body. Was this a trick? Was he planning something? Were we going to make a quick getaway?

"I'll keep them entertained until he's ready," Jaeger whispered in my ear. He released me and turned back to Megan. "Let's go."

Megan sneered at me as she slid her arm around Jaeger's waist, and suddenly they were both gone.

I hurriedly teleported back home and ran into my room, locking the door behind me. I grabbed my .45 and slumped to the floor next to the bed, resting my back against the box springs, waiting for Megan to come crashing through my door. I suddenly noticed something hard digging into my spine between my shoulder blades. I reached back and felt something in the hood of my sweatshirt. As my fingers closed around it, I realized what it was. It was Trent's watch. That was why Jaeger insisted upon hugging me – he needed to slip that into my hood.

I didn't know how to feel about Jaeger. I didn't like him, but I didn't exactly dislike him, either. Jaeger had saved my life. Those reflexes I had cursed earlier had stopped me from taking a knife through the skull. But if he hadn't gone behind my back and taken Trent's watch, I wouldn't have been in that situation in the first place. I know he did it because he thought it was what needed to be done – he thought it was the right thing to do – but it was still a betrayal of the limited amount of trust I had given him.

But…what now? Jaeger was in the hands of Megan and SABER, and Trent was still out of commission. Was I just supposed to leave Jaeger? I looked at the watch in my hand. If he had kept Trent's watch, I could've tracked him. I didn't know how to track Jaeger's watch, though. It frustrated me at how much I still didn't know how to do. I stood up and set the gun on the nightstand, my adrenaline rush now ebbing. I reached down and strapped Trent's watch on his wrist. I allowed my fingers to linger, running them down to his hands. I laid his hand on top of mine and inspected his fingers. I noticed his knuckles were less knobby than they used to be, though his fingers were still long and slender. I laid his hand back on the bed and turned away from him. I grabbed the gun off of my nightstand, stuck it in my waistband, and walked out of the bedroom.

I paced and fretted all evening, uncertain of what I should be doing. I was so tense that I almost had a heart attack when my phone rang. It was my mother, calling to let me know she had made it home safely.

"I hope you aren't still mad at me," my mother said.

"I still think the things you said were shitty, but I'm not mad anymore. I, um…I don't think it's going to work out with Trent, anyway."

"Oh, honey, already? You two seemed to be getting on so well on Friday."

"Yeah, well…people change."

"Yes, sometimes they do. And there's nothing you can do about that. But don't worry. You're a beautiful girl and you'll land yourself a good, hard-working man someday."

"I think I'm done looking for a while."

"Now, don't say that. You don't want to wait too long. The older you get, the harder it is to find someone."

I gave a disgusted sigh. "Jesus, Mom, you act like I'm some kind of old spinster."

"No, nothing of the sort! I'm just saying…if you're going to want kids someday, you're going to want to get on that sooner rather than later."

"I'm not particularly worried about that."

"When you find the right man, you will be."

"You know when I said I wasn't mad at you anymore? I think I might have to revise that if we keep this conversation going much longer."

"Goodness, you are snippy tonight! Breakups are never easy, but it does you no good to take it out on those who love you. I wish you'd quit pushing people away every time things get a little rough. You can't just shut down like that."

"I don't shut down."

"Yes, you do. You withdraw into yourself, everyone else be damned."

"Well, that's not what I'm doing this time."

My mom sighed. "For your sake, I hope not. That's a lonely way to live. You need to let people in. It's better to have your heart broken than to have no heart at all."

"I think I would have to disagree with you on that."

"Don't say things like that. You sound like a sociopath."

"I'm not a sociopath," I said. I felt a twinge in my heart when I heard Trent's voice in my head saying, "I do wonder." "Mom, I have to go. I need to make dinner."

"Well, I love you regardless of whatever choices you make and regardless of how salty you are."

"I love you, too."

I ended the call with my mom and went into the kitchen. I didn't have the energy nor the desire to make dinner, so I sat at the table with a sleeve of crackers, a chunk of teriyaki flavored tofu, and the tray of cheeses I had left over from my parents' visit. Cattiel strolled into the kitchen and rubbed against my shin with a purrrt while I snacked.

"This sucks, kitty. I don't think I can go back to doing this by myself every day. How do you go back to being lonely after finding out what it felt like to be happy?"

I finished my "dinner" and got ready for bed. It wasn't all that late, but I had no idea how long I had been awake and I was tired. When I walked into the bedroom, I saw that Cattiel had made his way back into the room and was curled up next to Trent.

"I don't even recognize him anymore, but you seem to know it's him," I said to the cat as I slipped into my pajamas. Before shutting off the light, I stood and gazed at Trent's face. Any familiar trace of his old appearance was gone now, having changed into a man my brain had a hard time seeing as "Trent." He was slightly thinner. His chin and nose were both quite a bit narrower. His ears were smaller, and his eyes were much bigger. His eyebrows looked thicker and darker, but his hair hadn't changed. He was still attractive, but he looked so different that I had difficulty feeling any amorous feelings for this stranger lying in my bed. I blinked the tear from my eye and shut off the bedroom light. I climbed into bed, leaving a cat-sized distance between myself and Trent.

"I'm afraid, Trent," I whispered in the darkness. "My head and my heart can't seem to reconcile their differences. They don't know how to interpret your change. I love you, but…god, I can't believe I even have to put 'but' after 'I love you.' I never thought I would ever do that. I'm sorry. I'm failing you. The more you change, the further I feel from you. I hate the way this feels, but there's nothing I can do to stop it. I keep doubting myself. I just need a little reassurance, but no one seems to want to give me any…so I guess it's up to you now. I don't need much. Just something. One little thing. When you wake up, just give me one tiny little sign to show me that you're still in there. Help me find you. Well…that is, of course, assuming you even remember me when you wake up." I rolled over and faced the window, turning my back to Trent. "Who am I kidding?" I said aloud to myself. "I'm being entirely too optimistic. He's going to open his eyes and look at me blankly, and it's going to kill me."

At 7AM, my alarm clock went off. I reached over and snoozed it without even opening my eyes. I started to snuggle further under my covers when I felt the bed suddenly jostle. I looked over just in time to see Trent bolt upright in bed with a loud, dramatic gasp. My heart was instantly in my throat. He looked around wildly.

"What? Where am I? What's going on?!" He paused and ran his tongue across his teeth. "My mouth feels weird. My teeth…" He reached up and ran his hands over his face, inspecting every feature with his fingers. He ran his hands through his hair, causing it all to stand up on end. He glanced over at me in the midst of his inspections and froze. Our eyes locked, and in the dim, predawn light, I could see the moment of recognition in his new, expressive eyes. They were the color of rich black coffee when the sun shone through it. "Roselyn," he said in a low, unfamiliar voice, almost more to himself than to me. He held his hands out and looked at them, wiggling his fingers as he scrutinized them. He looked back at me, knitting his eyebrows. "I'm so sorry, Roselyn."

My heart was awash with relief. "You remember me."

"You're the one person I never seem to forget," he said with a slight smile. "What happened? Where am I?"

I frowned. "You're in my house."

Trent looked at Cattiel, who was sitting at the foot of the bed with his ears back, having been startled from his sleep by Trent's dramatic awakening. "Oh, a cat! I love cats, I think!"

The relief in my heart gave way to anxiety. "You don't remember Cattiel?"

"Is that her name?"

"His name."

"I might later. I'm always a bit foggy when I first rouse."

"Listen, there's some shit going on that I need to tell you about. SABER took Jaeger."

"Jaeger who?"

"Jaeger Novak."

"That's a neat name. I like it. Why would SABER take him?"

"They thought he was you."

"Why on Earth would they think that?"

"Because he looks like you did originally."

"Well that's quite a coincidence. I suppose we'll have to devise a plan to rescue the poor chap. But first I need to eat. I can't do anything until I eat. I'm famished!" Trent jumped out of bed and immediately fell onto the floor.

"Good lord, are you ok?!" I asked as I scrambled over to the side of the bed.

"Well, that's embarrassing," he said from his sprawled-out position on the floor. "I feel like a baby…um…you know, those gangly critters with the outlandishly long necks?"

"Giraffe?"

"Yes! Like a baby giraffe. New bodies take time to get used to."

I climbed out of the bed and helped him to his feet. "You're taller," I said. He had to be a little over six feet tall now.

"I feel thinner," he commented as he looked down at himself. "Hey, where are my clothes? Why am I walking around in my pants and undershirt?"

"Oh…They got left behind in Glasgow."

"What happened in Glasgow?!"

"You passed out."

"But I wasn't wearing any clothes?"

"Yeah, you were, but after you passed out, we took off your suit."

"Who's 'we'?"

"Jaeger and me."

"Why did Jaeger want to undress me?" Trent asked, raising one bushy eyebrow.

"We didn't know how much you were going to change, so we thought it would be better if you weren't wearing any restrictive clothing."

"Oh, that makes sense," Trent said as I helped him to a chair at the kitchen table. I went to the cupboard and grabbed a package of toaster pastries.

"Here. These are your favorite," I said as I handed him the pastries.

He ripped open the package and took a huge bite out of the first one. He chewed for a couple of seconds, then gave me a disgusted look.

"I don't think I like these," Trent said as he slid the uneaten portion back across the table toward me.

I stared at him in disbelief as I felt tears welling up in my eyes. "But…but you love toaster pastries…"

He shook his head. "Not so much. It tastes a bit like chocolate cardboard. What else do you have?"

I was suddenly angry with him.

"You can eat the pastries or you can get your own food," I hissed through clenched teeth as tears streamed down my cheeks. I started to walk out of the kitchen.

"What have I done? Why are you cross with me?" Trent asked as he reached out for my arm on my way by.

I yanked my arm back, out of his reach. "Because you aren't you!"

He looked wounded. "I can't help it, Roselyn! I didn't ask for this to happen either!" Trent shouted back.

"I know!" I cried. I walked over and sat on the edge of the couch in the living room and buried my face in my hands. "I know."

"Roselyn, come sit with me. Please."

I ignored him.

"Are you really going to make me slide out of this chair and army crawl across the floor to you?"

"Don't."

"Are you going to come over here and talk to me?"

"No."

Trent sighed. "Bollocks." I heard a thump and felt the floor shake. I looked out from behind my hands and saw Trent squirming across the floor toward me, a toaster pastry in his hand.

"Are you serious?"

"I told you I was going to," Trent replied as he pulled himself up onto the couch next to me and slumped back against the cushions. He looked so unruly in his underwear and hair sticking up every which way. He shoved a bite of toaster pastry into his mouth.

"You don't have to eat that if you don't like it," I said quietly.

"If it makes you happy, I can pretend to like anything."

"I don't want you to pretend, Trent. That's the problem. I want the old you who didn't have to pretend."

Trent's big brown eyes were like giant windows to his soul – and I could see that I had crushed him. He turned his reddening eyes away from me and took another bite of toaster pastry.

"You know, my mind might not always remember everything, but my heart will always remember the feelings," Trent said after a long silence. He looked back at me. "I don't remember all of what I used to be, but I know I loved you…and I still do. I know it's hard for you to see me right now. I know you might not love me yet because you can't find me in this," he said, gesturing to his new body, "but if you loved me the way I think you did, you will find me again."

I wiped the tears from my eyes and rose from the couch. I went to the kitchen and opened the fridge. I pulled out the egg carton.

As grabbed a skillet and set it on the stove, I asked Trent, "Do you remember when you took a cooking class while I was sleeping so you could learn how to make me breakfast? You made that amazing omelet with truffles. Do you remember it?"

I heard only silence behind me. I felt my lower lip tremble.

"I'm sorry, Roselyn."

I cleared my throat. "What kind of cheese did you put in it?" I asked him curtly.

"Roselyn…"

"You need to remember!" I shouted, turning to him.

"I can't, ok?! It's gone! Maybe it'll come back to me, but maybe it won't! I remember you, and I remember how I feel about you. Isn't that enough?"

"No, of course it isn't enough! I want you to remember why you love me! I want you to be able to remind me why I love you!"

Trent looked at me with a somber expression. "Or maybe we'll have to find new reasons to love each other. Is that so bad? Is that such a terrible thing to be able to fall in love all over again?"

I rested my hands against the front edge of the stove and bowed my head. "And what if the opposite happens?"

"Are you already placing your bets against us?"

"No. I'm just being realistic."

"Try being optimistic. It's so much more."

"More what?"

"Just…more."

I said nothing as I turned on the burner on the stove and stuck two slices of bread in the toaster. I looked at the clock on the stove in front of me. There was no way I was going to work today. I couldn't leave Trent here by himself in this state, especially if Megan happened to make a surprise visit.

I called into work and made up a story about having a stomach virus while I cooked Trent's breakfast. When I got off the phone, I started working out a plan in my head. It was obvious I needed to buy myself time. There were things that needed to be dealt with, and I couldn't get Trent back on track and rescue Jaeger if I had to worry about work on top of everything. I needed to take Trent somewhere else until we figured everything out.

"So, tell me about Jaeger," Trent called from the living room. "Was he our companion? Why did he look like me? How did SABER get a hold of him?"

I told Trent all about who Jaeger was, and I filled him in on what had happened with Megan. When I had explained everything, I brought his breakfast to him in the living room. I sat down on the other couch across from him.

"He saved your life," Trent said.

"Yeah, he did. He saved yours, too. He could've easily given you up, especially considering the state you were in, but he took the fall for you instead."

"He sounds like a good man."

I hesitated. "He sounds like one, doesn't he?"

"We'll get him back. Don't worry," Trent assured me.

"I know we will. What about the history that Megan changed? Are we going to have to go back and fix that?"

"I'll have to take a look at the data before I know for certain, but I think we got lucky. I don't think this change was enough to cause much of a ripple. I think history will remain intact. Besides, Jaeger may have fixed the event simply by showing up when he did, so it might not be possible for me to change it back now. Either way, I'll deal with it if it needs to be dealt with."

As Trent started to dig into his food, he glanced up at me. "Aren't you eating?" he asked.

"I'm not hungry." I said.

"Oh. Well, thank you. I appreciate this."

"When you're done eating, we need to get out of here. We need to go somewhere and somewhen else so you can recover without me having to lose days from my own time period. Any ideas where we could go?"

"I hear Nebraska's nice," Trent said.

"Nebraska?"

"I remember having a house there. I'm not sure when, but I can find it." He opened the holographic display on his watch. He squinted at the interface in front of him for a moment, then looked over at me with furrowed brows. "Do I have glasses somewhere around here?"

"No, not here. You still need them, even after the change?"

"I think I need them even more now," Trent remarked.

"Doesn't that get fixed by the nanobots?"

"It isn't an injury. It's just part of the genetics, so it isn't something that gets 'repaired.' Sometimes it's worse, sometimes it's not so bad, depending on how my DNA gets rewritten and rearranged with each change."

"Well, maybe you have some glasses at your Nebraska house."

"...Assuming I send us to the right place..."

"You'll get us there. Finish eating. I'm going to go get dressed before we blow this joint." As I got up and started to head down the hallway, I was reminded of the dress in Trent's closet. I stopped and turned to him. "I know this is a long shot, seeing as you aren't remembering much yet, but...whose dress was in your closet in Glasgow?"

He looked at me blankly. "A dress? I haven't the foggiest."

I walked back to my room and closed the door. It was hard to accept that there were huge chunks of Trent's life that I would never know about. Every time I thought I had come to terms with it, something would happen that proved otherwise. I hated it. That dress was like a scar. Trent didn't develop scars on his body, as he always healed perfectly, but he left items scattered through his past that revealed things about the life he had lived much in the way a scar does. If he retained a scar for every person he loved and forgot, I wagered he would be covered from head to toe. I might never know who wore that blue maxi dress, but I knew a man didn't keep a woman's dress in his closet without a certain level of intimacy. How much time did I have before I became an unclaimed dress in his closet?

Chapter 8

Trent finally found his legs – his no longer bowed legs, I had noticed – after he had eaten. He was able to teleport us to his place in Nebraska in the year 2434, and after we arrived, he took a quick shower and got himself dressed. When he walked into the living-room-turned-library, he had his hair styled differently – he wore it messy in the front now instead of swooped over. He still wore a tweed suit, but I noticed he had tennis shoes on instead of his usual boots or oxfords. His feet weren't as awkwardly big as they used to be, so he probably didn't fit in his other shoes. I saw he was wearing his thick-framed glasses, too.

"You look like a new man," I joked. Even when I was in a foul mood, the opportunity for a bad joke wasn't lost on me.

He pressed his lips together in an amused smirk. "That I do."

"Why did you change your hair?" I asked.

"Don't you like it? I thought it looked better with this face."

"I like it, it's just…not what I'm used to."

"Let's face it, Roselyn. None of this is what you're used to."

"Yeah, don't remind me."

Trent stuck his hands in his pockets and gave me a stern look. "Do you realize that when you say things like that, it hurts me? You wishing for who I used to be is to be expected, I know. I get it. I wish I could be who you want me to be, too. But it's also a rejection of who I am now, and like it or not, the man you knew is dead, and this is who you're stuck with."

"So, what, I'm not allowed to miss him?"

"I'm not saying that. But being disgusted with me because I'm not him anymore? I don't think I can bear that."

"I'm not disgusted with you. I just…need time."

Trent looked at the floor and nodded.

"I see you found your glasses," I said, trying to change the subject.

"Yep."

"Are we going to get Jaeger now?" I asked.

"Soon. I need to eat again. Changing takes a lot of energy," he said as he walked out of the room. I got up and followed him into a large, high-tech kitchen. He stood in front of what looked like a short fridge or a freezer with a big window on it. I could see what looked like single-servings of food that reminded me of the kinds of things I'd find in the frozen dinner section at a grocery store. He opened the door, and I noticed this "freezer" wasn't cold. He grabbed what looked like a desiccated sub sandwich encased in shrink wrap, and he put it into a boxy device that looked like a microwave sitting on top of the "fridge." He pressed a button that showed water drops on it. The "microwave" made a low humming sound that lasted about five seconds, then beeped. Trent opened the appliance and pulled out the sandwich. It was still in the shrink wrap, but it now looked like it was freshly prepared. He leaned over the counter on the island in the middle of the kitchen and unwrapped his sub, taking a bite out of it nonchalantly.

"What was that?!" I asked in awe.

He looked at me like I was crazy. "Hydrator," he said as though it were obvious.

I inspected the sandwich in his hands. "It looks like someone just made it!"

"I did. You watched me."

"No, I mean it looks like it just came from the deli. Does it taste normal?"

"Why wouldn't it taste normal?"

I leaned over from the opposite side of the counter where I had been standing and took a bite out of his sandwich while he looked on with a raised eyebrow. It tasted like it had just come from the deli.

"Holy shit, that's amazing," I said around a mouthful of sub.

"Have you never had a sarnie before?"

"I'm not talking about the sandwich. I mean it's amazing that it went from a dried-up, sad-looking thing to a real, fresh sandwich."

"Oh, that's right. You don't have this technology yet. This particular process of dehydrating and rehydrating food cut down on worldwide food waste by something like fifty-percent almost overnight."

"Why do you remember that?"

Trent shrugged as he took another bite of his sub.

"Are you starting to remember more things yet?" I asked.

"A little. I'm starting to remember Jaeger. I can picture him now. It's weird, though, because thoughts of him are accompanied by a certain sense of unease. Did something happen? Is there reason for concern?"

"You two had your moments. Jaeger is…well…he's kind of a jerk."

"No, this is something else. Distrust, maybe?"

"Probably."

Trent stared at me, like he was trying hard to concentrate to remember something.

"Why are you staring at me like that? You look like you're trying really hard to hold in a fart."

He scrunched his face at me like I was absolutely ridiculous. "That's—OH! He fancied you!" he exclaimed with a wild snap of his fingers. "That was it! Now I remember."

"Yeah, you mentioned that before, but I think you might be wrong about that one. Like, really wrong."

"Really? You think so? I'm not usually wrong."

"Well, you are this time, so just sit there in your wrongness and be wrong and eat your wrong sandwich."

Trent narrowed his eyes at me. "Well, I guess we'll see about that."

"Should I write him a letter? 'Do you like me? Circle yes or no.'?"

"No, of course not…obviously I have to rescue him first," Trent jested.

"Ah, yes. We'll have to settle it afterward." I rested my elbows on the counter and looked at Trent. "So, how are we going to rescue him? I can't imagine it's going to be as easy as teleporting in, snagging him, and popping back out again."

"No, it won't be that easy. Also, you aren't going."

"Bullshit. I'm going. When are you going to learn?"

"When are you? You're a liability. You make me weaker."

I raised my eyebrows in shock. "What the hell did you just say to me?"

"I don't mean it as an insult to you. I simply mean that there is no limit to what I would do, to what I would sacrifice to save you. Please don't put me in a position like that."

"Oh, you mean so I can sit here and wonder if you're ever coming back? Because if you don't then I'm coming in for you anyway. Wouldn't you rather me come with you so we can work together rather than having me show up later on my own?"

"I'll take your watch."

"I'd love to see you try to pry this watch off of my wrist," I taunted.

"I'm not putting you in the path of danger."

"Dammit, Trent! I'm mortal. I'm always in the path of danger! I could choke on a chunk of chicken in my kitchen while sitting around waiting for you. I could get in a car accident. I could get sick. Like it or not, I'm never out of the reach of death. You might as well accept that and just let me live my life as I choose – even if I make a risky decision. You don't get to decide that for me. You used to understand that."

"I used to be reckless! But after you told me about what happened with Megan…you could have died back in Jordan, Roselyn. That was too close of a call. No more."

"No more? That's it? No more? Who the hell do you think you are?"

Trent's demeanor became melancholy. "I'm the one who loves you, even when you don't love me."

Those words worked to subdue my anger, but they didn't dampen my resolve. "If you love me, then you know better than to try to control me. I'm not doing this to put myself in danger – I don't want to die. I'm doing this because it's right. Jaeger deserves my help."

We stared at each other stubbornly, neither of us willing to budge.

I added, "Besides, how much can you possibly love me if you can't even remember why you love me? Don't use 'love' as a tool to try to make me obey you."

Trent looked at me solemnly. He turned away from me and slowly walked out of the kitchen.

"Robiola," he said as he paused with his back to me. He turned his head to the side, but not far enough to look at me. "It was robiola."

By the time I understood his meaning, he had walked out of the room. The truffle omelet…he did remember. I took a step in the direction he had gone, but I hesitated. That was a horrible thing for me to have said to him. He didn't like this any more than I did, and I was making it harder on both of us. What was wrong with me? Why couldn't I stop being angry at him for changing? It was like I viewed the man he was now as some kind of villain who took away my

Trent. It was such an absurd feeling to want so desperately to love someone when all you feel is resentment.

After a while of sitting by myself in the kitchen, lost in my thoughts, I headed back to the library and found Trent sitting at his desk. He had a journal sitting open in front of him on the desk, and he was scrolling through the information in his watch. He didn't acknowledge that I had entered the room.

"Finding anything good?" I asked.

"Unfortunately, no."

"Does this mean we don't have a plan?"

"No, it just means we don't have a good plan."

"All right…so what do we have?"

"The bad news is that tracking Jaeger's watch has proved to be problematic. I had it synced to mine, so I should be able to find it without an issue, but something's blocking out part of the coordinates – namely, the time portion. I can find exactly where on earth it is, but I don't know when it is."

"But is he going to be with his watch? I have to imagine they would've taken it away from him as soon as they brought him back to their time."

"Yeah, I'm sure they took it from him, but if they are assuming he is me, then they have no reason to try to hide it. They probably wouldn't be expecting anyone to track it. It's probably still in the same compound where they're keeping him."

"So what do we do?"

"We lock onto his location and take a guess on time."

"That sounds like a terrible plan," I remarked.

"I told you it wasn't a good plan."

"Yeah, but you didn't say it was terrible."

"I know. You did."

"Do you think this is really going to work?"

"Did you miss that part earlier where I said it wasn't a good plan?"

I sighed. "Maybe we should wait until we come up with a better one."

"I hate to say it, but I don't think there is a better plan."

"What do we do when we get there? How are we going to find him?"

"Still working on that one."

"Great."

Trent turned to me. "It's not too late. You can still opt out of this."

"No. I'm going."

"This is going to be incredibly dangerous. If you run into Megan—"

"I know the risks. Let's just do it."

Trent closed the display on his watch and stood up. "Don't you dare get hurt. I'll never forgive you if you do."

"Never forgive me? I thought you'd say you'd never forgive yourself."

"Hey, I tried to stop you, but you insisted. This is all on you, love."

I rolled my eyes. "I'll be fine."

"Before we go, I want you to save this location in your watch. If we get separated, we can reconvene back here."

After Trent had helped me save Nebraska 2434 in my watch (for the return trip) and handed me a translator to put in my ear, he sidled up next to me and put his arm around me. He turned and looked down at me.

"Ready?"

"Ready."

As our surroundings started to change, there were strange flashes of colors and light around us, as though the teleporter had glitched. It reminded me of something you'd see in a sci-fi movie wormhole. After a second, we landed in wide open desert.

I looked around, confused. "What happened? Where are we?"

"Right where we need to be. Let's hope we're when we need to be."

"What are you talking about?! We're in the middle of a desert!"

"Take a closer look," Trent said as he pointed in front of us.

I shaded my eyes with my hand and squinted. I noticed there was something off about the landscape in front of me – I couldn't place my finger on it, but something didn't look quite right. Trent took a few steps forward and put his hand out – and it rested against the side of an invisible wall. It looked like a mime trick. I followed him and reached out, feeling a cold, hard wall. Now that my hand was on it, I could see it was like a bunch of computer screens put together to form a wall.

"The whole compound has been camouflaged. These screens take visual information from the opposite side of the building and display them on this side. It's like that all the way around the building. Even the roof is covered in monitors that look like the ground to avoid detection from the sky. Brilliant, isn't it?"

"How do the people who work here and visit here ever find it?"

"I'm guessing the people who work here don't leave. And they probably don't get many visitors, either." Trent held his watch up to eye level and activated the holographic display. "Look at that – no thermal signature, either. That's amazing."

"Is this camouflage technology the reason we had such a weird teleport?"

"No, that wasn't the camouflage. Our trip went wonky because they've warded the building against teleportation technology. This must be why I had such a hard time finding Jaeger's location."

"What the hell are they keeping in there, the Ark of the Covenant?"

"No, SABER never had an interest in that. It's buried deep underground on an island in Canada."

"...Canada?"

"Canada. But don't tell anybody."

"I don't foresee it coming up in conversation," I replied. "So...how do we get into this place?" I asked, looking for any kind of indication of a door on the camouflaged building in front of us.

"Very sneakily," Trent said. He started to walk around the building while using the display on his watch to examine the structure. I followed behind him until he suddenly stopped and held his hand up. "I think we've found a side entrance."

It just looked like another invisible wall to me. I looked on as Trent used his watch to manipulate the door configurations. He had the door opened in less than a minute.

As we walked through, I looked over at him and said, "You really need to teach me how to do that."

I saw his eyes widen as he stopped in his tracks, looking forward. I followed his eyes and felt my heart leap into my throat. We had stepped into what appeared to be a large hangar housing several sleek, black aircraft. And there were at least ten armed men and women in bulky-looking synsuits staring at us. They all raised their strange gun-like weapons. They reminded me of the kind of gun that Jaeger had.

"You should all be ashamed," Trent said boldly. "You've just failed your security inspection! No, no, this will not do. This will not do at all."

Everyone lowered their guns and looked at each other in confusion.

"Did Shoruku send you?" a man with a gun asked.

"What do you think?" Trent sassed.

"I'm sorry, sir."

"What's your name?" Trent asked.

"I'm MPLA67, sir."

"Ah, yes. Lovely. Must be a family name."

"Beg your pardon, sir?" the man asked, puzzled.

"I need you to come with me, MP...can I just call you MP?"

"Of course, sir."

Trent put his arm around MP's shoulders and started walking through the hangar with him as I quietly followed behind. "Listen, MP. I need to ask a favor of you. I need to take a look at your security system to figure out why it failed so epically. Could you point me in the right direction of where I need to be?"

"I can take you to the security hub, sir. You will have access to everything there."

"Brilliant. Lead the way, MP."

I followed Trent and MP through the hangar and into a long corridor. We took a lift up several floors and then walked down another long corridor. MP led us to a large metal door and stopped in front of it.

"Here you are, sir."

"Thank you, MP. Say, do you think you could get the door for me? My clearance ID has been on the fritz lately."

"Sorry, sir, I don't have authority to enter this room. Should I call someone?"

"No, no, that's all right. I'll give it a try." Trent turned his back to MP and used his watch on the door. It clicked open. "Well, look at that! They must have fixed the glitch."

"What's going on? Who's there?" a woman called from inside the dim room. I peeked around Trent and saw a room filled with monitors and rows and rows of what looked like computer towers.

"It's ok, Kaz. I have, uh…" MP turned to Trent. "What's your name, sir?"

"Mr. Holmes."

"I have Mr. Holmes here to look at the security system. He was sent by Shoruku. He found a defect in the system."

A small woman with large, blue eyes walked to the doorway. She was wearing a white synsuit that hid the rest of her features, but I could see some kinked blond hair sticking out around her face.

"Hello, Mr. Holmes. I'm KAZ2Y5, but most people just call me Kaz." Kaz looked past Trent at me. "And who is this?"

"Oh, this is my assistant, Billie," Trent replied. "Now, if you don't mind terribly, I will need a few minutes alone to assess the condition of the system. It's simply protocol, to help avoid any outside influences and interferences. I'm sure you understand. You can just wait out here if you'd like. I'll only be a moment or two."

"Oh…well, all right," Kaz said hesitantly.

Trent walked into the room and closed the door behind him, leaving me outside with Kaz and MP. We all stood and stared at each other in uncomfortable silence.

"I guess we're lucky they didn't send Megan this time," Kaz said to MP.

"I wouldn't be here right now if they had," MP replied.

"You're familiar with Megan?" I asked.

They both looked at me like I had two heads. Kaz asked, "Why are you speaking English?"

I felt my ears start to burn. "Oh, um…It's just something I do. It's cool." When they continued to stare at me, I prodded them about Megan. "So, you said you knew Megan?"

"Who doesn't?!" Kaz replied. "With her reputation, everyone knows her even if they haven't met her. Last time she came here, she smashed a bloke in the head so hard his eyeball popped out."

"Good grief! What did he do to deserve that?"

"He smiled at her," Kaz said.

"Yikes. She threw a knife at my face once for talking out of turn," I confessed.

"You talked to her and lived?!" MP said in astonishment.

"Only because my friend had some quick reflexes."

"Did she kill him?" Kaz wanted to know.

"…I don't know. I haven't seen him since then."

Kaz and MP looked at each other knowingly, but neither of them said anything.

When Trent finally emerged from the dark room, his face was pale. He swallowed hard and clenched his jaw.

"Is everything all right?" Kaz asked.

Trent quickly put on an upbeat front. "Yep! All set! It was just a minor malfunction, but I got it squared away. Now, since I've really taken to you two, maybe we can keep this little issue among the four of us to prevent any possible repercussions. Deal?"

MP and Kaz agreed, and Kaz went back to work. MP stood there, looking at us expectantly, waiting to take us wherever we needed to go next.

"Thanks for your assistance, MP," Trent said, "but I think we can take it from here. I have a friend over in the east wing I'd like to stop and see before I leave."

MP headed back from where we had come, and Trent led me in the opposite direction. Once we rounded the corner, I saw the sickened look cross Trent's face once more.

"What did you see in there? What's wrong?" I asked him as we walked quickly down the corridor.

"He's in bad shape, Roselyn. You're not going to want to see him. You should go home."

"I'm not going home. What did you do in there?"

"I disabled their teleportation firewall, retrieved Jaeger's watch, and located Jaeger."

"How did you retrieve the watch?"

"Are you even listening? I disabled their teleportation firewall. I teleported."

"How long before they notice?"

"I don't know, but we need to move quickly." Trent stopped, looked around, and then grabbed me and ducked into a dark nook. "I can teleport us to Jaeger's location. But…I wish you would just go home."

"What am I going to see, Trent? What did they do to him?"

"He's…he's in pieces, Roselyn."

I covered my mouth, horrified. I felt like I was going to be sick. I could taste the bile rising up my esophagus.

"…Pieces?" I whispered.

"I need to teleport in there, grab him, and send us back to Nebraska. We can figure out what to do about Megan and her time-traveling after we get Jaeger back."

"Won't they be able to track you if you teleport?"

"It's a risk we're going to have to take. We've got no choice."

"Well, we could take him back to my house. You put up that cloaking device, remember?"

Trent's eyes widened. "Yes! That's right! Oh, Roselyn, you clever girl!" He grabbed my face and planted a quick kiss on my lips. "I'll meet you back at your house!"

"No, I'm going with you. If Jaeger is in…if he's in…pieces…you'll need my help."

"I can't ask you to do that."

"You don't have to ask. I'm doing it. Now, quit wasting time and let's bring Jaeger home."

Chapter 9

When I saw Jaeger, the horror was seared into my brain forever. He was lying naked on a metal examination table, his flesh ripped and splayed open from his neck to his pelvis. His severed leg and one of his arms were on a gurney nearby, and I could see the other leg and arm had been stitched back onto his body, presumably after having been severed as well. The most gruesome scene, however, had to be his scalp pulled back from his cranium, revealing a missing chunk of skull and an exposed section of his brain.

"Oh my god," I whispered in revulsion.

Jaeger opened his eyes and turned them toward me. I felt my stomach heave. I couldn't believe he was conscious.

"Stow it, Roselyn!" Trent ordered sternly as he ran over and grabbed Jaeger's leg. "Help me!"

In a shocked trance, I hurried to assist Trent and retrieved Jaeger's arm. Trent folded the flesh closed over his chest cavity and abdomen and placed the severed leg unceremoniously on top of him. He took the arm from me and stacked it on top of the leg.

"I'm sorry, Jaeger," Trent apologized.

Trent and I did our best to hoist Jaeger into our arms without causing any further damage, but Jaeger cried out in pain when we moved him. Trent quickly teleported all three of us to my bedroom, and we deposited Jaeger's bloody, dismembered body onto my bed while he screamed in agony. I stepped back and watched as Trent moved the severed leg and arm off of Jaeger and laid them on the bed next to him.

"Why...why so long?" Jaeger murmured, barely coherent.

"Don't talk," Trent commanded. "There'll be time for that later. I need to get you stitched back together first."

Trent suddenly teleported out of the room, and I just stood there chewing my lower lip nervously, staring at Jaeger. He gazed back at me, his eyes communicating his anguish wordlessly.

"I'm so sorry," I whispered.

Jaeger said nothing, only staring silently.

Trent reappeared with a big medical bag. "Roselyn, I'm going to need your assistance. We need to put him back together." He started pulling items out of the bag.

"Where did you get those medical supplies?" I asked.

"This isn't my first rodeo," Trent replied simply. He pulled out a syringe and injected Jaeger with a sedative. "We'll talk when you wake up," Trent said to Jaeger. "The worst is over now."

I handed Trent tools, snipped thread, and held things together while he stitched for over four hours. When we were done, we were covered in blood. My bed was completely ruined. But Jaeger was back in one piece, and that was all that mattered.

Trent and I washed up, and I changed my clothes. I followed Trent out to the kitchen and watched him start digging through my fridge.

"How can you be hungry after that?" I asked.

"I'm still recovering from my transformation. I needed to eat three hours ago." He held out a plate of ham. "Is this still good?"

"Yeah, you can eat it." I sat down at the table and rested my chin in my hand while Trent dived into the ham like a starving wolf. "Is Jaeger going to be ok?" I asked. "What if he gets an infection? My room is hardly a sterile environment. Shit, I didn't even wash my damn hands before we started sewing him up."

"He'll be ok. We don't get infections. We don't get sick. Now that he's back together, his body will heal itself."

"How long will that take?"

"I don't know. A day? Maybe two?"

"How long was he at the SABER compound?" I wondered.

"I don't know, but...I get the feeling it was a long time."

I felt sick. "What do you mean by a 'long time'? Like, as in weeks?"

"Possibly years."

"Jesus."

"Yeah."

"There are going to be mental repercussions. He's not going to be the same man," I surmised.

"I know." Trent glanced over at me and did a double take. He squinted his eyes at me, then pointed at my neck. "You've got red on you."

"Red on me? You mean blood?" I said, rubbing my neck in the location where he was pointing.

"Yes, blood. But I thought it might sound less gruesome if I just said 'red.'"

"I think I've been desensitized to blood at this point." I looked over at him shoving ham into his mouth just as quickly as he could chew it. "Looks like you have been, too."

"That happened a long time ago." Trent finished off the plate of ham.

"Better?"

"For now." He smiled at me. My eyes already enjoyed looking at his new face, but when he smiled at me just then...I felt it in my heart.

"You know, you were pretty amazing today," I said. "That was top notch manipulation and charisma you used at the SABER compound. You had me almost believing your bullshit. You just made that all up as you went, didn't you?"

He beamed with pride. "Yeah, but I did a proper good job, didn't I?" he said more as a statement than a question.

"And then you got Jaeger home and put back together...all in the same day you woke up as another person. You're a damn superhero."

"No, I'm not. I may be good at certain things, but a superhero I am not."

"You've tried many times, but you'll never convince me that you aren't a superhero."

Trent chuckled.

"Oh! That's the first time I've heard you laugh since you changed!" I exclaimed. "Wow, you have changed. It seemed like old Trent was always laughing about something, even when it wasn't funny. Especially when it wasn't funny." I suddenly felt sad, and I wished I hadn't said that out loud.

"Well, I haven't had a whole lot to laugh about today. Sorry I haven't been terribly jolly," he replied sourly. "I wake up with a new face and a girlfriend who hates me for it, and then I have to rescue and sew together my tortured friend whom I failed horribly by picking the wrong year to rescue him from. So sorry laughter hasn't flowed freely from my lips."

I felt the sting of his words and the guilt I deserved. I looked down at the table. "I'm sorry. I've been a real jerk ass."

Trent didn't disagree with me. "Well...at least you don't smell like cabbage." I looked up at him, and the corner of his mouth turned up slightly.

"At least there's that," I said with a little smile.

I heard Jaeger mumbling from the bedroom. Trent and I jumped up and dashed down the hall to check on him.

"Where am I? What are you doing to me?" he growled, his eyes darting wildly around the room.

Trent approached him slowly, holding his hands up in a defensive position. "Easy, Jaeger. You're safe now. Roselyn and I got you out of the SABER compound."

Jaeger looked over at Trent and me, and after a moment of recognition, he started to calm down. His breathing slowed to normal and his body relaxed.

"You were supposed to come get me when you woke up," Jaeger said bitterly.

"I did," Trent said, "but SABER had some kind of time-traveling, teleporting firewall in place that blocked the time portion of the signal from your watch."

"So how did you find me?"

"I guessed."

Jaeger gave a humorless laugh, then cringed in pain. "You guessed wrong."

"I'm so sorry."

"I was there for years, Trent. Five. Fucking. Years."

Trent rubbed his hands down his face. "I didn't know how to find you. I'm sorry."

"They tortured you for five years?" I asked, horrified.

Jaeger turned his eyes to me. "Once Megan realized she couldn't coerce me into doing her bidding, I was turned into a guinea pig. They would cut parts off of me and see how long my severed limbs would stay viable. Did you know we can regrow appendages?" Jaeger asked, looking at Trent. "Because we can. They also messed with my brain. They tried to insert a mind-control device in my head, but my body and immune system attacked it as an unrecognized foreign object. They tested all kinds of experimental drugs and devices on me that they wouldn't normally have tested on humans, but since I couldn't die, they saw that as a green light. And it was all headed by Megan. She oversaw everything they did to me. I'm not even sure the rest of SABER knew what she and Doctor Simian were doing." Jaeger was shaking. "Did you kill them? Are Megan and Doctor Simian dead?"

"That's not what I do," Trent said. "I don't kill for vengeance. I only kill when it's absolutely necessary."

Jaeger's eyes filled with fire. "Are you taking the fucking piss?! Those two needed to die yesterday! After what they did to me, you let them just walk away? They'll be after us! You know that, right? What are you going to do when they get their hands on her?!" Jaeger shouted, using his eyes to indicate he was referring to me.

"They weren't there," I said, trying to calm Jaeger. "Our top priority was getting you out of there. We can deal with the rest when you're healed."

"It could be too late by then. They're probably tracking us right now!"

"My house is hidden to them. They can't track us here."

"You need to blow it all up, Trent. Just like you did in my world. Kill them all," Jaeger said.

Trent hesitated. "I can't do that."

Jaeger looked at him incredulously. "Why the bloody hell not?"

"It's too big of an incident. It could alter the intended course of time. It's why I haven't destroyed them yet. I stop them when they mess with history, but I don't exterminate them completely."

"You did it in my world with hardly a thought," Jaeger pointed out.

"I gave it three years of thought. Since it wasn't my world and they posed a real threat to my world…and they had my Roselyn…I decided the rules didn't apply."

"It's time, Trent. It's time to take them out. They're too powerful to be ignored. They have technology that can undermine everything you've fought your whole life to protect."

"It isn't my call to make."

"Then I'll make it for you," Jaeger warned.

"Ok, ok, let's take a night to think about it, all right?" I mediated. "You both have made good points, but this isn't going to be decided right now. Come on, Trent, let's let Jaeger recuperate," I said as I tugged at Trent's jacket sleeve.

"Wait," Jaeger said. "Roselyn, can I talk to you alone?"

Trent stepped in. "What for?"

"It's fine," I said, guiding Trent toward the door. "I'll just be a minute."

Trent looked at me with a suspicious frown as I closed the door between us. I went over to Jaeger and sat on the edge of the bed next to him.

"You need to talk to him. I understand why he chooses to be passive, but this is something that requires action. If our roles had been switched, I know he would sympathize with me. I know he'd want them all dead. You met Megan. You saw what a ruthless psychopath she is, and that was barely scratching the surface. She thinks humankind is a plague on this planet, and she will tear this world apart from its very foundations if she isn't stopped…and the only way to stop her, is to kill her. She won't be reasoned with, and she's too clever to safely keep imprisoned."

"Is she like you and Trent? Is she engineered?"

"Somewhat. But she's more super-soldier than super-genius, and she isn't immortal."

"How the hell would we kill a super-soldier?"

"How the hell did you get into the SABER compound?"

"Trent's quick-thinking."

"Exactly. Brains. The most powerful weapon in the world."

"I don't know, Jaeger. I don't know what the right move is here."

"I do. I'm not asking for your opinion. I'm telling you what the right answer is. What I'm asking is that you help Trent to see it because he'll listen to you. He doesn't want to listen to me because he looks at me like the little devil on his shoulder. You're the angel. Make him listen."

"It's not that easy. Things are little tense between us right now."

"Oh, that's right. What's been five years in hell for me has only been a day for you. You're still dealing with his change. Well guess what? Get over it. We've got bigger problems."

"This isn't even your world, Jaeger. Why do you care what Megan does to us? You can just go back to your world and wash your hands clean of us."

Jaeger broke eye contact with me and didn't immediately respond.

I prodded, "Are you sure this isn't just about getting revenge for what they did to you?"

Jaeger scowled at me. It was an intimidating scowl, especially now that he looked like Frankenstein's monster.

"This isn't about me. If it were, I'd head for the bloody hills. Is it so difficult for you to believe that I'm not just a selfish wanker? Is it so difficult for you to believe that I may have an interest in protecting this world?"

"Why? Just because you want to learn from our history to—"

Jaeger interrupted, "What difference does it make what my motives are?"

"It makes all the difference. It tells me how sound your reasoning is regarding the matter."

"My reasoning is sound, all right?"

"Are you motivated by love or hate? When it all boils down, it's either one of those two things."

Jaeger looked out the window. "I'm not motivated by hate. This isn't about revenge. I just…I want to make sure you and Trent have a world to continue saving after I leave."

That wasn't the answer I was expecting. I sat silently, unsure of how to proceed.

"What, nothing to say now?" Jaeger pressed.

"You should rest. I'll talk with Trent. I'm not going to try to persuade him one way or the other, but I will make sure he explores all of our options." I stood up. "Now, get some rest. Hopefully you'll be good as new before too long."

"'Tis but a scratch. I've had worse," Jaeger jested. I don't think I had ever heard a more perfectly fitting joke in all my life (albeit terrible, given the circumstances), but I found myself able only to muster a weak smile.

"Your arm's off," I replied, unable to resist.

"No it isn't."

"I didn't peg you for a Monty Python fan," I said.

"Trent made me watch a couple of the skits because I didn't understand a joke he had made in reference to it."

"Yeah, that sounds like him," I acknowledged. "Goodnight, Jaeger. Trent will probably check on you in a bit." I walked out of the room, leaving the door open behind me.

When I walked into the living room, I found Trent sitting on the couch with his head slumped to the side, snoring, with Cattiel curled up in his lap. I'd never seen Trent sleep. I'd seen him unconscious, of course, but not just asleep. I knew he did sleep a little bit here and there, but he never did it around me. I sat across from him and looked him over. He really was handsome. If my mother saw him now, she'd still say he wasn't my type because he wasn't a thick-necked jock, but she'd be wrong. He might not be the Trent I'd fallen in love with, but...he was still in there somewhere. I'd seen little glimpses of him, fleeting though they might've been. His face and mannerisms may have changed, but his heart was still the same. He was still a good man. Was it possible that I could love him the same as I used to? Was it possible that I was already starting to?

I grabbed a couple of pillows and blankets out of the hall closet and set them on the chair in the living room. I scooped Cattiel up out of Trent's lap and put him on the floor, much to Cattiel's displeasure. Trent groaned and opened his eyes, lifting his head.

"Did I fall asleep?" he asked.

"Looks like it," I replied. "I didn't know you did that sort of thing."

"I don't, usually. I'm still feeling the effects of the change." Trent rubbed his eyes and rested his head against the back of the couch.

"Blimey, I'm knackered. I don't know how you lot deal with this feeling on a daily basis."

"Did you want to sleep on the couch? I got you a pillow and blanket."

"You really need to invest in a bed for one of your spare bedrooms," Trent said. "Any chance your parents happened to leave their air mattress behind?"

"Sorry, it's either the couch or a sleeping bag on the floor in one of the spare rooms."

"Well, I guess the couch is better than the floor." Trent slipped his suit jacket off and loosened his tie while I laid one of the pillows and blankets on the couch next to him. When I tossed the other pillow and blanket on the other couch, Trent gave me a puzzled look. "What are you doing?"

"What?" I asked, turning to him.

He looked over at the other couch. "You're sleeping over there?"

"Is there something wrong with that?"

Trent furrowed his brow as he unbuttoned his shirt. "I just thought maybe you would want to sleep next to me. I mean, it isn't very often, or ever, really, that we get to actually sleep together." Trent paused, then held his finger up. "Wait, not sleep together sleep together, but you know what I mean. And I'm not expecting anything like that, in case you were worried."

"Oh. Well...I just thought, you know, with things being the way they are, it might be a little...weird."

"It doesn't have to be weird, Roselyn. It's still me."

After a brief pause, I responded with, "I think that's still up for debate."

Trent closed his eyes for a moment. "I don't want to argue. If you want to sleep on the other couch, go ahead. I'm not going to push the issue any further." Trent kicked off his shoes and lay down on the couch, turning his back to me as he covered himself with his blanket. "Goodnight, Roselyn. I love you...always."

I shut off the living room light and climbed under my own blanket on the couch opposite of Trent. I stared at his back in the darkness, wondering what was going through his mind. Was he as upset with me for being so distant as I was with him for changing? Hell, I was upset with me, too.

"Trent? Can we talk?"

"Are we going to talk or are we going to argue?"

"It's about Jaeger."

"Still doesn't answer my question."

"I don't want to argue. I just wanted to tell you what he said tonight."

"Let me guess – he wants you to persuade me to go along with his plan?"

"Well, of course he wants that. But I just wanted to tell you what he had to say, and I don't intend to try to persuade you."

"What did he say?"

I told Trent about Megan's ambitions to destroy human civilization. "I think he is genuinely concerned for us. I know I've been distrustful of Jaeger before, but I believe him on this. Whether killing her is the right move to make, I don't know. What I do know, though, is that he fully believes it's the only way to stop her."

"I'm not against stopping her. I'm not against killing her if she does prove to be a threat to this world. What I am against is destroying all of SABER to do it. We could end up doing more harm than good."

"I just thought of something. Jaeger made a comment about Megan being more like a super-soldier than a super-genius. If that's true, then where did she get the time travel device?"

"It isn't the first time SABER has developed the technology. That's why I'm always on watch."

"If you destroyed them once and for all, you wouldn't have to continue to worry about them," I pointed out. "You'd be free."

"If I destroy SABER, someone else will take its place. Possibly someone even worse."

"If someone even farther into the future takes over and tries to change the past, wouldn't you have already encountered them by now?"

"Yeah, you'd think so…but I haven't, and I'd like it to stay that way."

"But…ugh. I hate trying to keep up with these conversations. It all seems so counter-intuitive."

"Intuition has no place in this kind of physics, and you can't apply everyday cause-and-effect logic to time travel. It doesn't always work that way in reality."

"You know, I often wonder what it's like in that incredible brain of yours. Mine must seem so boring in comparison. I can't even begin to comprehend the things you seem to understand so plainly."

"Hardly. There isn't much I can't figure out – but you? You're so often a complete mystery to me. What I wouldn't give to have a day inside your brain…I'd love to know what's going on in there."

"I think you'd be disappointed."

"Yeah, I probably would be."

I was instantly offended. "Hey! You aren't supposed to agree with me when I say I'm dumb!"

"What? No! No, that's not what I meant. Ugh. Never mind."

"What did you mean, then?"

"Go to bed, Roselyn."

"What did you mean?"

Trent was silent.

I lay on the couch in the darkness. I had felt weary earlier, but now that I was lying down, trying to sleep, it eluded me. I had a tightness in my chest that always manifested when I felt like Trent was upset with me, and it was keeping me awake. I threw the blanket aside and sat up. I gazed across the room at the man-sized mound on the other couch. Why was I fighting so hard to keep my distance from him, when all my heart really wanted was to reconnect with him? That was what I truly wanted after all, wasn't it? Why was I doing this to myself? I was so afraid of not being able to love him that I was avoiding the opportunity completely. I'd put up a wall between us to try to keep out the uncomfortable feelings, but it was time to knock down a few bricks. I wasn't ready to let the old Trent go yet, but it didn't mean I had to shut out the man he had become.

I slowly rose from the couch and tip-toed over to Trent. I carefully slipped under his blanket and nestled my body up next to his back, sliding my arm under his and wrapping it around his torso. I rested my cheek against his back and closed my eyes. For the first time since the change, it felt like him. I squeezed him against me, and I felt his hand slide up over top of mine. He entwined his fingers with mine and held my hand without saying a word.

I woke up in the dim light before dawn to the sound of my fridge door creaking open. My eyes flew open. I was lying on my stomach with the left half of my body on top of Trent, and I had my face buried in his shoulder. I turned my head quickly and saw Jaeger standing in the kitchen, staring into the fridge.

I rolled over and sat up on the edge of the couch. "What are you doing out of bed?" I chastised. "There's no way you're healed enough to be up walking around yet!"

Jaeger reached into the fridge and pulled out a container of yogurt. "I think you forget who you're talking to," he said as he hobbled to the living room. He sat down in the chair near the couch and popped the top off the container. He raised it to his lips.

"Hey! No! Get a damn spoon and a bowl, you barbarian." I reached over and snatched the container from him and brought it back to the kitchen. I dumped a generous portion into a bowl, grabbed a spoon, and brought it to him. "How are you feeling?" I asked as I sat back down next to Trent, who was staring to stir.

"Good, not great. I'm back together, but I don't think all the nerves and muscles have completely healed in my leg. I still don't have much feeling in it. My arm's good, though," he said, moving it around and opening and closing his fingers to demonstrate.

"What about your head? And your...guts?"

"My skull hasn't fully regenerated. I still have a weird soft spot, but it's getting smaller. I think my guts are all right. All right enough for me to be hungry, anyway."

Trent sat up behind me, so I moved over a little. He ran his hand through his messy hair and looked over at Jaeger. "Hey, not too shabby," he said. "I think it's possible you may heal faster than I do."

"I've had a lot of practice," Jaeger said humorlessly. "Have you had time to think over what we're going to do about Megan and SABER?"

"Right to it first thing in the morning, eh?" Trent said begrudgingly. "Don't you know you're more likely to start an argument with someone if you bug them when they've only just woken up?"

"I don't care," Jaeger said as he slurped down his yogurt. "We need to get a plan together."

"I need time to think."

"We don't have time for that."

"It's never a good idea to charge into something, guns blazing, without having properly thought it through."

"And sometimes you don't have a choice."

"We have a choice, Jaeger. We have time. We need to talk this through before we do anything."

"But we are going to kill Megan and take down SABER, right?"

"I don't know. If we need to kill Megan – if she gives us no other choice – we will. But as far as taking down SABER, I don't know about that." Trent rose from the couch and went to the kitchen to make coffee.

Jaeger got up and limped after him. "I know you're afraid that destroying them will alter things. But if you don't, eventually they're going to succeed at altering the past. Megan already has. I know you aren't a fan of either choice. But you still have to choose. You have to do something."

"I have been doing something. I've been doing something for hundreds of years. I monitor. I keep them in check. I do what is necessary to keep civilization on track."

"Then you know you have to do this."

"I know no such thing. SABER may be a necessary evil."

"That may be, but I think they've outlived their necessity."

Trent slammed his hands on the counter. "Come off it, Jaeger! Why is this so important to you? What difference does any of this make to you?!"

Jaeger dug his heels. "Why isn't it important to you? What about Roselyn?!...and the rest of humankind? Don't you care what could happen to her and everyone else if you do nothing?"

Trent nosed up to Jaeger. I noticed that, in his new form, he was now the same height as Jaeger. He spoke in a low but threatening voice. "Roselyn is my concern. I will make sure she is safe from SABER. Don't you dare question my ability to do so."

"Oh, but I am questioning it. You don't exactly have a stellar track record."

Trent was seething. "Once. And you saw what I did to them."

"They got me once. And you saw what they did to me."

"You know, as I recall, it was your fault the SABER from your world knew about her in the first place. So you're in no position to be criticizing me."

I couldn't stand it any longer. I jumped up. "For Pete's sake, just stop! If you're going to talk about it, talk about it like adults. Quit squabbling like children!" I walked past them into the kitchen and pulled a bowl from the cupboard for oatmeal.

After a long pause, Trent asked Jaeger, "So, you're proposing we just destroy everything. Is that correct?"

"It's the only way to be sure. Take out the whole organization, all their technology, all their people. Erase them, and you'll never have to worry about them again."

Trent sighed. He turned away from Jaeger and poured himself a cup of coffee. "That simple? Just kill everyone?"

"That simple."

Trent sat down at the table with his coffee. "Except it isn't. You know, when you read it in books and see it in movies, no one ever thinks about the rest of the victims. No one thinks about the collateral damage. They always think, 'Oh, the bad guys got theirs! They got what was coming to them! Justice was served!' No one thinks about the innocent people caught in the blast or the people who will suffer because their father or sister or son was blown up in a 'lab accident.' No one thinks about what comes next. Well, I do. I've made my share of mistakes. I've done horrible things – I'm not pretending I haven't. I do what is necessary, but I don't take killing lightly. And I certainly don't take wiping out an entire super power lightly. This could have tremendous ramifications for all of humankind. There must be another way. We can find another way that doesn't involve mass murder. I've been down this road so many times…there has to be another road."

Jaeger shuffled to the table and sat across from Trent. "Do you honestly still think of yourself as 'good'? Are you so naïve? We're gods, Trent. We aren't good or bad. We do what we must for our world, regardless of the cost. You know why you think you can do this another way, without killing? It's because you get to forget everything you've done. Your memory loss isn't a curse – it's a blessing. You get to walk away, change your face, and forget what you've done, and it allows you to mistakenly believe that you have some kind of moral code. But you're no better than me. We both do what we have to do. The difference between you and me, though, is that I remember everything, and I've learned to live with it. You never did, because you never had to. So don't look at me with that condescending, better-than-thou expression. I have embraced everything that I am – the so-called 'good' and the 'bad.' When are you going to?"

Trent took a sip of his coffee. "I refuse to embrace it. Do you know why?"

"Because you lack a spine?"

"Because I know I can do better. I can be better. And so can you."

Jaeger scoffed at Trent. "You do know you can't actually kill someone with kindness, right?"

"I don't think we have to kill anyone."

"What do you suggest we do, then? Sit on our asses and wait for the apocalypse? Been there, done that, and I wouldn't recommend it."

"We prepare."

"How?"

"You do have a brain like mine, don't you? We can figure this out. If I managed to walk right through the doors of SABER and collect you without killing anyone – flying by the seat of my pants, mind you – then imagine what we can do together with a little thought and effort."

Trent got up and went to the cupboard and pulled out the box of toaster pastries. I gave him a puzzled look as he ripped open the package and started eating one.

"What are you doing?" I asked.

"Eating," he said as though it were obvious.

"I thought you didn't like those."

"I know. But I've had a weird craving for them."

Jaeger held up his hands. "Toss me one, mate."

As I finished eating my oatmeal at the counter, I watched Trent and Jaeger sit at the table, tentatively discussing their options. Who knew the fate of SABER, and possibly the fate of humankind, would be decided at my kitchen table over chocolate toaster pastries?

I left Trent and Jaeger to it while I got ready for work. As I showered, I thought about what I would do if I were in their position. Would I be all right with destroying SABER and Megan? If it were me – if I was the one who would be directly responsible for the deaths of everyone involved with SABER – would I be able to do it? After seeing what they'd done to Jaeger, the clear answer seemed to be yes. But what about MP and Kaz? They seemed to be as much victims of the people they worked for as anybody else. If we destroyed SABER, they would have to die too, though, wouldn't they? I didn't know if I could do that.

When I was dressed in my athleticwear, I went back out to the kitchen to pack myself a quick lunch, and I found Trent and Jaeger with a long section of untorn paper towels on the table, drawing on it with markers. It appeared they were sketching out floor plans.

"Has my kitchen become the war room?" I asked.

Trent glanced at me, then did a double-take. "Why are you dressed for work? You aren't actually thinking of leaving the house, are you?"

"I have to. If we're going to hide out in my time, then I have to go to work. I can't keep calling in. Don't worry, though. I'll leave the watch here so I can't be tracked in any way," I explained as I dumped a spring salad mix into a storage container and threw it in my lunch box. I reached for the boiled eggs that had gotten pushed to the back of the fridge, but I was suddenly yanked back.

Trent whirled me around to face him. "You can't leave this house."

"Watch me."

"Roselyn!"

"Trent! I have a life here, remember? I have responsibilities!"

"So do I! And, whether you like it or not, right now you are one of those responsibilities!"

"I'm just going to work! Without my watch, I'm just a regular Jane. Nobody is going to come after me if I'm not carrying around a time-traveling beacon."

Trent looked over at Jaeger, seeking support. Jaeger looked at me. "It isn't a good idea, Roselyn," Jaeger said. "Don't be foolish."

"What are the chances of anyone from SABER finding me at work today? I mean, really. It'd be like trying to find a needle in a haystack…if the haystack could be at any point in time in the history and future of civilization."

"I get your point," Trent conceded, "but I'd rather err on the side of caution."

"Well…too bad it isn't up to you," I said. I took my lunch box cooler and walked to the closet to get my coat.

Trent followed on my heels. "Why are you doing this?"

I threw my coat on and slung my purse over my shoulder. "You act like I'm disrespecting or slighting you by going to work."

"I'm uncomfortable with it."

"I'll be fine."

"Oh, well, in that case…" Trent said sarcastically.

"I'll tell you what, Trent. I'll worry about me, and you can worry about everybody else. Ok?"

"You're rubbish at worrying about yourself. That's why I always have to do it."

"I'll see you after work," I said as I slipped out the door and hurried to the car. I was running late.

Being back at the gym was refreshing. I did a quick workout on my first break between clients, and it made me feel normal and sane again. It reminded me why I loved my job, and why I refused to let Trent, or anyone else, try to take me from it. By the end of the day, I had almost forgotten about SABER and their homicidal madwoman.

That is, until I walked into the locker room.

Chapter 10

Megan was leaned against my locker in her black leather jacket with her arms crossed, a smug smirk on her lips. My blood ran cold and my legs suddenly turned to lead. I was afraid to open my mouth to ask how the hell she had found me.

"Well, isn't this just the happiest of accidents?" Megan said cheerily. "I thought I recognized you through the window when I walked by here earlier." She stared at me, waiting for me to speak. When I remained silent and frozen, she pouted. "Oh, you don't look very happy to see me. I was afraid of that."

"You..." I squeaked. I cleared my throat. "You tried to kill me..."

"Oh, that?" Megan gave a dismissive wave of her hand and walked toward me. "Don't take it personally. I do that a lot. It's part of my charm."

"What you did to Jaeger...wasn't very charming," I mumbled.

Megan raised an eyebrow at me as she circled me. "Who's Jaeger? A friend of yours?" She then held up a hand to stop me from responding. "Actually, you know what? I don't care. What I do care about is your friend Trent, and how the holy hell you managed to smuggle his chopped-up ass out of dear Dr. Simian's lab."

That's right...she thought Jaeger was Trent. But after five years, they never figured out that he wasn't? I stared at her silently.

"Oh, come now, you can tell me. You can brag a little. I'm not even mad. I'm impressed. But I will need him back."

"What makes you think it was me?"

Megan stopped her circling and stood in front of me, giving me a knowing look. "Let's not be coy. Just tell me."

"It wasn't me."

"You're starting to piss me off. There's nothing I hate more than a liar."

"I'm not smart enough to pull off anything like that."

"I know you aren't. That's why I'll also need to know who helped you do it."

"No one. I did it on my own."

Megan gave me an unamused smile. "Oh, so now you did do it?"

"Yes."

"How?"

"I walked through the front door, wandered around, found him, and teleported him out."

"No one just walks through the front door of a SABER compound."

"I did. Didn't your people tell you?"

Megan giggled. "Silly...dead people don't talk." She turned around and walked back to my locker. She grabbed a hold of the handle and yanked the metal locker door right off its hinges in one powerful movement. "This one's yours, right?"

"How did you find me?" I asked quietly.

"Would you believe it was a complete coincidence?" She watched me as I stared at her in disbelief. "Well, you'd be an idiot if you did. I tracked you."

"Impossible."

She threw her head back and laughed. "Just because you can't figure out how it was done it doesn't make it impossible. I could tell you how I did it. I'm not afraid to brag. But I want you to ask nicely."

I scowled at her. "How did you do it?" I murmured.

"Well fuck you very much. That wasn't nice at all."

"It doesn't matter," I said. "You found me. Now what?"

"Oh, come on, you're like the fourth least fun person I've ever met. And I killed those other three, so...maybe you should try a little harder at entertaining me. One more time: ask me nicely."

I gritted my teeth. "Please...please tell me how you tracked me."

Megan started rummaging through my locker. "Wow, you suck at this. Whatever. It's Trent. Dr. Simian had injected him with some experimental nanobots to see if they could be used to interrupt the function of his already existing nanobots. Well, they didn't do shit, but Dr. Simian did find that they gave off a unique and trackable signature." She paused and looked at me expectantly. Her face fell. "You're looking at me like you still don't understand. You don't, do you? It's his blood. You must have gotten some of those nanobots on you when you bafflingly nicked him from the lab, because I was led right to this time and this gym."

But...I changed my clothes! I showered! I...I didn't wash my hair. Was she really able to track me through a miniscule droplet of Jaeger's blood in my damn hair?!

"If that's true, then why would it take you to me? Why wouldn't it take you to him?"

"I was hoping you could explain that to me."

"I'm sure I don't know."

"If you have his blood on you or your clothes, then you've been with him recently. Where is he? Is he still... a man apart?" Megan snickered. "He had to pay for deserting SABER…it cost him an arm and a leg."

"Jokes? Nothing about this is funny."

"Oh, lighten up. Everything about this is funny. Now, enough bullshit. Where is he?"

"Why don't you track him yourself?"

"Because obviously he bled out all his nanobots on you. Where is he?"

"I don't know."

Megan pulled my car keys out of my purse. "Do you drive a fast car?"

"No."

"God, you're boring," she said as she dropped them onto the floor. "I hope you're more entertaining when I kill you."

My heart pounded violently in my chest.

She turned to me with an exasperated expression. "Where. Is. He?"

"Why do you want him?"

"Simple. You took something of mine, and I want it back."

"He's not yours."

"He is. He belongs to SABER, and SABER gives me everything I want – and I want him. Ergo, he's mine."

"All you want to do is torture him!"

"No, I want to study him. You see, I want his power."

"What power? His intelligence?"

"Pffff!" Megan scoffed. "Of course not. I want the secret to his immortality."

"If SABER created him, shouldn't they already know?"

Megan gave me a conspiratorial sideways glance. "Oh, you don't know? See, when he escaped, he destroyed everything used to create him – all research data, experimental embryos, computer files, papers…everything. He even went through and systematically murdered everyone who had anything to do with his creation. I must say, he might be an even more heartless killer than I am. And that's saying something."

"You're wrong about him. He's not heartless. Everything he does, he does for humanity."

"I'm sure all the people he killed would agree," she said sarcastically.

"And what's your excuse?" I asked.

"I don't need one. I just like killing people. I mean, seriously, you are the most disgusting, selfish creatures to ever plague this planet."

"We aren't all bad," I argued.

"Yes, you are. You're like a virus that just keeps multiplying and spreading and mutating and defiling everything you touch."

"You're human too."

"But I'm not equal to. I'm greater than. Like Trent."

"So, you want to wipe the rest of us out, then, right?"

"Did Trent tell you that? It's an idea I've been throwing around the ol' noggin, but I haven't decided yet. Maybe you can change my mind." Megan gave me an earnest look, then burst out in laughter. "No, I'm just kidding. Uck. No one wants to hear your blubbering."

I heard someone opening the first door into the locker room. "Roselyn? Are you all right? You've been in there a while. I'd like to lock up..." my manager's voice trailed off as she walked through the second door and saw Megan. "Oh, I didn't know anyone else was in here," she said in confusion.

Megan walked up and stood next to me. She grabbed a big handful of my buttcheek, looked my manager right in the eye, and said, "We need just a few more minutes of girl time, if you don't mind."

"Oh! Um...I um...I'll...give you a moment..." my manager said as she quickly turned tail and hurried from the locker room.

"Get your hand off my ass," I ordered.

"Oh, don't be a prude," Megan said. "Now, tell me where Trent is and I'll be off."

"Yeah, right after killing me."

"I'll make it quick."

"Why haven't you killed me yet? I mean, you threw a knife at my face without a second thought last time we met, and now you're standing here bantering with me. What is the point of this?"

"I like to play with my prey."

"No, it's more than that. You said I was boring. No…you need me," I surmised.

Megan narrowed her eyes at me. "I don't need you."

"Then why haven't you killed me?"

"I could kill you if I wanted to. I'm just choosing not to yet."

"But why?"

"I'm sorry, are you seriously demanding to know why I'm not killing you?"

"What do you need me for?"

"I need to know where Trent is."

"And when you find him? What then? What makes you think you can get him back into that compound?"

Megan looked at me expectantly and raised an eyebrow. "Almost there."

I furrowed my brow at her. "Almost where?"

She rolled her eyes. "Good golly, you're thick. I'm bored now. Let's go." She pressed some buttons on her watch and quickly snatched my wrist before I could dodge her.

We were suddenly in a dirty, dimly lit room with a big metal door to our left and a smaller hatchlike door to our right. Along the wall stood several dusty…spacesuits?

"Where did you take me?!" I asked, feeling panicked.

Megan giggled mischievously. "Let's play a game of hide and seek, shall we? I'll hide you, and let's see if Trent can find you!"

"Where am I?!"

"That is the question, isn't it?" Megan said with a sinister giggle. "A word of advice: I wouldn't go outside if I were you. All right! Have fun! Au revoir! Oh, and try not to die." Megan stepped back, waved at me with a wild grin on her face, and teleported out of the room, leaving me on my own.

My mind raced. Where could I be? What were the spacesuits for? Were they…real? Jesus, I wasn't on the International Space Station, was I?! No, that couldn't be. I wasn't floating. But…I took a step, and it felt strange. Something wasn't right. I jumped up into the air, and I almost threw up due to the sensation – it was like I was too light. Was I in some kind of simulation room? I moved around cautiously, making sure to keep down my lunch. I felt like Neil Armstrong hopping around on the Moon.

NO. No, no, no, no. NO. IMPOSSIBLE. I can't be…

I made my way to the small hatchlike door. It had a big wheel on it, so I started to turn it. As I did, red lights started flashing and alarms started going off. What did I do?! I hopped back away from the door as quickly as I could. Should I turn the wheel back the other way? As my breathing accelerated from the adrenaline rush, I realized I was starting to feel light-headed. I looked over at the spacesuits. They were held up on stands that appeared to be designed to help facilitate getting into the suits independently. I climbed into the cumbersome suit and was surprised when an indicator light flashed brightly on the stand in front of me that said "Activated." The suit suddenly sealed shut on its own up along my back. I saw the helmet portion sitting in its own designated spot, and I grabbed it. My spacesuit gloves were surprisingly nimble and had excellent grip. I placed the helmet on my head and heard a "whoosh" of air as it sealed to the suit.

Suddenly, I heard a feminine robotic voice speaking through the helmet. It was a language I didn't understand.

"What the hell is this? I don't understand," I said aloud.

There was a brief silence, then the robotic voice said, "Language set to English. Suit status: oxygen levels charged. Eight hours remaining. Pressure stable. All systems go."

"Whaaaaat…?" I murmured to myself.

"I'm sorry, I didn't understand. Could you repeat that?" the robotic voice said.

"You can hear me?" I asked aloud.

"Yes, I hear you. What is your question?"

"Who are you?"

"I am Neeri. I am the voice-activated interface for the MoonBase1 system. It appears the system is on standby. Would you like me to reboot the system?"

"Yyyyyyes. I think so? What will that do?"

"It will start up the life support and communication systems. Oxygen levels inside the base are at critical levels. Pressure is stable. Temperature is 27 degrees Celsius. Airlock Hatch A ajar."

"Can I open that door?" I asked.

"I do not know what door to which you refer."

I looked at the white hatch door and saw that it had a large letter A on it. "Can I open door A to the airlock room?"

"Airlock Hatch A is ajar."

"I know, is it safe to open it?"

"The life support system will take an hour to stabilize conditions in the base. It is not safe."

"Can I enter if I'm wearing the spacesuit?"

"You can go anywhere in the spacesuit."

"Can I go outside with this suit?"

"You can go anywhere in the spacesuit."

"Neeri? Where am I?"

"You are inside the airlock of MoonBase1."

"So, I'm on the Moon."

"Yes."

"How do I get back to Earth?"

"GSF must send a transport ship. Would you like me to contact GSF?"

"What is GSF?"

"Global Space Federation."

"Neeri, what year is it?"

"It is 3156 AD."

Shit. "No, don't contact GSF. There'll be too many questions. I'll probably be treated like a spy or something. There must be another way. I need to get back to Trent to warn him that Megan is coming."

"Would you like me to contact Gatekeeper3000 currently in lunar orbit?"

"In orbit around the Moon?"

"Yes, that is what lunar orbit means."

"Damn, you're sassy. Why is it in orbit around the moon?"

"Gatekeeper3000 is a lunar space station that will replace the obsolete International Lunar Station and provide docking services for future Martian colonist ships. It is currently under construction."

"No, don't contact them just yet. Wait…did you say Martian colonists?"

"Martian colonist ships."

"There are Martian colonies?"

"There have been attempts to create Martian colonies, but the effort has been abandoned until terraforming is completed."

"Oh, that's right. Trent had mentioned that once. How long will that take?"

"It should be complete within the next fifty years."

"I'll have to remember that. Maybe I can visit a Martian colony someday."

I made my way back over to the hatch and finished opening it. I stepped through the door and closed it tightly behind me. I was in what looked to be a small break room. I saw labeled, packaged food in small bins on a shelf along the wall. Well, at least I wouldn't starve.

"Is there drinkable water?" I asked Neeri.

"Yes. The water tank is full."

"How much water is in the tank?"

"Five thousand gallons."

"Well, at least I'm not going to die."

"On a long enough timeline, everyone dies."

"Thanks for that, Neeri."

"I am glad to help."

I walked through the break room carefully, still trying to get used to moving around with the low gravity, and I found a bigger room that looked like it could be a lounge. I turned and looked to my right and my breath caught in my throat. There was a large window, and through it I could see the Earth.

"Holy shit."

"I'm sorry, I didn't understand that."

"Shut up, Neeri."

"Yes, ma'am."

I saw someone had pulled up a rickety old metal folding chair to the big window. Sitting down was tricky, as the bulky suit was awkward to maneuver, but I managed. I sat and stared at my planet in awe. If I did die up here, at least I had a great view.

"Why is no one here, Neeri?" I asked.

"May I speak?"

"Yes."

"The last astronauts were here twenty years ago."

"When are the next ones coming?"

"No future arrivals have been scheduled."

"So, I'll be on my own for a while, then."

"I will be here to assist you."

"Do you have an android form? Or are you just an interface?"

"I do not have an android form."

"...Be a lot cooler if you did."

"I do not understand."

"Yeah, you probably don't say 'cool' anymore."

"Cool is a term to indicate a relative lack of heat."

"Ok. Thanks."

As I gazed at Earth, I wondered if Trent was down there. The Trent I knew wouldn't be, as he didn't like to go to the future past his own time. But, if he truly was immortal, he would eventually have to go into the future, wouldn't he? He would run out of days in the past. He'd have to push into the future to avoid crossing his own timeline. Therefore...it would be perfectly reasonable to assume Trent could be down there somewhere. So, if Trent was down there, how could I get his attention? I needed to get him to rescue me so I could rescue him. I didn't want to get the "Federation" involved. Even if they didn't interrogate and detain me (but it seemed very likely that they would), they wouldn't be able to help me find him once I was down on Earth anyway – he could be anywhere. No, I had to do something big. Something he could see from anywhere.

Then it hit me.

I was going to steal the Declaration of Independence. No, wait…That wasn't it…

I was going to blow up the Moon base.

Chapter 11

It was going to be a risky move. A stupid one, even. But I had to do something. I needed to get back to him before it was too late. Blowing up the base would have to register on his radar, wouldn't it? I would be altering time. I was already altering time just by being here. Now, I didn't want to blow up the entire base. If I did, he might not have anywhere to transport himself to – I didn't know if he would keep a spare spacesuit lying around for just such an occasion. Of course, if he was living in the future, I supposed anything was possible.

"Neeri, is there a way to close off sections of the base in case of fire or explosion?"

"The base is divided into five separate sectors that can be sealed off from each other with a secure hatch in case of emergencies. Sector D has already been sealed off due to fire damage."

"What happened?"

"Uncontained fuel ignition."

"What was in Sector D?"

"Sector D is the rover port."

"Is the rover still functional?"

"The rover is offline. I am unable to diagnose."

"What are the other four sectors?"

"Sector A is the recreation center. It is where I detect you are now. Sector B is the living quarters. Sector C is the mess hall and kitchen. Sector E is the communication and mining operations control center."

"Mining operations?"

"Yes."

"What mining operations? What the hell would anybody want from the Moon?"

"This base was established as the headquarters for the MoonLife company's mining operations. They mine rare earth elements, helium-3, and ice."

"Why did they stop?"

"They didn't. Mining operations are still underway."

"Then where are all the people?"

"It is an automated system that no longer requires human workers. Instructions are sent to the system remotely."

"So who does the mining? Just a bunch of self-driving robot bulldozers?"

"Autonomous heavy equipment, which does include bulldozers of sorts. Excavated material is transported to the processing facilities and subsequently shuttled to Earth."

"Are there people at the processing facilities?"

"Negative."

"What about the shuttles? How often do they come?"

"The shuttles come once a week."

"Maybe I could stow away on one and hitch a ride back to Earth...but, I guess that still doesn't solve my problem, does it?"

"What is your problem?"

"I need to get back to my own time. I need to find Trent from now so he can help me save himself."

"Who is Trent?"

"That is always the question, isn't it?" I replied. As I stared out the big window, I saw a giant dump truck rolling by off in the distance. "Is that the autonomous heavy equipment you were telling me about?" I asked.

"Is what the autonomous heavy equip—"

"That big dump truck I see outside."

"Yes. Rough Transport 78 is likely in view at the moment."

"Wait, you know which one it is? How do you know that?"

"All machinery is connected to my system."

"Do you control them?"

"I relay commands to them when I am directed to do so."

I suddenly had an idea. "If I asked you to change their course, could you do that?"

"I can only take commands from the head of operations."

"But I'm the only one on the base. Doesn't that automatically make me the head of operations?"

"Negative."

"Then who is the head of operations?"

"Norland Solovic."

"This is an emergency. I need your help, Neeri!"

"In the case of an emergency, protocol dictates that the highest-ranking team member on the base assumes the role of head of operations until the emergency is under control. However, I detect no emergency."

"So, if there is an emergency, would I be the highest-ranking person on the base?"

"Yes. You are the only person on the base."

I smiled. "Does an explosion on the base count as an emergency?"

"Yes, an explosion is an emergency."

"Awesome. Neeri, where would I find a map of the base?"

"Sector E. I will bring up the floor plans for you."

Neeri directed me to Sector E. When I opened the hatch and entered the large room, I saw a digital map of the base displayed on a large screen amid what appeared to be an elaborate control panel. It looked as though the base was arranged like spokes on a wheel, with one main hub.

"Neeri, is there anything flammable in the base?"

"All flammable items are kept in Sector D."

"You said it was locked off. Can I still access it?"

"You must access it from outside. Hatch D is sealed."

"Well, shit. How do I get outside?"

"Through the airlock."

"That was where I started from, right? Does the big metal door lead to the outside?"

"Exterior Door A1 opens to the outside."

I looked at the floor plans in front of me. Which sector was I going to blow up? I supposed the living quarters were probably my safest bet. If my plan didn't work and Trent didn't come for me, I was going to need to be able to survive in this base until I could be rescued, and the living quarters seemed like the least essential portion. I could camp out on the recreation room floor if I had to.

"Neeri, can you show me where all the bulldozers are at right now? Do you have a radar or something that shows their location?"

"I can bring it up." The floor plans of the base disappeared and were replaced with an image full of little slow-moving dots. They were spread out all over the screen.

"Which ones are the bulldozers?" I asked.

"They are all bulldozers. Did you want me to include the other machinery?"

I grinned. "Damn, this might just work."

I hurried back to Sector A and opened the hatch that led into the airlock. The alarms started going off again. I closed it behind me and they stopped.

"Am I clear to go outside? Is my suit, well, suitable for a brief excursion outdoors?"

"You must reduce the pressure in the airlock before opening Exterior Door A1. Would you like me to do so now?"

"Yeah, go for it."

"Reducing pressure in the airlock. Do not attempt to open Airlock Hatch A or Exterior Door A1."

A loud hissing sound filled the room, and I felt my suit puff up a bit. After several minutes, I saw a green light flash next to the metal door that said "A1" on it.

"You may now exit the base," Neeri said.

I walked to the door and pressed the green light. With an obnoxious but brief scraping and whining sound, the door slid open. Everything was suddenly silent. I looked out at the barren, crater-pocked landscape before me. The sky above the horizon was black, but the surface of the Moon was quite bright – bright enough to make it difficult for me to see many stars in the black sky. It seemed strange. I stepped out the door and planted my foot on the surface of the moon. Damn it, I had to say it.

"That's one small step for man…one giant leap for mankind."

"The quote is actually, 'That's one small step for a man, one giant leap for mankind,'" Neeri said through my helmet.

"Are you sure?"

"Yes."

"Damn it. Pretend I said it right."

"I am not programmed to pretend."

"Did they program you to sass?" I asked snidely.

"I am programmed to assist and inform. I do not intend to offend."

I hopped my way around the outside of the base, trying to keep focused on my task even though my entire being wanted to freak out over the fact that I was walking on the moon. I did, however, stop for a moment to use my boot to write "Roselyn Wolff" in the dirt. But then it was right back to business.

I found a long section of the base that was windowless and had what looked like a huge hangar door. It said "D1" on it.

"Neeri, can you still hear me?"

"Yes. How can I assist you?"

"I need you to open this big door that says D1 on it."

"There should be a control button on the right side. Press it to open Exterior Door D1."

I found and pressed the button, and the massive door shook. I was afraid it wasn't going to open, but it finally broke free from whatever was binding it and started to slide upward, reminiscent of a garage door. I was expecting groaning and screeching like the other door, but it was eerily silent.

"Why is that door so quiet?"

"There is no air outside, so sound waves do not have a medium through which to travel."

"Oh. Duh. You know, Neeri, you're making me feel really stupid."

"I am sure you have a wonderful personality."

I laughed. "Yeah, someone definitely programmed you to sass." I walked through the door into Sector D. It was dark inside, though, and I couldn't see much. "Can you turn on the lights in Sector D?"

"I cannot. The systems in Sector D were damaged by fire. Would you like to activate your flashlight?"

"I have a flashlight? In the suit?"

"It is on your helmet. I can activate it for you if you wish."

"Yes, please."

The room suddenly lit up. I was immediately surprised by the dump truck-sized rover parked in the middle of the room. I looked around at the other tools and crates and containers and canisters…it was like a Moon garage. I could tell there was some severe fire damage throughout, but I was hoping to find some fuel or something else flammable that hadn't been touched by the previous fire. I wandered around, looking through crates and opening up canisters, but I wasn't sure if I even knew what I was looking for.

"Neeri, is there some kind of gas or fuel in here? Something that could be ignited?"

"The fuel reserve is a combustible liquid."

"Where is it?"

"It is near Exterior Door D1."

I turned around and saw a cylindrical metal container roughly the size of a refrigerator standing in the corner. That had to be it. Now…how was I going to get the fuel to Sector B? I retrieved some of the empty metal canisters I had found earlier and brought them to the fuel tank. I wasn't sure if they were suited for holding whatever kind of fuel was in the tank, but they didn't need to hold it for long. I lifted the nozzle from the tank, which was connected to the bottom of the cylinder with a long hose.

"Ok," I said to myself, "it should be just like pumping gas…I hope." I stuck the nozzle from the tank into the first empty canister and pulled the lever. I could feel the slight movement of the nozzle from the pressure of the liquid fuel being ejected from the hose, but it was odd to hear no sound from it. I'd never realized until now how much I relied on the sound of liquid filling a container to know how full the container was. I let the fuel flow for a few moments, then stopped to inspect the container. It was only about a quarter filled. I continued in that manner until I had filled the first container, then moved on to the second. By the time I got the third container about halfway filled, the pressure in the hose dropped to nothing. The tank was out of fuel.

"Son of a bitch!" I cried in frustration. "Neeri, is this all the fuel there is? Is there another tank somewhere?"

"There is only one fuel tank on MoonBase1."

I looked down at the measly two and a half canisters at my feet. I had about five gallons of fuel. I could probably make an explosion with it, but would it cause enough damage? It would start a fire, surely, but I imagine the living quarters probably had some kind of fire suppression system in place. I couldn't risk failure. I needed a bigger explosion. I surveyed the room one more time, trying to think of anything else I could use. My eyes fell upon the enormous rover.

"Does the rover have fuel in its tank?" I asked.

"The rover is offline. I cannot access that information."

"How do I get it back online?"

"Its electrical systems must be charged and rebooted."

"Neeri, if the rover were to, I don't know, crash into the base, would that count as an emergency?"

"If it compromised the integrity of the structure, it would be considered an emergency."

"Fantastic. How do I charge and reboot the systems?"

"Are you planning to crash the rover into MoonBase1?"

"Nnnooo, of course not. I was just curious. So, how do I charge and reboot the systems on the rover?"

"It has solar panels. It must collect sunlight."

"Where are the solar panels?"

"They are attached to the roof of the rover."

I looked at the behemoth before me. How was I going to get that thing out into the sunlight? I climbed up the steps to the door and opened it. It was surprisingly spacious, with room for at least ten people. It was like a church van. I sat down in the driver's seat and inspected the gauges and levers around the steering wheel. One of the levers had an arrow pointing up and an arrow pointing down.

"What does this black lever with the up and down arrows do?" I asked.

"It operates the speed of the rover."

"How do I put it in reverse?"

"Pull the red knob on the underside of the steering wheel."

I found the red knob and pulled it. "Does this thing have a parking brake I need to know about?"

"To activate the parking brake, press the left pedal on the floor under the steering wheel."

"How do I turn it off?"

"Press the left pedal a second time to release the brake."

I pressed the pedal and felt it pop up. I must have released it. I climbed out of the rover and made my way around to the front of it.

I braced my shoulder against the wide bumper and gave it a shove – and the rover began to roll backwards.

"I'm beginning to love this low gravity," I said. "I could never do this on Earth."

"Do what?"

"Move this monstrosity of a rover."

"Be aware that low gravity does not affect inertia."

I stopped pushing and watched the rover continue to roll backwards toward the open door. "Say what now?"

"Gravity affects acceleration. But once an object is in motion, the low gravity does nothing to reduce inertia, since that is determined by mass, and gravity does not affect mass."

"Are you saying I can't stop this thing?"

"It will eventually stop due to friction. I am simply advising you not to get in the way of the rover when it is in motion. It is easy to move it, but harder to stop it."

I tried to hop quickly to the rover, but my movements were so awkward and slow in this strange environment that I had a hard time catching up to it. When I got close enough, I made a desperate grab for the rail attached to the steps. I clung to the rail and lifted myself up onto the bottom step just as the opposite side of the rover made contact with the door opening. I felt the rover slow and shake, and I saw metal and plastic pieces come flying off the side of the rover. I climbed the steps and entered the cabin. I grabbed the steering wheel and turned it to direct the rover away from the door framing. I watched out the windshield (which seemed an odd thing to call it considering there was no wind on the Moon) as the rover continued to move backward, away from the Moon base. When I was certain the rover was in sunlight, I pressed the parking brake. The rover shuddered to a halt.

I stepped out the door and looked up at the roof of the rover. The solar panels were covered in a layer of Moon dust. I pulled myself up and used my hand to swipe the dust off of the panels.

"How long will the system take to charge?" I asked Neeri.

"It takes roughly one hour to charge. Once it is charged, it must be rebooted."

"What, do I unplug it and plug it back in?" I joked.

"Negative."

"Control alt delete?"

"Negative. You must press the power button."

I slid down off the roof and looked into the cabin. "And which one is the power button?"

"It is the small red button in the uppermost left corner of the control deck."

I spied the button. "Cool. Got it." I climbed out of the rover and headed back toward the base to collect my fuel containers. I still didn't have a fully formed plan, but I knew if I rolled with it long enough, some resemblance of a plan would materialize. I knew I was going to light this fuel on fire in the Sector B, and as a backup plan, I was also going to crash the rover into the side of it so I could assume control of the MoonBase1 system. How I was going to accomplish these things without seriously maiming or killing myself, I wasn't sure. All I knew was that I needed to get Trent's attention. Sure, I was going to attract attention elsewhere, too, but as long as I signaled Trent, he could rescue me and get me back to my own time and my own Trent long before anyone else had time to come and investigate.

I carried the fuel back to door A1 and brought it into the airlock with me. After closing the door, Neeri began to pressurize the chamber so I could enter the base. As the pressure increased, however, I watched in horror as the fuel containers I had with me began to crumple.

"What's going on?! Why are my containers collapsing?!" I shouted.

"If you bring sealed containers from the low pressure outside to the higher pressure inside the base, the pressure on the outside of the container will be greater than the pressure inside the container and may crush it."

I quickly backed away from the metal fuel containers. "Are they going to explode?!"

"They may implode."

"But they have fuel in them!"

"What kind of fuel?"

"I don't know! Whatever fuel was in the tank in Sector D!"

"It will not explode from this pressure change."

I cringed in the corner as far away from the canisters as I could get while the room finished pressurizing. When Neeri informed me that it was safe to open the hatch, I entered the base and left the fuel containers in the airlock.

"Is there a cart or a wagon or something for hauling things in here?" I asked.

"There are wheeled transport wagons in Sector D."

"I'm not going back out there right now. What else? Is there a laundry cart or a dinner cart or something?"

"There is a laundry cart in Sector B in the laundry room."

"That'll do. Hey, can I take off this suit yet?"

"Life support systems are not yet stabilized. I will inform you when you are able to safely remove your suit."

I hopped through Sector A to the hub. I located the hatch that had a "B" on it and went inside. It looked like an apartment hallway, with numbered doors on either side. I made my way down the hall until I found the laundry room. Sure enough, there was a canvas-sided laundry cart. I grabbed it and wheeled it back to Sector A. I gingerly transported the crumpled canisters from the airlock to the cart, and wheeled them back to Sector B. I shoved the cart through the hatch and closed it. I'd deal with them after the rover was charged and the base was filled with oxygen. I couldn't have an explosion if I didn't have oxygen.

Now that I had set things in motion, I needed to work out the details. I wandered back to the recreation room, sat in the metal folding chair, and stared at the Earth while I pondered my next move.

Chapter 12

"Neeri, are there any flares on the base?"

"There are flares in both Sector E and Sector D."

"How long do they stay lit?"

"They burn for approximately fifteen minutes."

"Do they require oxygen to burn?"

"No. That would be disadvantageous on the Moon."

"Yeah, I suppose you're right." I got up and went to Sector E to collect the flares. When I found them, with Neeri's assistance, of course, I was pleased to see there were nine of them in the emergency kit, along with the flare gun. I brought the whole kit back to Sector A with me. I would collect the additional flares from the "garage" when I went back out to reboot the rover.

As I waited impatiently for the base to fill with oxygen and the rover to charge, I wandered around the recreation room. They had a ping-pong table, a giant screen on the wall that I assumed was a television of sorts, and something that looked like a blacked-out shower stall with gridded dots, which Neeri told me was a virtual reality platform. I wanted to try it, but Neeri informed me that it couldn't be used in conjunction with my spacesuit. Disappointed, I decided to push a more comfortable chair over to the window and sit.

"Why aren't there more chairs by the window here? You'd think this would be the best place to sit in the whole base."

"You may change your mind when you are able to try the virtual reality platform."

"I don't think I'm going to have time to give it a whirl. I've got business to attend to soon."

"Do you need assistance?"

"Not just yet. I'll let you know when I do."

I had formed a plan, but I was still missing one little piece. I was going to blow up Sector B and crash the rover into it for good measure, and then I was going to take over the bulldozers to write a message to Trent on the surface of the Moon. But what was it going to say? I couldn't just write "TRENT SOS." That would definitely get his attention, but I might not be the only one looking for him in this time. Surely there were other Trents in the world down below, but anyone who was looking for Trent Morgan would have to investigate a big "TRENT SOS" on the Moon. No, it would have to be something that he would know was uniquely meant for him, but that everyone else would just think was a prank or something silly. It had to be something he would know was from me. But what?

As I sat and pondered, Neeri finally informed me that the pressure and oxygen levels in the base had stabilized and it was safe to remove my suit.

"Great! I'll do that in just a second. Hey, are these suits fire-proof?"

"Yes."

"Perfect. How long has it been since I moved the rover out into the sun?"

"Give me a moment to search the log." Neeri paused, then said, "Thirty-two minutes."

"Damn it. Well, I'm going to get started anyway. Maybe it'll be charged by the time I get out there."

"May I be of assistance?"

"Soon."

I grabbed my flare kit and headed to Sector B. I went inside and looked at the crushed canisters sitting inside the laundry cart. I needed to open them, but I was terrified that they would somehow explode. I had no idea how flammable the liquid inside was. I picked up one of the containers and carefully twisted the cap. It didn't budge. I put a bit more effort into it, and finally felt it come loose. At that moment, I heard a loud hiss of air and the canister popped back into shape. I shrieked and dropped the can back into the cart as I turned and covered my helmeted head with my hands.

"Are you all right? Have you suffered an injury?" Neeri asked through my helmet.

When nothing happened, I replied, "I...I think I'm ok." I looked back over my shoulder cautiously. The canister was on its side in the cart, leaking fluid into the canvas bottom. "Yeah, I'm fine, Neeri. Don't mind me."

I leaned over the cart and righted the container. I then opened the second and third canisters and luckily didn't trigger any explosions while I was in the room. I used the half-filled container to soak the canvas laundry cart with fuel, then screwed the cap back on one of the other two containers. I thought it might create a better explosion if it could build up pressure inside while being heated by the fire in the cart, but I wasn't sure if it would work. So, I left the cap off of the other container, just in case. Before heading back to the hatch, I went up and down the hall and opened all of the "apartment" doors to allow a free flow of air through the sector. I left the cart in the middle of the hallway and hurried from the room as quickly as I could (although with low gravity and a spacesuit, I wasn't particularly quick).

I crouched outside the hatch with my emergency kit. As I loaded the flare into the gun, my hands were shaking. I held the hatch door slightly ajar and pointed the gun at the laundry cart. I took a deep breath, aimed, and fired. I quickly withdrew my hand from the doorway and slammed the hatch shut behind me, turning the wheel frantically. I waited for the big boom. And I waited. And waited.

"Shit, I don't think it worked," I mumbled.

"I'm sorry, I didn't understand," Neeri said.

"Not now, Neeri."

I loaded another flare into the gun and slowly opened the hatch. The flare was burning away harmlessly on the floor way beyond the laundry cart. I'd failed to take the gravity into account – I was aiming based on Earth gravity. I fired again, trying to aim lower to get the flare inside the cart, and quickly shut the door. Again, nothing happened. I repeated the exercise until I was down to my last flare. That was when I realized I was probably better off if I threw the flare into the cart. I loaded the last flare into the gun, aimed it at the wall behind me in the central hub, and fired it. When the flare ignited and bounced off the wall, I quickly kicked it over to the hatch. I opened the hatch, picked up the flare with my gloved hand, and lobbed it in the room. I watched it arc right into the cart milliseconds before I slammed the hatch closed for the last time.

That had to do it! I thought.

It didn't. Nothing happened. I felt my heart fall into the pit of my stomach as I slid to the floor with my back against the door.

"Neeri, I thought you said that fuel was flammable?!"

"The fuel is a combustible liquid. It can be ignited, but it takes more effort to ignite than a flammable liquid."

"Goddamn it! Now you tell me! Shit. Shit shit shit shit."

I felt the tears welling up in my eyes. No. There's still Plan B. Don't give up yet. I stood up, punched the wall, cursed profusely, and stormed back through Sector A toward the airlock.

There was no marveling at the fact that I was walking on the Moon during this excursion outside. I was on a mission. I went around to Sector D, where I had likely irreparably mangled the door frame (but I wasn't sure, as I hadn't actually tried to close door D1 yet) and rummaged around for the flare kit. When I couldn't find it, Neeri informed me that it was located inside the rover.

"Why didn't you tell me that from the start?!" I cried.

"The rover is housed in Sector D."

"Yeah, but I moved it outside, remember?"

"It is in the log. However, by default, I locate the rover through its tracking beacon, and since it is offline, it is assumed to be in Sector D."

"You're a shitty assistant," I said sourly.

"I am sorry you feel that way."

I went out to the rover and climbed inside. It had to have been close to an hour by now, I hoped. I pressed the red button as Neeri had instructed, and the lights on the control deck flashed on.

"Rover is online," Neeri said. "Fuel levels critical."

"Well, it doesn't have to go far. It just has to go fast."

I started up the engine. "Neeri, how the hell does this engine work without oxygen?"

"It is a combination of combustion and electric. It runs on electric by default, which requires no oxygen, but it reverts to combustion when the battery runs out or when more power is needed. There are compressed oxygen tanks connected to the unit."

"How far can I get on the fuel and oxygen we have if I run this rover at maximum speed?"

"The fuel levels are critical. The rover will exhaust its reserve in approximately three miles."

"That'll do. Like I said, I'm not going far."

I lifted the lever to accelerate the rover forward. The gauges showed a response to the accelerator, but the unit wasn't going anywhere.

"Why won't this bastard go?"

"You left the parking brake on."

Of course I did. I released the parking brake and the rover jolted and began accelerating backwards. I forgot I had left in in reverse. I slammed on the parking brake again and pushed in the red knob under the steering wheel to take it out of reverse. I released the parking brake one more time, and the rover began to accelerate forward. Operating the rover with a lever for the throttle took some getting used to. I steered the monstrosity in a wide arc around the base until I could see the spoke that was Sector B. I pointed the nose of the rover at the building and put it in reverse. I wanted to give it a good running start.

Once I was a good distance from the building, I stopped the rover and located the flares. There were three left in the box. I had an idea.

"Neeri, where are the oxygen tanks located on the rover?"

"They are on the underside. Oxygen tanks can be accessed through the floor of the rover."

I climbed in the back and found the metal door that opened to the tanks. I disconnected one of the tanks, with Neeri's instruction, and used the winch on the front of the rover to attach the tank to the bumper. I figured that if the tank was punctured upon impact with the building, the pressure might blow the tank and cause even more damage to the structure. Hey, if you're going to make a scene, make a good one.

I got back into the rover, loaded a flare into the gun, and threw the vehicle into full throttle toward the base. As it approached, I quickly fired all three flares into the compartment that held the remaining oxygen tanks and then jumped from the rover. I landed and rolled, then fumbled to my feet, quickly looking up to watch as the rover made contact with the base. It looked like the tank blew as the rover plowed through the side of Sector B, and there was an explosion of debris. I was surprised to see how far the rover penetrated into the base before finally coming to a halt.

"Emergency," Neeri alerted me through my helmet. "Sector B has been compromised. The structure has been breached. Please attend to the breach immediately."

Mission accomplished. I grinned, dusted off my spacesuit, and started back toward the base. "I'll be there in a jiffy," I said cheerily.

Suddenly there was a bright burst of light from Sector B. I glanced over and saw the explosion disappear as quickly as it had erupted.

"Emergency. Fire detected in Sector B. Please attend to the fire immediately."

"I think it's out already, Neeri."

"Checking...fire has been resolved. Oxygen levels critical in Sector B. Please attend to the breach immediately."

"Chill out, I'm coming. I have something I need to take care of first. Seal off Sector B until I can get it repaired."

I hurried back to the base in an awkward hopping manner and took off my space suit once the airlock was pressurized. It felt good to finally be free of that cumbersome suit. I opened the hatch and rushed into the base, headed for Sector E.

"Neeri, can you hear me?" I asked aloud as I entered Sector E.

"How may I assist?" I heard Neeri say. She was speaking through some kind of intercom.

"I'm assuming control of all operations until this emergency can be resolved."

"Confirmed."

"Show me all the bulldozers on the radar again, please."

"It is not a radar."

"Whatever. Just show me."

Neeri brought up the grid on the screen that showed all the bulldozers as little dots. Each dot had a number associated with it. Following the grid pattern coordinates, I instructed Neeri in how to change course for each bulldozer and when to make them drop their blade. I made sure to have her accelerate all bulldozers to full speed as well. I had her mark it out on the grid as I went, and when I was done, the screen had two giant words on it: TIME THIEF.

That ought to get his attention.

Neeri pestered me to attend to the emergency at hand, but I ignored her. Then she informed me that GSF was attempting to contact the base, and I ignored that too. I just sat and watched the little dots on the screen as they plowed out my message.

"MoonLife headquarters is attempting to take command as head of operations," Neeri said.

"No. I'm still dealing with the emergency on the base. They can't just take over again if there's still an emergency, can they?"

"Not without your consent. It is protocol."

"I do not consent to it."

"Understood."

After a few hours and several attempts of MoonLife and GSF to contact me, I was starting to worry. The bulldozers had almost finished the message, and I had to seriously consider the possibility that Trent wouldn't get it, or that Trent wasn't down there. What would I do then? I should at least make a backup plan in case this ridiculous, elaborate scheme didn't work.

"GSF has deployed a shuttle to the base," Neeri said. "It will arrive in approximately fifteen hours."

"Well, with any luck, I won't be here."

"Someone has entered the base."

I jumped up, my heart in my throat. "What do you mean? Did they come through the door?"

"Exterior Door A1 has not been opened. Human life form detected in Sector A."

"Trent!" I shouted as I hopped quickly toward Sector A, knowing I must've looked like an uncoordinated kangaroo. "Trent, it's me!"

When I entered Sector A, I saw a person in a spacesuit standing with their back to me, looking out the window. It wasn't a spacesuit from the base.

"Trent?" I called hesitantly.

The person turned around. When they saw me standing there without a suit on, they pulled off their helmet. It was a man who appeared to be in his early forties. He was over 6 feet tall and lean with dark hair speckled with gray. His eyes were grayish-blue. He had a handsome face.

"Roselyn," he said, a look of utter disbelief on his face. "I didn't believe it, but there you are…"

"It's me! Yes! Are you…are you Trent?"

He nodded. His eyes were misty. "It's been…too long."

I looked at the man before me, hardly able to believe it myself. He looked older. "Trent, I don't mean to sound rude or ruin the moment, but why are you older? You don't age."

Trent gave a short laugh. "I do, apparently. Just on a really long timeline."

I hesitated to ask, but I had to know. "How old are you?"

"Somewhere in the ballpark of 2,400 years."

"Oh my god," I gasped.

"I know. Time flies when you're having fun," he joked.

I stepped closer to him. He smiled, but his eyes were full of sorrow and regret.

"I need help, Trent," I pleaded as I grabbed his hand. "I need to get back to my own time, and back to you. You're in danger." As I looked earnestly into his eyes, a tear rolled down his cheek. "What's wrong?"

"I'm sorry," he said as he quickly swiped the tear away. "I'm just having a moment. I guess old age will do that to you," he joked.

That was when I realized what was wrong. "How long has it been?"

He looked away. "A very, very long time."

The mournful look on his face said it all. "You watched me die, didn't you?" I asked quietly.

He didn't answer, and that answered everything. I suddenly didn't know how to feel.

He brought my hand to his lips and kissed it. "You're here now, you need me, and that's what matters."

Tears filled my eyes. "Even after all this time…"

"Love is forever. Even when it hurts."

"You never forgot."

"How could I?"

"What about this? Surely I must tell you about this when I get back. Why do you seem so surprised to see me?"

"I remember you, always, but I do still forget things."

"Where did you get a spacesuit?" I asked, looking him up and down. "It looks more advanced than the one I've been using."

"It is. I nicked this from a Mars shuttle base in 3519."

"You've been to Mars? What's it like?"

"In 3519? Not terribly exciting. We've terraformed it, which basically means we've made it into mini-Earth. However, if you visit much later on, say, in the 8000s, things get much more interesting."

"If it's terraformed, why do they need spacesuits?"

"They don't need them for Mars. They need them for traveling to and from Mars."

"So, you aren't afraid to go to the future anymore?"

Trent laughed. "No, that's a thing of the past," he punned.

I grinned. "I'm glad to see that your sense of humor hasn't changed the way the rest of you has."

"Perhaps that's my curse," he said with a chuckle.

"What changed your mind about visiting the future?"

"You'll find out." Trent looked out the window at the Earth. "Well, shall we?" He held his hand out to me.

"We shall. I need to get back to March 5, 2018. Do you remember where my house was? If you could bring me to my house at, like, 4:45PM, that would be great. Just a fair warning, though – your past self will be there. And so will Jaeger. Do you remember Jaeger?"

"I don't need to remember him. I still see him regularly. Bastard still doesn't look a day over thirty-five," Trent mumbled. He looked at me sadly. "I know this may seem a silly request to you, but…I will take you back to the time you wish, I promise, I just…I've missed you terribly, and this may be the last time I ever see you. Perhaps you could allow me to steal just a little bit of your time, for old times' sake? Just an hour or two?"

I couldn't imagine the way he was feeling at that moment. I'd been spending the past day or two (or three? I didn't know anymore) giving my Trent grief over his change, wondering if I could love him the same if his personality changed, and here he was, countless changes and 1,800 years later, still hopelessly in love with me. I didn't deserve him. He looked at me with affection and adoration, and it made me feel like absolute garbage for my behavior.

"Sure, of course," I said quietly.

I went to him and tucked myself under his arm. In an instant, we were in a library. The books on the shelves looked positively ancient.

"How did you do that?" I asked. "Where is your watch?"

Trent stepped away from me and started removing his spacesuit. "It's been biomechanically installed into my wrist, and I control it with my mind. Isn't that brilliant?"

"It is. I wish I had mine biomechanically installed into my wrist. Then I wouldn't have ended up in this situation in the first place."

"I know it's incredibly selfish of me, but…this situation has brought us together one last time. Forgive me if I'm not disappointed."

When he had his spacesuit off, I threw my arms around him and hugged him tightly. My heart ached for him. "I'm so sorry, Trent."

Trent enfolded me in his arms and stroked the back of my head with his hand. "There's nothing to be sorry for."

"I've been terrible to you. You've just recently changed and I've been treating you like it's your fault. Instead of trying to get to know the new you, I've been pushing you away. I'm sorry for that."

"Don't be so hard on yourself. I had never expected any of that to be easy for either of us."

I felt a pang in my chest. "I must be a ghost to you. To hear you talk about us in the past tense…"

"It wasn't my intention to make you feel badly."

I looked up into his eyes. "Do we make it? Do we stay together?"

"I can't answer questions like that. You'll just have to find out."

I searched his eyes. If there's one lesson I've learned in life, it's when you ask someone a question, don't pay as much attention to what they answer as to how they answer. Just because someone refuses to answer a question doesn't mean you can't get an answer. People's faces betray them. Trent's voice had an optimistic tone to it, and his lips curved into a slight smile. I could almost see the memories flooding into his eyes as he looked down at me. He didn't say yes with words, but his expression shouted it.

"Is there something you'd like to do? Somewhere you'd like to go?" Trent asked eagerly, smiling hopefully at me.

I rested my head against his shoulder. "The longer I stay, the harder it is going to be for you to say goodbye…again," I said softly.

He was silent.

"We both know I need to go home now. All I'm doing here is causing you more pain."

"It was worth it," he said in a low, husky voice. He cleared his throat. "Even a time-traveler longs for the past, it seems."

In an instant, Trent and I were outside my house, near the back porch.

"Do me a favor, will you?" Trent requested.

"Anything."

"Do what makes you happy. Always. Life's too short to spend it any other way."

I smiled and nodded. I raised myself up on my tip-toes and pressed my lips to his lightly. "Can you do me a favor?"

"Name it."

"Let me go. Find someone new. Do what makes you happy. Don't let my memory haunt you forever."

"I've tried."

"Try harder. It's ok to forget me now. I give you permission. If that's what it will take to give you peace, forget about me. You've held on to me for long enough." With tears in my eyes, I squeezed his hand. "Goodbye, Trent."

He smiled sadly at me. "Goodbye, love."

Then he disappeared.

My heart was a mess of emotions, but I didn't have time to be sad. I turned on my heel and ran up the back porch to the back door and started knocking frantically.

"Let me in! Megan is coming! We need to run!"

I heard the door handle jiggle as the door was being unlocked, and when it flung open, Trent was standing there staring at me, like he was looking at a ghost. He turned and looked back inside, and I tilted my head to follow his gaze. He was looking at Megan, who was standing in my living room with my purse in her hand.

Megan's eyes locked with mine, a look of pure disbelief on her face. Then she smiled, almost proudly. "Oh, Rosie. You are full of surprises! I did not see this coming."

"You just lost your bargaining chip," Jaeger said smugly, slowly standing from the kitchen chair.

"So I have. For now." She dropped my purse onto the floor. "Let's do this again sometime, shall we? Too-da-loo!" Megan said as she raised her arm and reached for her watch.

Jaeger suddenly lunged at Megan (with surprising speed considering the injuries he was still healing from) and grabbed a hold of her before she could press the button. He ripped the watch off of her wrist and flung it across the room. It hit the wall with a loud crack.

"You're not going anywhere," he said between gritted teeth.

Chapter 13

Before I had a chance to say anything, Trent scooped me up into his arms and hugged me tightly, lifting me from the ground.

"God, I thought I'd lost you!" he said, his voice muffled against my neck.

"You won't be rid of me quite so easily."

Trent set me back on my feet and held me at arm's length, looking me over. "Are you all right?"

"I'm fine. I just spent that past couple of hours working to escape from the Moon, but I'm fine."

"What?! That's where she was hiding you?!"

"Yeah, that bitch just dropped me on a base and left."

"Hey, lovebirds – a little help?" Jaeger called to us. He had Megan on the floor, her cheek pressed into the floor with his knee in her back and her arm twisted behind her to incapacitate her. The look on her face was one of contempt.

"I might have some rope in the garage," I offered.

"How about zip ties? I could use some of those, too."

I ran out to the garage and retrieved rope and zip ties. Jaeger tied Megan to one of my kitchen chairs, zip-tying her hands and her feet together.

"Is this really necessary?" she asked.

"Shut up," Jaeger spat. "If it were up to me, you'd be dead already."

"So why aren't I? Why isn't it up to you?" she asked snidely.

"Because I'm not Trent."

Puzzlement crossed Megan's face. "What do you mean you aren't Trent?"

"I mean I'm not Trent. I'm Jaeger."

"Then why do you look like him?"

Jaeger smirked at her. "Wouldn't you like to know?"

"If you aren't Trent, then where the hell is he? Why do you have his powers?!"

"Do you have any idea how satisfying it is to see you looking so genuinely out of sorts? After all those years of torment – all those years of you smiling smugly at me while Dr. Simian cut into me and sawed off limbs – I finally get to be the one to see you squirm."

Megan looked over at Trent and me, then a smile slowly spread across her face. She returned her attention to Jaeger. "She isn't with you at all, is she? She's with him. You're not the star-crossed lovers I originally pegged you for. No…you're the third wheel!"

"That's not what this is!" Jaeger shouted.

Megan laughed. "Oh, your face! I love it! You're in love with her and she's in love with him! Is that why you're so angry? Is that where all this pent-up rage is coming from?"

"Shut up! You know nothing!"

"He's Trent, isn't he?" Megan asked as she nodded her head toward Trent. "How does it feel? You stood in for him for, what, five years to protect her? You let us rip you apart piece by piece and sew you back together so we wouldn't come after her, and you don't even get to reap the benefits? Wow. That's sad. Even I feel for you."

Jaeger opened his mouth to reply, but Trent interrupted him. "Don't bother arguing with her. She's only trying to rile you up."

"And it's working," Megan sneered. "I've hit a sore spot."

Trent ignored her. "What are we going to do with her?" he asked Jaeger and me.

I shrugged. "Oh, I don't know…maybe we should drop her on Mars without a teleporter and see how long it takes SABER to find her," I suggested.

"We need to kill her," Jaeger asserted.

"You don't have to kill me. I can be of use to you," Megan bargained.

Jaeger turned to her. "What use could we possibly have for you?"

"Easy. I have sway with the higher-ups in SABER. I can keep tabs on them for you. All I want in return is your secret."

"My secret?"

"Or his," she said, looking to Trent. "Either one will do, really. I just want to be immortal. If I don't need SABER to achieve that, then…screw them. I'm opportunistic."

Jaeger looked over at Trent. "You can't seriously consider this. She can't be trusted."

"I know. But…"

"No! No 'but'! Absolutely not!" I exclaimed. "She left me on the Moon. Did you already forget that? She tortured Jaeger! She threw a knife at my face! This bitch is not on our side and she never will be!"

Megan rolled her eyes at me. "Oh, honey, you hold a grudge like no one I've ever met. Yeah, I threw a knife at you. Yeah, I left you on the Moon. But did you die? Seriously, if I wanted you dead, you'd be dead."

"You fully intended to kill me with that knife."

"Yeah, ok, I did. But I didn't continue to try to kill you when my first attempt failed. You know why? Because I didn't give a shit enough about you to care if you lived or died. You were just a thing. A snail under my boot. It was of no consequence to me what happened to you – that is, until I got to know more about you. It turned out you were useful to me. You gave me leverage against your lovers, here. You gave me this tall drink of water," she said as she smiled at Jaeger. "Then, after you stole him away from me, you led me right back to him! You aren't the brightest, but holy hell you've got balls, sister. And I commend you for that. Because of that, you've earned my respect. I won't try to kill you. Like I said – if I wanted you dead, you'd be dead already."

"Can we put some duct tape over her mouth or something?" I asked Trent.

"Just listen to me," Megan said in exasperation. "Give me what you have, and I'll return the favor by sabotaging SABER when need be. We'll be square."

"We'll never be square," Jaeger hissed.

"Oh, come off it. You're fine," Megan said dismissively.

"Let me torture you for five years and then you can tell me how fine you are."

"That's enough," Trent said firmly. "Jaeger, I need you to calm down."

"Calm down? Don't tell me to calm down! Have you lost the plot?! She should be dead! This shouldn't even be a discussion!"

"A wise man once said, 'A quick temper will make a fool of you soon enough.' Let's try to keep a cool head, shall we?" Trent reasoned.

"Sounds like a sissy," Jaeger retorted.

"It was Bruce Lee. Definitely not a sissy."

"Yeah, well, he might feel differently if he were in this situation."

Trent pulled Jaeger aside, away from Megan, and I followed them. "Listen," Trent said in a low voice, "I'm just saying we need to think this through before we act. We need to at least get as much information out of her as we can. We will kill her if we have to, but what if we don't have to?"

"Trent, even if we wanted to bargain with her, we can't give her what she wants," Jaeger said. "We were created this way from an embryonic state. We can't just give her immortality. It's impossible. Besides, why would we want to make someone like that immortal? Isn't that what you've been spending your entire life working to prevent?"

"Yes, I know, but imagine how useful it would be to have an inside person in SABER—"

"I am imagining it, and it's a goddamn nightmare. You can never trust her. You'd never know if she was spying for you or spying for them or both. Do you know what her ultimate goal is? It isn't just immortality. She wants to eliminate civilization. She isn't on our side, and she never will be. It's time to be realistic."

"Maybe you should try being optimistic," Trent suggested.

"Optimism gets you killed…or worse," Jaeger countered.

"She'll always be a threat," I added. "Jaeger's right. We'll never be able to trust her. Not after everything she's done."

Trent turned to me. "Do you want to be the one to do it? Do you want to pull the trigger or slit her throat?"

"If I have to," I said.

"Do it, then." Trent challenged. "Go kill her."

I hesitated. "What, right now?"

"Yes. Do it."

I looked at Jaeger, but he looked just as stunned as I felt.

"Is this a joke?"

"Do I look like I'm joking?" Trent asked with a stern expression. "Kill her."

"…Ok…" I went to my room and grabbed my .45. My hands were shaking and my heart was beating out of my chest as I checked the clip and racked one into the chamber. I walked back down the hallway and stopped to look at Trent. "Are you sure about this?"

"Are you?" he asked.

"Why does she get to do it?" Jaeger wanted to know.

Trent held up his hand to quiet Jaeger without replying.

I walked over to Megan and stood in front of her. Her dark eyes stared into mine as I raised my gun and pointed it at her. My whole body was trembling at this point, and my heart threatened explode. My vision began to blur as my eyes welled up with tears.

"You don't have to do this," Megan said. "I like you, Roselyn. You're tough, like me. We can work together."

"Shut up!" Jaeger shouted from the living room. "Trent, why are you letting her do this?"

The gun was suddenly too heavy for me to hold. My arm dropped to my side and I clicked the safety on. As the tears ran down my cheeks, I felt weak everywhere. I turned my reddened eyes toward Trent.

He turned his head to Jaeger. "Because she can't do it."

"Why?" I asked angrily. "Why did you make me do that?!"

Trent walked up to me and took the gun from my hand. "Because you needed to be reminded that this isn't the kind of person you are. You needed to understand what you were asking of me."

"I've never killed anyone. You have."

Anger flashed in Trent's eyes. "Do you think killing someone is easy for me? Is that who you think I am?"

"It'll be easy for me. Let me do it," Jaeger said, holding his hand out for the .45.

"This isn't about revenge, Jaeger. It never was," Trent said.

"It is for me," I said with a shaky voice.

"Revenge isn't a motive. It's a disease. It will consume you. You think killing her will change what's happened? It won't. It won't change how you feel about what happened either. Now, I'm not saying she isn't going to have to die – I don't know that yet. I'm just saying that if she does, it won't be because you two are hellbent on revenge."

"The world is better off without her," Jaeger asserted.

"It very well may be," Trent conceded. "But that is yet to be determined."

"And who determines that? You?" Jaeger asked.

"We all do. But only after we know everything she knows and we've had time to properly think this through. In the meantime, Jaeger, why don't you accompany Roselyn back to the gym so she can retrieve her vehicle."

"I can get it myself," I said as I snatched my purse up off the living room floor.

"I know you can. But I think Jaeger needs time to cool off. He could use a nice long ride."

Megan chimed in, "Not the jealous type, hey?" she asked Trent.

"I've no need to be jealous."

"No? Why not? Jaeger is clearly in love with her and, I mean, look at him. He's not so hard on the eyes. Roselyn would have to be blind to not appreciate that—"

"He has nothing to worry about," I snapped.

"They all say that," Megan replied.

Trent gave a humorless chuckle. "Is this the part where you try to divide us? Try to plant little seeds of doubt toward each other to take some of the focus off of you? Because that's not going to happen."

"I'm not trying to divide you. I'm just observing."

"Well, observe a little less vocally," Jaeger growled from across the room.

Trent brought me my watch and helped secure it to my wrist. "I'm never letting you leave the house without this again," he said.

"I'm sure I'd eventually find my way home."

"I know you would. You're too stubborn to let time and distance stand in your way."

"Well, I can't just leave Cattiel on his own. Someone needs to feed him and scoop his crap box."

"And what about me?" Trent asked, looking injured.

"You won't scoop the damn thing."

"…That's not what I meant."

I gave him a weak smile. I was still shaken up from earlier and wasn't quite feeling myself yet, but I was trying my best to brush it off. I understood why Trent did what he did, but I wasn't happy about it.

Jaeger and I teleported to the gym locker room so I could grab the rest of my belongings. I threw on my jacket and changed my shoes while Jaeger stood by. When I was ready, he teleported out to the car while I walked out of the locker room to the front door. My manager had seen me in the locker room earlier, so I needed to make sure I walked back out again. My manager called out to me as I started to push the front door open to leave. I stopped and turned.

"Roselyn, we need to have a talk."

"Listen, I'm sorry about my friend. She was trying to pull a prank on me, and it wasn't funny at all. I'm so sorry."

"I don't care what you do at home. I don't care who your friends are or how you spend your time together," my manager scolded. "However, there is a code of conduct I expect my employees to follow, inside and outside of the locker room, and you were in clear violation of that code. This may not be a typical office setting, but I expect you to behave professionally. What I saw in the locker room was anything but professional behavior. If that ever happens again, you're going to be out of a job. No excuses. Do you understand?"

I nodded my head. "I understand. I'm sorry. It won't ever happen again."

I walked out to my car with my head hung in shame. I was embarrassed all over again.

"What's wrong with you?" Jaeger asked as we climbed into the car.

"Megan almost cost me my job," I said.

Jaeger shook his head. "We need to do something about her. If we don't kill her, she's going to be a constant threat looming over our heads. Trent may not want her dead yet, but you and I both do. I think our vote should count for something."

"Trent has his reasons. I get it," I replied. "I may not agree with him, but I get it."

"After everything she's done to you and me, he should want her dead. The fact that he's allowing her to live and is talking about creating an alliance with her is a slap in the face. He about lost his mind when Megan showed up and said she had taken you. We were prepared to do whatever she asked if it meant keeping you safe. Now, though, it's like he's completely forgotten about it."

"He hasn't forgotten. He's not disregarding what she's done. He's just trying to figure out the right thing to do," I defended. "He's not going to kill her out of revenge. That's not who he is. And it's one of the reasons I love him."

Jaeger grunted and looked out the window. "I thought we were in agreement. Why are you jumping to his side now?"

"I'm not. I'm defending his position since he isn't here to do it himself. I'm not going to talk shit behind his back."

"Are you suggesting I am?"

I didn't reply.

"Well, I'm not," Jaeger said. "I'm just voicing my own opinion regarding the matter."

In the ensuing silence, I heard my stomach gurgle. I hadn't eaten since before the Moon.

"Do you like pizza?" I asked Jaeger.

"I suppose so."

I whipped into the drive-thru pizza shop and ordered two of their large, ready-to-go pizzas. When the teenager working the drive-thru window handed them over, I gave them to Jaeger to hold on to. As I pulled back out onto the road to head home, the intoxicating smell filled the car and made my mouth water. I reached over and opened the lid to the top box and grabbed a slice of pizza. As I brought it to my mouth, a piece of pepperoni fell off and landed on my leg. I looked down at it and cursed profusely as I started to feel it burning my leg through my athletic leggings. I didn't have a free hand with which to remove it.

Jaeger looked over at me when I started swearing and saw the situation. He reached over, snatched up the hot pepperoni, and popped it into his mouth. "Better?" he asked.

For the first time since I'd been abandoned on the Moon, I laughed a real, genuine laugh. "Why did you eat it?!"

"What else was I going to do with it?"

"Throw it away! It was on my dirty leggings. They probably still have Moon dust on them."

"Nonsense. It was still perfectly good."

"That's nasty," I chuckled.

"I've eaten worse," he said. "I think you've forgotten what kind of a world I come from."

I paused. I actually had forgotten for a while. "Well, as long as you're with us in this world you won't have to eat anything too gross. Trent might disagree, though, because he'd rather live on toaster pastries and Chinese takeout than eat a damn salad once in a while, but I digress."

"So, what's your deal with kale?" Jaeger asked inquisitively.

I scoffed. "I don't have a deal with kale. Trent got it in his head once that since I enjoy healthy eating habits, I must love kale. He's been convinced of it ever since, even though I've told him time and time again that I don't particularly like kale, and I haven't bought it the entire time he and I have been together."

"He makes it sound like that's all you eat."

"He's a dirty liar," I said around a mouthful of pizza.

After a long silence, Jaeger asked, "So, how did you get off the Moon, anyway? What was that all about?"

"Megan dropped me in an abandoned Moon base in the future, and I blew it up and took over its system to send a message to Trent of the future. He brought me home."

"...You blew it up?" Jaeger asked with a raised eyebrow.

"Just part of it. I drove a rover into it. I'm still not sure if the rover exploded or if it was the fuel canisters I put out, but there was a brief yet glorious burst."

"You purposely drove the rover into the base?"

"It was part of my plan."

Jaeger chuckled. "I like your style."

I laughed. "It's hard to believe how much different I am now from the emotionally-damaged divorcee I was when Trent showed up on my doorstep."

"You mean you haven't always been a rover-smashing, ass-kicking time traveler?" he asked sarcastically.

"Shocking, isn't it? I know, I seem like such a natural," I jested as I took another bite of pizza.

When we arrived home, I walked through the door, carrying the pizzas.

"Dinner's ready!" I shouted. But there was no reply, because Trent and Megan were gone.

"What?! Where are they?!" Jaeger shouted as he pushed past me and dashed into the kitchen where Megan had been. He picked up a piece of paper from the table. "He left a note. It says, 'I brought her to a proper containment cell. Bring food.' Then there's coordinates." Jaeger looked up at me. "Do you think it's a trick? A trap? Do you think she has him?"

I sighed. "I doubt it. Why don't you take the pizza and go meet him? I'll be along shortly. I'm in desperate need of a shower after the day I've had. I feel like I have Moon dust in my hair."

"Are you sure? I can wait if you'd like me to."

"No, go ahead. I'll be right behind you."

Jaeger entered the coordinates and teleported from the house. As I started down the hall toward my room to get some fresh clothes, Jaeger came back. I hurried back anxiously.

"Is everything ok?" I asked.

"I forgot the pizza," he said sheepishly. "Everything's fine. Well, except for the fact that your boyfriend has a dungeon in his basement…that could be a red flag, but I'm not usually one to judge these kinds of things…"

"Sounds about right. I'm not concerned. Off you go," I said as I handed him the pizza boxes from the table and headed off to take a shower.

As I scrubbed my hair (remembering that there was very likely a small amount of Jaeger's blood in it), my brain kept replaying the moment I aimed my gun at Megan with the intention of pulling the trigger. I had thought it would be easy. I hated her for what she had done to us. She deserved to die, didn't she? She was a danger to us and to everyone she might cross paths with. But I couldn't do it. I couldn't pull the trigger.

What if I had? What if Trent had misjudged me, and I had splattered her brains all over my kitchen? It wasn't the idea of killing or the gore that had stopped me – I'd hunted and killed game animals before. It was the idea of killing another human being. It was her eyes when she'd looked at me – she had one hell of a poker face, but the eyes don't lie. She was truly afraid of dying, and when I had pointed that gun at her, her eyes were filled with primal fear. It was at that moment I realized that if I had ignored her fearful gaze and pulled the trigger, I would be no better than she was. If I was being honest with myself, I knew that the real reason I wanted her dead had nothing to do with making a better world. It was strictly out of fear and anger. I had learned a long time ago that actions taken out of fear and anger tend to elevate rather than alleviate the problem, and this was exactly why Trent didn't want us to kill Megan.

I stepped out of the shower and started to towel off. As I carefully dried my wrist around and under the watch (yes, it was waterproof and I wore it in the shower), I thought about how much I missed Trent. Things had become so crazy that we'd barely had any time to ourselves, and what little time we did have I'd spent being disagreeable. I wanted to get to know my new Trent. I had finally accepted the loss of the old Trent, and, while I would miss him, I was no longer hung up on worrying about whether I still loved him. Trent had changed, but he was still Trent. That was all that mattered.

When I was dressed and ready, I followed Trent's directions and teleported to 1824 Ireland. When I arrived, I looked around at the spacious room in which I found myself. The ceiling soared high above me, and the walls looked to be made of stone. The architecture appeared incredibly old, much older than the 19th-century. I wandered down the wide hall and glanced into the expansive rooms as I passed. I was beginning to understand.

His "house" was an old castle.

Chapter 14

I called for Trent and Jaeger as I made my way through the old castle until I finally saw Trent enter the hallway from an archway ahead to the right.

"There you are," he said as he walked toward me.

"Here I am. You never told me you had a castle."

"Well, it's not really mine. I borrow it from time to time in the periods when it's uninhabited. I thought the dungeon would come in handy for our current situation. We couldn't leave Megan tied to a chair indefinitely."

"So, you put her in a dungeon. I know you intended for that to sound better, but…that doesn't sound better."

"Not better, per se, but more secure. Better for us."

"Have you decided what to do with her yet?" I asked.

Trent gave me an uneasy look. "I know you don't agree with it, but I don't think killing her is in our best interest."

"I know. I think you're right."

His lips formed and upside down "U" and he raised a brow at me. "You've changed your stance?"

"She could be useful. But, if she ever comes after me again, all bets are off," I warned.

"I won't let that happen," Trent assured me.

"Where's Jaeger?" I asked, looking around.

"He's keeping an eye on our guest."

"Aren't you afraid he's going to kill her?"

"He won't."

"I'm not so sure. He sounded quite hellbent on it when I spoke to him last."

"He may be angry and vengeful, but he isn't stupid. As much as he wants her dead, he knows we might need her."

"You can't blame him for wanting to kill her."

"And I don't. I just think there is a better way to deal with this."

"Can I ask you something? I know you've killed people. Megan even mentioned that you killed everyone associated with creating you. Hell, you killed an entire building full of innocent people just to get to a few bad ones. Taking all of that into account, it makes me wonder what is different in this situation. What is it about Megan that warrants giving her a second chance that none of those other people possessed?"

Trent sighed. "Every life I've taken has been taken because I thought it was necessary to ensure the continuance of humanity as we know it. But Megan could be different. If we can get her to join our side, she could work to sabotage SABER and prevent them from doing the kinds of things that require lethal intervention."

"She kills people for fun, Trent. I just want you to remember that. She would probably cause a net loss of life rather than a surplus of saved lives."

"Let's hope you're wrong about that."

I followed Trent down a long stone staircase to a dark, dingy, musty smelling dungeon. It had a cell with thick iron bars across the front. I could see shackles hanging from the wall opposite the bars. Megan paced around in the center, kicking dirt and debris up like a bored child.

"Oh hey, the gang's all here!" she exclaimed when she saw me walk in with Trent.

"Shut up," Jaeger said in annoyance. He was sitting near Megan's cell on a rickety stool that looked entirely too frail to be holding a man of his size. He handed me the pizza box he had in his lap. "We saved you a slice."

I held my hand up and scrunched my nose as I looked at my surroundings. "No thanks."

"Suit yourself," he replied as he helped himself to it.

"Are you ready to talk yet?" Trent asked Megan as he approached the bars with his arms crossed.

"Are you ready to make me immortal?"

"I want information first."

"I thought it was your job to know things. A man with a time machine teleporter strapped to his wrist has access to all the information he could ever want. What could you possibly need from me?"

"I want to know where you got your time machine teleporter. Who made it?"

"It was a gift."

"From whom?"

"You."

I felt as though someone had kicked me in the stomach. "Are you saying he made you a watch?" I asked in disbelief.

"No, that wouldn't be his style, now would it? He made himself a new watch and gave me his old one. Mine is the original. Well, at least it was," she said sarcastically as she looked askance at Jaeger, "until someone threw it against the wall like a maniac."

I looked to Trent for answers. "What is she talking about?"

Trent seemed to be as confused as I was. "That's impossible. I…I wouldn't do that…I don't know you…"

"Oh, you know me. You've forgotten me, of course, because, well, that's kind of your thing."

"You're lying," I hissed.

"Am I? What did you do with your original watch, Trent?"

Trent frowned. "I…I thought I must have destroyed it, but…I don't really remember."

The pit in my stomach grew.

"She's having you on, Trent!" Jaeger exclaimed. "You can't trust her!"

"Your original watch had a defect," Megan said to Trent. "Do you remember that? If you tried to go to midnight on any given day, it would short out."

When I saw the look on Trent's face, I could see it was true. He looked horrified.

"You tortured Jaeger for five years thinking he was Trent!" I shouted angrily. "If you had been close to him, why would you do that to him? It doesn't add up!"

Megan chuckled snidely. "Haven't you ever heard the saying about a woman scorned?"

Trent turned and walked briskly out of the room. He looked pale.

I pointed at Megan. "I don't know what kind of a game you're playing, but it stops now."

"The game is over," Megan replied with a shrug. "It was fun while it lasted, but it's done. All Trent has to do is make me immortal, and we'll be square."

"It doesn't work that way."

"He's a clever boy. He'll figure it out."

"I think I'm regretting not killing you."

"I was getting that vibe from you all of a sudden. But I don't regret not killing you. I think you and I will end up being the bestest of BFFs." It was impossible to tell if she was being serious.

"That will never happen," I growled. I turned my back to her and went after Trent.

I found Trent standing in the hallway at the top of the stairs with his hands in his pockets. He was looking down at the floor, deep in thought. I stood next to him.

"I don't believe her," I said.

"I do," he confessed quietly.

I felt sick. "You can't possibly."

He pulled his hand out of his pocket. His was holding a mildly damaged watch. "I went back to your house. I had to see." He looked down at the watch. "She wasn't lying. It is the original."

"That doesn't mean you gave it to her."

"I don't know how else she would've gotten it."

"Maybe you lost it. Maybe that's why you built a new one."

"If I had lost it, I wouldn't have rested until I'd found it," Trent said with a heavy sigh. "I'm sorry. I leave a goddamn mess everywhere I go," he said bitterly. "The longer I live, the more I grow to regret. I'm not a watchman. I'm a wrecking ball, leaving a trail of destruction and suffering in my wake."

Trent reached for his watch and suddenly teleported from the castle. If he thought I was just going to let him run off to wallow in his own self-loathing, he had another thing coming. I used my watch to lock onto his location and I followed him to Venice, Italy, 2005.

"I need a moment alone," Trent grumbled, annoyed at my persistence. He walked away from me through the small studio apartment we had landed in.

"That's the last thing you need right now." I followed him and grabbed his hand to stop him. "You can't run from this. Don't shut me out," I begged.

He paused with his back still turned to me, but he didn't pull his hand away from mine. "I don't know what to do," he admitted.

"About Megan?"

"About everything. Every time something bad happens, it's always because of me. It's always because of something I did. Maybe it's time I just…stopped."

"What do you mean 'stopped'? You're just going to give up? You're going to throw in the towel, just like that? All because Megan might be your crazy ex?"

"It's more complicated than that, and you know it."

"I know you, and this…whatever this is…this isn't you," I said with concern.

He pulled his hand away from mine. "Or maybe you just don't know me that well."

I stepped around him and toed up to him, raising my chin and looking him in the eye. "Don't I? Have you changed that much? I don't think so. I think you're throwing yourself a little pity party and you need a swift kick in the ass, which I am gladly here to provide. So what if Megan is telling the truth? We'll deal with it. Sure, we've been thrown a curveball, but that's never stopped you before and it won't stop you now. So, stow your crap and let's get back to doing what we do – fixing things and protecting people."

My pep talk did nothing to change Trent's demeanor. He just gazed back at me regretfully. "You could end up like her someday. I know you see the parallels just as I do."

I was taken aback. "Is that what this is about? Me?" The ensuing silence had me fuming. "How could you ever believe that I could be like her?!"

"I don't mean a monster like her. I mean…forgotten." Trent said, his voice full of shame. "It's something I try not to ruminate on, but then things like this happen and…all I can think about is what I would be putting you through if I did forget, and everything I would lose without even knowing I'd lost it."

My anger dissipated. "I would track your ass down and make you remember me," I said, pointing to my watch. When I saw pain fill Trent's eyes, I realized that what I'd said sounded almost exactly like what Megan had been doing. I sighed. "Trent, my biggest fear isn't that you'll forget me. It's that you won't ever forget me."

"I don't ever want to forget you."

"Someday you will wish you could."

He looked at me questioningly. "Why are you saying that?"

"Because I've seen a glimpse of your future, Trent. When I was stranded on the Moon, I met a future version of you. The way you looked at me...even in a different body with different eyes, I saw every ounce of your heart pouring out. And it broke mine." I gazed into his rich brown eyes – eyes that were now so familiar and comforting to me – and I asked him, "Why me? Why am I the one you always remember? And what did I do to deserve such incomprehensible devotion?"

Trent gathered me into his arms, a tender smile caressing his lips. "You have become a part of me. You are the breath in my lungs. I'm hopelessly devoted to you because, without you, I would completely lose the desire to function. Without you, I'm not me. Perchance I'll never forget you because I stubbornly refuse to allow myself to let you go – an act of sheer willpower that keeps your memory tethered to the very essence of my being."

"I don't deserve love like that."

"Everyone deserves love like that. Unfortunately, most people never get to experience it. Lucky for us, I had all the time in the world to find you."

"It's too bad you didn't find me a little sooner," I remarked. "I could've done without the Barry years."

Trent gave me a knowing look. "Your experiences – the good and the bad – are what made you who you are today. You were forged in the kind of fire that might break someone with a weaker constitution. But you persisted. You overcame your adversity, and you grew stronger from it. Don't wish you'd had an easier life – take pride in the fact that you had the strength to rise above it. See, there's no reason to wish we had met sooner. We met at just exactly the right points in our lives."

"How can you say such nice things to me after I've been so terrible to you recently? I've doubted you. I've doubted us."

"Am I supposed to be angry? Did you think that would change how I feel? Of course you had second thoughts. I mean, look at me!" he exclaimed, gesturing to himself. "When you look at me, you don't see the man you fell in love with. Not yet, anyway. You see an imposter. A stand-in. And that's ok. I'm not upset with you. That would be absurd. I think I'd be more concerned if you weren't a bit wary of this new face."

"But I'm not anymore," I said as I reached up and touched his cheek. "I'm not worried or afraid or doubtful. When you changed, I thought I was losing the Trent I loved, and I was heartbroken. But I've come to realize that was the wrong way to look at it. I wasn't losing you. I was just given access to a new layer – a new version of you. I was getting more of you. You aren't a stranger, like I had feared. You're still Trent Morgan. And you're still mine."

I raised up on my toes and touched my lips gently to his. He reciprocated timidly at first, as though he were afraid I was going to suddenly change my mind, but when I forked my fingers into his wild hair and pulled him closer, he groaned and leaned into me, his kiss deepening. I slipped my hand under his suit jacket and slid it off over his shoulders. He responded by quickly yanking my shirt off over my head and shoving me roughly against the wall. I felt a heat growing in my belly as his mouth descended upon my breast and his knee worked its way between my knees, the lean muscle of his thigh rubbing pleasurably against me. My skin tingled as his attentive tongue swirled over my tender mounds. I threw my head back as his lips skimmed lightly over the delicate skin on my neck on his way back up to my mouth. He brought his hands up and cupped my face, his lips crushing against mine, stealing my breath away as his tongue ravaged mine.

My fingers worked to loosen his tie, then moved down to the buttons on his shirt. When Trent felt his shirt sliding off onto the floor, he pulled away from me slightly and looked into my eyes. I could see that he was mustering every ounce of restraint he possessed, yet he still appeared on the brink of losing control.

"Are you sure?" he asked as his eyes flicked briefly down to my bare torso, his breath heavy. He looked absolutely ravenous.

I nodded eagerly. With that, Trent scooped me up and brought me to the bed, quickly removing my jeans and freeing himself from his trousers. He climbed onto the bed, running his hand slowly up my inner thigh as he made his way toward me. My breath caught in my throat as I felt his nimble fingers gently nestling between my legs, stroking me sensually. His lips tenderly caressed my neck, his breath leaving a hot trail on my skin as he worked his way down between my breasts and over my belly. When I felt his tongue dip into my feminine folds, I bit my lip with a soft moan and closed my eyes.

He brought me right to the brink before he suddenly stopped. "I need to be inside you. Now," he pleaded, gazing up at me longingly. When I nodded eagerly, he grinned at me devilishly and climbed over top of me. He positioned his waist between my thighs, one hand cupping my backside, as he slowly pressed into me. I watched his face as he entered me, and I relished in the way he groaned and closed his deep brown eyes as he felt my body squeezing around him.

I hadn't realized how much I had needed him until now. I'd missed our intimacy. I thought it would be weird to be like this with him now that he had changed, but it wasn't. Yes, he touched me with different fingers, tasted me with a different tongue, and pleasured me with a different manhood, but as far as our hearts were concerned, nothing had changed. He still felt like him. I clung to him as he ravaged me, panting in his ear and grinding my hips against his as I felt the rising need for release. When he brought me over the edge, coming right along with me, I felt like a wall had been shattered. We had become one again. He wasn't strange and new anymore – he was just my Trent.

Trent lay on top of me as we savored the aftershocks of our release, his forehead resting against mine. He looked into my eyes, and all I could see was the love welled up behind them.

"I love you," I whispered.

He smiled. "To the Moon and back?" He kissed my lips tenderly before rolling over next to me.

"To the Moon and back," I giggled. I propped myself up onto my elbow, resting my head on my hand. I looked at him lying next to me and smiled.

"So…does the new model perform as well as the old one?" he asked with a raised eyebrow.

I laughed. "It would seem so, but I might need to take another test run before I give an official verdict," I jested.

Trent's face grew serious. "I've missed you," he said. He reached over and caressed my cheek. "I've missed this."

I placed my hand over his. "Me too."

As we lay and gazed at each other, Trent said in a disappointed tone, "We should probably get back to Jaeger and Megan, shouldn't we?"

"Yeah," I agreed regretfully. I nestled up next to him and draped my arm over him. "But not quite yet."

After a long silence, Trent sighed. "I really wasn't sure if we were going to make it through this."

"What do you mean?"

"I thought there was a real chance you might leave me after I changed. You seemed so repelled by me. I was scared I was going to lose you, and it was destroying me."

"You've got nothing to worry about, Trent."

"I always have something to worry about. I'm just glad that you leaving me high and dry isn't one of those things anymore."

I lay with my ear against his bare chest, listening to his steady heartbeat. Sometimes, in moments like this, especially, I felt like that heart beat only for me. He'd had a long life full of adventures, excitement, and women before me, and he'd likely have a long life of that after me, but at this moment in time, he belonged only to me. His time with me might only take up a small portion of his life, but I knew it was an important part. I knew I wasn't just another woman. I would be the one he remembered.

I looked up at him. "Do you think you loved her?" I asked suddenly.

His dark brows furrowed. "Megan?"

I nodded.

He sighed and looked up at the ceiling. "I don't know. I must have trusted her at some point, I suppose, but I don't know the nature of our relationship. I couldn't say if it was love or not."

"I think she must have loved you once," I surmised.

"What makes you say that?"

"Because nobody hates as hard as someone who used to love. Loving someone does something to you. It's great when it's returned, but when it isn't…that's one of the fiercest kinds of anger there is. If she hadn't ever loved you, I don't think she'd be this obsessed with hurting you."

"How does all of this make you feel?" Trent asked me.

"I don't know. I'm angry with her for what she's done, of course, and there's also a bit of jealousy. But…I'm beginning to kind of understand, too. I never thought I'd say that," I admitted. "Obviously what she's done is wrong and horrible, and she's completely devoid of common human decency, but almost nobody starts out that way."

"Another love story gone wrong," Trent suggested.

"Most of them do," I replied. "And it's never pretty when it falls apart."

"Well, the only way to know for sure what we're dealing with is to get back and talk to Megan."

Trent and I gathered up our clothes from the floor and got dressed. He took me under his arm and teleported us back to the castle in Ireland.

Chapter 15

When Trent and I returned to the dungeon, Megan looked through the bars at us and raised her eyebrows.

"How was it?" she asked.

"How was what?" Trent responded.

"Oh, don't act so oblivious. It's obvious you had sex."

"Oh, nice," Jaeger said in annoyance, standing up from his rickety stool. "Leave me here in a dank dungeon with a psychopath so you can run off and shag." Jaeger scowled at Trent.

"It wasn't by design!" I cried defensively.

"It was an accident? He tripped and fell on you?" Megan teased.

"Just shut it, will you?" Trent said in disgust. He turned to Jaeger. "Did she say anything while I was gone?" he asked, tipping his head toward Megan.

"The annoying hag never shuts up! It wasn't anything of any importance, though. Mostly complaining about her accommodations."

"Seriously, though," Megan said. "It is a bit dramatic, don't you think? A dungeon? I thought you wanted to get information about SABER from me, not give me typhoid."

Trent pulled up the stool that Jaeger had been sitting in and sat across the bars from Megan. "You want out of here? Start talking. What's your role in SABER?"

"I'm like you. Modified to serve a purpose. But Jaeger knows this already. I answered all kinds of questions for him in the compound when I thought he was you. Care to share with the class, Jaeger?"

Jaeger spat on the ground and glowered at her. "I'm not here to parrot answers for you."

"Such a poor sport," Megan said as she shook her head. She rested her elbows on the horizontal bars of her enclosure, clasping her hands together outside of the cell. She looked at Trent. "It feels strange telling you this for a third time. Well, to be fair, the second time wasn't technically you, but I digress. I was part of another one of SABER's failed GE projects. They were trying to design super-soldiers, but most of us weren't particularly stable. I was the only one they kept."

"When did you and I first meet?" Trent asked.

"You said you were 68. I have no idea how long ago it's been for you, but it's been about eight years for me. You broke into the SABER compound because you needed parts for a new watch. I tried to kill you when I caught you in the engineering lab, but…well, we found something more entertaining to do instead."

I felt ill as an image of Trent and Megan together flashed into my mind.

"What, and I just gave you my watch after that?"

"Of course not. When I found out who you were, I realized what you had to offer me. Everyone at SABER knows the legendary Trent Morgan. Number Thirty. The anomaly. I helped you get your parts, and you took me with you."

"Why would I do that?"

"I don't know. I get the feeling that's kind of what you do."

Trent looked over at Jaeger and me. I shrugged. It didn't sound entirely off-base for a young Trent.

"So how did you end up with the watch?"

"We spent quite a lot of time together. Almost two years. You grow to trust someone when you've spent that much time with them."

"But I don't understand why I kept you around so long. I mean, you're quite horrid. Really, properly terrible."

Megan smirked. "I'll allow you that. I can be. But I wasn't to you – not back then. You were quite possibly the only person I ever cared about. Then you had to go and shit all over everything and disappear like I meant nothing to you. You said you had something you had to do and you'd be right back."

"And I never came back," Trent said with a sigh.

"Maybe now you can understand a little more clearly as to why I didn't feel too badly about keeping you in a lab for five years."

"You mean keeping me in a lab," Jaeger piped up.

Megan waved her had. "Whatever, same thing."

"So how did you get the watch?" Trent asked.

"You left it behind."

"I didn't actually give it to you, then."

"Not directly, no. But I think by you leaving it in my possession and not returning, I kind of inherited it."

"What did you do after that?" Trent inquired.

Megan blew a loose piece of hair out of her face and tilted her head to the side. "Well…I didn't know how to use the watch very well, but I knew enough to get me back to my own time. I was barely missed at SABER because to them I had only been gone for a couple of days. I picked up where I had left off with my old life."

"Then how did you find Jaeger? Why did you go to the Middle East and blow up two ancient cities? What has been the point of all of this?"

"Finding you became my quest. I used to just wander aimlessly through time, looking for you, but it's hard to find someone when you don't know what face to look for. It wasn't like I even wanted you anymore. You'd already burned that bridge. No, you owed me for what you'd done. You still owe me. All I want is for you to make me immortal. That's all I'm after."

"I can't do that."

"You can figure it out. You're supposed to be the genius to end all geniuses. You figured out time travel, but you can't figure out how to make one measly human body keep ticking forever?"

"SABER made me this way. Ask them."

"You destroyed all records, research, and scientists associated with you. You left nothing behind to learn from. I thought about going back to when they were creating you and trying to make them help me then, but I was afraid I would alter something and ruin their single successful outcome. If that happened, I'd have nothing."

"Why do you want to be immortal?" I chimed in.

Megan looked over at me. "Are you serious? Don't you? Doesn't everyone? I don't want to get old, to slowly waste away into a husk of who I once was. I don't want to watch my health and my mobility deteriorate and lose the clarity of my mind. I can't bear the idea of becoming so frail and full of aches and pains that I might one day welcome the end. I don't want that! No one wants that! I want to be like this – young and athletic and beautiful – forever."

"You would outlive anyone you ever loved. You would have to watch everyone else around you go through that, and there would be nothing you could do for them. You don't want that, Megan," Trent said quietly.

Megan looked at him flatly. "I don't love anyone. I don't care if people die around me. They usually do anyway."

"Why didn't you just go to the future?" I asked. "I have to think there would be some kind of technology like that in the far future past your and Trent's time."

"They don't offer the kind of immortality I'm after. I want this body, not a semi-realistic, robotic surrogate implanted with a virtual world option. I mean, when you look like this, why would you want a surrogate?"

"How far into the future have you been?" Trent asked, his interest sparked.

"I've been far enough to see humanity destroy this entire planet like a disgusting plague," Megan said angrily. "You greedy sloths just use it up and fill it with trash until you have to evacuate to Mars. If you'd spent half the effort in cleaning up this world as you did in terraforming Mars, Earth could've easily been resuscitated. But no, that wasn't glamourous enough. You wanted a new planet...you spoiled rotten shits," Megan spat.

Jaeger scoffed. "You realize that if you become immortal, you'll live right through all of that. You'll get a front row ticket to watch it all unravel."

"Maybe I can stop it," Megan replied.

"How? You know we won't let you eradicate humankind," Jaeger said.

"And you better believe you aren't leaving here with that watch," Trent added. "Your time traveling days are officially over."

Megan rolled her eyes. "We'll see about that."

"What's SABER's role in the future?" Trent wanted to know.

"I don't know. I wasn't interested in what SABER was doing in the future. Why don't you go see for yourself if you're so curious?"

"What's SABER up to right now? Are they still working to develop their own time travel device? Did they know you had my old one?"

"They are always working on time travel. And no, I didn't tell them I had your watch. If I had, they'd want me to use it to go back in time and try to avert the 2033 Crisis, and I'll be damned if I'm going to try to prevent something that takes out so much of the human population. If anything, I wish that flu had been more successful. I want nothing to do with their attempts at managing history – my idea of a 'perfect' history deviates drastically from theirs."

I looked over at Trent questioningly. "What is she talking about? What happens in 2033?"

"We'll talk about it later, Roselyn," Trent said dismissively.

"No, I want to talk about it now," I demanded.

Megan crossed her arms and leaned her shoulder against the bars, facing me. "Oh, I'll be glad to tell you all about it. There's a global flu pandemic. That particular strain was actually created in a lab for testing, but people are clumsy and stupid and someone was exposed. It spread like wildfire from there. So many people died that it triggered a global economic collapse and basically sent the world into a second Dark Age. It took over a century for society to recover. They estimate that if they'd been able to prevent that outbreak, we would've been lightyears ahead of where we currently are technologically in my time." Megan squinted at me. "Let's see, you must be, what, twenty-eight? Thirty? Which means you'll be forty-five-ish when the outbreak occurs – so yeah, you'll probably die of the flu if you stick around your own time."

I gave Trent a look of betrayal. "How could you not warn me about this?"

Trent stood up from his stool and turned his back to me, running his hand through his hair without replying.

"Trent! Answer me!"

He turned to me, remorse in his eyes. "Because there's nothing I can do about it! I didn't want it festering in the back of your mind knowing that nothing can be done to stop it!"

I couldn't believe what I was hearing. In fifteen years, my world would collapse, and Trent had allowed me to remain ignorantly unaware.

Jaeger gave a disgruntled sigh. "Can we save the domestics for another time? We're dealing with a more pertinent problem right now."

"That bitch can wait," I growled, pointing in Megan's direction.

"Hey! What'd I do?" Megan cried innocently.

I ignored her and returned my attention to Trent. "I can't believe you've been purposely hiding this from me this whole time! What about my family? Am I just supposed to let them suffer through the goddamn apocalypse?"

"It isn't an apocalypse," Trent countered.

Megan interjected, "It's pretty damn close. It was bad."

Trent shot her a look that could kill.

"Well?" I commanded his attention. "What were you planning to do when 2033 rolled around? Are you going to at least save my family?"

"Roselyn, there's nothing I can do."

"Bullshit!" I shouted. Hot, angry tears filled my eyes. "We can move them! We can bring them to the future!"

"We can't do that. We have no idea what the repercussions would be," Trent said calmly, avoiding my eyes.

"Why not?" Megan jumped in. "All four of us time travel. What's a few more?"

"You are not a part of this conversation!" Trent barked.

"I'm just saying…" Megan mumbled.

I glared at Trent, unable to comprehend how he could be so cold-hearted and so unyielding. I felt like a rift had just formed between us. I shook my head at him, raised my watch, and teleported back to my house. I snatched up Cattiel and buried my tear-streaked face in his soft fur.

I barely had time to gather my thoughts before Trent appeared.

"Roselyn, listen—"

"No! I feel like I don't even know you!"

"Oh, no? Roselyn, you knew who I was right from the beginning! I told you about the things I had to do and the things I couldn't do in order to keep time on the proper course. You knew about the people I've had to either kill or let die. You knew all of this! It didn't bother you then! But now that the burden is being placed on your shoulders, you cry foul. That isn't fair."

"It's not fair? Screw you, Trent. Were you planning to leave me behind, too? To let me weather the collapse of the 21st century with my family?"

"No, of course not."

I looked at him incredulously. "Do you even realize what a hypocrite you are?"

"You're different. You travel and move around with me. They would be placed in a permanent time setting, which could drastically change the natural course of events in that time."

"It's just my parents and my brother. That's three people! That seems hardly enough to overthrow the balance of time."

"You wouldn't think so, but it is. Please, just trust me, Roselyn. They need to stay right where they are."

My lip trembled as I stared hatefully at him. I never thought I would feel this way about him. "Then I will save them. I don't need you," I hissed through clenched teeth.

He shoved his hands in his pockets and looked at me sorrowfully. His eyes looked a deeper shade of brown. "I can't let you do that."

My heart stopped. I set Cattiel on the couch next to me and stood up, facing Trent confrontationally. "Excuse me? Are you telling me you're going to stop me from saving my family?"

He maintained steady eye contact. "Yes."

"What, are you going to kill me like you did all those other people who wanted to change history?" I challenged him.

"No, of course not. But I will stop you."

It took every ounce of my being not to give him a stiff right hook. My hands were shaking and my eyes were burning right through his.

"Please don't look at me like that," he pleaded, his eyes reddening. "Don't look at me like you hate me. I can't bear it."

"Then don't make me hate you," I implored as my voice broke.

"There are things you don't understand right now, Roselyn. No one should know too much about their own future, and that's partially why I haven't told you about the 2033 Crisis. The other reason is this, right here. I knew you'd ask this of me, and I knew I'd have to tell you no. But it isn't because I'm a heartless bastard. It's because your parents, and subsequently your brother, have an important role to play. I can't take them out of their timeline."

"I don't believe you. You're just trying to placate me."

"If I were trying to do that, I'd tell you I was going to save them."

"I don't care what role they have to play. I want them safe, with me. If you won't save them, and you won't let me save them, then I'm not going with you, either. If they stay, I stay," I said stubbornly.

"You still have fifteen years to think this over. Don't make such assertions yet."

"You think time is going to change my mind? Do you think I'm going to suddenly become selfish in the next fifteen years?"

"I think you're being selfish right now."

I took a deep breath. "Get out."

Trent gave a surprised, humorless laugh. "Well, there we are then." He looked at me with upturned brows, a pitiful expression on his face. "Is that really what you want?"

I nodded, even though my heart was starting to second-guess my decision.

"Very well, then, if that's what you want. But I'll be needing that watch back," he said, pointing to my wrist. When he saw my shocked expression, he added, "I can't have you popping off to the future to retrieve your family from 2033."

"It isn't your watch. It's Jaeger's."

"Quite right. I'll return it to him for you."

As I fumbled to remove the watch with shaky fingers and blurry eyes, I felt like my world had just come crashing down around me. Was this it? Why did this feel so permanent? I knew it couldn't possibly be, but...why did it feel that way, then? When I had the watch off, I whipped it at Trent. He looked startled as he caught it against his chest.

"It doesn't have to be this way, Roselyn," he said in a last attempt at reconciliation.

In my current state of angst, words flew from my mouth that I wished hadn't. "Yeah, it does. All you ever did was screw up my life anyway."

I hated myself for those words.

Trent nodded and looked at the ground as the corners of his mouth turned downward. "I suppose you're right." He lingered for a moment, then mumbled, "I just...I don't..." Without finishing his sentence, he sighed, nodded, and disappeared.

This wasn't real. This couldn't be real. He'd be right back, wouldn't he? He'd come back and say he'd found a way to save my family and everything would be ok. Right? That was how this worked, wasn't it? He wouldn't really leave my family and me to endure an apocalypse. He couldn't. He loved me. I knew he loved me. But...

Suddenly Jaeger appeared in my kitchen. He immediately started looking around on the floor.

I quickly swiped my tears away. "What are you doing here?" I asked, trying to sound normal.

He glanced up at me briefly, surprised to see me. "Oh! I didn't realize you were here! Say, do you happen to know where I could find the watch Megan had?"

"Trent has it."

"Oh. Of course he does," he said, annoyed.

"Why are you looking for it? Are you trying to make sure I don't go to the future to save my family too?"

"What?" Jaeger asked, bewildered. "Is this about that 2033 thing you and Trent were arguing about?"

"Never mind."

Jaeger looked more closely at me. "Hey, are you ok?"

"I'm fine."

"You don't look fine. Where's Trent?"

"I thought he'd gone back to Ireland with you."

"Oh. I hadn't seen him. Did you two have a go at each other?"

"I don't want to talk about it."

Jaeger stood in awkward silence for a minute before asking, "I know this sounds like an odd request, but can I borrow your watch?"

"For what?"

"I just want to try something," he replied vaguely.

"You'll have to get it from Trent. He took it."

Jaeger was taken aback. "What do you mean he took it?"

"I mean he took it. I don't have it."

"What, is he on some kind of watch nicking spree? When are you getting it back?"

"I don't think I am."

"Roselyn, what happened?" he asked with concern.

"I can't really say," I said, my voice starting to crack. I cleared my throat and blinked my tears back. "I don't want to talk about it."

"Are you and Trent...over?"

"I don't know."

"But...I thought you were getting on again."

"We were. But I guess we've reached an impasse." I then changed the subject. "Jaeger, why are you still here? I don't have a watch for you. What did you want to test?"

"Oh, I just wanted to calibrate the quantum temporal nonlocality entangling synchronizer."

"That sounds like something you just made up."

"Well, I suppose I did. I did create this watch, after all."

"Good point." When Jaeger continued to stand there in uncomfortable silence, I said, "You can go now. I promise I'm fine."

"Are you sure?"

"Yeah. Go get your watch from Trent so you can calibrate your quantum location temperature tangling symphonizer."

Jaeger chuckled. "Ok. I'll see you soon, maybe?"

I doubted it, but I nodded anyway. Then Jaeger teleported from the house, leaving me all by myself again. It was a strange feeling to not have my watch anymore. I had grown so accustomed to being able to just go to Trent whenever I wanted to. Now, I felt helpless and alone, and I didn't know if he was ever coming back for me. I had to believe that he would return for me, but he'd made me no promises before leaving. He hadn't even told me he loved me.

He'd left so much unsaid when he left. What was so important about my family that they couldn't be moved from this timeline? Why couldn't he just tell me? What else was he keeping from me? I understood that there were dangers to knowing too much about one's own future, but I didn't understand how he could stand to keep such a big event secret from me. My trust in him was completely shattered – as was my heart. I had always felt safe with him before, and I thought he would never let anything happen to me. But now I wasn't so certain. If time demanded it, would he stand aside and watch me die?

I felt like I needed to talk to my parents. I grabbed my phone and rang their house.

My dad answered the phone. "Two calls in one week? To what do we owe the pleasure?"

"Oh, jeez, it's only been like a day or two, hasn't it?"

"I take it you've had a hectic couple of days?" Dad asked.

"You could say that. I was actually calling for a bit of advice."

"Well, I can't promise it'll be any good, but I'll do my best."

"If you knew something bad was going to happen to someone, but there was absolutely nothing that could be done to stop it, would you warn them?"

"Nothing they could do could change it, either?"

"Let's assume not."

"What is this all about, Roselyn?" he asked, concerned.

"It's private. Something going on with a friend."

My dad sat in thoughtful silence for a moment. "That's a tricky question. On one hand, you'd want to warn them so they wouldn't be taken by surprise, but I suppose if nothing could stop it from happening, what would be the point in making them worry and dread it before it even happens? Maybe it'd be better to allow them to be happy while they can because you know they'll be unhappy later. I don't know. I'd need more context to know what to do."

"If you were the one the bad thing was going to happen to and you found out someone knew and didn't tell you, would you be mad?"

"Is something bad going to happen to me and you're trying to decide whether to tell me?" my dad asked jestingly. It made a knot form in my chest.

I forced a laugh. "This isn't about you, Dad. Just answer the question."

"I don't know. I might be. I can see both sides of it, though. And now I'm dying to know what this is all about."

"It's really not a big deal," I lied.

I was startled from my conversation with my father when Jaeger reappeared in my kitchen. He looked disheveled and he was breathing heavily. When he looked at me, I could tell something was wrong.

"Dad, I have to let you go. I'll talk to you later. I love you." I ended the call and turned to Jaeger. "What's going on now?"

"I can't find Trent."

"What? Can't you track him from your watch?"

"Not like I normally can. I think he's unsynced our devices. Do you know where he might've gone?"

I frowned, suddenly worried. "Why would he do that? I have no idea where he would go. Do you think something happened to him?" I felt panic rising in my chest.

"Did he say anything before he left here?"

"Not really. Do you think something happened to him?" I repeated.

"I don't know," Jaeger confessed. "I'm at a loss."

"I'll try to call him," I said as I brought up his weird number on my phone. It beeped and buzzed, but there was no answer. Something was definitely wrong. Jaeger looked at me expectantly. "He's not picking up," I said as I shoved the phone in my pocket. "Do you suppose maybe he's just mad?" I asked.

"Well, he's always been a bit odd, I thought."

"No, not crazy. Mad as in angry."

"Oh. I suppose that's possible, too. Are you going to tell me what happened between the two of you now?"

I gave Jaeger a brief overview of what had transpired. He seemed sympathetic.

"You know what bothers me the most?" I asked him. "Why didn't he put up more of a fight to stay? Why did he just leave like that?"

"You told him to get out."

"I know, but if he really wanted to stay with me, why would he just step aside and let it all fall apart like this? It was like he didn't care enough to try."

"Or maybe he respected your choice and did exactly what you asked." Jaeger pointed out softly.

"That's rich. Since when does he ever listen to me?"

Jaeger shrugged his shoulders. "I don't have answers for you. Sorry."

I felt my eyes starting to water up. "I don't know what I'm supposed to do now."

Jaeger looked uncomfortable. He came over and sat down next to me. "Please don't cry. I really don't know what to do with crying."

"I'm not crying," I maintained as I turned my head away from him. "I'm fine."

"You know, just because he took your watch, it doesn't mean you can't still travel."

I gave him a curious glance.

He looked down at his hands nervously. "You could always travel with me."

My eyes widened in surprise.

Before I could respond, Jaeger rushed to explain. "Listen, I'm not asking to be his replacement. I'm just saying that if you and he aren't on the best of terms right now, I'd be glad to help you out. You can accompany me on our adventures...until things smooth out again."

"And if they never do?"

"Well...we'll talk about it then." Jaeger stood up and held his hand out to me. "So, what do you say?"

I suddenly felt a small sliver of hope. "Will you help me save my family from 2033?"

Jaeger turned his eyes away. "Don't ask that of me, Roselyn."

"Why not? You said you'd be glad to help me out."

"If Trent wouldn't do it, there must be a good reason. Besides, this isn't my world and it isn't my place to interfere."

"It could be your world, if you wanted it to be. You could stay."

One corner of Jaeger's mouth lifted in a half-smile. "It's a nice thought, but Trent would never allow that."

I thought back to when Trent from the future brought me back from the Moon, and he'd said he still saw Jaeger regularly. Did that mean that Jaeger didn't go back to his own world after all? Or did it just mean that he visited often?

"Oh, I don't know about that. If you had the option to stay, would you?" I asked.

He looked thoughtful. "I don't know. The whole reason I'm here is to figure out how to fix my own world, not to assimilate to this one. But…"

"But what?"

"But I do like it here."

"Then maybe this world has already become home to you. And maybe it wouldn't be so wrong for you to help me, if that's the case."

Jaeger looked conflicted. "I want to help you, Roselyn, I do, but you know I can't."

I glanced down at the watch on Jaeger's wrist that was so temptingly close to my hand as he sat next to me on the couch.

Forgive me for what I am about to do, I thought.

I slid my right hand over and intertwined my fingers with Jaeger's. His eyes widened, and he looked at me as though I'd suddenly grown two heads. I leaned my head against his shoulder.

"I'm glad you're here," I said as sweetly as I could. Guilt was already knotting my chest, but I persisted. I lifted my head and looked up into Jaeger's hazel-green eyes, and he gazed back at me with confusion, but not an ounce of rejection. He would never forgive me for this, but I had to do it. He and Trent had left me with no choice.

I crushed my lips against his and kissed him like my life depended on it. While his attention was drawn to our kiss, I quickly brought my left hand over and unhooked the strap on his watch. When I had it worked free, I slipped the watch from his wrist and bolted for the bathroom, vaulting over the couch in my path.

If I hadn't completely blindsided him with such an effective distraction, I never would've escaped Jaeger's quick reflexes and agility. By some miracle, I managed to slam the bathroom door and lock it just milliseconds before Jaeger reached it. But in that moment as I was shoving the door shut, I caught a brief glance of Jaeger's face as he lunged for me. As if in slow motion, I saw the entire range of emotions in his eyes in that fraction of a second – the shock, the betrayal, and, ultimately, the devastation.

"I'm so sorry, Jaeger," I cried as I fumbled with his watch, my back pressed against the bathroom door. It shook and vibrated under his fists.

"Open the door, Roselyn! Don't you dare run off with my watch! You can't do this!"

I blinked through the blurry tears, trying to read the display on his watch.

"I'll come right back!" I promised.

"It won't work!" he shouted.

I knew he would be through the door in a matter of seconds.

"I have to try!"

"No, that's not what I mean! The watch—"

Before he could finish his sentence, I quickly entered 2033, keeping the current coordinates, and teleported from my time, leaving Jaeger behind.

Chapter 16

I found myself in a disgusting, unkempt bathroom. It was still my bathroom, but it appeared that no one had cleaned it or been in it in a very long time. It smelled rancid, the toilet water was black, and there was mold growing along the back of the sink. I covered my nose and quickly exited the room, only to find that the rest of the house was in similar condition. How had this happened? If the pandemic had only started in 2033, why did my house already appear to be abandoned and dilapidated? I glanced down at the watch in my hand, and that was when I realized my mistake. In my haste, I had entered 2043, not 2033. I was ten years into the apocalypse.

I tried to enter 2033 and teleport to the time I had originally intended, but the screen suddenly went blank. I opened up the holographic display, but all it showed was a message reading, "Host tether not found." What did that mean? I put the watch on my wrist, wondering if it needed to be worn in order to function further, but the same message continued to flash at me. What was a host tether?

I was gripped by panic as it dawned on me that I was stuck here with a malfunctioning teleporter, and I had left Jaeger deserted in my time while Trent was MIA. I had no idea what kind of world I would find outside my front door, and no idea how I would get to my parents or brother. Hell, I didn't even know if they were still alive in 2043.

I went to the window and looked outside. The lawn was overgrown, and the small trees and shrubs had grown larger, but other than that, nothing seemed out of the ordinary. It was encouraging to see a black car sitting in the driveway, too. It wasn't the one I have in my own time, but I assumed it must be mine. It looked like it had been sitting for a while, though, as it had a grimy film on it and the tires looked like they could use some air. I hurried to the counter where I normally would leave my keys, and, thankfully, there were keys sitting there. I snatched them up and ran outside to the car.

I gave it a quick once-over, and it looked to be sound. I opened the door and climbed into the driver's seat, praying to whatever god would listen that the car would start. I stuck my key in the ignition and turned it.

Click click click. Then nothing. The battery must be dead after sitting for an extended period of time. I slammed my hands against the steering wheel in frustration and threw myself back in the seat, butting the back of my head against the headrest.

"Son of a bitch!" I roared.

There was a sudden knock on the window next to me, and my hands flailed wildly in surprise as a shriek escaped my lips.

"This seems familiar," Trent said through the window. "I think our second run-in started like this."

I opened the door, swinging it fast and wide to make Trent jump back to dodge it, and climbed out of the car. I headed toward the garage.

"Where are you going?" Trent asked.

"To look for a new battery or some way to charge the current battery in my car." Trent grabbed my arm to stop me, and I tore it from his grasp. I whirled around. "Go home, Trent! ...Wherever the hell that is."

Trent ignored my demand. "Where's Jaeger?" he asked, looking down at the watch on my wrist.

"Not here," I responded vaguely.

"He didn't give you his watch willingly, did he?" he asked as he began to unstrap it from my arm.

"What makes you say that?"

"Because it doesn't work without him." He shoved the watch in his pocket.

"It got me here, didn't it?" I countered.

"Yeah, but it's not going to take you anywhere else. He installed a security biosensor on it that allows it to work only if it can detect him within a certain vicinity. It was meant to prevent someone from stealing the watch. Now, tell me what happened."

"Go ask him yourself. He's back in my time, probably having a meltdown in my hallway or bathroom."

"So he's not with Megan."

"Obviously."

Trent folded his hands together and rested them on top of his head with his elbows pointed outward. "Oh, Roselyn, you just don't get it, do you?" he sighed. "You just don't see the bigger picture!"

"I've seen all I need to see."

"No, you really haven't."

I rolled my eyes at him and continued toward the garage.

"Any car battery or charger in the garage is going to be dead, too," Trent advised me. "They've been sitting too long."

I stopped and threw my hands in the air. "Fantastic!" I shouted sarcastically. I turned around. "Why don't you just take me where I want to go, then? Or better yet, give me back my watch so I can get there myself!"

"Where are you trying to go?"

I looked at him flatly. "Where the hell do you think I'm trying to go?"

"I would hope back home."

"I'm going to my parents' house. But you knew that already."

Trent held his hand out to me. "Fine. You want to go to your parents' house? I'll take you."

I looked at him in disbelief. "…Really?"

He gave a nod. "Really."

I eyed him suspiciously as he started to enter coordinates into his watch. "No, you're trying to trick me, aren't you? As soon as I take your hand you're going to bring me back home again!"

Trent shook his head. "I promise I'm not going to do that. Trust me."

I scoffed. "Trust you? After everything I know now?"

Trent held up his watch. "Would you like to look for yourself?" he asked in exasperation. "I mean, if you don't want to take the quick route, I can sit here and watch you waste time looking for a way to get that car started. Either way. Your choice."

I reluctantly trudged over to him and took a glance at his watch. I had no idea if the coordinates were my parents' house or not, but the year was still set to 2043, so at least I knew he wasn't taking me home. I stood next to him and waited to be teleported. Instead of putting his arm around me, he looped his arm through mine while he initiated the teleport. It felt so…impersonal.

When we arrived, I was looking upon a house that I barely recognized. It was the house I had grown up in, and the house that held all of my childhood and adolescent memories. As I looked upon it now, however, it didn't fill me with warm nostalgia like it ordinarily would. It filled me with grief. The siding was cracked and grimy, and every window was broken. Some of the wooden boards on front porch had caved in, and the front door was hanging loosely on its hinges as though it had simply given up its will to hold the outside world at bay.

I stepped carefully onto the porch, finding footing in a section that still seemed sturdy. Trent reached for my hand.

"It isn't safe," he warned.

"Since when has that ever stopped me? Or you, for that matter?"

I made my way to the door and pushed it aside. It groaned in protest and scraped along the floor as I stepped inside. Trent followed on my heels.

"They aren't here, obviously," I said as I looked around at the peeling paint on the walls and the cobwebs hanging from every corner. It's amazing how quickly a dwelling can deteriorate when left uninhabited. "I'm afraid to ask where they've gone." I turned and looked at Trent, fearful of what I was going to see in his eyes.

His expression was soft. "They aren't far away. Only about six miles north."

"In town?" I asked, surprised. Trent nodded. "Why would they be in town? There was hardly anything there before the apocalypse started, so I can't imagine what would..." My voice trailed off as a terrible though occurred to me. "Oh, god, you don't mean the cemetery, do you?!"

Trent's eyes widened. "What? No! Good lord, I'm not that cryptic!"

I expelled a sigh of relief. "Well, where are they? I want to see them."

Trent gave me a hesitant grimace. "Yeah, about that...you can't let them see you."

"Why not? How can I save them if I can't let them see me?"

Trent frowned at me. "You aren't going to save them. I don't know how many times I have to tell you that."

"Oh, yes I am. That's why I'm here."

"No, you're here because I'm allowing you to be here. And that is all I'm allowing. Only you and I will be going when we leave this place."

"You're a heartless bastard," I hissed.

"There's nothing heartless about this," he argued.

"I don't know how you can honestly believe that."

"Because you don't know anything. You don't understand anything. You're trying to proceed on your own without having all the facts and it could be potentially devastating."

"More devastating than allowing my parents to weather the apocalypse?"

"Quit calling it that. It isn't the apocalypse," Trent said disagreeably.

"I don't give a shit what you call it. Tell me why I can't save them. I don't mean give me some bullshit vague excuse about 'time can't be changed,' either. I want to know exactly what purpose is served by leaving them here."

Trent pressed the heels of his palms against his eyes in a gesture of frustration, then ran his hands up through his hair again. "Fine! You want to see? You want to know the truth? Come with me!" He quickly entered coordinates into his watch and grabbed my hand. Before he sent us off, he looked down at me. "But don't you dare let them see you."

"Why can't I let them see me?"

Trent averted his eyes. "Because they think you're dead."

Before I could respond, we teleported to a playground. I recognized it as the playground behind the school in my hometown, not far from my parents' house. Trent pulled me back along the brick wall, trying to stay out of sight. I watched a couple of small children playing on the slide, and when a man came to assist the younger one with an untied shoe, I realized I was looking at my brother. Were those his kids? I saw an older couple, probably in their 70's, standing near the swings, smiling at my brother and the kids.

They were my parents.

I turned to Trent, giving him a questioning look. I hadn't expected to see such a happy, peaceful scene. I thought it would be constant violence and chaos and pestilence.

Trent looked out at the kids playing. "Your parents are important people now," Trent informed me. "It turns out your mother is immune to the virus. When the hospital here filled up, most people died. Most of the doctors and nurses contracted the disease and died, too. Your mum was one of the only nurses who remained, and she found herself in a position of leadership. She took the reins and kept the hospital open and running as best she could, and her persistence saved lives. One of the people she nursed back to health was a young medical student who had come home from university, since the schools all closed down due to illness. That student, who went into medical research, developed a highly effective universal vaccine against all strains of influenza, including the one that caused the pandemic. So, in a roundabout way, your mother is responsible for saving countless lives, including your nephews over there. Things are bad economically, and the big cities and industry remain in crisis for a long time yet, but because of your mum, at least the worry of pandemic flu is behind them." Trent gave me a meaningful look. "That's why she has to stay here. That's why they all have to stay here." He looked out at my parents. "One seemingly unimportant person in one seemingly unimportant little town can have an impact so profound it can change the world. It's amazing," Trent marveled.

I was speechless. If I had succeeded in changing the future, if I had taken my mom from her timeline, it would've changed so much more than I ever could've imagined.

Trent teleported us back to the yard in front of my run-down house. "Do you understand now? Or do you still think it would be better to rescue your parents from their timeline?"

I swallowed hard. "I understand."

"You understand that you aren't the center of the universe? You understand that there is more at stake than you can even begin to comprehend? Or you just understand that you were wrong?"

I crossed my arms and looked at the ground. "All of it, ok? I get it. You don't have to rub it in."

"Actually, I think I do," Trent said seriously. "I need you to completely understand the gravity of your indiscretion. I thought you had a better grasp of what our role was in the grand scheme of things. I thought you took this seriously. I thought you were capable of seeing a world outside of yourself. You have no idea how much it injures me to find out how wrong I was about you."

I felt a shame so deep I didn't think I would ever be purged of it. "I'm sorry," I whispered. "I didn't know."

"That's the problem, Roselyn. You didn't know, but you didn't care. You were reacting emotionally and you weren't listening to what I was trying to tell you. In the moment when your trust in me was truly tested, you turned on me. When are you going to learn that I have a pretty good idea of what I'm talking about when it comes to matters of time?" Trent thrust his hands in his pockets and looked at me the same way Jaeger had looked at me as I was slamming the bathroom door in his face. I hadn't just angered him. I'd let him down. I'd betrayed him. I'd failed him.

I stood before him completely humbled and deflated. "Where do we go from here?" I asked hesitantly, afraid of the answer. "I'm not getting my watch back, am I?"

Trent shook his head. "No, I don't think that's a good idea."

I nodded and sniffled. "That's fair. I understand." I brushed a stray blond hair from my face and looked over at the dilapidated house. "So I suppose this is what I have to look forward to."

Trent knitted his brows. "What, this?" He pointed at the house, looking confused. "What makes you say that?"

"I tried to alter the future – or history? Past, present, future, I never quite know what tense to use with you. Either way, I almost ruined things. And I did ruin things between us. And between Jaeger and myself. Ugh, Jaeger. I don't want to go back home and face—"

Trent stopped me. "Wait, who said you ruined things between us? You think this is over?"

"Isn't it? I was terrible to you. I betrayed you."

"Is that supposed to matter? Betrayal can be forgiven. It already has been."

I looked into those deep brown eyes. "You don't hate me?"

"What? Of course not! Disappointed and upset, yes. But I don't hate you. I think I'm quite incapable of hating you."

I felt like he had just lifted a boulder off of my chest. "Does that mean you aren't leaving me, then?"

"I never wanted to leave you. You're the one who keeps telling me to go. If you want me to stay, all you have to do is say so." He looked at me earnestly.

I stepped close to him and rested my head against his chest and wrapped my arms around his torso. "Please stay," I begged as I squeezed him tightly. "I'm so sorry."

Trent enveloped me in his arms and I knew that all was forgiven.

"Now, before we go back, maybe you should enlighten me as to how you nicked Jaeger's watch from him. He's not easily tricked."

I felt a surge of guilt. "Well...he came to see where you had gone off to..." I stopped and looked up at him. "Where did you go off to? He said he couldn't track you."

He looked embarrassed. "Oh. I, um...I needed a moment to myself. After our exchange, I was feeling not quite myself."

"You were moping."

"I was indeed moping," he admitted. "But what happened with Jaeger? Regale me."

"I was sitting and talking with him, and I distracted him just long enough to snag the watch and make a run for the bathroom. He didn't really have time to warn me that it wouldn't bring me back."

Trent eyed me suspiciously. "Is that really all there was to it?"

I didn't want to tell him the truth. I didn't want to tell him how despicable I had been, and how I had used Jaeger's feelings for me and his trust in me against him. "I'm not proud of it. I don't really want to discuss it in fine detail."

"Very well, then. I'm sure he'll have more than enough to say about it when we get back."

"Trent, wait!" I protested, but before the words had rolled from my tongue Trent had already pressed the button on his watch. We were suddenly in my living room, and Jaeger was standing in the hallway with his forehead pressed against the bathroom door, his shoulders slumped.

When he noticed our presence, a look of relief washed over his face briefly. It was quickly replaced by rage, however.

"Are you out of your mind?!" he shouted, jabbing his finger toward me. "Do you have any idea what could've happened?!"

Trent stepped in. "Luckily, catastrophe was averted." He pulled the watch out of his pocket and handed it to Jaeger. "I believe you'll feel better having this back."

Jaeger snatched the watch from Trent's hand and quickly secured it to his wrist. "Did she tell you what she did?"

"I got the gist."

"I'm sorry, Jaeger," I said. "I didn't mean to cause so much grief. I thought I'd be able to come right back. I didn't know what would happen."

Jaeger's eyes were piercing. "Trent may be quick to forgive, but you'll find me less so. I trusted you. I'll not make that mistake twice."

I knew I deserved that, but it didn't make it sting any less.

"We can hash this out later," Trent said. "We've got a problem in a dungeon in Ireland that requires our attention."

Jaeger flared his nostrils in annoyance, but he said nothing as he quickly teleported from the house. Trent took me under his arm and sent us to Ireland. When we arrived at the castle, I could hear Jaeger's heavy footsteps already descending the stairs ahead of us. We followed, and when we got to the bottom, I saw Jaeger standing there, staring at the cell. I followed his gaze.

The cell door was open, and Megan was gone.

Chapter 17

"No, no, no!" Trent cried. "How did she get out?!" He checked his watch. "She was only here on her own for five minutes!"

"She can't be far, then," I reasoned.

Trent and I started to look around frantically, but I noticed Jaeger was just standing there looking wholly unconcerned.

"Aren't you going to help look for her?" I asked.

"Maybe we should just leave her," he said without looking at me. "She has no watch. What harm can she do in 1824 Ireland?"

"Plenty!" Trent replied. "She doesn't belong here!"

"You're the one who brought her here," Jaeger said.

"Exactly, so it's my responsibility to get her back out of here!"

Suddenly, Trent's watch started beeping. He pulled his glasses from his pocket and pulled up the display, quieting the beeping. After swiping through several different holographic screens of data, he turned and looked at Jaeger in dismay.

"What have you done?" Trent asked accusingly.

Jaeger froze in a moment of uncertainty, looking as though he was contemplating how to proceed. "I did what needed to be done!" he shouted defensively.

"That was not your decision to make!"

"You two left it up to me! You ran off, nowhere to be found, and Roselyn seemed to suddenly be out of the picture, so what was I supposed to do? Twiddle my thumbs and wait? I did what was necessary!"

I interjected. "Can someone please explain what the hell is going on? What did Jaeger do?! Why was your watch beeping?"

"Megan's changed something in the future – something beyond the time I normally stick to."

"If you haven't been there, then how do you know she's changed it?" I wondered.

"The future influences the past. Cause and effect can run both ways. Changing the future can change the past, and my watch detected such a change." Trent turned to Jaeger. "What did she do?"

"She took down SABER in exchange for immortality."

"We can't give her immortality!" Trent argued.

"Oh, I have no intention of holding up my end of the bargain," Jaeger said flatly. "I'm killing two birds with one stone. Now, if you'll excuse me, I need to finish this." He suddenly teleported from the dungeon.

"Wait here," Trent ordered as he manipulated his watch.

"Like hell," I said defiantly. I grabbed his arm as he pressed the button to teleport to the future.

When we arrived, we were standing in the desert before a pile of rubble, and I was reminded of the scene Jaeger and I had witnessed the day we first met Megan. It seemed this was her trademark. I saw her and Jaeger standing together off in the distance, their silhouettes facing each other against the backdrop of blue sky. They appeared to be talking, but their voices were carried away by the wind long before they reached my ears.

Then I saw him raise his arm and point his gun at her. I saw the jolt of the recoil through Jaeger's arm a fraction of a second before I heard the blast. But it wasn't Megan who fell. I suddenly realized someone else was standing between Jaeger and Megan, and I watched as the man's silhouette staggered backward slightly before dropping to his knees in front of Jaeger.

I turned to Trent to see his reaction, only to find that he was no longer next to me. I looked back to the scene in horror as I heard Jaeger shouting, holstering his weapon as he rushed to aid the man he'd just shot. Megan just stood silently and unmoving, but from this distance I couldn't tell if she was frozen in shock or just standing in a state of general apathy, waiting for the next move.

I bolted toward them, my feet pounding the compacted, dry ground almost as quickly as my heart pounded in my chest. As I approached, Jaeger saw me coming. He quickly stood and held his hands up defensively.

"Don't panic! He'll be ok, I swear it," he promised. "He's going to be just fine."

I looked down at Trent, kneeling in the dirt with blood dripping through his fingers as he applied pressure to the gunshot wound in the middle of his chest. He turned his big brown eyes up to me and gave me a grimacing grin. "I'd forgotten how much getting shot hurts," he said almost jokingly.

I kneeled next to him, unsure of what to do. "How can I help?" I asked desperately.

"Don't let him shoot anyone else."

"Why did you do that? Why did you save her?" I was still in a state of shock.

"Because she doesn't have to die."

I looked over at Megan, scrutinizing the expression on her face. She was staring at Trent in utter disbelief. It was as though she couldn't comprehend that someone had put himself in harm's way to protect her. It must've been a concept that was completely foreign to her.

She asked, "After everything I've done, why do you care?"

Trent turned his head slightly, but he couldn't move far enough to make eye contact with Megan. He replied, "Because if I cared about you in my past, then you must be worth caring about."

"You don't even know me anymore," she countered. "I'm not the same person I was then."

Trent stumbled to his feet and turned around to face Megan. He smirked. "Neither am I. And that's why you need to let go of all that bitterness and hatred you've been harboring toward me all these years. It's time to move on. I can't make you immortal, and even if I had that ability, I wouldn't. So, maybe instead of obsessing over an everlasting life, you should try to understand the value of life. What is the point of living forever if you're gleaning so little happiness from life? Instead of seeking immortality, you should be figuring out how to actually live."

"Oh, spare me the bullshit," Megan said, rolling her eyes. "I'm perfectly happy with the way I live my life. Just because it isn't how you envision what happiness should look like it doesn't make it wrong."

Jaeger scoffed, "If your happiness is killing everyone who looks askance at you, then yes, yes it does make it wrong."

"It isn't killing people that makes me happy so much as the idea of having less people alive. Give me a world without other people, and I'd call that bliss."

"Well, how about a dungeon cell all to yourself? That's the best I can offer you," Jaeger said.

"I should've found a way to kill you when I had the chance," Megan retorted.

Trent raised his hand. "Sorry to interrupt, but I've been shot, remember? Could we possibly continue this after I've had a little medical attention?"

Megan shrugged. "To be fair, you willingly and knowingly put yourself in front of that bullet, so…"

I scowled at her. "He did it to save you, so maybe you should shut your trap and be grateful that he did."

"I think you forget how easily I could snap your neck," Megan shot back at me.

Jaeger stepped up next to me, facing Megan. "And I think you know I'd never allow that."

I gave Megan one last side-eye as I turned away to tend to Trent. It appeared that his bleeding had slowed, but he was starting to look pale and unsteady on his feet.

"Should we get you to a hospital?" I asked.

"No, I just need to get somewhere where I can dig this bullet out and stitch myself up. It's lucky for Megan that it didn't go right through, but not so lucky for me, I suppose."

"You shouldn't have done that," I chastised. "She wasn't worth it. I know you heal quickly and survive things most people wouldn't, but it doesn't mean you can't die."

"Eh, I'm too stubborn to allow that nonsense."

"Where did you want to go? I think your medical bag is still at my house, if I remember correctly."

"I can take the murder princess back to her dungeon while you take care of that," Jaeger offered.

Trent glowered at him under heavy brows. "If you think for a minute I'd trust you on your own again, you are mistaken. Roselyn will accompany you. I can tend to this on my own." He tapped the buttons on his watch, and before disappearing, he looked at Jaeger and me. "Don't disappoint me again."

I looked over at Jaeger as Trent teleported away, but I couldn't bring myself to maintain eye contact. I was still ashamed of how I'd manipulated him, but I was also upset with him for going behind our backs and taking action against Megan and SABER on his own. We'd all been deceitful toward each other, and it had taken its toll on our group dynamic.

"I'm not going back to that dungeon," Megan declared.

"Like hell you aren't," Jaeger said. He quickly snatched her arm firmly. He glanced at me. "Grab on," he ordered.

Back in Ireland, Jaeger shoved the struggling Megan back into her dungeon as I looked on. Once she was locked up, she started in on us.

"You know he betrayed you and Trent," she said, pointing at Jaeger. "He isn't your friend. He hasn't an ounce of loyalty to you. The only reason he tried to kill me was because he got caught and he didn't want me telling you the truth. You can't trust someone who plays both sides of the fence."

I sighed. "He did what he thought he had to." Out of the corner of my eye, I saw Jaeger's head turn toward me in surprise. I looked over at him. "I know you thought you were doing the right thing. I know you didn't intend for it to end up like this. We've all made some stupid mistakes lately and let our little unit break down because we each thought we knew best. Obviously, we were wrong. I'm sorry for what I did, Jaeger. I truly am. I wish I could take it all back."

Jaeger grunted. "Does Trent know?"

"No. But it doesn't matter because it didn't mean anything."

Jaeger's hazel green eyes looked stormy. "It was a shitty thing for you to do."

I hung my head. "I know, and I'm sorry. But please understand why I did it. If you thought you had to do it to save your family, wouldn't you do the same?"

"I don't have a family. You and Trent have become the closest thing I've ever had to family, but now..." Jaeger's voice trailed off and he left his sentence unfinished.

I gave him a half-smile. "Well, if there's one thing I know about family, it's that they can suck sometimes. Sometimes they hurt each other, whether intentional or not, but you know what? Family forgives."

Jaeger just sat silently, but I hoped he was taking the words I'd said to heart.

Megan guffawed obnoxiously. "Oh, please. Family forgives? Could you be any more cliché? I don't know what you three fuckateers have been up to, but let me tell you what I do know: if someone screws you, you don't give them an opportunity to do it again. Forgiveness is for the weak who are too afraid to stand up for themselves."

"Without forgiveness, this would be an awfully bleak and hateful world," I argued.

"Isn't it, though?" Megan replied.

"Maybe at times, but I'm pretty sure it's never caused by too much forgiveness. Quite the opposite."

"And what about me, Roselyn? Have you forgiven me for trying to kill you? For leaving you on the Moon? For playing Frankenstein with your pal Jaeger? For being Trent's companion before you?"

I stared at her briefly before breaking eye contact with her.

"Didn't think so," Megan continued. "Don't preach forgiveness to others when you're seeking it if you aren't willing to give it as freely. Hypocrite."

Jaeger stood up suddenly. "Shall we check on Trent? He shouldn't have to deal with that wound on his own."

"What about her?" I asked, hooking my thumb toward Megan.

"She's not going anywhere. Not this time."

Jaeger teleported us to my house. I couldn't believe it was still only Tuesday in my time. It felt like weeks had passed.

"Trent?" I called as I walked down the hall looking for him. When I entered my room, I saw him sitting on the floor, slumped against my bedframe with his medical bag sitting on the floor between his outstretched legs. He had a bloody pair of forceps in his hand and his shirt was unbuttoned, blood spilling from the bullet hole in his chest. "Jesus, Trent, are you ok?" I rushed to his side.

He looked up at me. "I guess I'm still not quite back to one hundred percent after the change. It can take a while to fully recover from the process. I might need some help getting this piece of lead out."

I quickly stripped the bloody sheets off of my bed from when Trent and I had sewn Jaeger back together and put a clean blanket down over the bed, and Jaeger helped me get Trent onto the bed. Jaeger dug the bullet out of Trent's chest, and I assisted with the stitching.

"I feel like I should've been a nurse," I joked once we were done treating Trent.

"A time-traveling RN," Trent quipped.

I grinned, glad to see his sense of humor had returned. "I never knew time-traveling would be this bloody."

"Have you changed your mind about wanting to be part of it?" Trent asked.

"No, I haven't changed my mind. But...it occurred to me that recently I've spend a lot of time away from home, but only a couple days have passed here. I can't keep going at this pace. I mean, I'm a personal trainer, and I haven't had time to work out or barely even eat. At this rate, I'm going to end up crashing hard. I'm not going to be able to keep up with my regular life if I spend this much time away from it."

"It doesn't always have to be like this. I won't keep you away from your life. I don't want to take that from you. But it doesn't mean we can't have date nights, right? Or mini holidays?"

I smiled. "That sounds perfect."

Jaeger cleared his throat as he walked into the room, wiping his hands on a towel. "Not to change the subject, but what about Megan? We can't leave her in that dungeon indefinitely. Obviously you don't want her dead, but what are our other options? We can't just let her go because I can guarantee she'll end up being a problem again at some point. She'll probably start a new SABER organization that'll be even worse than the last."

A thought suddenly occurred to me. I asked Trent, "What would happen if Jaeger didn't go back to his world? What if he stayed here?"

Jaeger frowned at me. "We're talking about Megan right now, not me."

"No, I know that, but didn't you say you wouldn't mind staying in this world if you had the option? This is relevant, I promise."

"Where are you going with this?" he asked impatiently.

"Think about it! Megan wants to be in a place with no people, and Jaeger wants to be here. Are you following me yet?"

Trent's eyes lit up. "Oh! OH! Blimey, that might just work!"

Jaeger looked skeptical. "You're suggesting we give her an entire world?"

"You don't want it!" I argued. "It's the perfect solution! She'll be out of our hair and unable to hurt anyone else, and she'll finally get a world free of people. Everybody wins."

Jaeger stood silently.

"If you're against it, we don't have to do it," Trent said. "It was just an idea."

"Well, I didn't say I was against it. I don't know." Jaeger looked to Trent. "What do you think?"

"Honestly, I think it's our best option."

Jaeger sighed. "Fine. Ok. Let's do it, then."

"We don't have to if you aren't ok with it," I said, picking up on his reluctant tone.

"No, it isn't that. I just…are you sure it's all right for me to stay? I don't belong here."

Trent smiled. "Yeah, you do." He stood up from the bed and flinched, but when I reached out to assist him, he held me at bay. "No, I'm ok. Come on, let's go and finish this ordeal."

We teleported back to the dungeon and presented Megan with our decision. She looked at us like we were insane.

"Let me get this straight: you're going to banish me to a parallel universe now, like some kind of comic book villain?"

"That's exactly what we're going to do," I said smugly.

"We can't let you run amok in our world," Trent said. "Not after everything you've done and everything you know. Even without a watch, you're a threat."

"Wouldn't it be easier to kill me?"

"We could do that if you prefer it," Jaeger offered.

Trent held up his hand to quiet Jaeger and continued talking to Megan. "It would be easier to kill you. But easy doesn't mean right."

"So you're going to ship me off to another world to be somebody else's problem?"

"You won't be anybody's problem. You'll be alone," Trent replied.

Megan furrowed her brows. "What do you mean?"

"I mean there are no other people. You will be utterly alone in the world. Isn't that what you wanted?"

"Is it even habitable?"

"Assuredly."

Megan eyed us suspiciously. "What's the catch?"

"There is no catch. It's a win-win."

Megan crossed her arms and nodded slowly. "Fine. I'll go."

"It's not like you had an option," Jaeger grumbled as he opened the door to Megan's cell and grabbed her arm.

I turned to Trent. "Is he taking her?"

"He has to. He's the only one with the capability to teleport from our world to his. But the jump has to be made from your house, so we'll be heading there first." Trent hooked his arm through mine and sent us back to my living room. Jaeger and Megan appeared moments later.

As I watched Jaeger lead Megan roughly down the hall toward my room, I leaned in toward Trent and whispered, "Aren't you afraid he's going to kill her as soon as he is alone with her?"

"Oh, he's not going alone," Trent replied as he started after them, his movements slowed somewhat by his injury. "I'm going, too."

I followed him down the hall and to my room where Jaeger and Megan were waiting. Jaeger was adjusting the settings on his watch, presumably preparing for the leap between worlds. When I tried to enter the room, however, Trent turned and stopped me.

"What are you doing?" I asked. "Aren't we all going?"

He looked at me regretfully. "No. I've stolen enough of your time already. There's no telling just how much time will pass in your world before we get back. It could be a few minutes, or it could be a few weeks. You need to stay here and live your life. That's what you wanted, isn't it? Besides, I'm sure Cattiel will be glad to have you to himself for a while."

A slow ache was growing in my chest. "I don't like this. Just let him go by himself."

"It will be fine. I promise I will be back." Trent leaned forward and touched his lips to mine gently. I closed my eyes tightly and gripped the nape of his neck, holding him to me a few moments longer to elicit a deeper kiss from him. I wanted to wrap my arms around him and press my body against his, but I knew I couldn't do that with that blasted bullet wound in his chest. I didn't want to let him go.

When we parted, he gazed down at me lovingly. "See you in a bit, love." He winked at me and turned away to join Jaeger and Megan. I watched from the doorway as he placed his hand on Jaeger's shoulder and turned his head. We locked eyes for a brief moment, and then he was gone.

Chapter 18

In the following days, I tried to fall back into my old routine, but everything was off. I had lost weight and was sleep deprived from all the recent shenanigans, but even though I was home and free to do as I pleased, I found I had no appetite and had a hard time sleeping. I was waiting for Trent to come home, and I wasn't going to feel quite at ease until he did.

Days turned into weeks, and weeks turned into months. I expected him to show up at any time, but he didn't. I thought surely as a time traveler, even if it took him months to get back, he could go back in time after coming back to our world to at least let me know that he was ok and tell me when he would be home. But there was no sign of him. My days became monotonous – go to work, come home, and wait. I felt like my life was on hold, and my worry and loneliness were slowly turning into resentment and bitterness.

It hit me especially hard on my birthday. I was turning another year older, and it made me realize that time was marching forward for me, with or without Trent. Age didn't matter to him, and he barely noticed the passing of time, but for me, it was different. I had a limited amount of time, and I couldn't waste it waiting for him to come back to me. What if it took him years? What if I didn't see him again until I was sixty? How long was I willing to sit in standby mode before I had to get up and get on with my life? I loved Trent, of that there was no doubt, and I knew he was coming back someday – but I had no way of knowing when "someday" would come.

But I couldn't stop waiting. I tried, but regardless of what I did, I always had Trent in the back of my mind. All of my plans for the future had caveats for when Trent returned. My brain was trying to force me to move on, but my heart wouldn't let me exclude him from my future.

Then, a little over a year after Trent disappeared on his errand to another world, my wait ended. I was in the bathroom in the morning, wearing a bath towel while applying my makeup in the mirror, when I suddenly heard two English-sounding voices from my bedroom. I gasped and quickly slammed the bathroom door shut. My heart was attempting to beat itself right out of my chest and a flood of emotions threatened to overwhelm me. I sank to the bathroom floor with my back against the door, trying to compose myself.

"Roselyn?" I heard Trent say. Hearing his voice calling my name felt more like home than this house ever did, and there was nothing I could do to stop myself from calling back to him.

"I'm here!"

"Oh good! You're home! Can I come in?" he asked as he knocked on the bathroom door.

I clenched my towel tightly around me. I wanted to fling the door open and leap into his arms, but after all this time, I found myself feeling apprehensive. "No, I'm not dressed," I said hesitantly.

He chuckled. "I don't mind if you don't."

I felt a tear roll down my cheek. "I mind."

There was a pause on the other side of the door. "Oh. Did you want me to pop back in later?"

"No!" I cried, a little too desperately. I took a deep breath. "No, don't leave. Please, just don't leave." I instructed him to bring me the clothes I had sitting on my bed, and when he opened the door and handed them in, I quickly snatched them from his hands from behind the door and slammed it again. I dressed as quickly as I could, but my hands were trembling so badly that it made it difficult. When I was finally dressed, I dabbed my eyes and opened the door, stepping out into the hallway.

He was standing there nonchalantly with his hands in his pockets, wearing the same bullet-torn suit he'd had on when he left. Our eyes met, and he grinned at me.

I rushed to him and hugged him tightly, afraid that he might disappear if I let go. I felt him flinch, and I remembered his wound. I released him and stepped back. "You left me. I waited so long, I thought you weren't coming back," I said. I had to fight to keep my tears in check.

He looked down at me in surprise. "What do you mean? How long has it been?" He looked down at his watch and pressed a button. His face dropped. "Oh...oh no." He looked at me with upturned brows. "I'm so, so sorry," he apologized. "I suppose we have some catching up to do."

All the anger and resentment that I had allowed to build up over the past year bubbled suddenly to the surface. "Oh, do you suppose? Is that it? 'I'm sorry, let's catch up'?"

Jaeger piped up, "We had no idea it would be this big of a time difference." It was only then that I realized Jaeger was standing in the hallway behind Trent the entire time.

I cast a glare at him. "If we'd been able to trust you, Trent never would've had to leave, and I wouldn't have had to spend the past year in a state of perpetual uncertainty."

Jaeger narrowed his eyes at me, but he didn't dispute my accusation. He huffily brushed past Trent and me and headed to the kitchen.

I directed my attention back to Trent. "You need to go back in time and see me. You need to fix this!"

Trent shook his head. "You wanted to have time to live your life. I'm not going to go back and interfere with that."

"What life?! I felt like I was living in a state suspended animation while you were gone!"

"Didn't you get out and about and have your own adventures? Didn't you enjoy having your world to yourself for a while without worrying about me sweeping you up into some dangerous situation?"

I couldn't believe what I was hearing. "No! I was waiting and hoping for you to come back and save me from this ordinary life! I tried to move on, knowing there was a possibility you weren't coming back for a very long time, but I couldn't do it. You're like a damn tornado – an unstoppable force of nature. You ripped through my life and took me up in a whirlwind, showing me things I never could've imagined, making me feel things I had never felt, and forever changing my perspective on everything – and then you just dropped me and disappeared for a year. Was I just supposed to get up, dust off my pants, and walk it off?"

"I'm truly sorry, Roselyn. I don't know what you want me to say. I didn't know it would be a year for you. But I'm here now, and I'm willing to do whatever it takes to make it up to you."

"I want my year back. I wasted a year without you, and I want it back," I choked angrily through my tears.

"You'll have the rest of your life with me, if you'll have me. Someday you might look back on the year you were free of me and wish you could have another one."

"And what about when I'm old and you still look thirty-five? I'm another year closer to that reality now. What kind of a relationship will we have then? You'll wish then that you'd gone back and spent that year with me while I was still young."

"I suspect I will always wish for more time with you. But some things happen for a reason, and some things should be allowed to play out without interference." I opened my mouth, prepared to deliver a rebuttal, but Trent grabbed me and pulled me against him in a tight embrace and my voice was muffled against his shoulder. I struggled feebly to wriggle free, but I wasn't truly committed to the effort. He held on tightly. "Good heavens, I feel like I'm trying to hug Cattiel. Just love me!" he demanded jokingly.

I sniffled, then sighed. I allowed myself to meld against him. "I do love you," I whispered.

"Then let's quit wasting precious time arguing, shall we?"

I nodded.

I suddenly heard Jaeger yell from the kitchen, "Trent! Come quick!"

Alarmed, Trent and I quickly rushed down the hall. I saw Jaeger standing in front of the snack cupboard with the door open. He reached inside and pulled out a crinkly chip bag and held it out toward Trent. As soon as I saw what he had, I knew I was never going to hear the end of this.

"Are those...kale chips?!" Trent exclaimed. He moved closer to inspect the bag. "They are kale chips!" He turned to me with a teasing look of utter betrayal. "I knew it! You do like kale!"

As I stood there and tried to explain that my appreciation for kale chips was only a recent development, I realized that this moment was the happiest I'd been all year. The empty feeling I'd almost gotten used to was suddenly gone. Everything finally felt like it was as it should be. The trust among the three of us would still need to be rebuilt, but, much like the wound in Trent's chest, I knew the healing had already begun.

Before Trent and Jaeger had left me, I thought I had wanted to slow down, to have a little of my old life back. I thought I needed to have my work and my independence to maintain my own identity. But I now knew that that wasn't what I wanted at all. What I truly wanted was for time to slow down because I needed more of this. I didn't need to be on my own to know who I was, because that wasn't who I was anymore. I needed these two infuriating, insufferable, but incredible time travelers in my life to feel complete, and there was nothing wrong with that. I had finally realized that it was ok to depend on others and to need more than just myself and my cat. It didn't make me weak. When the three of us were together, we were stronger than any one of us could ever be on our own. It may have taken a few monumental mishaps and a year of their absence to fully understand how much I needed them, but, in the end, it all came together as perhaps it was always meant to.

I'd also grown to understand that it didn't matter that Trent bore a new visage from the one I had first fallen in love with – the man that he had always been still shone out from the inside, and that was where my love resided. Even if I couldn't count on him always looking like the man I knew, I could count on him always being the man I loved and the man to whom I would gladly give every last minute of my time.

When Trent and Jaeger finally relented their teasing, Trent turned to me and asked, "Well, are you ready?"

"Ready for what?"

"The future. It's time to go see what kind of a mess Megan has made."

"I thought you were afraid to go to the future," I pointed out.

Trent grinned. "Oh, I don't know. Maybe it's time to change the rules. New face, new rules. Come on. It'll be fun."

And just like that, my life went back to the wild, perfectly chaotic "normal" that I'd grown to love.

THE END

Also by Jacqueline Richardson:

The Burning Side
Dream Jumper
Beyond Reason
Scars